Double
TROUBLE

February 2014

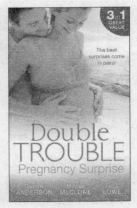

March 2014

Double
TROUBLE
Newborn Twins

Rebecca
WINTERS

Marie
FERRARELLA

Victoria
PADE

Published in Great Britain 2014
by Mills & Boon, an imprint of Harlequin (UK) Limited,
Eton House, 18-24 Paradise Road, Richmond, Surrey, TW9 1SR

DOUBLE TROUBLE: NEWBORN TWINS
© 2014 Harlequin Books S.A.

Doorstep Twins © 2010 Rebecca Winters
Those Matchmaking Babies © 2000 Marie Rydzynski-Ferrarella
Babies in the Bargain © 2004 Victoria Pade

ISBN: 978 0 263 24573 8

011-0214

Harlequin (UK) Limited's policy is to use papers that are natural, renewable and recyclable products and made from wood grown in sustainable forests The logging and manufacturing processes conform to the legalenvironmental regulations of the country of origin.

Printed and bound in Spain
by Blackprint CPI, Barcelona

Doorstep
TWINS

REBECCA WINTERS

Rebecca Winters, whose family of four children has now swelled to include five beautiful grandchildren, lives in Salt Lake City, Utah, in the land of the Rocky Mountains. With canyons and high alpine meadows full of wild flowers, she never runs out of places to explore. They, plus her favourite vacation spots in Europe, often end up as backgrounds for her Mills & Boon® romance novels, because writing is her passion, along with her family and church.

Rebecca loves to hear from her readers. If you wish to e-mail her, please visit her website at www.cleanromances.com.

CHAPTER ONE

"I'M SORRY, Ms. Turner, but Kyrie Simonides says he can't fit you in today. If you'll come next Tuesday at three o'clock?"

Gabi's hand tightened around the leather strap of her taupe handbag. "I won't be in Athens then." The outcome of this visit would determine how soon she left Greece...that was if she were allowed to see him now.

She fought not to lose her composure in front of the retirement-age-looking receptionist who was probably paid a lot of money not to lose *hers*. "After waiting over three hours for him, surely he can take another five minutes to talk to me."

The woman with heavy streaks of silver in her hair shook her head. "It's the weekend. He should have left Athens an hour ago."

At twenty after six on a hot Friday evening Gabi could believe it, but she hadn't come this far to be put off. There was too much at stake. Taking a calming breath, she said, "I didn't want to have to say this to you, but he's left me no choice. Please tell him it's a matter of life and death."

Because it was the truth and her eyes didn't blink, the receptionist's expression underwent a subtle change. "If this is some kind of a joke, I'm afraid it will backfire on you."

"This is no joke," Gabi replied, standing her ground at five feet five in her comfortable two-piece cotton suit of pale lemon. She'd already undergone a thorough vetting and security check upon entering the building, so the receptionist knew she didn't pose a threat.

After a slight hesitation the taller woman, clearly in a dilemma, got up from her desk and walked with a decided limp back to her boss's office. That was progress.

While businessmen came and went from his private domain on top of the building complex in downtown Athens, she'd been continually ignored until now. If Gabi had just come out with it in the first place, it might not have taken her most of the day to get results, but she'd wanted to protect him.

Gabi only knew three facts about the thirty-three-year-old Andreas Simonides: First, he was the reputed new force majeure at the internationally renowned Simonides Corporation whose holdings were tied up in all areas of metallurgy, including aluminum, copper and plastics.

Her source confided that their vast fortune, accumulated over many decades, included the ownership of eighty companies. With a population of twelve thousand employees, the Simonides family ruled over a virtual empire extending beyond Greece.

Second, if the picture in the newspaper didn't lie, he was an exceptionally attractive male.

The third fact wasn't public knowledge. In truth no one knew what Gabi knew...not even the man himself. But once they talked, his life would change forever whether he liked it or not.

While she stood there anticipating their first meeting, she heard the woman's footsteps. "Kyrie Simonides will give you two minutes, no more."

"I'll take them!"

"You go down the hall and through the double doors."

"Thank you very much," she said with heartfelt sincerity, then rushed around the reception desk, her golden jaw-length curls bouncing. At first she didn't see anyone as she entered his elegant inner sanctum.

"Life and death you said?" came a voice of male irony from behind her. Though deep, it had an appealing vibrant quality.

She spun around to discover a tall man shrugging into an expensive-looking gray suit jacket he'd just taken from a closet. The play of rip-cord muscle in his arms and shoulders beneath a dazzling white shirt attested to the fact that he didn't spend all his time in the confines of an office. Helpless to do otherwise, her gaze fell lower to the fabric of his trousers molding powerful thighs.

"I'm waiting, Ms. Turner."

Heat stole into her cheeks to be caught staring like that. She lifted her head, but her voice caught as she looked up into eyes of iron gray, half veiled by long black lashes that gave him an aloof quality.

He possessed a healthy head of medium-cropped black hair and an olive complexion. Rugged of feature, his dark Greek looks fascinated her. The picture she'd seen of him hadn't picked up the slight scar partially hidden in his left eyebrow, or the lines of experience she could detect around his eyes and wide male mouth. They revealed a life that had known every emotion.

"You're a difficult man to reach."

After shutting the closet door, he walked across the room to his private elevator. "I'm on my way out. Since you refused to come back next Tuesday, say what you have to say before I leave." He'd already stepped inside the lift, ready to push the button. No doubt he had a helicopter on the roof waiting to fly him to some exotic vacation spot for the weekend.

Standing next to him, she'd never felt more diminutive. Even if she didn't have an appointment, his condescension was too much. But because she might never have another opportunity to get this close to him, she hid her reaction.

Without wasting time she opened her handbag and pulled out a manila envelope. Since he made no move to take it, she undid the flap and removed the contents.

Beneath a set of DNA results lay the front page of a year-old Greek newspaper revealing him aboard the Simonides yacht, surrounded by a crush of people partying the night away. Gabi's elder half sister Thea, whose dark Grecian beauty stood out from the other women on board, was among the crowd captured in the photo. The headline read, "New CEO at Simonides is cause for celebration."

Along with these items was a photograph taken a few days ago of two baby boys wearing diapers and shirts. Gabi had gone to a store to get it enlarged into an eight-by-ten.

She held everything up so he couldn't miss looking at the identical twins who had a crop of curly black hair and gorgeous olive skin like his and Thea's. He'd had his hair cut since the photo.

Up close she picked out many of the other similarities to him, including their widow's peaks and the winged shape of their dark eyebrows. The strong resemblance didn't stop there. She quickly noticed they had his firm chin and wide mouth. Her list went on and on down to their sturdy bodies and same square-cut fingertips.

Yet nothing about the set of his features indicated the picture had made any kind of impression. "I don't see *you* in the photograph, Ms. Turner. I'm sorry if you're in such a desperate situation, but darkening my doorstep wanting a handout isn't the way to get the help you need."

Gabi's jaw hardened. "And you're not the first

man to ignore the children he helped bring into the world."

His black eyes narrowed. "What kind of a mother sends someone else on an errand like this?"

Somehow she got around the boulder in her throat. "I wish my sister could have come herself, but she's dead."

The moment the words left her lips, she sensed his body quicken. "That's a tragedy. Now if you'll excuse me."

Andreas Simonides was a cold-blooded man. There was no way to reach him. As his hand moved to the button on the panel, alerting her that this conversation was over, she said, "Are you saying you never saw this woman in your life?"

Gabi pointed to Thea's face in the newspaper picture. "Maybe this will help." She put the items under her arm while she pulled out Thea's Greek passport. "Here."

To her surprise he took it from her and examined the photo. "Thea Paulos, twenty-four, Athens. Issued five years ago." His black brows formed a bar. He shot her a penetrating glance. "Your sister, you say?"

"My half sister," she amended. "Daddy's first wife was Greek. After she died, he married my

American mother. After a while I came along. This was the last passport Thea held before her divorce." Gabi bit her lip. "She…celebrated it with friends aboard your yacht."

He handed the passport back to her. "I'm sorry about your loss, but I can't help you."

She felt a stab of pain. "I'm sorry for the twins," she murmured. "To lose their mother is tragic beyond words. However, when they're old enough to ask where their father is and I have to tell them he's alive somewhere—but it doesn't matter because they never mattered to him—*that* will be the ultimate tragedy."

The elevator door closed, putting a definitive end to all communication. Gabi spun around, angry and heartsick. For two cents she'd leave the incriminating evidence with his receptionist and let the other woman draw her own conclusions.

But creating a scandal within the Simonides empire was the last thing Gabi wanted to do, not when it could rebound on her own family, especially on her father whose diplomat position in the consulate on Crete might be compromised. In his work he met with Greek VIPs in business and governmental positions on a regular basis. She couldn't bear it if her presence here brought on unwanted repercussions.

No one had asked her to come. Except for Mr. Simonides himself now, no one knew the nature of this visit, especially not her grieving parents. Since Thea had died in childbirth from a heart condition brought on by the pregnancy, Gabi had taken it upon herself to be the babies' advocate. Every child deserved its own wonderful birth mother and father. Unfortunately not every child was so lucky.

"Mission accomplished," she whispered to the empty room. Her heart felt like an anchor that had come loose and had plunged through fathoms of dark water to the lowest depths of the Mediterranean.

Once she'd put everything back in the envelope and stashed it in her handbag, she left his private office. The venerable receptionist nodded to Gabi before she disappeared into the hall. In a few minutes she arrived at the ground floor of the building and hurried outside to get a taxi back to her hotel.

To her surprise, the chauffeur of a limo parked in front got out and approached her. "Ms. Turner?"

She blinked. "Yes?"

"Kyrie Simonides said you had to wait a long time to get in to see him. I've been asked to drive you wherever it is you wish to go."

Her adrenaline kicked in, causing her pulse to speed up. Did this mean the twins' father wasn't a complete block of ice after all? Who wouldn't melt over seeing a photo of his own flesh and blood? If the boys' picture didn't completely convince him, the printout of their DNA would provide infallible proof of a match.

By sending a limo for Gabi, it could mean he planned for a second meeting with her, but he was forced to be discreet. With his money and power, not to mention his looks, the head man had learned how to keep his former liaisons private.

"Thank you. If you wouldn't mind taking me to the Amazon Hotel?" She'd purposely checked in there because it was near the Simonides building in the heart of the Plaka.

He nodded as he helped her in.

Before carrying out her plan to meet with Mr. Simonides today, Gabi had told her parents that one of her female coworkers from Alexandria, Virginia, was in Athens on a trip. They'd decided to get together and see a little of the sights. Gabi felt awful for outright lying to them, but she didn't dare let them know her true agenda.

Until Thea's fifth month of pregnancy when she'd developed serious heart complications and was hospitalized, Gabi hadn't even known the name of the babies' father. But as the end drew near and it became apparent Thea might not make it, she told Gabi to look in her jewel box at home and bring her the envelope she'd hidden there.

Gabi brought it to the hospital. Thea told her to open it. She took one look and gasped when she realized who the man was. "This is all I have of him. Like everyone else on board, we'd both had way too much to drink," Thea whispered. "We were 'strangers in the night' kind of thing."

Her confession elicited a moan from Gabi.

"It didn't mean anything to him. He didn't even know my name. I'm ashamed it happened and he shouldn't have to pay for a mistake which was as much mine as his. I wanted you to see him so you'll know what kind of genes the children have inherited. Now promise me you'll forget everything."

Gabi understood how Thea felt and planned to honor her wishes. Besides the unsuspecting father, she realized that any news would be exploited if linked to the Simonides family. As they had recently lost the daughter of her father's first marriage, Gabi wanted to save her parents any added grief.

While she sat there deep in thought the rear door opened. Surprised they'd already arrived in front of the hotel, she gave a start before getting out.

"Please thank your employer for me."

"Of course."

Once he'd gone, she hurried inside, anxious to eat something at the snack bar before going up to her room. Whatever Mr. Simonides intended to do, he was in the driver's seat and would be the one to set the timetable for their next conversation. *If there were to be one...*

She could only hope he would make the arrangements before morning. Tomorrow she needed to fly back to Heraklion on Crete and rejoin her family. On top of their sadness, they had their hands full with the twins who'd been born six weeks premature.

When it had looked as if Thea was in trouble, Gabi had taken an undetermined leave of absence from the advertising agency in Virginia to fly to Heraklion. Since then she'd taken over the care of the babies because her busy parents' demanding diplomatic position didn't allow for the constant nurturing of the twins without full-time help.

That was four months ago and Gabi's job as public relations manager had been temporarily filled by someone else at Hewitt and Wilson, so she had a vital decision to make. If Mr. Simonides chose to claim his children, then she needed to get back to her work in Virginia ASAP.

Her immediate boss had been made regional director of the East Coast market and hinted at an important promotion for her. But she needed to get back home if she wanted to expand her career opportunity with him. The only other career more important would be to become the mother to Thea's children. But if she chose to do that, then it meant she would have to give up her advertising career until they were school age.

Having been burned by Texas rancher and oil man Rand McCallister five years ago, Gabi had no intention of ever getting married or having children, but if the twins' birth father didn't want them, then she would take on the responsibility of raising them because they were her family. As such, she needed to go back to Virginia where she could rear them in familiar surroundings.

Her family's home in Alexandria was the perfect residence in a guarded, gated community with other diplomats' families, some of whom had small children. Gabi had always lived in it with her parents when they weren't in Greece on assignment. Since Gabi's father owned the house outright, she wouldn't have to deal with a mortgage payment.

If she combined the savings from her job with her dad's financial help, she could be a stay-at-home mom until they were both school age, then get back to her career. It could all work. Gabi would *make* it work because she'd grown to love the twins as if they were her own babies.

In all likelihood Mr. Simonides wasn't interested in the children and had only made certain she got a ride back to wherever she'd come from. Therefore she would fly the twins to Alexandria with her next week.

After a quick meal, Gabi went up to her room on the fourth floor, reasoning that her mother would go with her to help the three of them settle in before returning to Crete. The consulate was no place for two new infants. Her parents would never admit it, but the whole situation had grown out of control.

No sooner did she let herself inside with the card key than she saw the red light blinking on the telephone. Her mother could have left a voice message rather than try to get her on her cell phone. Then again…

With an odd combination of curiosity and trepidation, she reached for the receiver to retrieve it.

"Another limo is waiting for you in front of the hotel, Ms. Turner. It will be there until eight-thirty p.m." Her watch said eight-ten. "If you don't appear with your luggage by then, I'll understand this isn't a life and death situation after all. Your hotel-room bill has been taken care of."

Gabi hung up the phone feeling as if she were acting in a police procedural film, not living real life. He'd had her followed and watched. The fabulously wealthy Mr. Simonides inhabited a world made up of secrecy and bodyguards in order to preserve, not only his safety, but the privacy he craved.

She imagined the paparazzi constituted a living nightmare for him, particularly when someone unknown like Gabi materialized. Her intrusion reminded him there were consequences for a night of pleasure he couldn't remember because everyone partying on the yacht had been drinking heavily.

Thea had confided he was a Greek god come to life. Unlike Gabi, who'd inherited her mother's shorter height and curves, Thea had been fashionably tall and thin. Growing up, she could have any boy she wanted.

She'd always had a man in tow, even the bachelor playboy Andreas Simonides touted in the press, now the crowned head of the Simonides empire. When he'd picked Thea out from the other women on board and had started making love to her in one of the cabins, she'd succumbed in a moment of extreme weakness.

How tragic that in celebrating her divorce she'd become pregnant, the consequences of which had brought on her death…

Gabi couldn't imagine Mr. Simonides forgetting her sister no matter what. But if he'd been like Rand, then there'd been many beautiful women in his life. As both sisters had learned, they'd only made up part of the adoring horde. What a huge shock it must have been to discover he'd fathered baby boys whose resemblance to the two of them was nothing short of astounding.

Gabi only had a few minutes to freshen up and pack her overnight bag before she rushed down to the lobby. It was a simple matter since she hadn't planned to be in Athens more than a night and had only brought one other change of outfit with her.

Through the doors she spied a limo with dark

glass, but a different driver stood next to it. She assumed she would be driven to an undisclosed location where Mr. Simonides was waiting for her.

"Good evening, Ms. Turner." He opened the rear door to help her in with her case. "I'll be taking you to Kyrie Simonides."

"Thank you."

Before long they were moving into the mainstream of heavy traffic circulating about the old Turkish quarter of Athens. Again she had the feeling she was playing a part in a movie, but this time she experienced a distinct chill because she'd dared to approach a complete stranger who had all the power.

The sky was darkening into night. If she were to disappear, her family wouldn't have a clue what had happened to her. Their pain at such an eventuality didn't bear thinking about. In the desire to unite the babies with their only living parent, she'd been blinded to the risks involved. Now it was too late to pull out of a possibly dangerous situation she'd created.

At this point she wasn't quite sure what she'd hoped to achieve. Unless a bachelor who partied and slept with women without giving it a thought were to give up that lifestyle, he wouldn't make the best father around. But for the sake of the twins who deserved more, she couldn't just take them back to Virginia and raise them without first trying to let their father know he *was* a father. Would he want any part in their lives?

She wanted him to be a real man and claim his children, invite them into his home and his life…be there for them for the whole of their lives. Give them his name and seal their legacy.

But of course that kind of thing just didn't happen. Gabi wasn't under any illusions. No doubt he was convinced she'd approached him to extort money and was ready to pay her off. He would soon find out she wanted nothing monetary from him and would be leaving for the States with her precious cargo.

Before Thea died, she'd asked Gabi to help get the babies placed for adoption with a good Greek couple. She wanted them raised Greek. Both sisters realized the impossible burden it would put on their older parents to shoulder the responsibility of raising the children. For all their sakes Gabi had made Thea that promise.

But after her death, Gabi realized it was a promise she couldn't keep. In the first place, the twins' birth father *was* alive. Legally no one could adopt them without his permission.

And in the second place, over the last three

months Gabi had learned to love the boys. She'd bonded with them. Maybe she wasn't Greek, but, having been taught Greek from the cradle, Gabi was bilingual and would use it with them. They would have a good home with her. No one but their own father could ever pry them away from her now.

Suddenly the rear door opened. "Ms. Turner?" the driver called to her. "If you'll follow me."

Startled out of her thoughts, she exited the limo, not having realized they'd arrived at the port of Piraeus. He held her overnight case and walked toward a gleaming white luxury cabin cruiser probably forty to forty-five feet in length moored a few steps away along the pier.

A middle-aged crew member took the bag and helped her aboard. "My name is Stavros. I'll take you to Kyrie Simonides, who's waiting for you to join him in the rear cockpit. This way, Ms. Turner."

Once again she found herself trailing after a stranger to an ultraleather wraparound lounge whose sky roof was open. Her dark-haired host was standing in front of the large windows overlooking the water lit up by the myriad boats and ferries lining the harbor. The dream vessel was state of the art.

Since she'd last seen him in the lift, he'd

removed his suit jacket and tie. He'd rolled his shirtsleeves up to the elbow. Thea had been right. He was spectacular-looking.

She understood when the man announced to her host that the American woman had come aboard. He turned in her direction. The lights reflecting off the water cast his hard-boned features into stark relief.

"Come all the way in and sit down, Ms. Turner. Stavros will bring you anything you want to eat or drink."

"Nothing for me, thank you. I just ate."

After his staff member left the room, she pulled the envelope out of her purse and put it on the padded seat next to her, assuming he wanted a better look at everything. He wandered over to her, but made no move to take it. Instead his enigmatic gaze traveled over her upturned features.

She had an oval face, but her mouth was too wide and her hair was too naturally curly for her liking. Instead of olive skin, hers was a nondescript cream color. Her dad once told her she had wood violet eyes. She'd never seen wood violets, but he'd said it with such love, she'd decided that they were her one redeeming feature.

"My name's Andreas," he said, surprising her. "What's yours?"

"Gabi."

"My sources tell me you were christened Gabriella. I like the shortened version." Unexpectedly he reeked of the kind of virile charm to turn any woman's head. Thea hadn't stood a chance.

Gabi understood that kind of potent male power and the money that went with it. Once upon a time she'd loved Rand. Substitute this Greek tycoon's trappings for seven hundred thousand acres of Texas ranch land with cattle and oil wells and voilà—the two men were interchangeable. Fortunately for Gabi, she'd only needed to learn her lesson once. Thea had learned hers, too, but it had come at the cost of her life.

One black brow quirked. "Where are these twins? At your home in Virginia, or are they a little closer at your father's consulate residence in Heraklion?"

With a mere phone call he knew people in the highest places to get that kind of classified information in less than an hour. Naturally he did. She wanted to tell him that, since he possessed all the facts, there was no need to answer his question, but she couldn't do that. Not after she'd been the one to approach him.

"They're on Crete."

"I want to see them," he declared without hesitation, sending Gabi into mild shock that he'd become curious about these children who could be his offspring. She felt a grudging respect that he'd conceded to the possibility that his relationship with Thea, no matter how short-lived, had produced them. "How soon are you due back in Heraklion?"

"When I left this morning, I told my parents I was meeting a former work colleague from the States in Athens and would fly home tomorrow."

"Will they send a car for you?"

"No. I told them I wasn't sure of my arrival time so I'd take a taxi."

He shifted his weight. "Once I've delivered you to Heraklion, there'll be a taxi waiting to take you home. For the time being Stavros has prepared a room for you. Are you susceptible to the *mal de mer*?"

They were going back by sea?

"No."

"Good. I'm assuming your parents are still in the dark about the twins' father, otherwise you wouldn't have needed to lie to them."

"Thea never wanted them to know." She hadn't wanted anyone to know, especially not Thea's ex-husband Dimitri. For the most part their marriage had been wretched and she hadn't wanted him to find out what she'd done on the very day she'd obtained her divorce from him. Dimitri wouldn't hesitate to expose his ex-wife's indiscretion out of simple revenge.

"Yet she trusted *you*."

"Not until she knew she might die." Thea hadn't wanted to burden anyone. "Though she admitted making a mistake she dearly regretted, she wanted her babies to be taken care of without it being Mom and Dad's responsibility. I approached you the way I did in order to spare them and you any notoriety."

"But not my pocketbook," he inserted in a dangerously silken voice.

"You would have every right to think that, Mr. Simonides."

"Andreas," he corrected her.

She took a deep breath. "Money isn't the reason I came. Nor do you have to worry your name is on their birth certificates. Thea refused to name the father. Though I promised to find a good home for the twins with another couple, I couldn't keep it."

"Why not?"

"Because you're alive. I've looked into the law. No one can adopt them unless you give away your parental rights. In truth, Thea never wanted you to know anything."

He shrugged his elegant shoulders. "If not for money, then why didn't you just spirit them away and forget the legalities?"

Gabi stared hard at him. "Because I plan to adopt them and had to be certain you didn't want to claim them before I take them back to Virginia with me. You have that God-given right after all." She took a fortifying breath. "Being their aunt, I don't."

Her lids prickled, but she didn't let tears form. "As for the twins, they have the same God-given right to be with their father if you want *them*. If there was any chance of that happening, I had to take it, thus my presence in your office today. Naturally if you do want them, then I'll tell my parents everything and we'll go from there."

The air seemed to have electrified around them. "If you're telling me the truth, then you're one of a dying species."

His cynical remark revealed a lot. He had no qualms about using women. In that regard he and Rand had a lot in common. But Gabi suspected Mr. Simonides didn't like women very much.

"One day when they're old enough to understand, I wouldn't be able to face them if I couldn't tell them that at the very beginning I did everything in my power to unite them with you first."

His eyes looked almost black as they searched hers for a tension-filled moment. "What's in Virginia when your parents are here in Greece?"

"*My life*, Mr. Simonides. Like you, I have an important career I love. My parents' responsibilities are here on Crete for the time being. Dad has always had connections to the Greek government. Every time they're transferred, I make the occasional visit, but I live at our family home in Virginia."

"How long have you been here?"

"I came a month before the children were born. They're three months old now." *They're so adorable you can't imagine.*

"What's your routine with them?"

Gabi thought she understood what he was asking. "Between naps I usually take them for walks in their stroller."

"Where?"

"Several places close by. There's a small park with a fountain and benches around the corner from the consulate. I sometimes go there with them."

"Let's plan to meet there tomorrow, say three o'clock. If that isn't possible, phone me on my cell and we'll arrange for another time."

"That will be fine," she assured him.

"Good." He wrote a number on a business card and handed it to her. In the next breath he pulled the phone out of his trouser pocket and asked Stavros to report.

Half a minute later the other man appeared. "Come with me, Ms. Turner, and I'll show you to your cabin."

"Thank you." When she got up, she would have taken the envelope with her, but Andreas was too fast for her.

"I'll return this to you later. Let's hope you sleep well. The sea is calm tonight."

She paused at the entrance. Studying him from across the expanse she said, "Thank you for giving me those two minutes. When I prevailed on your receptionist, she said you were already late leaving your office. I'm sorry if I interrupted your plans for the evening."

He cocked his dark head. "A life and death

situation waits on no man. Go to bed with a clear conscience. *Kalinihta*, Gabi Turner."

His deep, attractive voice vibrated to her insides. *"Kalinihta."*

As soon as Stavros saw her to her cabin, Andreas pulled out his cell phone to call Irena for the second time this evening.

"Darling?" she answered on the second ring. "I've been hoping to hear from you."

"I'm sorry about tonight," he began without preamble. "As I told you earlier, an emergency came up that made it impossible for us to join the family party on Milos."

"Well, you're free now. Are you planning to come over?"

He gripped the phone tighter. "I can't."

"That sounded serious. Something really is wrong, isn't it?"

"Yes," his voice grated. In the space of a few hours his shock had worn off enough for agony to take over.

"You don't want to talk to me about it?"

"I will when the time is right." He closed his eyes tightly. *There was no right time. Not for this.*

"Which means you have to discuss it with Leon first."

What did she just say?

"Judging by your silence, I realize that came out wrong. Forgive me. Ever since we started seeing each other, I've learned you always turn to him before anyone else, but I said it as an observation, not a criticism."

She'd only spoken the truth. It brought up a potentially serious issue for the future, but he didn't have the time to analyze the ramifications right now. "There's nothing to forgive, Irena. I'll call you tomorrow."

"Whatever's disturbing you, remember I'm here."

"As if I could forget."

"*S'agapo*, Andreas."

In the six months they'd been together, he'd learned to love her. Before Gabi Turner had come to his office, he'd planned to ask Irena to marry him. It was past time he settled down. His intention had been to announce it at tonight's party.

"*S'agapo*," he whispered before hanging up.

CHAPTER TWO

THE next afternoon Gabi's mother helped her settle the babies in their double stroller. "It's hot out."

"A typical July day." Gabi had already packed their bottled formula in the space behind the seat. "I've dressed them in their thinnest tops and shorts." One outfit in pale green, the other pastel blue. "At least there's some shade at the park. We'll have a wonderful time, won't we?"

She couldn't resist kissing their cheeks. After being gone overnight, she'd missed them horribly. Now that they were awake, their sturdy little arms and legs were moving like crazy.

"Oh, Gabi…they're so precious and they look so much like Thea."

"I know." But they also looked like someone else. That was the reason they were so gorgeous. She squeezed her mother around the shoulders. "Because of them, Thea will always be with us."

"Your father's so crazy about them, I don't know if he can handle your taking them back home to Alexandria to live. I know I can't. Please promise me you'll reconsider."

"We've been over this too many times, Mom. Dad can't do his work the way he needs to. It's best for both of you with your busy schedules. At home I'll be around my friends and there'll be other moms with their babies to befriend. We'll see each other often. You know that!"

Right now Gabi had too many butterflies in her stomach at the thought of meeting up with Andreas to concentrate on anything else. She slowly let go of her. "See you later."

Making certain the twins were comfy, she started pushing the stroller away from the Venetian-styled building that had become a home to the consulate with its apartments for their family. From her vantage point she could look out over the port of Heraklion on the northern end of Crete, an island steeped in Roman and Ottoman history.

Normally she daydreamed about its past during her walks with the children, but this afternoon her gaze was glued to the harbor.

Somewhere down there was the cabin cruiser that had brought her from Piraeus.

The trip had been so smooth, she could believe the sea had been made of glass. She should have fallen into a deep sleep during the all-night crossing, but in truth she'd tossed and turned most of it.

That was because the man she'd labeled bloodless and selfish didn't appear to fit her original assessment. In fact she had trouble putting him in any category, which was yet another reason for her restlessness.

As a result she'd slept late and had to be awakened by Stavros, who'd brought a fabulous breakfast to her elegant cabin with its cherrywood décor. She'd thanked him profusely. Following that she'd showered and given herself a shampoo. After drying her hair, she'd changed into white sailor pants and a sleeveless navy and white print top.

Once her bag was packed, she'd applied lipstick, then walked through to the main salon before ascending the companionway stairs in her sandals. She'd expected to find Andreas so she could thank him for everything, but discovered he was nowhere in sight. Somehow she'd felt disappointed, which made no sense at all.

Since Stavros had let her know her ride was

waiting, she'd had no choice but to leave the cruiser from the port side. He'd carried her overnight bag to the taxi and wished her a good day. After thanking him again, she'd been whisked through the bustling city of close to a hundred and forty thousand people. Further up the incline they reached the consulate property and passed through the sentry gate.

After her arrival, she'd made some noncommittal remarks to her parents about having had an okay time in Athens, but she'd missed the children too much and wanted to come straight home. The babies had acted so happy to see her, her heart had melted.

Closer to the park now, she felt her pulse speed up. Though the heat had something to do with it, there was another reason. What if Andreas took one look and decided he *did* want the children? Though that was what she'd been hoping and praying for, she hadn't counted on this pang that ran through her at the thought of having to give them up.

The park held its share of children, some with their mothers. A few older people sat on benches talking. Several tourists on bikes had stopped to catch their breath before moving on. It was a benign scene until she noticed the striking man who sat beneath the fronds of a palm tree reading a newspaper.

There was an aura of sophistication about him. A man in control of his world. One of the most powerful men in Greece actually. Everywhere he went, his bodyguards preceded him, but she would never know who they were or where they were hidden.

Today he'd dressed in a silky blue sport shirt and tan trousers, a picture of masculine strength and a kind of rugged male beauty hard to put in words.

She glanced at the twins. They didn't know it, but they were looking at their daddy, a man like no other who wasn't more than ten feet away.

His intelligent eyes fringed with inky black lashes peered over the newspaper at them before he put it aside and stood up.

Gabi moved the stroller closer until they were only a few feet apart. Hardly able to breathe, she touched one dark, curly head. "This is Kris, short for Kristopher. And this…" she tousled the other gleaming cap of black curls "…is Nikos."

Andreas hunkered down in front of them. Like finding a rare treasure, his eyes burned a silvery gray as his gaze inspected every precious centimeter, from their handsome faces to the tips of their bare toes.

He cupped their chins as if he were memorizing their features, then he let them wrap their fingers around his. Before long both his index fingers ended up in their mouths.

Gabi started to laugh. She couldn't help it. "He tastes good, huh. You little guys must be hungry." She undid the strap and handed Nikos to him. "Sit down on the bench and you can feed him." In a flash she supplied him with a cloth against his shoulder and a baby bottle full of formula.

"If you've never done this before, don't worry about it. The boys will do all the work. Let him drink for a minute, then pat his back gently to get rid of the air bubbles. I'll take care of Kris."

For the next little while, she was mostly aware of the twins making noisy sounds as they drank their bottles with the greatest of relish. Afterward they traded babies so he could get to know Kris.

Every so often the sounds were followed by several loud burps that elicited rich laughter from Andreas. When she'd approached him in his office yesterday, she hadn't thought he was capable of it.

Any misgivings she'd had about starting up this process fled at the sight of him getting acquainted with the boys. It was a picture that would be impressed on her heart forever. Wherever Thea was, she had to be happy her sons were no longer strangers to their father, even if he'd never sought her sister out again.

Gabi didn't know the outcome, but this meeting was something to cherish at least.

"We'll have to make this fast because I don't want to keep them out in the sun much longer." She flashed him a quick glance. "Next time—if you want there to be a next time—you can take them for a walk on your own."

He made no response. She didn't know what to think. Another five minutes passed before she said, "There now. They're as sated as two fat cats." Again she heard laughter roll out of him.

Together they lowered them back into the stroller. Her arm brushed his, making her unduly aware of him. She put the empty bottles and cloths away. When she rose up, their glances collided. "I have to go," she said. Maybe she was mistaken, but she thought the light in his eyes faded a trifle. "If you want to see them again, call me on my cell."

Pulling out his phone, he said, "Tell me your

number and I'll program it into mine right now."

Maybe that was a good sign. Then again maybe it wasn't. A small shiver ran down her spine in fear that when he contacted her next, he would tell her that, cute as the boys were, he was still signing his rights away and they were all hers with his blessing.

After she'd given him her number, he pushed the stroller toward the path leading out to the street. One of the older women caught sight of the twins and shouted something about them having beautiful children.

"Efharisto," Andreas called back, thanking the woman as if this were an everyday occurrence.

Gabi didn't want to tear herself away, but her mother would worry if she wasn't back soon and would want to know why the delay. "I really have to go."

"I know," he said in a husky tone before giving the boys a kiss on their foreheads. "I'll be in touch."

With those long powerful strides, he left the park going one way while she trundled along with the stroller going the other. The farther apart they got, the more fearful she grew.

He wasn't indifferent to the twins. She knew

that. She'd felt it and seen it. But one meeting with his children didn't mean he wanted to take on the lifetime responsibility of parenting them. Between his work and girlfriends he wouldn't have much time to fit in the twins.

She'd told him she'd be leaving for Virginia next week. If he didn't want her to take them away, he needed to make up his mind soon.

Maybe he would compromise. She'd raise them and he'd be one of those drop-in daddies. For the boys' sake Gabi couldn't bear the thought of it, but having a daddy around once in a while, even if he only flew into D.C. from Greece once a year with a present, was better for them than no daddy at all, wasn't it? Gabi loved her own father so much, she couldn't imagine life without him.

The only thing to do now was brace herself for his next phone call.

Accompanied by his bodyguards, Andreas rushed toward the helicopter waiting for him at the Heraklion airport. Once he'd climbed aboard, he directed his pilot to fly him to the Simonides villa on Milos where the whole clan had congregated for the weekend.

Last night there'd been a party to celebrate his sister Melina's thirtieth birthday, but he'd been forced to miss it because of a life and death situation. *Gabi Turner had been right about that.*

Though his married sister had been gracious over the phone, he knew she'd been hurt by his excuse that something unavoidable had come up to detain him in Athens. He'd promised to make it up to her, but that kind of occasion in her honor with extended family in attendance only happened once a year. Now the moment was gone.

Yet, sorry as he was, he had something much more vital on his mind and couldn't think about anything else. Throughout the flight he still felt the strong tug of those little mouths on his fingers. Their touch had sent the most peculiar sensation through Andreas.

Even though he had ten nieces and nephews, he hadn't been involved in their nurturing. The closest he'd come was to hold their weightless bodies as they were being passed around at a family party after coming home from the hospital.

Today had been something totally different. It was as if the blinders had come off, but he hadn't known they existed until contact was made. Kris and Nikos weren't just babies. Those excited bodies with their bright eyes and faces belonged to a pair of little guys who one day would grow up to be big guys. Guys who had the Simonides stamp written all over them.

As soon as he entered the main villa Andreas went in search of his vivacious mother, who was in the kitchen supervising dinner preparations with the cook, Tina.

"There you are, darling," she said the minute she saw him.

He gave her a kiss, already anticipating her next comment. "My absence was unavoidable."

Her expressive dark brows lifted. "A delicate merger?"

"Incredibly delicate," he muttered. The memory of Nikos and Kris so trusting in his arms as they inhaled their formula never left his mind.

"You sound like your father. I have to tell you I'm glad he's finally stepped down and you're in charge. He's a different man these days. Let's just hope that when you're settled down, hopefully soon, your wife will have more influence on you to take time off once in a while. You're already working too hard if you had to miss Melina's birthday party."

His mother could have no idea. He gave her an extra hug. "Where's everyone?" he asked, knowing the answer full well, but he didn't want to sound like anything out of the ordinary was wrong.

"Still waterskiing. Your grandparents are out on the patio watching your father and your uncle Vasio drive the younger children around. We'll eat out by the pool in an hour."

"That gives me enough time to get in a little exercise." After stealing an hors d'oeuvre from the plate Tina was preparing, he pecked her cheek to atone for his sin before walking through a series of alcoves and walkways to reach his villa with its own amenities farther down their private beach.

The massive family retreat—a cluster of linked white villas in the Cycladic style— had been the Simonides refuge for many generations. Because of business, Andreas didn't escape from his penthouse in the city as often as he wanted and had been looking forward to this time with the family.

Who would have dreamed that, before the lift door closed, an innocent-looking blonde female would sweep into his office like a Cycladic breeze, bringing a fragrance as sweet as the honeysuckle growing wild on the island before she dropped her bomb?

Still charged with adrenaline, he changed into

his swim trunks and hurried down to the beach where the family ski boats were in use.

"There's Uncle Andreas!" One of his nieces waiting on the beach for her turn screeched with joy and ran toward him. Her brother followed. "Now that you're here, will you take us? Grandpa hasn't come back for us yet."

His sister Leila's children were the youngest, seven and nine. "What do *you* think?" He grinned. "Climb in my ski boat. We'll show everybody! You spot your sister first, Jason."

"Okay!"

Happy chaos reigned for another half-hour, then everyone left the beach because dinner had been announced. Andreas secured his boat to their private pier. Things couldn't have turned out better than to find his brother Leon the last to tie up his own ski boat. His wife Deline had gone up with the others, leaving them alone for the moment.

"How was the party last night?" Andreas asked as he started tying the other end for him.

Leon shot him a glance. "Fine, but I have to tell you Dad wasn't too thrilled you didn't make a showing. He was hoping to see you there with Irena."

Irena Liapis was a favorite with the family

and the daughter of his parents' good friends who owned one of the major newspapers in Greece. It was the same paper that had shown Thea aboard the family yacht.

Everyone was hoping for news that a wedding was in the offing. With his four siblings married, his parents were expecting some kind of announcement from him.

Andreas groaned. No woman had ever been his grand passion. Maybe there wasn't such a thing and he was only deluding himself because he'd been a bachelor for too long. But his feelings for Irena had grown over the months. Besides being beautiful, she was intelligent and kind. He wanted his marriage to work and knew it could if she were his wife.

But last night Gabi Turner's explosion into his life had caused every plan to go up in smoke. Now that a certain situation had developed threatening to set off a conflagration, his whole world had been turned on its side. For the time being he couldn't think about Irena or anything else.

Andreas knew it wasn't fair to keep any secrets from the woman he'd intended to marry, but, as he'd just found out, life wasn't fair...not to the twins who'd lost their mother or to Gabi who'd taken on the awesome responsibility of raising her half sister's children.

By tacit agreement he and his brother started walking up the beach toward the pool area. Using his fingertips, Leon scooped up his sandals lying in the sand. "Your non-appearance was kind of a shocker. Normally Dad gives you a pass."

"It's because he has a soft spot for Melina." She was the baby in the family.

"If you pulled off the Canadian gold-refining merger, I'm sure all will be forgiven."

Andreas frowned. "That might not happen. I'm still debating if it's to our advantage."

"With the kind of revenue it could bring in, you must be joking!"

"Not at all. I think they're in deeper trouble than they've made out to be." He gave his brother a covert glance. "Speaking of trouble, there's something you and I have to talk about in private."

"If you're referring to the acquisition of those mineral rights in—"

"I'm not," he cut him off. "You made a brilliant move on that." Leon was his second in command. "I'm referring to something else that doesn't have anything to do with business. After we eat, come to my villa alone. Make it look casual. You need to see something."

Leon let out a bark of laughter. "You sound cryptic. What's gotten into you?"

"You'll find out soon enough."

For the next hour Andreas joined in with his family and gave Melina the gift he'd found for her on one of his business trips to the Balkans. She collected nesting dolls. The one he gave her proved to be a hit. Once dessert was served, he faded from the scene and headed for his place, nodding to one of the maids on the way. Not long after, Leon showed up.

"Lock the front door behind you. I don't want us to be disturbed."

Leon flicked him a puzzled glance as he pushed in the button. He walked into the living room. "What's going on? The last time I remember seeing you this intense was when Father suffered that mild heart attack last year."

Heart attack was the operative word.

Andreas was still trying to recover from the one Ms. Turner had given him. Without wasting any more time he handed the newspaper photo to Leon, who studied it for a minute before lifting his head. "Why are you showing me a picture of you? I don't understand." He handed it back to him.

"If you'll notice the date, this headline is a year old. When the picture was taken, I happened to be in the States on business with our big brother. As usual, the paparazzi got you and me mixed up. That was during the time you and Deline were separated. This tall, raven-haired beauty who's looking over at you was the woman, right?"

Only now did it strike Andreas that Thea bore a superficial resemblance to both Deline and Irena. Sometimes it astounded him that he and Leon had similar tastes, not only in certain kinds of foods and sports, but in women. They were all striking brunettes.

"Yes," he whispered. "And if I hadn't gone to Deline and told her the truth about that night, it could have cost me my marriage. I still marvel that she forgave me enough to give us a second chance."

Leon unexpectedly grabbed the paper out of his hand and balled it up in his fist. "Why are you reminding me of it? Look here, Andreas—" His cheeks had grown ruddy with unaccustomed anger.

"I *have* been looking," he came back in a quiet voice. "Because I love you and Deline, for the last twenty-four hours I've been doing whatever it takes to protect you and keep this news confidential."

"What do you mean?"

"I thought you'd like to know the name of the woman you spent that hour with on the yacht. Her name was Thea Paulos, the divorced daughter of Richard Turner, of the Greek-American Consulate on Crete. Her ex-husband Dimitri Paulos is the son of Ari Paulos who owns Paulos Metal Exports, one of the subsidiary companies we acquired a few years ago."

While his brother stood there swallowing hard, Andreas removed the twins' photo and DNA results from the manila envelope and handed everything to him.

Stunned into silence, Leon sank down on the couch to stare at the children he'd unknowingly produced. Though Andreas had it in his heart to feel sorry for his brother's predicament, a part of him thought Leon the luckiest man on earth to have fathered two such beautiful sons.

"I had our DNA compared to theirs. It's a match."

Leon's face went white.

"I've seen them," Andreas confided. Thanks to Gabi, he'd held and fed both of them, an experience he'd never forget.

His brother's dark head reared back. "You've *seen* them—" He sounded incredulous.

"Yes. They're three months old."

"Three months?" He mouthed the words, obviously in shock. "How did Ms. Paulos contact you?"

"She didn't. Tragically for the children, she died on the operating table giving birth to them."

"She's dead?" He kept repeating everything Andreas said, like a man in a trance.

"It was her half sister, Gabi Turner, who came to my office yesterday. She's the one who arranged for me to see the boys at a park near the consulate today."

His brother jumped up from the couch looking like a caged animal ready to spring.

"Take it easy, Leon. I know what you're thinking, but you'd be dead wrong. In the first place, she believes *I'm* the father."

Leon jerked around. "You didn't tell her *I* was the one in that news photo?"

"No."

His brother averted his eyes. "How much money does she want to keep quiet?" he asked in a subdued voice.

It was a fair question since the same one had dominated Andreas's thoughts when she'd first pulled out the photograph. "Forget about her desire to blackmail me. This has to do with something else entirely."

"And you believed her?" Leon cried, grabbing his shoulders.

Andreas supposed Gabi could have been lying through her teeth. If that were the case… He saw black for a moment before a semblance of reason returned.

"I'd stake my life on the fact that her only agenda for coming to me was to make sure I knew I had two sons before she left Greece."

"Why would she do that?"

He sucked in his breath. "Because she said they deserve to be with their real father if it's at all possible."

Leon's eyes clouded for a moment before he flashed Andreas a jaded look and released him. "It could be a ploy. Where's she supposedly going?"

"Alexandria, Virginia." To her home and her life, as she'd put it. "Her father started his diplomatic career there. I have confirmation of it."

While Leon stood there tongue tied, Andreas's cell phone rang. He checked the caller ID and clicked on. "Mother?"

"Where are you?"

"In my villa." He glanced at his brother. "Leon's with me."

"Can't you two stop talking business for one evening?"

"Yes. We'll be right over."

"Good. Everyone's wondering where you are. Deline's been looking everywhere. We're going to start some family movies."

"Tell her we're coming," Leon called out loud enough for her to hear before Andreas clicked off.

He went into the study and locked the envelope in his desk, then eyed his brother soberly. "Since Gabi thinks I'm the father, we'll leave it that way for now."

As soon as Leon handed the wad to him he set it in an ashtray on the coffee table and put a match to it. When the evidence was gone, he lifted his head. "Before you make a decision about anything, you need to see the twins for yourself."

Another odd sound escaped his brother.

"I'll phone Gabi and see if we can't arrange it for Monday. We'll make up some excuse to the family about a business emergency. We won't have to be gone long."

Leon buried his face in his hands. "How am I

going to be able to act like everything's normal until then?"

A shudder passed through Andreas's body. "We're both going to have to find a way."

His dark head reared back. "When Deline finds out about this... I swear I've been doing everything to make our marriage work. It only happened that one time, Andreas. It'll never happen again. I love Deline." The tremor in his voice was real enough.

"I believe you."

"You know the reason why we separated for those two months. We'd been fighting over my working too much. She got on that old rant about my being married to you instead of her. She said she was tired of being neglected and told me I was the reason we hadn't gotten pregnant yet.

"When she told me she wanted a separation because she needed time to think, I was in hell. After weeks of trying to get her to talk to me, she told me she was thinking of making the separation permanent. I was so hurt, I ended up taking the yacht out. Some of my friends came along and brought women. There was too much drinking. I never meant to lose my head."

Andreas had heard it all before. He'd seen

his brother was in anguish then, but this news added a terrifying new wrinkle.

After pacing the floor, Leon stopped and faced Andreas. "I know that was no excuse for making the ghastliest mistake of my life." His mouth formed a thin line. "Sorry you got involved in this mess." There was a lengthy pause. "It isn't your problem. It's *mine*, but I don't know what the hell I'm going to do about it yet."

At least Leon had admitted responsibility. "Once you've seen those babies, you'll figure it out." Of course Andreas could tell himself that now, but there was no sure way to know how his brother would feel after he'd gotten a look at them. "Let's agree that for the moment there's nothing else to be done. You go on back and find Deline. I'll be there in a few minutes."

Though he'd promised his mother he wouldn't be long, he found he didn't want to put off the phone call to Gabi until tomorrow. It surprised him how much he was looking forward to talking to her again.

Gabi had just finished changing the last diaper of the night when she heard her cell phone ring. She'd kept it in her jeans pocket to be certain she'd didn't miss Andreas's call if it came.

A peek at the caller ID and a rush of pleasure

filled her body. Since her parents had gone out to dinner with guests, she could talk freely and clicked on.

"Andreas?"

"Good evening," came his deep, compelling voice. She liked the sound of it. Thea had obviously found it attractive, too. The knowledge that she'd had an intimate relationship with him increased Gabi's guilt and anger at herself for having any thoughts or feelings about him.

"Am I calling at the wrong moment?"

"No." She left the bedroom that had been turned into a nursery and closed the door. "It's a perfect time." Gabi was the only person to speak for the children. He sounded eager enough to see them again. "The children are finally down until their three-o'clock bottle, thank heaven."

"Then you're going to need your beauty sleep, so I won't keep you."

She let the remark pass. His only agenda had to do with his children, who appeared to be growing on him. That was the result she'd been hoping for. Leaning against the wall in the hall, she said, "Have you decided you want to see the twins again?"

"Yes. Could we meet at the park on Monday?"

Her pulse sped up. "Of course. When would

you like to come? Morning or afternoon is fine with me."

"Morning would be an ideal time for me."

"Then I'll meet you at ten o'clock. After they've been fed and had their baths, I often take them on a walk when it's not so hot."

"I'm anxious to see them again."

That was an excellent sign. "The children love any attention." Especially when it was from their father. "I'll see you then."

"Gabi?" There was a nuance in his voice that caught her off guard.

"Yes?"

She heard him take a deep breath. "Thank you for being there for them."

It was too early for her to get a handle on his vision for their future. After his visit on Monday to see the children, there might not be another one. She had to prepare herself for that possibility. "You don't need to thank me. I wouldn't be anywhere else."

"I've noticed you don't accept compliments graciously, so I'll say it another way. Not everyone would do what you're doing. Not for your sister, not for anyone."

"Before you give me too much credit, don't forget I watched the twins being born. It was a life-changing experience for me."

"I don't doubt it. *Ta Leme*." She knew that phrase well enough.

Gabi hung up, wishing his visit was as soon as tomorrow instead of Monday. She would like to know his plans because she was leaving with the children next week. It was no good staying in Greece any longer. One way or the other, she needed to get on with her life and her parents needed to get on with theirs.

During Gabi's morning walk with the children, Kris had nodded off. Last night he'd played too hard after she'd gotten up to give him a bottle. Nikos, on the other hand was wide awake and raring to go.

When she reached the park bench beneath the shade, she undid the strap and picked him up. He clung to her as she showed him the fountain. The noise of the babbling water had captured his attention. She looked round to see if Kris was all right. As before, her breath caught to discover Andreas standing over the stroller looking down at him.

Every time she saw the boys' father, she experienced a guilty rush of excitement that was impossible to smother. He'd dressed in a light blue business suit with a darker blue shirt and no tie, the personification of male splendor in her eyes. Thea's, too.

There was a time when Gabi hadn't thought there was a man who came close to Rand in his cowboy boots and Stetson. While on her two-week summer vacation with Rachel McCallister, her friend from college, she'd fallen hard for Rachel's cousin and his Texas charm. Two weeks of a whirlwind relationship and she'd thought it would go on forever.

Too late she found out there was nothing deeper to back up his fascinating drawl and the smile in those dancing blue eyes. He'd let her go back to Alexandria without making any kind of plans to see her again. When she learned through Rachel that he was getting married to his old girlfriend, Gabi's heart withered.

Since then she'd met and dated some attractive, successful men at her work and at the consulate, but she took no relationship seriously. Her career had become her top priority, the one thing she could count on.

Thankfully she'd learned her lesson well before meeting the legendary Andreas Simonides. Though there was no male to equal his intelligence or incredible appeal, she wouldn't fall into that trap again. Once had been enough.

She walked toward him carrying Nikos. "Good morning."

"Kalimera." His voice had a lazy, almost seductive quality. She felt his gaze linger on her face before he switched his attention to Nikos. Again his gray eyes lit up. "Do you remember me?" He kissed the baby's cheek.

Nikos's eyelids fluttered in reaction. He was so cute.

"Gabi?" His eyes trapped hers once more. They held a trace of anxiety. "I brought someone with me I'd like you to meet."

Who?

Maybe it was a woman he was thinking of marrying now that he was running the Simonides company. Gabi fought to remain calm. Naturally that woman would be hopelessly in love with him. But when she learned he had two sons, would she be able to accept and eventually love the children he'd fathered with someone else?

Suddenly Gabi was feeling very possessive. No woman could mother them the way she could, but it was none of her business since she had no parental claim to the boys.

He put a hand on her upper arm and squeezed gently. "It's all right," he whispered, noticing how quiet she'd gone. "I trust him with my life."

Him?

While her heart picked up the lost beat, Andreas stepped around the end of the wall. Within two seconds he came back again, but at this point Gabi thought her vision had become blurred because she was looking at two of Andreas.

She blinked in alarm, but nothing seemed to clear her double vision. They came closer, in range now, she realized there was nothing wrong with her eyesight. Moving toward her was Andreas and his mirror image wearing a tan suit and cream shirt, only he didn't have a scar and his hair was the same style and longer length as in the news photo.

Gabi stared at Andreas in surprise. "You're a *twin*!"

"That's right. Gabriella Turner, meet my best friend and older brother by five minutes, Leonides Simonides."

"Hello, Mr. Simonides," she said, shaking his hand.

"Leon? Say hello to your sons."

CHAPTER THREE

Thea had been with Leonides Simonides, not Andreas?

"Ms. Turner? I hardly know what to say." Leon looked as stunned as she felt. In fact he barely got those words out because his gaze had fastened on the boys in visible disbelief.

"Gabi's holding Nikos," Andreas stated, filling in the silence. "Down there is Kris, who looks like he just woke up from his catnap."

Swift as the speed of light Andreas caught Gabi's eye and winked. Warmth flowed through her body as she smiled back, remembering the humorous comment she'd made on Saturday about the children being fat cats.

But she couldn't forget Leon. Though Andreas would have told him about the children ahead of time, this still had to be the most earthshaking moment of his life. She wasn't surprised he sank down on the bench literally stupefied.

"Would you like to hold Nikos?" she asked.

"I won't know what to do if he cries," he murmured, ashen faced.

"He won't." She handed the baby to him. By now Andreas had reached for Kris and was kissing his sweet little neck.

Deciding to give them privacy, she wandered to the other side of the park and sat down to finish reading the biography she'd picked up on the life of the French chef Julia Child.

She hadn't enjoyed a book as good as this in several years. Like Julia, Gabi had experienced an epiphany about food. But it hadn't happened until her father had been transferred to Crete where she'd tasted her first *pastitsio* and developed an instant love of Greek cuisine.

During the last few months she'd been practicing in the kitchen at the consulate, determined she would raise the boys on Greek food in honor of both their parents. By now she could make pretty good *spanakopita*.

When she realized she'd read the next page for the tenth time, she closed the book and looked across the park. The babies had been put back in the stroller. Both men stood next to them. It seemed as if Andreas was doing most of the talking. Gabi wasn't sure what it all meant.

Hesitant to interrupt, she waited until he

started wheeling the stroller toward her with a grave countenance marring his handsome features. She put the book back in her purse and stood up, noticing that Leon had walked out to the street.

"Let me apologize for my brother." He spoke without preamble.

"There's no need. It's not every day a man is confronted by instant fatherhood, especially when they're twins." The happiness she'd felt earlier to see the children united with Andreas had dissipated. Not in her wildest dreams would she have thought up a contingency where his twin brother was the father!

Andreas eyed her with a solemn expression. "Especially when he's been married three years."

A small gasp escaped her throat. Had Thea known he was married, or hadn't it mattered to either of them in the heat of the moment?

"Obviously he's going to need some time," she whispered.

"You're a very understanding woman. When he can gather his wits, I'm sure he'll want to talk to you." She was fairly certain Leon wouldn't, particularly when Andreas would have already told him she planned to go home to Virginia and raise the twins. But she didn't say anything.

"Thank you for making this meeting today possible, Gabi."

It sounded like a goodbye speech if she'd ever heard one. Leon had probably told him he couldn't deal with the situation. What man could? One night in a stranger's arms wasn't supposed to end up like this. He wouldn't be the first father to opt out of his responsibilities.

She felt sorry for Andreas, who clearly loved his brother and had done everything he could to support him. "Of course. I approached *you*, remember? Thanks to you I won't ever have to lie to the children."

After clearing her throat, she said, "When I get back to Virginia, I'll be reconnecting the phone and will leave the new phone number on a voice mail for you. That way if your brother ever wants to contact me, you can give him both numbers. One last thing. Please let him know I'll never try to get hold of him for any reason."

His eyes turned as black as his grim expression. "How soon are you leaving?" he asked in a gravelly voice.

"The day after tomorrow." She extended her hand, not wanting to prolong the inevitable. "Goodbye, Mr. Simonides."

* * *

Tuesday evening Gabi's phone alerted her to a text message while she was packing the last of the babies' clothes into the big suitcase. Her parents were in the nursery playing with the twins, their last night together for two months or more. Pretty soon it would be bedtime. Her dad wanted to put them down.

Since yesterday when she'd pushed the stroller in the opposite direction from Andreas and his brother, she'd tried hard to put the whole business behind her. She thought she'd been doing a fairly good job of hiding her feelings from her parents. Any pain they'd seen would have been attributed to tomorrow's dreaded departure.

Little did they know she'd met the boys' father. To her dismay he was doing nothing to prevent her from taking his children out of the country, out of his life.

Gabi hurt for his sons.

She hurt so horribly she could scarcely bear it, but she had to handle it because that was her agreement with Andreas. She would honor her commitment even if it was killing her.

With a tortured sigh she reached for the phone on the dresser. Her best friend Jasmin knew she was coming home and probably wanted to find out her flight number and time. But when she saw who'd sent the message, her adrenaline kicked in, causing her heart to thud.

I just arrived in Heraklion. When you've put the twins to bed, meet me at the park. I'll wait till morning if I have to because we need to talk. A.

She had to stifle her cry of joy. This meant Leon had been having second thoughts about letting his children slip away without making some arrangement to see them again. It meant she would have contact with Andreas one more time. Gabi wished her pulse didn't race faster at the thought.

After shutting the suitcase, she hurried to her bedroom to change. She slipped off her T-shirt and jeans, then reached for the tan pleated pants and kelly green cotton top she'd left out to wear on the plane tomorrow.

Once she'd run the brush through her curls and put on lipstick, she poked her head around the door of the nursery. Her parents were absorbed with the children, too busy to be unduly curious about her. "I'm going out for a few minutes to pick up some things at the store."

"Don't be too long," her dad cautioned in

between singing to Nikos off-key. The scene melted her heart.

"I won't."

A minute later she waved to the guard at the sentry and headed in the direction of the park. Because of the reflection from the water, twilight brought out the beauty of the Greek islands, but never more so than tonight. It was Andreas's fault. The knowledge he was waiting for her had added that magical quality.

Maybe this was how Thea had felt when she'd met Leon that evening aboard the yacht, as if the heavens were close for a moment and one of the twin gods from Olympus had come near enough for a human to touch.

He'd come close all right, so close he'd touched her with two little mortals, and now his twin, the powerful god Andreas, was here to parlay a deal between the two worlds. When Gabi thought of him in that light, the stars left her eyes and sanity returned.

Tonight he wasn't dressed like a god. She spied him at the fountain wearing a cream sport shirt and khakis. No one else was about. Instead of expensive hand-sewn leather shoes, he'd worn sandals like everyone else walking along the beachfront.

He watched her coming, but didn't make a move toward her. "*Yassou*, Gabi."

"Hi!" *Keep it airy.* "I came the minute I got your message because Mother and I have an early morning flight to Athens."

"I'm aware of that." He stood with his hands on his hips, emanating a stunning male virility. "Before you go anywhere, I have something in mind I'd like to discuss with you."

She blinked. "Why isn't Leon with you?"

Andreas studied her for a long moment. "I think you know the answer to that question."

Gabi was afraid she did, but Andreas's presence confused her. "Then I don't understand why *you're* here."

"Because I don't want you to leave Greece."

She struggled to stifle her moan. Of all the things he might have said, his blunt answer wasn't even on her list. Now if Rand had said, "I don't want you to leave Austin…" But he hadn't said anything. As for Andreas, she knew his agenda had nothing to do with her personally.

"I don't understand."

He took a deep breath. "Leon's in a panic right now, but in another day or two he's going to conquer it. When he does, the children need to be here, not clear across the Atlantic."

Gabi was the one starting to panic and shook her head. "I can't stay on Crete."

His pewter gaze pierced her. "Why not?"

"B-because my parents need to get their life back," she stammered. "The boys and I need our own home."

He took a step closer. "You've had a home here for months. I would imagine your parents will be devastated when the babies are gone. Therefore that couldn't be the real reason you're so anxious to take flight. Do you have a lover in Alexandria waiting for you?"

Taking the out he'd proffered, she said, "As a matter of fact I do. Not that it's anyone's business." While she spoke, she watched a young couple who'd wandered into the park and had started kissing.

"You're lying. Otherwise he'd have flown here to whisk you and the children back to Virginia weeks ago." The comment had come out more like a soft hiss. He would make a terrifying adversary if crossed.

She turned her eyes away from the amorous couple. "If you must know, I want the children to myself."

"So they'll know you're their mother," he deduced. "That makes perfect sense, but you don't have to go to Virginia to do that."

Gabi sucked in her breath. "I don't have the means to earn a living right now and Dad's home in Alexandria is paid for. With my savings and his financial help, it will work until they're in school and I can go to work."

He shook his dark head. "I've learned enough to know your father has the means to help you move into your own place here on Crete where you and the boys can be close by but still independent. Why are you afraid to tell me the truth? What's going on?"

Andreas saw too much. "There are already too many questions being asked about the paternity of the twins. My parents don't know anything. If it got out about your brother and Thea, my family as well as yours would suffer and you know it. That's why I want to take them back with me."

"Out of sight, out of mind, you mean."

"Yes."

He rubbed the back of his neck. "That might work for a while, but it's inevitable the day will arrive when the secret comes out. They always do. By then the damage will be far worse, not only for the families involved but for the twins themselves."

"I realize that, but for the present I don't know what else to do. There's—" She stopped herself in time, but Andreas immediately picked up on it.

"What were you going to say?"

"N-nothing."

"Tell me!" he demanded.

Feeling shaky, she said, "I should never have come to your office."

"That isn't what you were about to blurt."

The man had radar. At this point she had no choice but to tell him. Not everything, but enough to satisfy him.

Taking a few steps, she sank down on the park bench. He followed, but stood near her with his tanned fingers curled around the back railing. "Thea's husband would love to hurt our family for backing her in the divorce. He's capable of making trouble that could make things unpleasant for Leon, too."

"You're talking about Dimitri Paulos."

Gabi got up from the bench. "How did you know?"

His eyes played over her. "I did a background check. Thea's passport alerted me she has an ex. Has he threatened you personally, Gabi?"

She pressed her lips together. "No, but suffice it to say he was furious when Thea divorced him. If not for diplomatic immunity through Dad, I don't even want to think what might have happened to her. Dimitri considered her his possession. Thea was convinced he'd hired a man to follow her everywhere."

One black brow lifted sardonically. "My father and I have had business dealings with Dimitri's father in Athens. I'm familiar with his son's more devious methods."

That shouldn't have surprised Gabi. Andreas knew everything. "The trouble is, before she died she told me he was still out for blood wanting to know who made her pregnant. If he were to learn your brother is the father of her twins, he'd love to feed that kind of gossip to the newspapers just to be ugly."

"He can try," Andreas muttered with unconscious hauteur. After a palpable silence he said, "Since your parents must be waiting for you, I'll walk you back."

Gabi shook her head. "That won't be necessary."

"I insist."

He cupped her elbow and they started walking. Far too aware of his touch, she eased away from him as soon as they reached the street and moved ahead at a more brisk pace, but his long strides kept up with her.

When she nodded to the guard doing sentry duty, she thought of course Andreas would say goodnight. Instead he continued on through the front courtyard with her.

She halted. "You don't need to see me all the way to the front door."

"But I do. I want to speak to your parents."

What? Her body tautened in defense. "No, Andreas! My parents aren't involved in this. That's the way I want it to stay. If Leon decides to claim the children, then I'll tell them everything. If there's any discussion about this, he's the one who needs to do it."

He cocked his head. "In an ideal world, it would work that way, but he's not ready yet."

That was obvious enough.

Reaching out, Andreas grasped her upper arms gently. She wished he wouldn't do that. It sent too many disturbing sensations through her body. Her awareness of him was overpowering.

"I have a plan that will solve our immediate problem, Gabi, but you're going to have to trust me."

Her eyes filled with tears. "Thea trusted me. Now look what's happening because I broke my promise to her. After her wretched divorce and subsequent death, my parents have suffered enough pain." Her voice throbbed. "Please just go." She stepped away from him.

His jaw hardened. "I can't, not when things haven't been resolved yet. You know the saying about being forewarned. If our two families know the truth and unite now, no power later on can shake our worlds. Don't you see?"

Yes. She could see there was no talking Andreas out of this. He wasn't the acting head of the Simonides Corporation for nothing. Gabi had only herself to blame. He'd asked her to trust him. Up until a minute ago she'd thought she could. But to go any further with this was like flying blind.

"I—I don't even know if they're still up." Her voice faltered.

"Then call them on your cell and alert them you've brought someone home with you."

She lowered her head. "I can't do that."

"Then I *will* because they deserve to know exactly what's going on."

A shiver raced through her body. Andreas had just put his finger on the thing tormenting her most. She'd hated doing all this behind her parents' backs. Defeated by his logic and her own guilt, she opened her purse and pulled out her phone. When she pushed the programmed digit, her mother answered on the second ring.

"Hi, darling? Where are you? I thought you'd be home before now."

She turned her back on Andreas. "When I went out, it was to meet a man I arranged to see in Athens the other day. He's with me now and wants to talk to you and Dad. I realize this sounds very cryptic."

The silence on the other end told its own story. "Do we know him?"

Gabi swallowed hard. "No, but you know *of* him by reputation." *You and everyone in Greece.*

"What's his name?"

"Andreas Simonides."

"Good heavens!" When the Simonides yacht was occasionally spotted outside Heraklion harbor, the whole city knew about it.

Gabi closed her eyes tightly for a second. "I realize it's getting late, but this is of vital importance. Prepare Dad, will you?"

"Of course. The babies are asleep. We'll be waiting for you in the salon."

"Thanks, Mom. You're one in a billion."

Andreas eyed her as she put the phone back in her purse. "If you were looking for a job, I'd hire you as my personal assistant on your integrity and discretion alone."

She'd just received the supreme compliment from him, but the last thing she'd ever want to be was his personal secretary or anything else that put her in such close proximity to him for business reasons. No way would she allow herself to be put in emotional jeopardy like that again.

"Shall we go in?" She led the way to the front door and opened it. The salon was to the right of the main foyer where Gabi found her parents. Blonde and fit, she thought they were the most attractive people she knew. Andreas wouldn't be able to help but like their soft-spoken manner.

After she made the introductions, he sat forward in one of the chairs opposite the couch where they were seated. Gabi sat in another matching chair, knowing her parents were dying of curiosity.

"I've noticed you staring at me," Andreas began without preamble. "No doubt you've seen your grandsons' resemblance to me. That's because their father Leonides is my brother. We're identical twins, too. Twins run in the family."

While her parents digested that startling piece of information he said, "Nikos and Kris have an uncle Gus and two aunts, Melina and Leila. Until Gabi came to my office on Friday evening, my parents had ten grandchildren. But after our chat, I realized that number has grown to twelve."

"But this is unbelievable!" Gabi's mother

exploded. She actually sounded relieved as she looked at Gabi's father. His burnished face had broken out in a smile, the last reaction Gabi would have imagined from either parent.

Andreas sent Gabi a satisfied glance. "Later, she'll fill you in on all the hows and whys of our first meeting. The important thing to know is that on Saturday, Leon met the children at the park.

"Unfortunately he's not ready to claim them yet. His wife Deline knows about his one-night relationship with your daughter Thea while he and Deline were separated. His pain and guilt over what he'd done drove him to go home the next day and talk everything out with her.

"It took a lot of gut-wrenching sessions and tears, but she eventually forgave him because she wasn't without her faults in the marriage, either. But that was a year ago and she has yet to learn he fathered two children. That's the hurdle facing him as we speak."

Gabi's parents squeezed hands.

"When Leon tells Deline about the twins, it could break up their marriage, possibly for good. The irony here is that they've been trying for a baby since the day they got married. It was one of the reasons they quarreled in the first place. She claimed he worked too hard and wasn't home long enough for them to start a family. So far they haven't been successful."

The added revelation hurt Gabi a little bit more. There'd been too much suffering all the way around.

"They'd been separated a while at the time he met Thea aboard the yacht. She'd come with a big group of friends, but Leon didn't know them. His friends had arranged it in order to party and cheer him up. His wife Deline had just told him she wanted a permanent separation. In his grief, he acted out unwisely. It doesn't excuse him for what he did, but it does explain his actions that night."

Gabi's father sat forward. "I'm afraid my daughter acted just as irresponsibly. Her marriage never took. When she won her divorce after a long battle, she made a wrong choice that night."

Andreas frowned, his brows black above his gray eyes. "Even if he was separated from his wife at the time, my brother's in a bad way because of his shame over making love to a virtual stranger when he was already married. His shame is even worse because he knows your daughter has passed away leaving two beautiful little babies who are his. Believe me, he's in anguish right now."

"He would be," her father murmured.

"Leon's my best friend, Mr. Turner. I know his heart."

Gabi bowed her head. She heard the love and the caring in his tone. He really was a wonderful man.

"In another day or two when he's found the courage to tell his wife, he's going to want to see the children again and meet you. Hopefully at that point he'll be able to make some decisions in their best interest."

"I don't envy him," Gabi's mother murmured.

Neither did Gabi, but her thoughts were also on Andreas. This was no shallow man. The depth to his character kept hitting her harder and faster. Only a few days ago she'd thought he had ice water in his veins.

"I've come here tonight to urge Gabi not to go back to Virginia yet. I believe that if she stays in Greece another week where the children are accessible, something good will come of this.

"But she's told me her fears about Thea's ex-husband, Dimitri Paulos. I know him and his family through business. Apparently he became hostile when your daughter asked for a divorce. That's his way. Gabi's worried he's going to keep nosing around until he finds out who fathered

Thea's twins. She's afraid that if he learns it's Leon, he'll expose him to the press."

Her mother nodded. "He'd do it without a qualm."

By now Gabi's father had gotten to his feet. "I'm afraid he turned on me when I helped my daughter obtain her divorce."

"It happens. But by the time my brother comes to grips with this situation one way or the other, it will have lost its sensational value. For now I'd like to suggest Gabi and the children be removed to an undisclosed place that's still close enough for Leon to have immediate access."

Gabi blinked. "Where?"

Andreas shot her a penetrating look. "I know the perfect spot," he said with authority and got to his feet. "It's late. Walk me out and we'll talk about it."

The next few minutes were a blur while her parents thanked him for his frank speaking and dealing with this delicate situation head-on. Before he joined her at the front door, there'd been hugs to welcome the twins' uncle to the family. The man was endowed with charm from the gods.

She went outside with him. The balmy night air seemed to make the moment more intimate somehow. Strange little tingles brought an ache to her hands. When she looked up at him, she felt her body come to life with feelings she'd thought Rand had killed. But it wasn't true.

This couldn't be happening again. It just couldn't!

In the semi-darkness she felt his piercing gaze travel over her features. "Gabi?" he said her name in his deep voice. "Will you continue to trust me for a little while longer?"

It was hard to swallow. "After approaching you first, I'm hardly in a position to refuse now. Do your parents know anything yet?"

"No. Leon wants to tell them when he's ready."

"So you have to continue to be the keeper of all the secrets."

"I don't mind."

No, because she was learning what kind of a man he really was. "You have a lot on your shoulders."

"So do you. In fact you've inherited the bulk by taking care of the twins. I'd like to help you with that. We'll think of it as a vacation time for both of us. After all, they're part my flesh and blood."

"Andreas? Are you married, too?" Before she took another breath she needed the answer to that question. "I haven't seen a wedding ring, but I realize some men don't wear them."

In the silence that followed, she felt his sudden tension. "I'm still single. You don't need to be worried I'm keeping secrets from a wife or neglecting her for Leon's sake."

Single. His answer frightened her because she no longer trusted herself around him. When she'd promised to never let a man get under her skin again, Andreas had already found entrance, slipping past her guard totally undetected.

"W-where is this safe place?" she stammered.

"On Milos, in a little village called Apollonia. I realize you're leaving in the morning, but I hope you'll give my idea serious thought. Either way I'll expect a call from you later tonight. Sleep well, *despinis*."

CHAPTER FOUR

ANDREAS had two phone calls to make. The first was one he'd known was coming ever since Gabi had entered his office, or rather blown in with that head of curly golden hair and eyes like the periwinkle bougainvillea outside his villa door.

Like the Venus de Milo unearthed in the ancient town of Milos where he used to dig around the ruins as a boy, Gabi's feminine shape appealed to his senses. With his six-foot-three height, he'd never been partial to shorter women or blondes until now, a fact that surprised the daylights out of him.

Her guileless honesty combined with her intensity had intrigued him. If he were to admit to all the traits he'd found fascinating and endearing since watching her with the twins, the list would be endless.

Something earthshaking had happened to

him. Already he felt a changed man. Right or wrong, his desire to be with Gabi was so profound, he realized he had to break it off with Irena.

To feel this way about another woman wasn't fair to her. He hadn't planned for this to happen. It just did…

Maybe Andreas's feelings for Gabi would die a quick death, but until that eventuality he *had* to explore them because he'd never known this kind of excitement over a woman in his life. Somewhere in his gut he knew these feelings weren't all on his side. Gabi wouldn't have asked him if he was married if her emotions weren't involved, too.

Tonight, when they were outside the consulate, it was all he could do not to pull her in his arms and kiss them both into oblivion.

After his shower he hitched a towel around his hips and reached for his cell. It rang until Irena's voice mail came on. Frustrated because this wasn't something he wanted to do by phone anyway, he started to click off when he heard her speak.

"Andreas—don't hang up. I was in the other room and had almost given up on hearing from you tonight. I've missed you."

Guilt smote him. The last time they'd talked

had been Friday. Now it was Tuesday night. In that short amount of time he hadn't missed her at all. Another woman had filled his thoughts to the exclusion of everything else. How could that be?

"Irena? Forgive me."

"You know I do."

Yes, he knew.

"Something's definitely wrong. You sound so different."

Heaven knew his world had changed. "I'm not sure how to say this except to come straight to the point because you deserve my total honesty. Up until last Friday you've been the only woman in my life."

A long pause ensued. "And now you're telling me there's someone else?"

He bowed his head. "Let's just say I met someone." Andreas couldn't believe he'd admitted it to the woman he'd loved and had been planning to ask to marry him. It meant Gabi had a hold on him more profound than even he had realized. "I swear this was the last thing I ever expected to be saying to you."

More silence. "Does she feel the same way?" Irena finally asked in a subdued voice. There were never any tantrums with her. She wasn't like that. He wished she would rage at him.

Instead there was this condemning quiet that underlined her pain.

"I sense she's not indifferent to me, but I haven't acted on my feelings yet."

"But you *want* to?"

He drew in a ragged breath. "I would never hurt you purposely, Irena, but until I explore what's going on inside of me, being with you right now wouldn't be fair to you. That's why I'm calling."

More silence. "Won't you at least come to the house so we can talk about this?"

"I will when I'm back in Athens."

"Where are you?"

His hand tightened on the receiver. "I'm on Crete and can't leave." He was in a hotel, wondering how he would be able to wait until morning when he saw Gabi again.

"Does she know about us?"

There's no us. Not anymore. "No."

"Who is she?"

Irena deserved that much. "An American who came to my office because of a life and death situation. She had business with me no one else could help her with. I'm still helping her solve a very serious problem before she returns to the States."

"I see," she whispered.

Except she didn't see. How could she? Andreas wanted to tell her everything, but he couldn't until he knew what Leon was going to do. Irena was best friends with Deline. The whole situation was more complicated than anyone knew.

He clutched the phone tighter. "I know I've hurt you, Irena, but to be less than honest with you at this point would be unconscionable."

"Your father told me your courage is one of your most remarkable traits. After this conversation I have to say I agree with him. I love you, Andreas. I know you did love me in your own way. But you were never *in* love with me, otherwise—" She broke off talking. He knew what she was going to say, that otherwise they would have married months ago. "I'm going to hang up now." The line went dead.

Horrible as he felt for hurting her, relief swept through him that from here on out he wouldn't be lying to her or Gabi.

Before he let any more time pass, he had a second call to make to Leon, who was vacationing for the next two weeks on Milos with Deline and the rest of the family. With Gabi sequestered in Apollonia on the north end of the island nine kilometers from the Simonides villa, the timing and proximity couldn't be better.

In anticipation of her falling in with his plan, he'd made all the arrangements ahead of time. Now there was nothing left to do but inform his brother, who'd known this call was coming.

As soon as they spoke he'd never heard Leon sound so upset. He hadn't told Deline the truth yet, but knew he had to.

After encouraging him not to wait any longer, Andreas hung up to wait for Gabi's phone call. If she chose to fly back to the States in the morning, then he'd take her and the twins home in the company jet.

Gabi's father patted the side of the bed and stared at her with solemn eyes. "When did Thea tell you about Leon Simonides?"

With that question she realized it was going to be a long night. She sat down next to him. "Right before she died." After clearing her throat she said, "All along Thea thought the man she'd made love with was Andreas. That's why I went to his office."

Her parents listened intently as she explained what had happened to Thea. "When she swore me to secrecy, I intended to honor my promise to her. But after she died, I kept looking at the babies and thinking how terrible it would be if they never knew their father, either. I realized

I couldn't go through life with that kind of a secret."

"Of course you couldn't." Her father pulled her into his arms. "I love you more than ever for what you've done."

"So do I," her mother cried. "It took tremendous courage, darling."

"I'm sorry to have lied about my reason for going to Athens on Friday, but I didn't know if I'd be able to get in to see Andreas."

"Thank heaven you did. Honestly, when he walked in the salon, it was like looking at the children all grown up."

Her dad shook his head. "I'm still amazed by what we've learned. He's a very remarkable man. A good one. No wonder he's at the head of the Simonides empire."

"You should see him with the boys, Dad. The way he responds, you'd think *he* was their father." Her voice shook.

Her mother reached over to press her arm. "What's Leon like?"

"I can't tell yet. He was in shock on Saturday and hardly spoke, but the fact that he came at all speaks of his character." She wiped her eyes.

"Seeing those two brothers together will really be something," her mom said. "That's how it's going to be for Kris and Nikos."

Gabi nodded. "Thea was so beautiful, and they're so handsome already. When they've become men, they'll be as spectacular as Andreas—I mean Leon."

"Does he know Kris will have to undergo a series of surgeries in the future?"

"Not yet, Mom," she mumbled.

"Why didn't you tell him?"

"Because I knew Leon was in shock. When I put myself in his place, I realized how hard it would be for him to tell his wife. I suppose I didn't want to scare him off or have him thinking I was after his money to pay for the medical expenses."

Gabi's father patted her arm. "Tell Andreas. He'll know the best way to broach his brother."

Her dad was right. "I will."

"Do his parents know anything yet?"

"No."

"So where is this safe place he was talking about?"

She slid off the bed, too filled with nervous energy to sit any longer. "On Milos."

"Of course," her father said. "Their family compound is on that island in a private bay that is better guarded than the White House."

"Actually, he mentioned I'd be staying at a

nearby village called Apollonia, but I don't know any of the details yet. He said to leave everything to him, but I have to be sure it's the right thing to do. I told him I would have to think about it. He's waiting for a phone call from me tonight."

Her dad cleared his throat. "I guess your mother and I don't have to tell you how wonderful it would be to know you and the children are close by while Leon is deciding what to do. Naturally I'd prefer that you stayed right here and—"

"No, Dad," she interrupted him. "I don't know how you've done your work through all this, but it's time you were able to concentrate on the job you were appointed to. You have too many dignitaries coming and going to put up with so much distraction."

"You and the children are hardly a distraction, Gabi."

"You know what I mean. Your life isn't conventional. You need to get back to it. Andreas told me to think of this as a vacation."

Her mother flicked her a thoughtful glance. "If Leon realizes he wants his children, then you have to admit Andreas has come up with a temporary solution that suits everyone. A week from now and everything could be settled. But it's your decision."

That was what was haunting Gabi. No decision sounded like the right one.

If Leon wanted to claim his children and raise them, then she would be free to get back to her old life in the States. But her world had changed so dramatically since her arrival on Crete four months ago, she didn't know herself anymore.

The twins had come to mean everything to her. As for Andreas... She kneaded her hands. He was waiting for her to get back to him.

She paused in the doorway fighting conflicting emotions. "Andreas is doing everything in his power to unite his brother with his own babies. I started all this and need to finish it, so I'll tell him yes. See you in the morning."

Once out the door she rushed down the hall to her room to make the phone call. He answered on the second ring.

"Gabi?" came the deep voice she could pick out over anyone's. "Did you discuss this with your family?"

"Yes." She struggled to sound calm. "The children need their father. If my coming to Milos will hasten the process, then so be it."

"Good. Now here's what I want you to do. Follow through exactly with the plans you and your parents have for tomorrow morning. But when you arrive at the airport, tell the driver to take you through to the heliport where my helicopter will be waiting. I'll be there to help you and the boys aboard."

"All right." She gripped the phone tighter. "Andreas—there's something else you need to know. I should have told you before now, but I was afraid."

"Of what?"

"That you would believe what you first thought about me—that I was out to get money from you."

"Go on."

"This concerns Kris."

"What about him?" Just now she heard a raw edge to his voice.

"He was born with a defective aortic valve in his heart. No one knows why. He didn't inherit anything genetic from Thea. She didn't develop heart trouble until she became pregnant. His condition is called stenosis."

"I noticed he's a little smaller."

Most people saw no difference in the twins, but nothing got past Andreas. "According to his pediatrician here in Heraklion, he'll have to undergo his first operation next month. I'd planned to have the surgery done in Alexandria with a highly recommended pediatric heart specialist."

"We have one of the best here in Athens," Andreas murmured, sounding far away. "How many procedures will be required?"

"Maybe only one more after that. The doctor said most valves have to be replaced every two to three years, but with non-embryonic stem-cell heart tissue, the replacement valve should grow as Kris grows and no more surgery will be necessary. That's what we're hoping and praying for."

"Amen to that."

She put a hand to her throat. "When do you think you'll tell your brother?"

"Tonight. He needs to be apprised of all the facts before you're settled on Milos. In the next few weeks he and I will start giving blood for Kris's fund."

"Our family plans to give some, too. To look at him you wouldn't know anything's wrong. He's so precious."

"Until now I've never coveted anything of my brother's."

"I know what you mean. If the gods were giving out perfect children, you wouldn't have to look any further than Kris and Nikos."

"No," came the husky rejoinder. "Get a good

sleep for what's left of the rest of the night, Gabi. Tomorrow's a new day for all of us."

"Andreas—"

"Yes?"

"I just wanted to say that I think Leon is very lucky to have a brother like you. Would that the twins develop that kind of love for each other. Goodnight."

"We're coming up on the little fishing village of Apollonia, named after the god Apollo." Andreas had been giving Gabi an insider's tour of the Cyclades from his position in the co-pilot's seat.

She'd never been to Milos. As the pilot swung the helicopter toward the beautiful island sparkling like a gem in the blue Aegean Gabi's breath caught. She'd once visited the islands of Mykonos and Kea on the ferry, not by air. To see all the fantastic volcanic formations and colorful beaches from this height robbed her of words.

During the flight from Heraklion, her awe-struck gaze had met his many times. Maybe it was a trick of light from being at this altitude in a cloudless sky, but when he looked at her the gray of his irises seemed to turn crystalline, almost like a glowing silver fire.

The twins were strapped down in their carry-cots opposite her so she could watch them. They'd stayed awake during the flight, good as gold.

"Is that Apollonia down there hugging the bay?" she questioned as they drew closer.

Andreas chuckled. "No. That's the home of the Simonides clan. Apollonia is just beyond it."

Gabi was staggered. She stared at the twins. Little did they know the lineage they came from included a kingdom as magical as anything she'd seen in a fairy tale. But instead of towers and turrets and drawbridges, it was a gleaming white cluster of cubical beauty set against an impossibly turquoise-blue sea found only in this part of the world.

Further on lay the picturesque little town where she'd be staying. It was built in the typical royal blue and white motif along a sandy beach, the kind you saw in videos and on postcards advertising the charm of the Greek islands. Before the helicopter landed, she knew she was going to love it here.

She picked out the boats at the village pier. There appeared to be myriad shops and restaurants close by, an idyllic vacation spot if there ever was one. As soon as they landed and the blades stopped rotating, Andreas helped her and the twins into a car waiting by the helipad.

The pilot loaded her luggage and the stroller into the trunk. There was a considerable amount of stuff. She poked her head out the window. "Thank you!" she called to him. "When you travel with babies, there's no such thing as packing light."

Both men flashed each other a grin before Andreas took his place behind the wheel and started the motor. Seated across from his hard-muscled body, Gabi felt an excitement out of all proportion to the reason why she and the twins had been whisked to this heavenly place.

He drove them past tavernas and bars, pointing out a supermarket and a bakery where she could buy anything she needed. In a few minutes they turned onto a private road that wound beneath a cluster of trees and ended at a perfectly charming blue and white house with its own shaded garden and stone walkways.

Gabi let out a sound of pleasure. "This is an adorable place, Andreas."

"I'm glad you like it. From the front door you step right out onto the beach. The house is fully air-conditioned, another reason why I chose it."

"The babies and I will be happy as clams here."

He darted her a curious look. "That's an odd American expression. Do you think clams are happy?"

She burst into laughter. "I have no idea, but I know we will be."

His low chuckle followed her as she got out of the car to open the back door. By now the twins were so awake they were eager to escape their confinement. While she released Kris's carry-cot from the strap, Andreas removed Nikos. Together they walked toward the door where a pretty, dark-haired woman who looked to be in her mid-twenties held it open for them.

"*Kalimera*, Kyrie Simonides."

"*Kalimera*, Lena. This is Gabi Turner." The two women smiled. "Lena and her husband manage this resort. They have a son, Basil, who's five months old."

"Oh—I'd love to see him."

"He's with my husband right now, but I'll bring him out to the garden later in the day. How old are your children?"

"Three months."

"They are very beautiful." Lena's glance slid to Andreas, no doubt trying to figure out their relationship when the wiggling babies looked like *him*, not Gabi. "We have maid service. If you need anything, pick up the phone and the office will answer."

"Thank you. This is delightful."

"I think so, too. Enjoy your stay."

After she walked off, they moved through to the living room whose white interior was accented with dark wood furniture and blue accessories. "What a charming house!" she cried.

"I'm glad you like it." Andreas sounded pleased as she followed him through to one of the bedrooms down the hall where two cribs and a set of dresser drawers had been set up. Everything was impeccably clean.

Andreas helped her lift the boys out of their carry-cots and lay them down in their cribs. "I'll bring in your things."

"That would be wonderful." She kissed Kris. "The babies have been awake for a long time and are getting impatient for their lunch, but first they're going to need a diaper change."

"Afterward I'll help you feed them."

"That won't be necessary."

"What if I want to?"

His playful teasing didn't fool her. "You've done more than enough, Andreas. I can just picture your exceptional receptionist wondering where on earth you've disappeared to."

She watched him kiss Nikos. "Didn't I tell you I'm on vacation? The whole family's here for the next two weeks."

This time her heart really did get a major workout. "As I recall, you were going to give me an appointment at three o'clock yesterday afternoon."

"If *you* recall," he murmured, coming to stand next to her, bringing his warmth and enticing male scent with him, "a life and death situation altered the scheme of our lives."

Gabi gripped the railing of the crib tighter. *Our* lives was right. When she'd gone to his office in Athens on Friday, the idea that days later she'd be alone with him on Milos would have stretched the limits of her imagination. Yet here she was...

"For the time being, my first priority is to lend Leon moral support." On that succinct note he left the bedroom.

While he was gone she gave herself another lecture about remembering why she'd been temporarily ensconced in this corner of paradise. Leon was blessed to have his brother's backing. As Gabi's father had said, Andreas was a good man. *How* good no one would ever know who hadn't walked in her footsteps since last Friday evening when she'd first confronted him.

In a few minutes he'd returned with the diaper bag and bottles of formula already prepared. They changed the babies before going into the living room to feed them. He was as confident and efficient as any seasoned father. Whether Leon ended up raising them or not, Andreas had claimed his nephews. She had an idea he would be an intrinsic part of their lives from now on.

After they put the twins down for their nap, Andreas announced he was leaving for his villa. "I'll be back with food before they're awake." He flicked her a heavy-lidded glance before disappearing from the house.

While she was taking clothes out of the suitcase to hang up and put in drawers, she heard the car drive off. He'd told her the Simonides compound was only ten minutes away by car, but already she missed him. To keep herself busy she acquainted herself with the rest of the house.

A perfect little kitchen containing snacks and a fridge stocked with drinks connected to the living room. On the other side was a hall with a bathroom separating two bedrooms. Hers had a shady terrace with loungers and a table looking out on the translucent water. The pots of flowers and an overhang of fuchsia-colored bougainvillea on the trellis gave off a subtle perfume.

Gabi hugged her arms to her waist, hardly able to contain the rush of euphoria that swept through her. She was in that dangerous state where the lines were blurred and she was imagining something quite different than the reality of her situation.

The beach was calling to her, so, with Lena's assurance that she would watch over the babies, Gabi changed into her two-piece aqua-colored swimming suit. A month ago she'd wandered into a little shop in Heraklion and had bought the most modestly cut outfit she could find, but it still revealed more than she liked. A tan might have helped, but this hadn't been a summer to relax in the sun.

After smoothing on some sunscreen, she grabbed a large striped towel and left for the beach through the terrace exit. A person could step down to the sand where the sea was only ten yards away, no more. It shimmered like a rare aquamarine. She dropped the towel and ran out, luxuriating in the calm water whose temperature had to be in the seventies.

Gabi swam for a while, then floated around on her back while she watched various sailboats and the occasional ferry in the distance. There were a few other people farther down the beach, but for the most part she had this area to herself.

Doing a somersault, she swam underwater to examine the shallow sea floor before surfacing to reach the beach and stretch out on her towel.

While she lay there on her stomach thinking this was pure heaven, she heard a motor that signaled a boat was approaching. When the sound was suddenly cut, she lifted her head from her arms and realized a ski boat had glided right up on the sand.

Her double vision was back as two Greek gods in dark swimming trunks jumped down from the sides with the kind of agility any male would kill for and walked in her direction.

"Andreas—" She sat up with a start, taking the towel with her to give herself a little protection from his all-seeing eyes. Then she remembered her manners, her gaze darting to his brother. "How are you, Leon?"

A faint smile hovered around his lips. "More in control than I was a few nights ago. I apologize for my rude behavior."

She shook her head. "There's no need."

"There's *every* need," he insisted, reminding her of a forceful Andreas. "I should be the one asking you how you are. You've been taking care of my sons all this time and I never knew."

Gabi smiled. "They're my nephews so it's no sacrifice, believe me."

"May I go in and see them?" He was making the effort, she'd give him that.

"Of course. If they start to fuss, there are bottles of formula made up in the fridge. Just warm them up in some hot water. Andreas?" She flicked her gaze back to him. "Why don't you show him their room while I go for another swim? If they wake up, it will be lovely for them to see their daddy."

His white smile had a domino effect that slowly melted every bone in her body. "When you surface again, climb up the back ladder into the boat and I'll take you for a ride. While Leon gets acquainted with them, we'll enjoy a picnic on the water."

"That sounds good. I'm getting hungry." It was already three-thirty. She'd lost track of the time.

"So am I." His husky tone caused a ripple effect through her body.

The second they disappeared through the front door, she hurried into the bedroom via the terrace and grabbed a loose-fitting short sundress with spaghetti straps she often wore over her suit as a cover-up.

Their deep male voices faded as she rushed

back to the beach. After shaking out the towel, she walked in the water and chucked her things in the back of the boat before climbing in. By the time Andreas emerged from the house, she was presentable enough to feel comfortable being with him.

He ran toward her, shoving the boat back into the water, then he levered himself effortlessly over the side. His brief glance managed to take in all of her before he started the motor. "We'll head for Kimolos." He nodded toward an island that couldn't be more than a mile away. "The sight of the little village of Psathi is worth the short trip."

Halfway across, he turned off the engine and joined her in the back so they could eat. In the hamper were sodas, fruit and homemade gyros. No food had ever tasted so good. She didn't have to search for a reason why.

"Thank you for a wonderful meal. In fact this whole trip."

Andreas stared at her while he munched on an apple. "Thank *you* for not giving up trying to get in to see me."

Gabi knew what he meant. Her mouth curved in a half-smile. "We need to thank your receptionist. Without her going out on a limb for me, that would have been the end of it." Then a slight frown marred her brow. "But maybe it would have been better if she hadn't had compassion on me."

Lines darkened his striking features. "Don't *ever* say that. I don't even want to think about it."

Neither did she. A world without Andreas was incomprehensible to her. She finished her cola. "What are your brother's feelings by now?"

Letting out a heavy sigh, he closed his eyes and lay back on the padded bench to get the full effect of the sun for a moment. End to end, his toned physique with its smattering of dark hair plus his chiseled profile proved to be too much for her. She turned her head to stare anywhere but at him.

"If the twins hadn't tugged at Leon's heart the first time he saw them, he wouldn't have agreed to my plan for you to bring them here. When I told him Kris has to go in for heart surgery next month, that seemed to jar him to the reality of the situation. But he's terrified because he loves Deline and is afraid he'll lose her when she learns the truth."

"I can't imagine being in his position."

After a silence, "If you were Deline, do you think *you* could handle it?"

His searching question brought her head

around. They looked at each other for a long time. "I don't honestly know. She forgave him for what happened a year ago, but now that the other woman's children are involved…"

She bowed her head. "If I loved him desperately, it might be possible. At the time he didn't know he'd gotten my sister pregnant, but I'm not Deline. Do they have the kind of love for each other to deal with it?"

He jackknifed into a sitting position and put his feet on the floor of the boat. His eyes looked haunted. "After he tells her, I guess they're going to find out how solid their marriage really is."

Gabi stirred restlessly. "He needs to do it soon. Every day that passes while he keeps it from her will make it harder for her to trust him."

"I told him that the night he saw the children at the park."

"Andreas—much as I'd love to go sightseeing with you this afternoon to give him more time with the twins, I think we should go back. You need to impress on him that if he waits even another day, it might be too late to convince Deline of anything."

"I agree," his voice rasped.

"Trust is everything. If Leon wants to prove his love, then he needs to approach her *now.*"

He nodded. "Not only that, every day he's away from his sons, he's losing that vital bonding time with them." Andreas sprang to his feet. "Let's go."

With the sea so placid, they made it back to the beach in a flash, but Gabi had returned in a completely different frame of mind than when they'd headed for open water. She jumped into the shallows carrying her towel above her head and walked in the front door of the house ahead of Andreas.

To her surprise, Leon had brought the children into the living room. It was a touching scene to see the three of them spread out on the quilt together. Nikos lay next to his daddy, who held Kris in the air, kissing his tummy to produce smiles.

Andreas's eyes looked suspiciously bright as he darted her a glance that spoke volumes. While she held back, not wanting to interrupt, he lifted Nikos from the floor and cuddled him.

Leon stood up with Kris pressed against his shoulder. "I can't believe they're mine." He spoke into the baby's soft black hair. He was totally natural with the children now.

"I dare say you've produced the most beautiful sons in the entire Simonides clan."

He eyed Andreas with a soulful look. "No matter what, I have to tell Deline today. Come with me, bro."

What Gabi had been hoping for had come to pass, yet with those words *no matter what* she felt a door close on her secret dream of adopting the twins herself. It was as if her heart had just been cut out of her body.

CHAPTER FIVE

"GABI?" Leon had turned to her. "I'm not sure when I'll be back. Do you mind being responsible for the twins a while longer? You know what I mean."

Yes. She knew exactly, but by some miracle she didn't give in to the impulse to break into hysterical sobbing. "I've loved taking care of my nephews and want to help you any way I can. Why don't you put the children back in their cribs so I can change them?" she suggested in the brightest voice she could muster.

As they headed for the bedroom she was aware of Andreas's avid gaze leveled on her, but she managed to avoid contact. He could see inside her soul. If she were to make the mistake of looking at him, her composure would dissolve. This was a pivotal moment for Leon. An emotional meltdown on her part now could ruin everything.

Thankful after they'd left the room and she could hear the rev of the boat engine, Gabi put clean diapers on the twins and got them ready for an evening walk around the village in their stroller. Next to the bakery was a deli where she could buy some food ready to go.

Once she'd showered and had dressed in a matching blue skirt and sleeveless top, she wheeled them out of the back door. Lena happened to be pushing her little boy along in his stroller as she did some weeding.

The two of them talked and pretty soon they went into the village together. Gabi enjoyed the other woman's company. It helped not to think about the loss that was coming. If she were honest, it wasn't only the twins she was already missing...

Three hours later she was putting the babies to bed when her cell rang. The sight of Andreas's name on the caller ID caused a fluttery sensation in her chest.

"Hello?" She knew she sounded anxious.

"I called as soon as I could, Gabi."

"You don't owe me anything. H-has Leon told his wife?" Her voice faltered.

"Yes."

His silence made her clutch the phone tighter. "Was it awful?"

"I won't lie to you. It was a great deal worse." Tears clogged her throat. "I'm so sorry."

"So am I. She's threatened to divorce him and has flown back to Athens in the helicopter. I just drove him to the island's airport so he could take a plane to catch up to her."

A whole new world of pain had opened up for them.

When Thea had divorced Dimitri, Gabi had been overjoyed, but this was an entirely different situation. From all accounts Deline was a lovely woman who didn't deserve to have any of this happen to her. Neither did the babies. But the fact remained Leon and Thea had made a mistake that had caused heartbreak in every direction.

"Does your family know the reason they left Milos?"

"Not yet, but it's only a matter of time," he ground out.

She moistened her lips nervously. "What would your brother like me to do?"

"Stay right where you are. I'll bring the car around at eight-thirty in the morning. We'll drive to the pier where the cabin cruiser will be waiting. I need a solid break and intend to show you the sights of the island. Pack enough formula in case we want to dock somewhere overnight. Stavros will take care of everything else."

Her body trembled.

An invitation to party overnight on the Simonides yacht had proved too much of a temptation for Thea. Gabi wasn't any different. The desire to spend uninterrupted time with the twins' uncle aboard his cabin cruiser filled her with secret longings that had her jumping out of her skin.

When she thought about it, she would never again have the opportunity to be with a man who thrilled her the way Andreas did. In a few days Leon would make definitive plans where the twins were concerned and Gabi would be leaving Greece.

So why not enjoy this time with Andreas? As long as she recognized he was a bachelor who didn't take his relationships with women seriously, then she wouldn't either. She'd learned her lesson with Rand.

In the future she would come to visit her family and the twins from time to time, but she had a career waiting for her back in Virginia. The boys' lives were here with their father. They would need to get used to the nanny Leon would employ to help him.

Gabi couldn't possibly stay around, otherwise

none of it would work; therefore this little bit of time on Apollonia was all she was going to get with Andreas. As she'd told his receptionist on Friday, "I'll take it!"

"Eight-thirty's a perfect time. The three of us will be ready. Goodnight, Andreas." She hung up before she betrayed herself and kept him on the phone if only to listen to the sound of his deep, mellifluous voice.

With the babies down until their next feeding, Andreas instructed Stavros to bring the cruiser as close to the cave opening as possible. A side glance revealed that a golden-haired nymph had come to join him on the swim platform and was ready to dive with him.

Her modest two-piece suit only seemed to add to the allure of her beautifully proportioned body. Compared to the bronzed females he'd seen at various beaches throughout the day wearing little or nothing at all, her delicious femininity and creamy skin—unused to so much sun—drew his gaze over and over again.

"Are you sure you want to try this, Gabi? We've done a lot of swimming today. If you're tired, we can explore here in the morning."

She flashed him a mischievous smile that

gave his heart a wallop of a kick. "After the big buildup about an evening swim at your favorite beach, you couldn't stop me!"

Without warning she leaped off the side and headed through the cave opening to Papafragas beach at a very credible speed.

Andreas hadn't had this much fun in years and followed her into the cool water. Beyond the opening was a long, natural, fjordlike swimming pool surrounded by walls of white rock. He heard her cry of delight.

"This is fabulous, Andreas!" Her voice created an echo.

He caught up to her and they both treaded water. "You can see the deep caves where pirates used to hide."

Her lips twitched. "Even modern-day pirates like the Simonides twins, I would wager." She kept turning around, looking up at the incredible rock formations. "It's time for the truth, Andreas. Between you and Leon, how many girls did you used to bring here on an evening like this, pretending surprise that you were the only ones about?"

His laughter created another echo. "You've caught me out. We brought our share. It's true that this late in the day most tourists have gone back to wherever they came from." He'd planned it this way because he'd wanted Gabi to himself. "Come on. I'll race you to the beach at the other end."

Another fifty yards lay a strip of sand still warm from the sun, though its rays no longer penetrated here. She reached it first and sank down in it, turning over so she could look up at the sky. "Oh-h-h, this feels so good I'll never want to move again."

"Then we won't." Andreas stretched out on his stomach next to her. He couldn't remember the last time he'd felt this alive.

A come-hither smile broke one corner of her delectable mouth. "We'll have to, if only for the twins' sake."

"They're being watched over. For the moment I'd like to forget everything and everyone and simply concentrate on you." He raised up on one elbow. "You know what I want to do to you."

The little pulse at her throat was throbbing madly. "Yes," she whispered in an aching voice.

A moan sounded deep in his throat. That was all he was waiting to hear before leaning down to lower his mouth to hers. He needed her kiss as much as he needed air to breathe. At the first taste of her, he was shaken by her breath-taking response. After coaxing her lips apart he began drinking deeply. Back and forth they gave each other one hungry kiss after another until it all became a blend of needs they fought to assuage.

Heedless of the fine sand covering their bodies, he rolled her on top of him, craving the perfect fit of her in his arms, the sweet scent of her. "You're so beautiful, Gabi," he murmured against the side of her tender neck. "Do you have any idea how much I want you?"

"Andreas—" The tremor in her voice told him she was equally caught up in the surge of passion sweeping them into a world where nothing existed but their desire for each other.

"What is it?" he whispered after wresting another kiss from her incredible mouth.

"I feel out of control," she admitted against his lips.

He molded her body to his with more urgency. "That's the way you're supposed to feel when it's right. I can't get enough of you." So saying, he kissed her again until they were both devouring each other.

Never having known rapture like this, he wasn't prepared when she suddenly tore her lips away and rolled off him. "Where did you go?" he cried before sitting up. "We're not in any hurry."

"Maybe not, but I'm out of breath and need to slow down before we start back."

He kissed her shoulder. "If you're too tired when we're ready to go, I'll help you."

"You mean you'll get me out of here using the old reliable life-saving technique? Just how far do you think we'd get?" Gabi teased. She'd turned her head, focusing her dark-fringed eyes on him. Their color changed with the surroundings. Right now they'd picked up some of the gray-blue of the water.

"In my condition and the way I'm feeling at the moment, not far, but in time I'd manage it."

"I believe you would," she said with a smile that was too bright after what they'd just shared. His eyes narrowed on the erotic flare of her mouth, an enticement that lured him like Desponia's song. She could pretend all she wanted, but in each other's arms they'd both been shaken by a force that was only going to grow in strength.

"Sometimes I think you're half god the way you make things happen. It's like magic."

"Would that I had the magic to put my brother's world back together."

"I could wish for the same thing."

She got up from the sand and walked into the

water to wash off. Bringing her to this spot had been in the back of his mind since last night. He couldn't bear it that they were forced to leave, but they had to get back to the twins.

Although he'd allowed Gabi to believe otherwise, he'd never brought another woman here before, not even Irena. She liked an occasional dip in a swimming pool, but she wasn't adventurous, not like Gabi, who'd sprung onto the canvas of his life with an unexpectedness that had left him reeling.

Until today he could have told Irena that everything he'd done to help his brother through a nightmarish, unprecedented situation had been necessary and it would have been the truth. But being out here with Gabi would have been impossible to explain. More than ever he was thankful he'd broken it off with her.

She would have pointed out that the twins' aunt was already staying in a vacation spot that provided every possible distraction without requiring Andreas's assistance. He would have had no excuse for spending the rest of today and tonight with her on his cabin cruiser. No excuse for coming close to making love to her.

While she treaded water, he threw his head back and looked up at the darkening sky, wishing this night never had to end.

"We'd better go, Gabi." The words came out harsh, even to his own ears. "Do you think you're up to it?"

"I was afraid maybe you weren't and I would have to save *you*," she quipped. So saying, she took off like a golden sea sprite, leaving behind a trail of tinkling laughter he found utterly irresistible.

Gabi gripped the rings that helped her climb the ladder into the boat. After rinsing off in the shower of the swim platform, she wrapped up in a towel and moved toward the rear cockpit where Andreas was talking to Stavros.

She smiled at him. "Did you think we were never coming back and you'd have to deal with two howling babies wanting their feeding in the middle of the night?"

The older man's eyes twinkled. "We would have managed."

"Have they been good?"

"Like little angels."

"I'm glad, then." She raised up on tiptoe to kiss his cheek. "Thank you for being a wonderful babysitter."

Gabi was still trying to catch her breath, as much from the physical exertion of attempting to outdistance Andreas—which was an impossibility—as having been alone with him.

There'd been a moment on the sand when she'd wanted to know his possession so badly, she'd almost expired on the spot. But she knew better than to repeat the mistakes of the past.

She had no doubt Andreas wanted her. He'd been forthcoming about it, and the desire between them had been building until she was ready to burst. Those kisses on the beach were inevitable, but she was wise enough not to read anything more into them. That was why she'd swum for her life back there, so she wouldn't forget the promise she'd made to herself to focus all her energy on her career.

She flicked her host a steady glance. "When I'm back at my job inundated with work, I'll remember this glorious day. Thank you."

"There's more to see tomorrow before we get back to Apollonia," Andreas reminded her.

Gabi knew what that meant. Her pulse throbbed without her permission. "I'm looking forward to it," she said bravely. "Goodnight."

Not daring to meet his eyes this time, she darted down the steps to her cabin off the passageway. Relieved the children lay sound asleep in their carry-cots, she quickly showered again and washed her hair before climbing into bed.

Since spending time on the boat, she'd learned that his stateroom was on the other side of the wall. One more thing she'd picked up from Stavros. This cabin cruiser was Andreas's home when he really wanted to get away on his own.

Gabi realized the older man had let her know she was a privileged person, but she could tell him that without the babies she would never have been given entrée to Andreas's private world.

Almost a week ago today she'd gone to his office. Since then she'd spent some time with him, yet she still didn't know anything about his personal life. He'd only volunteered information on a need-to-know basis. Love for his brother was the sole reason she'd been invited aboard this boat.

With time on his hands, he'd done the natural thing and had kissed her because he knew the attraction was mutual. The same thing had happened with Rand. She'd been a guest on his ranch and he'd enjoyed her to the fullest *as long as she was there*.

Those were the key words to help her keep her head on straight with Andreas until she went back to Alexandria.

Three o'clock was going to be here before she

knew it. With the memory of him lying next to her on that sandy beach where she could still feel the taste of his mouth on hers, she closed her eyes, fearing she'd never be able to sleep. But to her shock the twins didn't start crying until seven-thirty the next morning.

Maybe it was the sea air or the gentle sway of the boat. Whatever, they'd actually slept through the night!

After she'd bathed and fed them, she got dressed in shorts and a top before carrying them up on deck one at a time. Already the sun was warm. Stavros had breakfast waiting for her on the up-and-down table, another remarkable invention aboard the cruiser.

"Mmm, that looks delicious. Good morning, Stavros. How are you?"

"Never better."

"I'm glad to hear it. Is Andreas still asleep?"

"No," sounded a familiar voice behind her. She swung around to discover him standing there in a sage-colored polo shirt and white shorts. There couldn't be a more attractive man anywhere in the Cyclades. His slate eyes collided with hers. "I've been waiting for you and the babies to appear. Let's eat. I'm ravenous."

"I'm hungry myself," she admitted. "It must

be this gorgeous air." Andreas sat down next to her. Gabi tried to act natural, but after her dreams of him it was close to impossible.

Andreas studied her for a moment. "How did you sleep?"

Was this god from Olympus psychic, too?

"Would you believe these two didn't start crying until seven-thirty? It's the first time I haven't had to get up in the middle of the night. The pediatrician said it would happen when the time was right. Isn't it strange how they both did it at the same time?"

His compelling mouth broke into a lopsided smile. "My mother could tell you endless stories about the mystifying aspect of twins."

"I don't doubt it." She would love to meet the mother of this extraordinary man, but held back from telling him so. Near the end of their meal he chuckled over Nikos, who gave a big yawn. In the next breath he got up and took the twins out of their carry-cots. Propping them in either arm, he moved over to the windows. "What do you think of this sight, guys?"

Gabi had been concentrating so hard on Andreas, she could tell him that the sight of him standing there holding his nephews was the most spectacular one in all Greece. Terrified to realize how emotionally involved she'd become with him, she found it a struggle not to let him know it.

When she could finally tear her gaze away, she noticed the cruiser was anchored off an unreal white outcropping of elongated rocks set against a brilliant blue sea. She stood up and joined him. "What is this place?"

"Sarakiniko, an Arabic word."

"It looks like a moonscape."

"That's what it's famous for. When we were boys, Leon and I would come here to play space aliens with our friends."

She laughed. "That beats the neighborhood park." Andreas's backyard was unlike any other. "Every time you show me a new place, I think it's the most fabulous spot around. I'll never be able to thank you enough for this tour. I'm very lucky."

He cast her a sideward glance. "Seeing everything through your eyes has taken me back to happier days and times. I'm the one indebted to you, so let's agree we're even."

Once again she sensed he was brooding. If he'd heard from Leon, he would have told her. His change in demeanor had everything to do with his brother.

Gabi knew most men stuck in this unique situation would have left her to her own devices while she waited for word from his brother. Not Andreas. His unselfishness meant he'd put his own needs aside, but it was wearing on him. She wouldn't allow this to happen again.

For the next while they lazed on deck and played with the babies. To convince him he wasn't the sole meaning of her existence she phoned her mother to let her know she and the children were fine. She hoped that if she played it breezy in front of him, he wouldn't suspect how on fire she still was for him.

Her mom was delighted to learn the boys had slept through the night. In front of Andreas she raved about her sightseeing trip and his kindness, then promised to phone again when she knew more about Leon's plans. He could probably see through her attempt to keep everything light and above board, but she had to try.

By the time she hung up, they were coming into port at Apollonia. Since Andreas was still having fun with the babies, she excused herself and went below to pack up the few things in her cabin. She found Stavros and thanked him.

Within a half hour Andreas had driven them back to the house. While he helped her and the twins inside, she sensed he had other matters on his mind. As he was bringing in the last bag, she met him at the door.

"Stop right there. You've done enough." She took the bag from him. "I had the time of my life. Now go. I know you'll get back to me when you have any news."

Gabi felt his gaze travel over her, turning her body feverish. He seemed reluctant to leave. "Promise me you'll phone if you need anything."

His entreaty spoken in that husky tone sent a weakness to her legs. She rubbed her palms against her hips nervously. "You know I will. Now I've got to take care of the babies."

"Before you do that, I need this." In the next breath he pulled her into his arms and started kissing her again. Caught off guard, she was helpless to stop him. Gabi had been dying for his touch since last night. Without conscious thought she slid her hands up his chest and encircled his neck, needing to get closer to him.

He was such a gorgeous man. With every caress her senses spiraled. The heat he created was like a fever in her blood. Another minute and she would beg him to stay. Through sheer strength of will she wrenched her mouth from his and eased away from him, breathing in gulps of air.

"I'll be back. Miss me a little." With another hard kiss to her trembling mouth, he strode off. She shut the door and fell against it while she waited for him to drive away.

As soon as she couldn't hear the car motor any longer, she made fresh bottles of formula, then put the twins in their stroller and headed out the door for a long walk. If her life depended on it, she couldn't have stayed in the house another second, not when she was feeling this kind of pent-up energy. She didn't plan to come back until she'd visited every shop in the village and had worn herself out.

At noon the next day Gabi left the house again, this time taking the twins with her to enjoy lunch in a delightful little restaurant she'd passed last evening. It was a good thing Andreas hadn't come back.

She blushed to realize how wantonly she'd responded to him at the door. Twice now she'd been playing with fire, but only she was going to get burned if she continued to let it happen every time he got near her.

During the delicious meal, the babies created a minor sensation with customers and staff alike. On her way out the door several tourists asked if they could take their picture because they thought the boys were so angelic.

Gabi supposed it didn't matter as long as no one knew they were the sons of Leonides Simonides. In that case their pictures would show up in the newspaper and on television.

Before long she reached the path to the house. As she was about to open the door she heard a female voice call to her. She turned around to see the manager come hurrying up to her. "I'm glad you're back. You have a visitor who's been waiting for a while. She's in the office."

"Who is it?"

"Mrs. Simonides."

Her heart pounded an extra beat. Deline? Was it possible? Where was Leon? Or maybe it was Andreas's mother. Had he dropped her off with the intention of coming by for her later? She could hardly breathe at the thought of seeing him again.

"While I take the children inside, would you please show her over here, Lena?"

"Of course." She rushed off.

Gabi looked down at the children. "Come on, you cute little things. Someone has come to see you. I want you to look your very best."

After wheeling them inside, she brought out

the big quilt and put it on the living-room floor where they could stretch out while she changed them. With that accomplished she put them in their white and yellow stretchy suits. The colors brought out the warm tone of their olive complexions. She kissed their necks. "Umm, you smell sweet."

When she heard the knock, she jumped up and darted over to the door to open it. The tall, slender brunette beauty on the other side couldn't be much older than Gabi's twenty-five years. She'd worn makeup but it didn't disguise the telltale signs of pain. Gabi detected a distinct pallor and her eyelids were swollen from too much crying.

"You must be Deline." She spoke first. Her heart ached for the other woman who'd found the courage to come and at least see the children.

"Yes. I understand you're Thea Paulos's half sister Gabriella."

"That's right. Please come in." She had a dozen questions, but didn't ask one. This was too significant a moment to intrude on Deline's personal agony. She followed her into the living room where the twins were lying on their backs making infant sounds. Their compact bodies were in constant motion.

Gabi's lungs constricted while she waited for

a reaction from Leon's wife. It wasn't long in coming.

A pained cry escaped her lips and she sank into one end of the sofa as if her legs could no longer support her. Tears gushed down her cheeks. "They look exactly like him, but they should have been *our* children," came her tortured whisper.

By now moisture had bathed Gabi's face. "I'm so sorry, Deline. I wouldn't blame you if you hated me for contacting Andreas. When I went to his office, I thought h-he was their father," she stammered.

"Andreas told me everything." Deline shook her head. "But a situation like this would never have happened to him. Unlike Leon, he doesn't lose his head when he's down or upset. That's why he was made the head of the company over Leon after their father suffered his heart attack."

"I didn't realize." Gabi knew so little really.

"When Andreas is married, his wife will be able to trust him to the death."

The blood pounded in her ears. "Is he getting married soon?"

"Irena's expecting a proposal any day now. She's his girlfriend and my best friend. Her family owns one of the major newspapers here in Greece. She heads the travel section department."

All of a sudden Gabi had to reach for the nearest chair and sit down. Swallowing hard, she said, "Will they be married soon?"

"Irena's hoping so. He's in Athens with her this weekend."

Gabi had to fight not to break down hysterically. It appeared Andreas and Leon had more in common than Deline knew.

Last night Andreas had kissed her senseless. If Gabi hadn't pulled away when she did, she'd have made the same mistake as Thea. When he'd told her he didn't have a wife, she'd taken it to mean he didn't have a romantic interest of any kind at the moment. What a naïve fool she was!

Yet none of it mattered in light of what Deline was going through. Gabi was being incredibly selfish to be thinking about herself at a time like this.

"How can I help you, Deline? I'd like to."

She looked down at the children. "You can't. I've loved Leon forever and always wanted his baby so badly, but it never happened. Now that I'm going to divorce him, there won't ever be that possibility. Life's so unfair." Sobs shook her body.

Gabi's heart sank to her feet. "I agree. My father lost his daughter early, and Thea didn't live long enough to raise her babies. I'm convinced that if she hadn't developed a heart problem, she would never have told me anything and this situation wouldn't have arisen."

"But it did," Deline stated flatly, "and Leon wants his sons, which is only natural. He's told his family, so that's it." She jumped up from the couch. "This morning he came to my parents' home and begged me to fly here and see the children before I did anything else.

"I know what he's hoping for, but he doesn't understand. Even if I wanted to stay with him and was willing to give our marriage one more chance, I don't see *me* in their countenances." Her voice broke. "I'm afraid I'll always see her and resent them even though they're innocent in all this."

Gabi felt such a wrench, she got up and put her arms around Deline. "I admire you for your gut honesty," she cried softly. "I can't tell you how sorry I am."

Deline relaxed enough to hug her back. When they finally let go she asked, "What will you do now?"

"As soon as Leon comes for the children, I'm going back to Crete and then on to the States. My job is waiting for me."

"What do you do?"

"I'm a manager at an advertising agency. It's a fascinating business I like very much." For the twins' sake if nothing else, she had to keep giving herself that pep talk in front of them. If she ever truly broke down, she might not get herself back together again. "Do you work?"

"Not yet, but I have a friend who has offered to let me work in a hotel gift shop. I'm thinking of doing that so I don't fall apart."

Good for her! Gabi could relate. Deline wasn't only wonderful, she had a backbone. "I wish you the very best. I hope you know I mean that."

While they'd been talking, Kris started to whimper. Gabi picked him up to comfort him.

Deline studied her for a moment while dashing the tears off her face. "I was prepared not to like you, but having met you I've discovered that's impossible."

Gabi's eyes filled again. Leon was losing a perfectly fabulous woman. How sad that he and Thea had ever met. Because of that pregnancy, Thea was no longer alive. But following that thought, if they'd never gotten together, there'd be no babies. She would never have met Andreas. No matter how hurt she was, Gabi could never wish the three of them didn't exist.

She walked Deline to the door. "Did you fly here?"

"In the helicopter with Leon. He's gone on to the villa. When he knows I've left the island, he'll be over."

Things were moving fast. "I hope you have a safe flight."

Before she could respond, the baby hiccupped, proving a distraction for Deline, who couldn't help examining his dear little face. "Which one is he?"

"Kris."

"The one who has to have the heart surgery?"

"Yes."

"He looks well."

"I know, but he tires more easily and fusses more than Nikos. He's a little smaller, too. When they're grown, he'll probably be an inch shorter. The doctor said this first operation is going to make a big difference."

Her lower lip quivered. "H-he's so sweet." Her voice caught before she turned away with

an abruptness Gabi understood. "I have to go."
She hurried off.

"Take care," she called after her.

Oh, Deline…

CHAPTER SIX

WITH a heavy heart Gabi closed the door. After feeding the babies, she put them down for their nap before checking her watch. It was ten after two. She phoned her mother, but all she got was her voice mail. Gabi left a message that she'd be returning to Heraklion without the children.

While she waited for Leon to come for his boys, she checked airline schedules and ferry crossings to Crete. There wouldn't be another flight out of the island airport until tomorrow, but there was a ferry to Kimolos leaving from the pier at five-thirty. From there she would take another ferry to Heraklion.

She needed one more day to be with her parents and get her packing done. Then she'd fly to Athens and make a connecting flight to Washington, D.C. Without the twins to care for, it was imperative she put an ocean between her and Andreas.

A knock on the door broke her concentration. "Gabi? Are you in there?"

It was Leon's voice. She hurried across the room to open it. He looked worse than Deline, as if he hadn't slept in days. "Come in. Your wife said you'd be over."

He followed her into the living room. "I'm not going to have a wife much longer."

There was nothing she could say to comfort him on that score. He knew better than to ask her questions about their conversation since she couldn't answer them out of respect for Deline. "But you do have two little babies who need their daddy. What plans have you made?"

"For the time being I'm going to keep them with me at my villa here. Estelle, the house-keeper, is going to take over as their nanny until I can find a permanent one. Mother will help. The family is around right now, turning one of the bedrooms into a nursery. Everyone's anxious to help me get them settled. Needless to say, my parents are eager to love their newest grandchildren."

"I'm sure they are."

"Gabi?" His bloodshot eyes had gone moist. "I'm aware of how much you and your parents love them. This has to be a very difficult moment for you."

"It is. I won't lie to you about that, but you gave them life. They need you more than my folks and I need them. The sooner you take over, the sooner they're going to become yours, heart and soul."

"You know my home will always be open to you."

"Of course. In two months I plan to fly back to Crete to see my parents for a week. By then Kris will have had his operation and be recovered in time for all of us to have a reunion."

"I'll be looking forward to it. We'll have a family party where everyone can get acquainted."

Gabi wondered how she would live until she saw them or Andreas again. "The next time you're with your brother, please tell him thank you for making the arrangements here. It's been a lovely vacation for me."

"Andreas is the greatest friend a person could have."

I know.

Together they packed up the children's things and put them in his car. Leon had already installed two infant carseats in the back. Then came time to carry the children out of the house and buckle them in.

Throughout the process they stayed asleep,

not having any idea that the next time they woke up, they'd be home with their daddy for the rest of their lives. And Andreas would always be their loving uncle…

Such lives they were going to lead being the sons of a Simonides!

She was thrilled for them. For herself, she was dying inside from too many losses in one day. *Don't lose it yet, Gabi. Remember why you sought out Andreas in the first place.*

Leon came around and hugged her hard. "You've been a guardian angel all this time. I'm never going to forget. Before I go, let's program in each other's cell-phone numbers. I'm afraid I'll be calling you pretty constantly until I get the hang of being a father. The children will be wanting you all the time."

"For a day or two maybe."

Gabi ran back in the house to get her phone. In a minute they were both set and there was nothing else to detain him. He climbed in behind the steering wheel. She shut the door. Leon pressed her hand one more time before turning on the motor.

Leave now before my little darlings open their eyes.

She waved until everything became a blur.

* * *

The minute the helicopter touched down on the helipad behind the villa on Milos, Andreas climbed out. He'd just come from Irena's, where he'd told her everything. She deserved to know about the twins and the strange circumstances that had brought Gabi into his life.

Even in her pain, Irena demonstrated a rare graciousness before he said goodbye. Now he was anxious to find his brother. He assumed everyone was out at the pool enjoying dinner. After he ate, he'd disappear with his brother.

As he drew closer he could hear his family talking. They sounded more animated than usual. He couldn't help but be curious over the reason why. When he descended the last flight of steps, he saw their large clan congregated around Leon and his parents. To his shock they were holding Kris and Nikos, but the babies weren't happy about it.

Andreas's heart thundered in his chest. He jerked his head to the side looking for Gabi. He felt as if it had been weeks instead of hours since he'd last seen her, but there was no sign of her.

Leon caught his glance and came striding toward him. He pulled Andreas over to the wall where they could talk in private.

"As you can see, the secret is out now. The family knows everything."

Andreas had to admit he was relieved. Now he didn't have to bear the burden of it alone. "Did Deline get a look at the twins?"

"This afternoon. Then she flew back to Athens. I'll be receiving divorce papers shortly."

Unfortunately he'd been afraid of that. "Where's Gabi?"

"On her way home."

It appeared Andreas had just missed her. "You mean the resort."

"No. I mean the States. She said she'd be back in two months for a visit with her folks. That's when I plan to get both our families together."

Two months?

His guts froze. "You mean she's already left Milos?"

Leon stared at him in surprise. "As far as I know."

"And you didn't stop her?"

His brother blinked. "Take it easy, Andreas. Why would I do that?"

"Why *wouldn't* you?" he fired back. "Gabi's been their mother for the last three months. She must be out of her mind with grief right now."

"I'm sure she is, but we both agreed it had to

be this way so I could bond with my sons. In this case a complete break was necessary if the babies are going to look to me for their needs now."

Andreas couldn't argue with her logic or Leon's, but after the brief intimacy they'd shared the knowledge that Gabi had left Greece made him feel as if his tether had come loose from the mother ship and he was left to float out into the dark void.

"She asked me to thank you for the vacation arrangements in Apollonia."

He rubbed the back of his neck while he tried to take it all in. When he thought of her response on the beach, and at the door yesterday… Didn't it mean anything to her?

"Bro?" Leon whispered. "Did you hear what I said?"

Yes. Andreas heard him, but he couldn't waste any more time talking. "Leon? Do me a favor and make my excuses to the family while I go inside for a minute. I'll be right back."

While his brother stood there looking visibly perplexed, Andreas raced up the side steps. When he was out of sight of the others he called the resort. "I'd like to speak to Lena. This is Andreas Simonides."

"One moment please." He paced until he

heard her voice. "Kyrie Simonides? What can I do for you?"

"I understand Ms. Turner checked out today. Did you order a car for her so she could be driven to the airport?"

"Not to the airport. She went to the pier to get the ferry."

That ferry only went to Kimolos.

His adrenaline surged. "Thank you. That's all I needed to know."

He hung up. Gabi would have to stay there overnight until there was a different ferry to Athens tomorrow. He had time to make plans.

With his pulse racing, he rejoined the family. Two extremely miserable babies were being passed around. They were looking for the one beautiful, familiar golden angel who didn't make up part of the dark-haired Simonides family.

No one—not his sisters, his mother or Estelle could calm them. Leon had to take over, but they still weren't completely comforted. Andreas knew in his gut Gabi wasn't in nearly as good a shape as the twins were.

His mother shot him a curious glance. "Where did you go? Why isn't Irena with you?"

Now was not the time to discuss his breakup

or the reason behind it. "She couldn't make it. I had an important phone call to deal with."

"Have you eaten yet?"

"I'm not hungry."

She shook her head. "Your brother told us the saga about the twins and the major role you and Gabriella Turner have played in all of it. You're a remarkable son, Andreas. I love you for your loyalty to him."

"Deline's destroyed all over again."

His mother nodded. "I'm afraid she might not be able to deal with his babies, not when she wants one so badly herself." Her eyes filled with fresh tears. "But the boys are so adorable. It's uncanny how much they resemble you and Leon at that age."

"They have the look of their mother, too. I saw pictures when I was at the consulate."

"The Turner family must be devastated over their loss. Your father and I would like to meet them."

"I'll arrange it." *Just as soon as I catch up to Gabi.*

The splotchy face and swollen eyes that looked back from the hotel-room mirror made Gabi wince. She could only hope that by the time she went aboard the ferry taking her to Heraklion later in the day, all traces of the terrible night she'd just lived through would be gone.

She finished dressing in jeans and a white sleeveless blouse. Her hair, still damp from its shampoo, was already curling. The heat would dry her out in no time. With a coat of coral lipstick, she felt a little more presentable to face the day.

After having given Leon all the babies' things yesterday, she had only her overnight bag to carry down to the pier surrounded with its assembly of fishing boats and other craft. Small groups of tourists were slowly making their way to the same embarkation point where they could see the ferry entering the port.

She hadn't been anywhere without the children for so long, she felt empty. Were they missing her? Her eyelids burned. The only way her parents were handling the loss was because they had each other. They were the great loves in each other's lives.

When she'd thought she'd be raising the twins, she hadn't met Andreas yet and had been glad she was single. Now she had nothing left except her dreams of a god who'd turned out to be too human after all. More than ever she was eager to get back to her career.

"Gabi?"

She thought she was hearing things and kept walking. When her name was called out a second time, she slowed down and turned around. By then it was too late to stifle the cry that sprang from her throat. Her overnight bag dropped to the ground.

Andreas studied her tear-ravaged face. "I thought so," his voice rasped.

Her mouth had gone dry at the sight of him. He looked impossibly handsome wearing white cargo pants and a blue crewneck shirt with the sleeves pushed up to the elbows.

"If something's wrong with the children, why didn't Leon call me? He has my number."

He scrutinized her for a moment. "Whatever happened to hello? How are you? Isn't this a beautiful day!"

Heat spilled into her cheeks, but she didn't look away. "A man with your kind of responsibilities doesn't show up at an obscure port off the beaten track unless there's a dire emergency."

"That's not always true or fair." He stood there with stunning nonchalance. "You're suddenly making judgments about me. What's changed since we last saw each other?"

For him, nothing. Though he had a serious girlfriend right now, he enjoyed being the quintessential playboy up to the very end. Why not?

Little did he know the experience with Rand had taught her two could dance to that tune.

"Absolutely nothing. Last week I told you that if Leon decided to claim the children, I had to get back to my job."

He rubbed the side of his hard jaw absently. "I'm the one who brought you to Milos. Why didn't you at least wait until I could make arrangements to get you back to Crete?"

She pasted on a phony smile. "Andreas—I'm a businesswoman, remember? I'm capable of looking out for myself."

His expression tautened even more. "Didn't it occur to you I wanted to do that for you?"

The fact that he'd shown up here proved he was hoping to pick up where they'd left off at the beach. If his girlfriend knew about the other women he played around with, then she had a high tolerance level. Gabi wasn't made the same way.

"It's not a case of occurring to me. You're probably the most generous person I've ever known. But you're also the head of your family's company. Now that Leon's been united with his children, you and I have other fish to fry, as we Americans say. I'm due for a promotion as soon as I return to Alexandria, so it's imperative I leave Greece on the next flight out."

His silvery eyes bored into hers. "Will one more day matter in the scheme of things?"

Yes, considering the convulsion he'd set off by his unexpected presence here. "Since my boss is expecting me, I'm afraid so. Now if you'll excuse me, people are starting to board the ferry."

"Let them," he declared. "My boat will take you wherever you want to go."

She sustained his gaze without flinching. Andreas had an agenda and insisted on taking her to her parents, so there was no point in fighting him. If she kept her wits about her, she ought to be able to handle a few more hours alone with him. Play along for a little while longer. That was the key.

"Okay. I give up. Hello, Andreas. It's lovely to see you again. What brings you to this island on such a beautiful summer morning?"

Laughter rumbled out of him. "That's better."

"I'm glad you think so." The charisma of the man had the power to raise her temperature. "My plan is to go back to Heraklion. I need to pack the rest of my things before I fly home."

He picked up her overnight bag. "Come with me and we'll reach Crete long before the ferry gets there."

Andreas walked her in another direction toward a sleek-looking jet boat tied up in one of the slips. The Simonides family had a different vessel for every occasion. For this trip it was going to be just the two of them. Though she forbade it, she couldn't stop the thrill of excitement that spread through her body to be with him again. She had to be some kind of masochist.

After helping her on board, he handed her a life jacket and told her to put it on. While she buckled up, he undid the ropes and jumped in, taking his place at the wheel. Before he could turn on the engine, she handed him a life jacket. "What's sauce for the goose..." she teased. "Do you know the expression?"

"I know a better one." He smiled back. "Never argue with a woman holding a weapon." He slanted her an amused glance before taking it from her and putting it on his hard-muscled frame. She felt relief knowing that if, heaven help them, something happened on the way to Crete, he was wearing a floating device, too.

The cold, implacable head of the Simonides corporation she'd first confronted at his office was so far removed from the relaxed man driving the boat, she had trouble connecting the two.

Before she knew it, they were idling out to sea at a wakeless speed.

"How long are you going to keep me in suspense about what really brought you here this morning?"

Andreas didn't pretend to misunderstand. "Not long." He engaged the gears and the boat burst across the water like a surfaced torpedo.

Gabi had to be happy with that explanation. She *was* happy. Too happy to be with him when he didn't know what it meant to be faithful to one woman. Gabi wished she didn't care and could give in to her desire without counting the cost.

Deline was a much better woman than Gabi. She'd forgiven Leon his one-night stand with Thea. *Until she'd found out about the twins...*

Resigned to her fate—at least until they reached Heraklion—Gabi put her head back to feel the sun on her face. Every so often the boat kicked up spray, dappling her skin with fine droplets of water. She kept her eyes closed in an attempt to rein in her exhilaration.

The problem was, she'd fallen irrevocably in love with Andreas, the deep, painful kind that would never go away. But she'd made up her mind he would never know he was the great love of her life. Nor would she ever dare to say it out loud. An ordinary mortal reaching for the unattainable might bring on the mockery of the gods.

"Tell me something honestly, Gabi. How wedded are you to returning to your old job?"

His question jolted her back to the real world. She sat up, eyeing him through shuttered lids to keep out the blinding sun. "I'm very wedded. Besides being stimulating, it provides me a comfortable living with the promise of great things in the future. Why do you ask?"

He cut the motor, immediately creating silence except for the lapping of water against the hull. In a deft motion he left his seat long enough to produce a couple of sodas from the cooler. After handing her one, he sat down again with his well-honed body turned toward her.

"Thank you. I didn't realize I was thirsty until now."

His eyes, a solid metal-gray at the moment, met hers over the rim of his drink. "I know what you mean." An odd nuance in his low voice caused her to believe he was referring to something else. Memories of the two of them communicating in the most elemental of ways on that beach never left her mind. Trembling, she looked away.

"What do you recall about my receptionist?"

The question was so strange, she thought she hadn't heard him right, but Andreas never said or did anything without a reason. "I suppose I thought she was firm, but fair...even kind in her own way."

"An excellent description," he murmured. "Anna's going to be seventy on her next birthday. She worked for my father forty-five years and never married."

"They must have been a perfect match for her to stay in his employ that long." Gabi imagined the woman had been madly in love with the senior Simonides. If he had a tenth of his son's brilliance and vitality, it all made perfect sense.

"When he stepped down, I kept her on with the intention of asking her to train a new receptionist before I let her go. However, after one day of working with her, I realized what a treasure she was and I refused to consider breaking in anyone else."

Gabi swallowed the rest of her drink. "If it hadn't been for her, the twins would still be without their father. For that alone, I like her without really knowing her."

She heard his sharp intake of breath. "Being a receptionist is only one of Anna's jobs. In a word, she's the keeper of the flame. Do you understand what I mean?"

"I think so," Gabi said with conviction. "She's a paragon of the virtues you admire most."

He nodded gravely. "But she needs to retire and get the knee replacement she's been putting off."

"I noticed her limping."

"It's getting worse every day. The trouble is, I've despaired of finding anyone else like her. Then I met *you*." His piercing glance rested on her, reminding her of something he'd said to her a week ago.

If you were looking for a job, I'd hire you as my personal assistant on your integrity and discretion alone.

The worst nightmare she could conceive of was upon her. She knew exactly where this conversation was going and shook her head.

"Before you refuse me outright," he said, "I'm only suggesting that I could use your help while I look around the company for the right person to replace her. It could take me several months. You'll be given your own furnished apartment on the floor below my office. There's a restaurant on the next floor down for the staff."

"Andreas—" she blurted almost angrily. "What's this really about?"

"I don't want you to leave Greece until we know Kris's heart operation is successful. If there are complications, you'll want to be here."

She didn't want to be reminded of that possibility. "I'm praying everything will go well, but if it doesn't, I'll fly over on the spot."

"That's not good enough."

What was going on inside him? She knew his request couldn't be for personal reasons. Besides his girlfriend, there were legions of women who'd love a fling with him. "Why?"

He seemed fascinated by the pulse throbbing in her throat. "I just came from being with the family. The babies were out of control. We both know they were looking for you." *They were?* "Let's be honest. With the operation coming up, Leon's going to need you. I know it in my gut."

Gabi bowed her head. "They'll get over the separation in a few days and cling to him."

"I don't believe that, and neither do you." Andreas leaned closer to her. "These things

take time. I know how much you love the boys.
Admit you're dying inside after having to give
them up."

"Of course I am." The tears started spurting.
Too late she covered her face with her hands.

"Gabi..." Andreas whispered in a compas-
sionate voice.

"When Thea asked me to find a couple who
would adopt the boys, it killed me because *I*
wanted to be the one to take over. She didn't
know that by then I was prepared to give up my
career for them. But the law forced me to come
to you."

"Thank God it did!" In a sinuous movement
Andreas pulled her into his arms. At first she remained stiff, but his gentle rocking broke down
every defense and she ended up sobbing against
his broad shoulder.

"I know how much you love them," he murmured into her silky curls. "That's why I don't
want you to leave. Stay and work for me until
Kris has recovered fully from his operation.
You and I can visit the twins after work every
few days. That way everyone will be happy and
it won't interfere with the bonding going on between them and their father."

When she realized she'd be content to stay

like this forever, she eased away from him and wiped her eyes with the backs of her hands.

Eventually she glanced at him, never having realized gray eyes could be so warm. His love of the twins produced that translucent glow. "When you put it that way, you manage to exorcize all the demons. Only Andreas Simonides can make everything sound so simple and reasonable, even if it isn't."

"That's all I needed to hear. The matter's settled."

No. It's not. "Nothing's settled. First I have to talk to my boss and determine if that promotion will still be waiting for me if I get back at a later date."

"After knowing you a week, I can guarantee he'll move mountains to accommodate you in order to get you in the end."

Andreas said whatever needed to be said in order to accomplish his objective. That was why he was the head of the family business. There was just one problem. She couldn't figure out his objective. She knew he loved the twins, but he was after something more.

"Tell me the real reason you're asking me to temp for you. By your answer, I'll know if you're telling me the truth or not."

"You're not just anyone. You're the twins'

aunt. There's no reason why you shouldn't be able to peek in on them from time to time. That's hard to do from across the ocean." A compelling smile broke out on his striking face. "I want to peek with you."

Andreas...

She averted her eyes. "That's the wrong answer."

"It's the only one I have," he answered with enviable calm.

"You mean the only one you're willing to offer me. Without knowing the truth, I can't stay in Greece even if my boss were willing to give me more time away."

His smile faded. "I didn't know there was more truth to tell unless it's my guilt."

She blinked. "About what?"

He eyed her intently. "About everything. It's my fault my brother's marriage is in trouble again. If I'd left everything alone after you walked out of my office, they wouldn't be headed for divorce and the twins would be in Virginia leading perfectly contented lives with you."

"Except that I couldn't have adopted them."

"They'd have still been yours, Gabi."

"And after they grew up and demanded to know about their father, what then? If I admitted that I'd known his name all along, they might never forgive me."

A strange sound came out of his throat. "You've just put your finger on my greatest nightmare. If I'd kept the secret of the twins over the years *knowing* Leon and his wife could never have children, I wouldn't have been able to forgive myself for playing god with my brother's life."

It was Gabi's turn to moan.

He reached out and grasped her hands. "The truth is, you and I are up to our necks in this mess together. Leon needs our help for a little while longer."

She sucked in her breath. "But you don't really need an assistant."

"Actually I do. Anna's got to get that knee operated on right away."

"You could hire any number of secretaries in your company to replace her."

"I could, but I thought one of the reasons you were leaving Crete was so your parents could get back to the lives they were leading before Thea became ill."

"You're right," she confessed quietly.

"By the time you leave my employ, I'll be hiring a permanent assistant." He kissed the back of her hands before letting them go. A tingling sensation coursed through Gabi's sensitized body and lingered for the rest of the trip to Heraklion.

CHAPTER SEVEN

THE blood donation area of the hospital in Athens had continual traffic. Gabi looked over at Andreas. Both of them were stretched out side by side on cots giving blood. They'd taken the day off from work. It was a good thing since they'd had to wait at least an hour after arriving there before their turn was announced.

In preparation for today she'd eaten a good breakfast and had forced down fluids. Before bringing her to the hospital where Kris would be having his surgery, Andreas had instructed the limo driver to drop them off at a fabulous restaurant in the Plaka for lunch. But instead of ordering the specialty of the house, they'd eaten iron-rich spinach salad followed by sirloin steak.

Andreas was remarkable. In the short time she'd been working for him, she'd learned that when he did something, he always did it right and thoroughly. She loved him with a vengeance. If Kris weren't facing an operation, Andreas wouldn't have asked her to stay on and none of this would be happening.

"This is kind of like lying on the beach at Papafragas."

For him to mention that night—out of the blue—when she'd lost almost every inhibition in his arms came as such a surprise, she almost fell off the cot.

"It's not as warm," she murmured.

"No, and we're not alone. It's a good thing we don't have to swim the length of that fjord later. We're not supposed to do any strenuous activity for the rest of the day. I wouldn't be able to save you."

In spite of that bittersweet memory, she couldn't help but laugh. "Then what are we going to do?"

"I'll tell the chauffeur to drive us back to the office and we'll watch TV in your apartment while we take it easy."

"If you get lightheaded, the long couch is yours," she quipped, but the second the words came out, she regretted saying anything. Since the day he'd shown it to her, he'd never asked to come inside and she'd never invited him.

To cover her tracks she asked, "Do you ever watch TV?"

"All the time."

"You're joking—"

He chuckled. "Leon and I are sports nuts."

"I can believe *that*, but when do you find the time?"

"My iPhone. Broadband is everywhere and performs almost every trick known to technological mankind."

"Aha! So in between important phone calls and meetings, you're watching soccer?"

"Or basketball or the NFL."

"How about NASCAR? The Grand Prix?"

"Love it all."

She frowned. "And here I thought you were different."

His smile was too much. "What do *you* watch?"

"When I'm in the States and have time, the History Channel and cooking shows, British comedies and mysteries. I also like bull-riding."

"You're a fan of the rodeo?"

"When I was in college, a friend of mine attending there asked me to go back to Austin with her during our two-week break. We met a couple of cowboys and got talked into going to one. I've been hooked ever since."

He stared at her as if trying to find a way into her soul. "On a certain cowboy?"

"For a time I was," she answered honestly, "but the illness passed."

"Have there been many?"

"Many what?" She knew exactly what he meant.

"Illnesses."

"Probably half a dozen." She didn't want to talk about old boyfriends. The man lying near her made every male she'd ever known fade into insignificance. "Andreas? Speaking of illness, what did Kris's heart surgeon tell Leon when he took him in for his checkup yesterday? You went with him, but you acted differently when you came back to the office."

"Did I?"

"You know you did. If you're trying to spare me, please don't."

Suddenly the curtain was swept aside and two hospital staff came in to finish up and unhook them. "You're all done." They both sat up and put their legs on the floor. "Take your time. There are refreshments outside before you leave the hospital."

When they were alone again, Gabi slid off the

cot and turned to him. "I'm still waiting for an answer."

By now Andreas had rolled down his shirt-sleeve and was on his feet. "The doctor couldn't promise the operation would be risk free."

"Of course not. No operation is."

"My brother's dealing with too many emotions right now."

They all were. She sensed Andreas was secretly worried, but he hid it well. "On top of Leon's pain, taking care of the twins is physically exhausting work no matter how sweet they are."

His eyes were almost slumberous as they looked at her. "We need time off from our fears, too. Since there's nothing more we can do for the moment, let's go home and relax."

She watched him shrug into his jacket. He sounded as if he meant that they would actually go back to her apartment and spend the rest of the day together, but it was out of the question. Andreas had a playful side that could throw her off guard at unexpected moments, but from the time Deline had told her he had a serious girlfriend, Gabi refused to play.

After they'd been served juice and rolls, the limo took them to the office. They rode his private elevator to her floor. Gabi's heart thudded heavily as they walked across the foyer to her suite.

She opened the door, then turned to him. "Thank you for accompanying me this far in case I fainted, but as you can see I'm fine. If you're feeling dizzy, there's a very comfortable couch to lie down on in the reception room of your office." A smile broke the corner of her mouth. "I know because I spent half a day on it waiting for you to give me an audience."

She heard him inhale quickly, as if he were out of breath and needed more air. "I'm sorry you were forced to wait so long."

"I'm not," she said brightly. "It gave me an opportunity to watch Anna at work. On that day who would have guessed I'd end up filling in temporarily after she left?"

When he still made no move to leave, she said, "Thank you for giving blood with me, Andreas. I'm glad I didn't have to do it alone. See you in the morning and we'll plan that big company party you want to give for Anna after she's recovered from her knee surgery."

Before the weakness invading her body smothered the voice telling her not to let him get near enough to touch her, she stepped inside and started to close the door.

"Not so fast." Andreas had put his foot there,

making it impossible to shut it. Quick as lightning he stepped inside and closed it. Her heart thumped so hard, she was afraid he could hear it.

"What is it?"

"What do you think?" he demanded in a silky voice.

Uh-oh. Gabi backed away from him. "I—I'm sure I don't know," she stammered.

He moved toward her. "When I left you at the resort on Apollonia after our night at Papafragas, I held a woman in my arms who was with me all the way. In the blink of an eye I learned she'd left the island. When I went after that woman and found her, she'd changed. Since then I've been waiting for her to re-emerge, but she hasn't. Now I want to know why."

She smoothed her palms against her hips, a gesture his piercing gaze followed while she tried to think up an answer. Unless it was the truth, nothing would satisfy him, but in doing so she would give herself away.

As the silence lengthened a grimace marred his handsome features. "At the hospital you admitted there was no other man in your life, or is that a lie and it's your boss you're in love with?"

Gabi had a hard time believing she'd injured

his pride by playing hard to get, because *that* was all this interrogation could possibly be about.

"No," she finally answered with every bit of control she could muster. "Like you, I don't have a significant other I'm keeping secrets from." She'd said it on purpose to watch for the slightest guilty reaction from him. Now was the time for him to admit his involvement with the woman Deline had mentioned, but nothing was forthcoming.

"If that's true, why do you rush away from me the second our business day is over? How come we never share a meal unless it's on Milos while we're checking on the twins?" His eyes narrowed on her mouth. "Have I suddenly become repulsive to you?"

She was aghast. "I'm not going to dignify that absurd question with an answer." If anyone were listening, they'd think he was her husband listing the latest problem in their marriage.

"Then prove it. I told you I'd like to spend the rest of the afternoon with you. We can do it here or at my penthouse."

There was no putting him off. She bit her lip. "Well, as long as you're here, y—"

"My thoughts exactly." He finished her sentence and removed his jacket, tossing it over a side chair. "When we get hungry later, we'll have the restaurant send something up."

She got that excited sensation in her midriff. "Excuse me for a moment."

"Take all the time you need to freshen up. I'm not going anywhere."

That was what she was afraid of as she darted from the living room. The second she saw herself in the bathroom mirror she groaned to see her cheeks were filled with hectic color. After giving blood, she was shocked by her body's betrayal.

When she returned a few minutes later her feet came to a standstill. Andreas had stretched out on her couch with his eyes closed. He'd turned on television to a made-for-TV Greek movie.

He was so gorgeous, she didn't dare move or breathe in case he sensed she was there and caught her feasting her eyes on him. Every part of his male facial structure was perfect. From his wavy black hair to the long, hard-muscled length of his powerful anatomy, he was a superb specimen. But it was the core of the remarkable human beneath that radiated throughout, bringing alive the true essence of what a real man should be.

Maybe it was the combination of giving blood

and the many hours of work he'd been packing into each day so they could spend time with the twins. Whatever, it all seemed to have taken its toll. She could tell from the way he was breathing that he'd fallen asleep.

He would never know how much she wanted to lie down and wrap her arms around him, never letting him go, but she couldn't. Feeling tired herself, she lay down on the small couch facing him so she could watch him as he slept.

The movie played on, but she had no idea what it was about. Her lids grew heavy. When next she became cognizant of her surroundings, Andreas had just set a tray of sandwiches and coffee on the table.

Surprised at how deeply she'd slept, she took a minute to clear her head before she sat up. Her watch said five to six! She glanced at Andreas. "How long have you been awake?"

"About twenty minutes. It's apparent we both needed the rest."

"I *never* sleep in the middle of the day!"

She felt his chuckle down to her toes. "You did this time." Did she snore? Help! "I'm going to take it as a compliment you felt comfortable with me."

"In other words it was the proof you needed to realize I don't find you repulsive?"

"Something like that," came the wry comment. "I've already eaten. Have some coffee." He handed her a cup.

"Thank you." She drank half of it before eating a sandwich. In a few minutes she sat back. "That tasted good."

He stood there surfing the channels until he came to another movie. Before she could countenance it, he sat down next to her and pulled her across his lap into his arms.

"This is what I wanted to do earlier."

Andreas moved too fast for her. She could no more resist the hard male mouth clinging to hers than she could stop breathing. Oh—he tasted so good, felt so good. Her body seemed to quicken in acknowledgment that they'd done this before.

Without conscious thought she curled on her side and wrapped her arms around his neck, wanting to get her lips closer to his face. The need to press kisses to each feature took over. She ran a hand into his hair, loving the texture of it.

On a groan he crushed her tighter, then his mouth covered hers again and she thought she'd die of the pleasure he was giving her. "I want you, Gabi. I want to make love to you."

She wanted it, too, more than anything she'd wanted in life, but enjoying a few kisses and sleeping together were two different things. Gabi refused to get in any deeper when she knew she wasn't the only woman in his life. Girlfriend or wife, there *was* someone else. The fact that he still hadn't admitted it revealed the one flaw in him she couldn't overlook.

These last three weeks she'd avoided this situation for the very reason that you couldn't go on kissing each other or it turned into something else. She needed to quit while she could still keep her head. That way she'd have fewer regrets when she got back to the advertising world.

The second he allowed her a breath she eased away from him and stood up. "Much as I'm tempted, I'd rather we didn't cross that line. Remember we're an aunt and uncle to the twins and will be seeing each other on the rare occasion throughout our lives. Many times I've heard you tell potential clients you like keeping things above board and professional. It's my opinion that line of reasoning works well in our particular case."

* * *

After his arrival on Milos, Andreas strode through Leon's villa looking for his brother. Estelle told him he was putting the babies down for the night. As he approached the nursery he saw Leon closing the door.

They glanced at each other. "Thanks for coming," he whispered. "Let's go to my room."

"Sorry I couldn't get here any sooner to help with the twins. I had an important meeting." He'd asked Gabi to type up his notes and leave them on his desk before he took off for Milos.

Since the night she'd delivered the coup de grâce, he'd only been functioning on autopilot. Gabi was keeping something from him and he was determined to get it out of her no matter what he had to do.

Leon shut the door behind them. "You're here now. That's all that matters."

Andreas stared at his brother. He'd lost weight and looked tired, but that was to be expected considering he was a new father. The look of anxiety in his eyes was something else again, kindling Andreas's curiosity. "What's this about? I thought you told me Kris was fine after his checkup."

"He is."

"Don't tell me you think they're still missing Gabi?"

"Not as much. After the first few days they both stopped crying for her and accepted me. Now when they see me, they reach for me and don't want anyone else except Gabi when she comes. It's an amazing feeling."

"I can only imagine." Andreas was longing for the same experience himself, but only under the right circumstances. "So what's wrong?"

"Maybe you ought to sit down."

Was it that bad? He remained standing. "Just tell me."

"You won't believe this. Deline called me this afternoon. She's *pregnant*."

The news rocked Andreas back on his heels. In fact it was incredible. He stared at his twin. Leon was now the father of a third child yet to be born.

"The doctor confirmed she's six weeks along. It was the shortest phone call on record. Before she hung up, she said she was still divorcing me, but wanted me to know the baby was due next spring."

"No matter what, congratulations are in order." Andreas gave him a brotherly hug.

Leon looked shell-shocked. "Ironic, isn't it?

I've got Thea's children, Deline's carrying mine, yet none of us will be getting together."

He'd left out a heartbroken Gabi who would have had every right to hold on to the twins without telling anyone, but she didn't have a selfish bone in her beautiful body. One thing was evident. Through this experience Leon had learned how much he loved Deline. Andreas could only commiserate with him.

"Don't despair. With time it could all work out the way you want it. As long as I'm here, why don't you fly to Athens and talk to her tonight? I'll do the babysitting duties here until you get back. If you need a couple of days, take it!"

Leon's eyes ignited. "You'd do that?"

His brother was in pain and needed help.

"What do you think?" After today's meeting he didn't have anything of vital importance on for tomorrow. If he went to Gabi's door, she wouldn't let him in. "I'm crazy about my nephews and want to spend some quality time with them."

His brother had difficulty swallowing. "Thanks. It seems like that's all I ever say to you. I haven't been to work in weeks. You've had a double load."

"Don't you remember you've been given

maternity leave? As Gabi once said to me, what's sauce for the goose..."

While Leon changed clothes, he shot Andreas a curious glance. "How's she doing as Anna's replacement?"

"Better than even I had imagined."

"Under the circumstances you were wise to break it off with Irena as soon as you did. Everyone in the family knows it now, but I have to tell you it came as a shock to Deline."

Andreas nodded. "Those two managed to grow even closer during the time I was seeing her."

"Deline says Irena is leaving for Italy for a long holiday. Before she does, she wants to take a look at the twins, so don't be surprised if she shows up. Sorry about that if it happens."

"I'm not concerned. If there's any problem with the boys that I don't anticipate, I'll call you."

As soon as Leon left the villa Andreas stretched out on top of his brother's bed and drew the phone from his pocket. He frowned when all he got was Gabi's voice mail. The beep eventually sounded.

"Gabi? Something has come up and Leon needs my help. First thing in the morning I'd like you to reschedule any appointments for the next two days, then I want you to fly to Milos. The helicopter will be standing by. I'll expect you in time to have a late breakfast with the boys."

She would never come for him, but an opportunity to see the twins was something else again.

The apartment in the Simonides office building was more fabulous than any five-star hotel. Every time Gabi stepped out of the shower of the guest suite, she felt as if she were a princess whose days were enchanted because she was allowed to be with Andreas while he worked.

If there was a downside, it came at the end of the day. When Andreas left his office and said he'd see her in the morning, the enchantment left with him. Except for the evening she'd talked to him about not crossing the line, she hadn't been with him in another setting away from the office.

Since she'd come to work for him, the nights had turned out to be the loneliest Gabi had ever known. To stave off the worst of it, she spent time after hours acquainting herself with the files stored on the computer and memorizing the names of his most important clients.

One night last week she'd come across the

merger with Paulos Metal Experts. To her astonishment she read that Dimitri had brought several unscrupulous lawsuits against the Simonides Corporation in order to get the judge to intervene.

Andreas had represented his father in court. Every attempt by the opposition was defeated. Photocopies of all the court documents were there. It had been a heated case. She didn't say anything to Andreas, but reading the material gave her a much fuller understanding of the disgusting man Thea had married.

This evening when Andreas had left the office, she could tell he was in a hurry. Naturally she imagined he was planning to spend the night with his girlfriend, a possibility too devastating to contemplate.

With an aching heart she reached for her cell phone to see if there'd been any calls from her parents or Jasmin while she'd been in the shower. To her shock, the only message she'd missed had come from Andreas.

She always loved the opportunity to fly out to Milos so she could hold her precious babies. This time she'd make it a short, drop-in visit and take some pictures of the twins with her cell phone to show her parents. After that she would ask the pilot to fly her to Heraklion for a surprise visit. They'd love to see how much their grandsons had grown.

Since Gabi needed a break to separate herself from Andreas, it was a good plan. In a few more days Kris would be having his surgery. After he'd recovered, she would resign her job with Andreas and go back to Virginia.

That would leave him free to do whatever. Everything would be wrapping up soon and she'd be gone for good.

Twelve hours later Gabi climbed aboard the helicopter atop the office building with her overnight bag. En route to Milos she informed the pilot she would only be there for a brief time. Afterward she wished to be flown to Heraklion.

Armed with her plans, she arrived at the Simonides villa where Andreas stood at the helipad, disturbingly handsome in an unfastened white linen shirt and bathing trunks. She'd been so used to seeing him in a business suit at the office, her heart skipped around, throwing her completely off-kilter.

As he stepped forward to help her out, his penetrating eyes seemed to be all over her, turning her insides to mush. She'd worn a summery print skirt and sleeveless blouse in earth tones on white with white straw sandals. It was an outfit he wouldn't have seen before.

"I'm glad you made it. You smell as delicious as you look this morning."

"Thank you." She hadn't been prepared for a comment like that. Her stomach clenched mercilessly. "It's a new mango shampoo I bought. Your pilot said the same thing. He's going to buy some for his wife."

His white smile was so captivating, her lungs constricted. "I know you can't wait to see the boys. They're in their new swings on the patio. Follow me."

She knew the way as they walked down several flights of steps past flowering gardens to the rectangular swimming pool of iridescent blue.

The Simonides compound was exquisite, surpassing what she'd seen from the air the first time they'd come. Each white villa was terraced with flowers and greenery, one on top of the other all the way down to the sea where the white sand merged with aquamarine waters. She paused on one of the steps to look around.

"Oh, Andreas… I know I say this every time, but this is all so gorgeous, I can't believe it's real." She couldn't believe *he* was real. "With a devoted father like Leon, the children have to be the luckiest little boys on earth."

"The real miracle is that they got their start with you and your family. They're waiting for you."

"I'm dying to see them." She trailed him down one more flight of steps and through an alcove. Out of the corner of her eye she saw the canopied swings propped near each other beneath an overhang of brilliant passion flowers. The seats were moving back and forth to a little nursery-rhyme song.

She ran toward the boys, then slowed down for fear she'd frighten them. They were dressed in identical blue sunsuits. No shoes or socks on because it was too hot.

"They've filled out!"

Andreas chuckled as he undid Kris and handed him to her. "Look who's here."

"Oh, you little sweetheart." She hugged him in her arms, unable to stop kissing his neck and cheeks. While she walked around with him, Andreas extricated Nikos and propped him against his broad shoulder.

"I've missed you," she crooned to him, rocking him gently. Finally she put her head back so she could look at him. "Do you remember me?" He blinked. "I don't think he knows me, Andreas." Her brows furrowed.

"Give him a minute. The sun's so bright. Here. We'll trade." He reached for Kris with one arm and handed Nikos to her with the other.

"How could you possibly be this adorable?" She kissed his tummy. "Do you take cute pills?" She lifted him above her head.

Andreas's happy laughter filled the air. "Kris recognizes your voice. See? He's craning his head to look at you."

"You think?" she cried out joyously. All of a sudden Nikos started getting more excited and made his little baby sounds. "Well, that's more like it." She kissed one cheek, then the other, making him smile each time.

"I'd smile like that if you kissed me that way all the time," Andreas said in a provocative aside. He was back to being playful.

Gabi ignored the comment, but felt the blush that swept into her cheeks. "I'm not sure this was such a good idea. I don't know how I'm going to tear myself away."

"No one's going anywhere quite yet. Estelle will be out in a minute with their bottles. We'll feed them before she puts them down for their naps."

"Maybe the two of you better do it. I don't

want my presence to upset them and undo the progress Leon has made."

She lowered Nikos into his swing so she could take pictures. Now that she had an excuse to capture Andreas at the same time, she took a dozen different shots of him and the children in quick succession.

"It's good for them to see you every few days," he murmured, brushing off her worries. "Their psyches have a greater sense of security knowing you haven't disappeared from their lives."

Gabi squinted at him. "Is that based on scientific fact?"

"No." His lips twitched. "I made it up because I know how much you need to hold them."

I love you, Andreas Simonides.

She found a chair beneath the overhang and put Nikos back on her lap so she could examine him. Andreas pulled up another chair next to her and sat down with Kris. Grasping the children's hands, they started to play pat-a-cake with each other. Gabi broke into laughter. Andreas joined her.

"Maybe we shouldn't interrupt them, Estelle. They're having too much fun."

Gabi heard an unfamiliar female voice and looked over her shoulder. She saw two women, each carrying a baby bottle. The older one was dressed for housework. The younger one was the epitome of the fashionably dressed, breathtaking, black-haired Greek woman, making a beeline for Andreas.

"Irena—" Andreas called to her.

Gabi wished she hadn't seen her. Ever since she'd heard about her from Deline, she'd wondered where she'd been hiding. Now that she'd appeared, Gabi found it was much harder than she'd thought to actually meet her. She hugged Nikos to her body.

Deep inside she wished the vision of this incredibly beautiful female weren't permanently etched in her mind. Her brown eyes looked like velvet. Taking the initiative, Gabi said, "You haven't interrupted anything. I'm Gabi Turner, the boys' aunt."

"How do you do?"

"You've come just in time to help Andreas feed the twins. I can't stay any longer. My parents are expecting me on Crete."

She got up and motioned for Irena to sit down before handing Nikos to her. Andreas's veiled eyes followed her movements. By his enigmatic expression, she had no idea what he was thinking. Estelle handed him the other bottle.

Gabi kissed Nikos before turning to Andreas.

"When the pilot flew me here this morning, I hope it's all right that I asked him to wait so he could fly me on to Heraklion."

"Of course," came the low aside.

If Gabi had taken license she shouldn't have, she didn't care. This was one time she needed an escape pod. The helicopter would do nicely. She gave Kris another peck on the cheek.

"See you at the hospital, my little darling." Before she lifted her head, the temptation to cover Andreas's sensuous mouth with her own was overpowering, but she resisted the impulse. "I'll let myself out."

As she hurried to retrace her steps back to the helipad she heard Kris start to cry. A few seconds later Nikos joined in. Their cries brought her pleasure as well as pain. In another minute they'd get over it and enjoy the attention of Andreas and his girlfriend.

Gabi, on the other hand, would never get over it. Her cries were loudest of all, but she would manage to stifle them until after she'd reached Heraklion.

By the time Andreas heard the helicopter and felt the paralyzing pang of watching it swing away with Gabi inside, the twins had settled down enough to finish their bottles.

Irena patted Nikos's back to burp him before putting him in his swing. She glanced at Andreas. "Forgive me for intruding on you and Gabi, Andreas. I didn't realize you were here this morning."

"You don't owe me any apology. Leon said you might come by to see the babies."

She nodded. "Deline was right. Leon's children are beautiful. What a tragic situation."

Andreas kissed Kris's head. "It's a painful time for everyone concerned including you, Irena. Heaven knows I never meant to hurt you."

"I'm going to be all right."

He had to believe that. "I understand you're leaving for Italy."

"Yes, but I'm glad I came by here first and happened to see you. The change in you since last month has been so dramatic, I don't know you anymore. When I saw you out here with her just now, I felt an energy radiating. It was like a fire burning inside of you. Seeing you with her explains several things I haven't understood and makes me want that kind of love for myself."

He got to his feet. "There's no finer woman than you. You deserve every happiness. How long will you be in Italy?"

"Why do you ask?"

"Because I'm concerned about you."

"Don't be. Your courage to break it off with me has opened my eyes to certain things about myself I haven't wanted to admit or explore. To answer your question, I'll be in Italy for as long as it takes."

Her cryptic remark surprised him. "Irena?"

"Don't say anything more. We already talked everything out at the house. Please don't walk me to the car. You stay with your nephews. *Adio*, Andreas."

"Adio." In a strange way he couldn't decipher, she'd changed, too. Something was going on... Bemused, he watched her until she disappeared, then he looked down at the twins. The time had come to get them out of this heat. He tucked a baby under each arm and carried them back to Leon's villa. Another diaper change and they'd be ready for their naps.

Once the boys were asleep, he found Estelle and told her he was going to do some laps in the pool. The energy Irena had referred to was pouring out of him. He needed to release it with some physical activity or he'd jump out of his skin.

On his tenth lap he heard the sound of a helicopter approaching. His heart knocked against his ribs to think it might be Gabi returning, but that was only wishful thinking. She'd run for her life earlier, just as she'd run from him at Papafragas beach, and again the evening she'd pushed him away at the apartment. He had yet to understand what was holding her back.

The rotors stopped whipping the air. Any member of his family could be arriving from Athens, a constant occurrence during the summer. It was probably one of his sisters with her children.

To his surprise Leon appeared minutes later and plunged in the pool. He swam like a dolphin to reach Andreas. The second he saw Leon's face, he knew the worst without having to be told anything.

"Thanks for watching the boys for me. It was a wasted effort. Deline couldn't get rid of me fast enough. Even with our baby on the way, the divorce is on."

"That's her pain talking right now."

Leon spread his arms and rested his back against the edge of the pool. "Apparently she and Irena have been discussing you and me. Before I left Athens she said, and I quote, 'It looks like your brother doesn't know how to be faithful, either. It must be another twin thing,' unquote."

Andreas frowned. "I don't understand."

"When Deline visited Gabi and the twins in Apollonia, I guess she didn't know you'd already broken off with Irena."

Air got trapped in Andreas's lungs. "You mean—"

"I mean she told Gabi the family was waiting for the announcement that you and Irena would be getting married."

Andreas swore violently and levered himself out of the pool.

"What's wrong, bro?"

"*That's* the reason Gabi's been fighting me." Now it all made sense.

"Ah." He eyed Andreas mournfully. "I wish my problem could be fixed as easily."

So did Andreas. Being twins, they understood each other too well. "I know how much you're hurting over Deline. Don't give up on her."

Leon gave him a mirthless smile. "I couldn't if I wanted to because she *is* the one woman for me. In the meantime the boys are keeping me sane."

"Gabi was here a little while ago. The children started crying when she left. Fortunately they settled down without too much trouble."

"I'm thinking of stealing her away from you," Leon admitted. "I need her help. The twins love Gabi and that's never going to change because she'll always be their aunt. Let's face it. Estelle's way too old for this sort of thing. She's been run ragged the last three weeks. It's not fair to her."

"I couldn't agree more."

"If nothing changes between Deline and me, I'm going to have to hire a permanent nanny. In the meantime I could use Gabi to bridge the gap, especially with Kris's operation coming up soon."

"Then call her!" Andreas cried excitedly. The very prospect had his adrenaline surging.

Leon lifted hopeful eyes to him. "You mean it?"

"Do it now! She can stay in one of the guest villas. Tell her what you just told me and she'll come in a shot. Let her know you're sending the helicopter for her."

His brother darted him a curious glance. "Who'll help you at the office?"

"Christine."

"Gus's private secretary?"

He nodded. "I like her. She's unflappable like Anna."

"Then she's the perfect choice to fill her shoes."

"I'll talk to our big brother. When he understands everything, he'll arrange for her promotion. As soon as you reach Gabi, tell her it's a fait accompli so she won't have any reason to turn you down."

"Who was that on the phone?"

Shaken by the conversation, Gabi hung up and turned to her mother. They were in the kitchen eating lunch while they looked at the pictures of the babies taken on her cell phone. "It was Leon Simonides. Would you believe his wife is pregnant?"

"You're kidding—"

"No. What's so terribly sad is that she wants the divorce more than ever. He's feeling over-whelmed. His mother has to look after his father, and he's worried because Estelle is too old to keep up the pace. He's asked me to come and help him with the babies until after Kris's operation."

"I don't envy that man the difficult position he's in."

"Neither do I. He's so hurt, Mom." Gabi let out a troubled sigh. "If I'm willing to come, Leon will send a helicopter for me in the morn-ing. All I have to do is say the word and he'll have my personal things moved out of the office apartment to the guest suite on Milos. After the operation he wants me to start helping him interview women for a permanent nanny position."

"That makes sense, but what about your job with Andreas?"

"Leon said not to be concerned. Their other brother's secretary is going to become Andreas's permanent assistant."

He'd already made the arrangements.

Gabi was like a hot potato...so hot Andreas had been willing to let her go without even telling her himself. She couldn't bear it.

Her mother moved around the table and hugged her. "I know you're torn because this means getting closer to the children, but think of it this way. If you decide you want to do this favor for Leon, then staying on Milos will definitely be easier for you."

She looked up at her. "Easier?"

"Oh, darling—I knew you'd fallen in love with Andreas the second he walked in our living room. Knowing he has a girlfriend, this period of time while you've been working for him has to have been very painful."

Gabi buried her face in her hands. "Was I that transparent?"

"Only to your father and me."

After taking a fortifying breath, she lifted her head. "I'll call Leon and tell him yes. With

Kris's operation looming, he needs all the support he can get." *And I won't have to face Andreas eight hours out of every day.*

CHAPTER EIGHT

GABI started out her fifth day on Milos with the same routine: baths for the babies followed by a bottle and a morning of playtime out by the pool. As he'd done every morning, Leon had flown to Athens early to put in some work. He always returned by four in the afternoon to take over and give Gabi a break. She'd seen nothing of Andreas, which came as no surprise.

While she was easing Kris into the shallow end of the pool, Estelle appeared. The two of them had developed a friendly rapport. While Gabi did all the carrying and running around, the housekeeper listened for the children when they slept.

"Leonides just phoned. He wants you and the boys to get ready for a boat ride on Andreas's cabin cruiser."

"Did you hear that?" She kissed Kris's cheek. "Your daddy's on his way home!" Kris's surgery was coming up the day after tomorrow. Since she hadn't been able to stop worrying about it, she welcomed the diversion that put a change in their schedule.

"The maids will pack and carry everything down to the pier. While you get ready, I'll stay with the twins. I've already made up their bottles."

Gabi wrapped Kris in a towel and handed him to Estelle. "I'll be right back."

She darted up the steps to the guest villa to throw on her beach cover-up over her swimsuit. In a bag she stashed a change of outfit, plus a towel and other essentials she might need. When she went back to the pool for the babies, Estelle told her they'd already been taken down to the pier. Leon must have arrived in the helicopter while she'd been packing.

"See you later, then."

Gabi hurried down to the beach and walked along the dock past all the different family ski and jet boats to board the cruiser. She frowned when she couldn't see or hear Leon or the twins.

"Hello? Anyone home?" she called out.

"We're all in the main salon."

She jumped at the sound of Andreas's voice and turned in his direction. The sight of his tall, well-defined body squeezed the air out of her lungs. He stood at the entrance to the companionway in a pair of sweats and nothing else. Beneath his hair more black than night, his silvery eyes swept over her. She might as well have been lit on fire.

"What are *you* doing here? I—I mean I thought you were at work," she stammered.

"At the last minute Leon went to see Deline in the hope that they could really talk. Now that he's found out he's going to be a father again, he's anxious to be with her and know how she's doing. I told him not to worry about his children and flew here as fast as I could."

Gabi was at a loss for words, still trying to recover from seeing him when it was so unexpected.

His lips curved upward, drawing her attention to his sensuous mouth. "Shall we start again? How are you, Gabi? It seems like months since we last saw each other. I've been all right, but, no matter how efficient Christine is, I must admit I've missed my American secretary who charmed all who came in the office or phoned."

Andreas...

He looked around. "I think it's a beautiful day. What do you think?"

It hurt to breathe. "Is Stavros watching the children?"

"No," he said. "Today we're on our own."

Don't tell me that.

Frightened by the primitive feelings he aroused in her, she darted past him and hurried down the stairs to check on the twins. She found them lying on a quilt he'd placed on the floor of the spacious salon. They were sound asleep on their backs, their arms at their sides with their little hands formed into fists. How would it be?

Andreas had followed her down and stood close enough that she could feel his warmth. "What would it be like to sleep like that without cares or worries? Nothing but sweet dreams until their next meal."

He'd read her thoughts.

"Let's get you up to the helm lounge," he whispered. His breath teased the nape of her neck, sending delicious chills to every part of her body. "I've turned on the intercom down here. If they breathe too hard, we'll hear them."

She didn't need an excuse to put distance between her and Andreas, but she felt self-conscious hurrying up the steps ahead of him. Her sundress only fell to mid-thigh, leaving a good expanse of leg showing.

He led her to the cockpit. "Make yourself comfortable while I untie the ropes. Then we'll be off to some other areas around the island you haven't seen yet."

Gabi sat down on the companion seat next to the captain's chair. Being perched this high with the sun roof open was an experience like no other.

"What do you think?" he asked after taking his seat. His arm and thigh brushed hers, increasing her sensitivity to his touch.

"Like I'm master of all I survey."

A chuckle escaped his lips. "It does feel that way." He started the engine and before long they'd idled out from the bay to head for open water. "When Leon and I were boys, he wanted a huge yacht where he could invite all his friends and sail the seven seas like Ulysses, but I dreamed about owning one of these to go exploring for plunder by myself."

"Naturally." She smiled. Andreas had always blazed his own trails, even if he was an identical twin. "A pirate needs to be able to maneuver in and out of coves, yet be able to outrace his enemies in a big hurry. Now that you've achieved all your dreams, it's going to be our little nephews below who will start dreaming their own dreams."

He cast her a shuttered glance. "You think I've achieved all my dreams?"

She averted her eyes. "It was just a figure of speech."

"For your information, I haven't even begun." He had to be talking about his future with Irena. "What about you?"

They were getting into a painful area. The only dream that truly mattered had been shattered when Deline told her Andreas had gone to Athens to spend time with his girlfriend.

"I've achieved a few little ones."

"For instance?" he prodded.

"I made it into the Penguin club when I was in grade school."

"And that was very important?"

"Yes. You had to be a good ice skater."

"Bravo." She laughed. "What else?"

"In high school I tried to make it on the debate team because I thought those kids were really smart. By my senior year I was chosen."

He turned to look at her. "Was it everything you'd hoped it would be?"

"Anything but. I missed too many classes going to meets, and my egghead partner drove me crazy."

"Male or female?"

"Male."

"I take he didn't grow into one of your past illnesses."

"No. Those came later."

"Have you ever been in love, Gabi? I'm talking about the kind you'd sell your soul for and didn't think was possible. The kind that only comes once?"

He'd just described the condition she was in. A band constricted her breathing. "Yes," she said quietly and got out of the chair. "Excuse me for a moment while I check on the twins."

"We haven't heard a sound from them yet."

"Maybe not, but they might be awake wondering where they are and why their daddy isn't with them. I don't want them to feel lonely."

"They have each other." He looked over his broad shoulder at her. The sun shone down, bronzing his skin. "Take it from me, that's the great thing about twins."

Their gazes fused. "Was it hard at first sharing Leon with Deline?"

An odd silence stretched between them. "Do you know you're the first person who ever asked me that question? You have great perception."

He took his sunglasses from a side pocket and put them on. "To answer your question, *yes*, but it helped that Leon and I do business together. Sadly it was Deline who suffered the most for having to share him. They'd been quarreling about it the night he took out the yacht with friends and met Thea."

Gabi moaned low in her throat. "After the twins were born, I bought some books to study up on the subject. One of the things I learned was to dress them differently, put them in different classes. Help them to be individuals. But the books also said that there's a bond connecting them like inner radar and has to be allowed for."

"That's true."

"Do you think it will be as hard on Leon when you get married one day?"

"Yes, because he's not used to coming in second with me."

Gabi didn't like playing second fiddle either. Sucking in her breath, she hurried below deck.

After learning the business alongside his father and grandfather, instinct told Andreas when it was the right or wrong time to make a crucial move. Now was not the moment to tell Gabi he was single. She was too worried about Kris and the upcoming surgery.

When the time came, he wanted her full attention in order to gauge her reaction after she learned he was a free man. Until their nephew had recovered and she couldn't use him for a distraction, Andreas would have to hold back, but the operation couldn't come soon enough to suit him.

"Wouldn't you know Kris was awake just lying there looking around making cooing sounds?" She'd returned to the cockpit holding the wide-eyed baby against her shoulder.

At a glance Andreas took in one head of jet-black hair, the other of spun gold. Gabi and child provided a live painting more riveting than the picturesque town in the distance.

"Look how beautiful, little sweetheart!"

Andreas could only echo the sentiment before he had to tear his eyes away and pay attention to steering the cruiser. He'd brought them into an inlet with a sweeping bay.

"Where are we?"

"Adamantas, the social center of Milos. This part of the island has a natural harbor. Everyone prefers this area because it's sheltered from the north winds."

"I'm sure your uncle knows every square inch of this paradise." She spoke to the baby, kissing his cheeks. For a second Andreas closed his eyes, wishing he could feel those lips against his skin, and jaw and lips and mouth. "Between him and your daddy, the day will come when you and Nikos will explore this place on your own. By then your heart will be as strong as your brother's."

Sunlight caught the well of her unshed tears reflecting the same blue as the deep water. The sight of them tugged at his heart. "He's going to be fine, Gabi." For Leon's sake, he *had* to be.

"I know." But the words came out muffled because she'd buried her face in Kris's neck. "He has no idea he'll be going into the hospital tomorrow to be prepped."

"We'll all be with him. I assume you've informed your parents they'll be staying in the guest suite at the office with you."

She lifted her head. "Yes. They're very grateful for everything."

"I've arranged for the helicopter to fly them from Heraklion."

"I know, but they didn't expect that. It's too much."

"The family insists. Our sisters plan to take turns tending Nikos at our parents' home, so there's no worry there."

"I don't think any babies ever had more love, but this has to be so hard on your brother."

Because Leon was his twin, maybe that was the reason Andreas felt the depth of his brother's anguish. "He needs comfort from the wife he has hurt too deeply. It's a tragedy."

"It *is*," she cried softly. "His pain must be exquisite to know she's carrying their child. I'd give anything to help them."

"Gabi," he said huskily, "don't you know you're saving his life right now?"

Her wet eyes swerved to his. "So are you. But who's helping Deline?"

Andreas loved this woman for her compassion. "She has a big supportive family."

"I'm glad for that." He watched her cuddle Kris closer. The pained expression on her face tore him up. In the midst of feeling helpless over her pain, he heard Nikos start to cry.

"I'll get him." He cut the motor and stood up. "When I come back, I'll bring their bottles and carry-cots. Shall I bring the stroller, too? We could go ashore in Adamantas and have a late lunch."

She stared up at him. "Are you hungry?"

He had to be honest. "No."

"Neither am I. Do you mind if we go back? This is a heavenly spot, but when Leon flies here, he'll expect to find his babies waiting for him."

Chills chased down his spine to realize how often he and Gabi were in sync, speaking each other's thoughts. In some ways it was like his connection with Leon, but much stronger.

Before the surgery, both sets of grandparents lingered in Kris's hospital room, hugging and kissing him. Gabi's father was visibly shaken. She knew he was seeing Thea. With her death so recent, his tears often lurked near the surface.

Leon hadn't let go of his mother. It was very touching. Andreas and their older brother Gus and his wife stood next to their father, who appeared emotional as well. A year ago he'd suffered a heart attack and had to be more aware of his mortality at a vulnerable moment like this.

Gabi found herself studying the impressive, black-haired Simonides family. They were tall people, each one incredibly attractive. Suddenly Andreas looked around and caught her gaze. He gave her a long, unsmiling look that penetrated to her inner core.

She had the feeling he was remembering their first encounter in his office when he was ready to shut the elevator door on her. The newspaper picture and photograph of the twins had changed lives, not only for the families here, but for Deline.

Gabi checked her watch. It was only

6:45 a.m. Kris was the heart surgeon's first patient on the morning docket. She was thankful for that. They'd all been waiting for this day, each of them doing a mental countdown.

The doctor had told Leon that the newest medical technology had made this a quick procedure. In another hour the surgery would be over. Soon life would return to a new normal, but Gabi couldn't go there yet, not when she knew Andreas wouldn't be in it.

You'd better get used to it, her heart nagged. No more thrilling cruises together with the twins like the one they'd gone on the day before yesterday to Adamantas. As long as she'd been helping Leon through this whole process of getting to know his instant family, Andreas had been a part of it. But those days were numbered and she would never experience such joy again.

She finally broke eye contact with him and hugged her mother, who knew her secret. Gabi needed her strength.

When the door opened, she saw the nurse who'd been working with Leon. She said it was time to take the baby and get the anesthetic administered. "There's a waiting room around the corner. If you'll all move there."

A sob rose in Gabi's throat to see tears trickle

down Leon's pale cheeks as he kissed his son one last time. He carried such a load of pain, Gabi marveled at his composure. Andreas was right there to steady his brother as the nurse disappeared out of the room with the baby Gabi had seen born. She felt as if a piece of her heart had been taken away.

Her dad reached for her hand and squeezed it. Slowly everyone filed out to the lounge for the long wait. Time was so relative. When Gabi was with Andreas, laughing and sharing while they played with the twins, an hour was but a moment that flew by unmercifully fast. But this hour was going to take a year to pass, she just knew it.

It didn't surprise her that Andreas was the one who brought in drinks and snacks, waiting on everyone. Before long his brothers-in-law arrived and the men congregated while the mothers started talking. Gus's wife Beril sat by Gabi. She couldn't have been nicer. They spoke quietly about Leon.

"Since becoming a father, he's changed for the better, Gabi. But taking responsibility has cost him his marriage. I was just talking to Deline yesterday. It's so sad."

Gabi shuddered. "Even though my sister had been drinking, I can promise you she wouldn't have done what she did if she'd known he was married. She wasn't even aware Andreas had a twin brother, but it's far too late to grieve over that now."

Beril wrapped a commiserating arm around her shoulder. Andreas happened to notice the gesture and left the men to come their way, causing Gabi's pulse rate to pick up.

"You look tired," Beril told him.

"Aren't we all, but Leon's the one on the point of exhaustion."

"I haven't had a chance to talk to him yet. Excuse me, Gabi. I'll be back in a minute."

After Beril walked off, Andreas sat down in her place. He smelled wonderful. The creamy sand-colored suit covered his hard-muscled body like a glove. He took her breath. His leg brushed against hers as he turned to her. "Are you all right?" His velvety voice resonated to her insides.

"I will be when the doctor comes in. It's already been an hour and a half. How are you doing?"

"You heard Beril. What can I do for you?"

She glanced at his striking features. Andreas hid his emotions too well. On impulse she said, "I should be asking *you* that question. You've been the one waiting on everyone else."

"Staying busy helps."

As Gabi nodded one of the doctors who'd assisted with the surgery came into the lounge. Like everyone else, she shot to her feet. He looked at Leon.

"Mr. Simonides? Your son's operation was a success, but he's having a little trouble coming out of the anesthetic." Gabi grabbed hold of Andreas's arm without conscious thought. "If you'll follow me. We've got him in the infant ICU."

Leon's anguish was palpable as he eyed Andreas. "Come with me, bro."

Andreas sent Gabi a silent message that he'd be back and left the room with his twin. Without his support, she hurried over to her parents. Her father hugged her for a long moment.

"I can't believe this is happening, Dad. Leon has already been through so much, and now this... Poor little Kris. He's got to come out of it."

"He will, darling."

When she pulled out of his arms, her mother was there to hug her. "We have to have faith that everything's going to be all right."

While everyone in the room was in agony, Gabi saw something out of the corner of her eye.

A dark-haired woman had entered the lounge. It was *Deline*! By then everyone had seen her.

"What's wrong? Where's Leon?" she cried in alarm.

Andreas's mother rushed over to her and explained.

"You mean Kris might not make it?" Deline's voice shook. Her face looked pale.

"None of us is thinking that way."

"But Leon is." Deline's response sounded like a wife who knew her husband better than anyone else. She still loved him, Gabi could feel it. "Where's the infant ICU?"

"Come on, Deline," Gabi answered before anyone else could think. "I'll help you find it."

Together they flew out of the lounge and down the hall to the nurses' station. Gabi spoke up. "This is Mrs. Simonides. She got here late. Her husband is in the infant ICU with Kris who was just operated on. Can she go in?"

"Of course. A baby needs its mother at a time like this." Neither Gabi or Deline bothered to correct the other woman. "Let me get a gown and mask for you."

When Deline was ready the other woman said, "Follow me."

They hurried down another hall and around

the corner where they saw Andreas standing outside the door. With the blinds down, you couldn't see inside.

Lines had darkened his arresting face, making him appear older than his thirty-three years. When he saw them coming, his eyes widened in shocked surprise.

The nurse opened the door for Deline who went right in, then she closed it again and walked away.

In the next instant Andreas gripped Gabi's upper arms. He was so caught up in emotions, he had no idea of his strength. "What's going on?"

Gabi shook her head. "I really don't know. Deline came in the lounge looking for Leon. Your mother told her Kris was in trouble. I thought Deline was going to pass out right there, so I told her to come with me and we'd find them."

Andreas couldn't speak. Instead he put his arms all the way around her and crushed her against him. She understood and didn't misinterpret what was going on while he rocked her.

This whole experience, from the first day Andreas had first found out about the twins, had been so fraught with emotion, he didn't know where else to go with all his feelings. Neither did Gabi, who held on to him, for once not worrying about Irena, who hadn't shared in this life and death situation from the beginning.

"Deline wouldn't have come this morning if she didn't still love Leon," he whispered into her silky gold hair. "She's known about this surgery from the start. To show up today has to mean something, doesn't it?"

Gabi had never heard Andreas sound vulnerable before. It was a revelation. "Yes, I believe it does."

"Oh, Gabi, if I thought—"

"That there might not be a divorce?" she finished what he was trying to say.

"Yes," he cried softly, kissing her forehead and cheeks.

"As my mom said a little while ago, we have to have faith." She buried her face in his neck. "Kris has got to make it, Andreas. Nothing will make sense if he doesn't."

She lost track of time while they held on to each other. This amazing man was actually clinging to her as if his life depended on it. His hands roved over her back. One found its way to her nape. His fingers stroked the curls, sending bursts of delight through her body. Gabi nestled closer against him, loving this feeling of safety and comfort. She'd never known anything like it before.

When another nurse came out of the ICU, Gabi had to force herself away from him, but she wasn't ready for the abrupt separation. It was a good thing there'd been an interruption, otherwise she would have stayed right where she was and Andreas would have figured out what was really going on.

"I'd better get back to the lounge and tell everyone there's been no news about Kris yet." Embarrassed to have revealed her terrible weakness for him, she started down the hall. In one long stride he caught up to her.

"We'll both go. There's no telling how long Leon and Deline will be in there. No matter what's going on with Kris, my brother has the person he wants and needs with him right now. As of this moment, we're both de trop."

Everyone's strained faces turned to them the moment they entered the waiting room. Andreas spoke for them. "We still don't know anything about Kris."

"Is Deline with him?" his mother asked anxiously.

"Yes."

Gabi could hear the questions everyone wanted to voice but didn't dare. "The nurse gave her a gown and mask to put on so she could go in with Leon." She saw glances being exchanged.

Andreas didn't miss them, either. "One thing we all know about Deline. She wouldn't be here at a precarious moment like this to cause Leon pain. Quite the opposite, in fact." He'd championed his sister-in-law. Everything Andreas said or did made Gabi love him that much more.

While he talked with his family, Gabi gravitated to hers, still experiencing the sensation of feeling his arms around her. All that strength was encased in one superb male who worried about his family and still had the stamina to carry the bulk of the load for those depending on him professionally.

She checked her watch for the umpteenth time. Another half hour had passed and still no word about Kris. It wasn't looking good. One glance at her parents' expressions and she knew they were thinking the same thing. The room had grown quiet. Like Gabi, who was fighting not to break down, they were all saying their own silent prayers.

While she was deep in thought she heard Leon's voice. "I have good news, everyone." She looked across the room. His gray eyes shone with a new light. "Kris is awake and breathing on his own. He's going to be all right." His voice broke.

Gabi watched Andreas race toward the entrance to give his brother a bear hug.

"Thank heaven!" She broke down and wept for happiness against her father's shoulder. At that point the whole mood of the room changed to one of jubilation.

"They're going to keep him until tomorrow, then I'll take him home. Deline's going to stay with me and help me." Leon's emotions were spilling out. "Thank you all for being here. I couldn't have gotten through this without you."

After hugging everyone, he hurried out of the room taking Andreas with him. No doubt he needed to talk to his twin privately.

Gabi's heart failed as she watched him disappear. Dying inside, she turned to her mother. "Mom?" she whispered. "Do you mind if we go back to the apartment and pack? I'd like to fly to Heraklion today, but let's go by plane. Even though Andreas has put the helicopter at our disposal, I don't want to take advantage now that Leon doesn't need me to help with the babies."

"I think that's a very wise idea." Her mother understood everything. "Let's go."

Once outside the hospital, they took a taxi back to the Simonides office building. Gabi put in the code so they could ride the private elevator to her floor. Relief that Kris was going to be all right took away all their anxiety in that regard, but Gabi was in too much pain over leaving Andreas to talk.

A clean break.

That was what she'd done with the twins a month ago. Now it was time for one more. She turned off her phone.

Her parents traveled a great deal so it didn't take them long to gather up their things and head for the airport in a taxi. While at the Athens airport waiting for their flight, she made the reservation for her trip to Washington, D.C., leaving the next day.

By late afternoon they reached the consulate. After a quick meal, Gabi showered and changed out of her suit into straw-colored linen pants and a mocha blouse in a silky fabric. With too much nervous energy to sit still, she got started on some serious packing. When she'd come here—five months ago now—she'd brought a lot of clothes. Enough to fill two suitcases and an overnight bag.

She'd left home in March and would be arriving in the August heat. An oppressive heat without the relief of a shimmering blue sea wherever you turned—without a pair of black-fringed gray eyes wandering over you like the sun's reflection off the water.

Gabi couldn't breathe for thinking about so many moments with Andreas preserved in her memory. Earlier today her body had memorized the feel of his while they'd held on to each other outside the ICU. She'd known it would be for the last time. That was why she hadn't been able to let go.

"Gabi?" Her father walked in her room. "I guess you didn't hear me. There's a man in the foyer wishing to speak to you. He says his name is Stavros."

She felt a quickening in her body. What kind of errand had Andreas sent him on? Her heart pounded so hard she got light-headed.

"What's wrong, honey? You paled just now. Who is he?"

"He crews for Andreas. I like him very much."

"Then you'd better not keep him waiting."

"You're right."

The urge to fly down the stairs was tempered by her fear that Stavros would know how excited she was. But that was silly because he was observant enough to know she was so hopelessly in love with Andreas, it hurt. He'd watched her in unguarded moments around his boss. She doubted anything got past him, either.

"It's nice to see you again, Stavros."

He smiled. "You, too. I brought the cabin cruiser over from Milos for Kyrie Simonides. A family gathering kept him in Athens longer than expected. His helicopter should be landing any minute now. To save time, he asked me to escort you on board and he'll join you for dinner to say goodbye."

That was the longest speech she'd ever heard him give, but the answer was still "no." No more. She couldn't take seeing him again.

"That sounds lovely. Please tell him thank you, but I'm flying to the States in the morning and have too much to do."

"I'll tell him." He started to leave, then stopped. "I shouldn't say this because it will spoil his surprise, but he's got Nikos with him."

Nikos—

Stunned by what he'd just told her, she was slow on the uptake. "Wait—" she cried because the taxi he'd taken here was about to leave. "I'll come. Give me a minute to grab my purse."

She dashed upstairs for it. When she returned,

her parents were talking to Stavros. "We heard," her mom said. "Give Nikos a hug for us."

Five minutes later the taxi dropped them off at the pier where she could see the cabin cruiser moored. As she stepped on deck Andreas came out holding Nikos against his shoulder.

She moaned inwardly because they looked perfect together, but it was all wrong. In an ideal world, Nikos should be Andreas's son... and *hers*.

He flashed her one of his enticing smiles. "We're glad you came, aren't we, little guy?" Andreas turned the baby so he could see her. Nikos's eyes lit up. He acted so happy to see Gabi, she let out a joyous laugh and pulled him into her arms.

"How's my big boy?" After smothering him with kisses, she carried him to the rear cockpit. Over his black curls she studied Andreas, who was standing there with his powerful legs slightly apart, looking impossibly handsome in a black crew neck and jeans. "This was a totally unexpected surprise. Thank you." Her voice caught.

"I knew you had to be missing him." His eyes narrowed on her upturned features. "It appears this was a day of surprises on both our parts, starting with your flight to Heraklion."

All of a sudden Gabi started to feel uncomfortable.

"I won't bother to ask why you didn't use the helicopter or why you didn't stay at the apartment long enough for me to take you and your parents out to dinner."

She hugged Nikos tighter. "We would have enjoyed that, but Leon needed you and you had your whole family to deal with."

"And?" he prodded.

"I didn't say anything else."

"Yes, you did," he came back more aggressively. She moved Nikos to her other shoulder and gave him kisses. "You were going to add Irena's name to the list."

Gathering up her courage, she asked, "What kept her from being at the hospital with you?"

"I didn't invite her."

"Andreas—" She stared at him, baffled. "That doesn't sound like you."

One eyebrow lifted. "An interesting observation. It connotes you're somewhat of an expert on my psyche. I like that," he drawled.

Gabi clung to the baby, growing more nervous by the second. "I shouldn't have said anything."

"You can say anything you like to me."

Exasperated, she cried, "That's what I

mean—you're normally so warm and kind about everyone. Did you and Irena quarrel? Otherwise I can't imagine her not being with you this morning w-when—"

"It was a life and death situation?" he finished for her.

"Something like that, yes." Getting agitated, she walked Nikos over to the windows looking out on the harbor. "I'm sure she's been upset since the moment she heard about this whole situation with the twins. But she doesn't have to worry now. The children are settled with their father and I'm leaving tomorrow so—"

"Gabi—" he broke in. "Before you say another word, there's something you need to know."

She struggled for breath. "What?"

"A week ago I learned from Leon that Deline had come to visit you and the twins in Apollonia. I understand she mentioned I'd gone to Athens to see my girlfriend Irena Liapis, the woman who was going to become my wife. Did I repeat that back to you correctly?"

Her body shuddered. "Yes."

He stared her down. "It's too bad Deline wasn't apprised of all the facts at the time."

"What facts?" she whispered.

"That I'd already broken it off with Irena. It's true that she used to be my girlfriend."

Used to be? Gabi's heart jumped. "But Deline said your family was expecting you to marry her."

"Up until you came to my office, that was my intention. Needless to say, my entire world got knocked off its foundation the moment I saw that photo of the twins. In order to deal with the ramifications of your unexpected visit, I was forced to put any plans I had on hold."

"Andreas..."

"As it turned out, it was a good thing. The time away from her made me realize that if I'd loved her the way a man should love a woman, we would have been married months earlier."

"How can you say that?" she cried. "I saw the look on her face when she came to the villa and saw us together with the children."

"What you saw was surprise that we were both there instead of Leon. She's very close to Deline and came by to see the famous Simonides twins before leaving for Italy on vacation."

By now Andreas had made himself comfortable on the leather bench with his arms outstretched and his hard-muscled legs extended in front of him. "Now that Kris is out of the woods, I thought we could relax over dinner and talk."

"There's nothing to discuss." She sank down

opposite him, still holding Nikos, who seemed to be content for the moment.

"You've made up your mind to leave, then?"

Her brows met in a frown. "You *know* I have."

"Would you mind putting it off one more day?"

Yes, she'd mind. It would kill her to be around him any longer. "I can't. After I got back with my parents, I phoned my boss at the advertising agency. He's meeting me for lunch the day after tomorrow to discuss my new promotion."

"I'm sorry to hear you're flying out that soon," he murmured. "Nikos and I will be disappointed. We were hoping to enjoy your company for another day."

Another day is all he wants, Gabi. Not a lifetime.

She kissed the top of the baby's head. "Why isn't he with your sisters?"

"They've already taken turns watching him. Now it's my turn to be responsible. If all goes well, Leon's bringing Kris home from the hospital tomorrow. He and Deline will need time alone with him, so I won't return Nikos until the day after tomorrow and could use your help. Our little nephew loves the sea. What better way to tend him than to cruise around parts of the island tomorrow you haven't seen?"

He sat forward with his hands clasped between his strong legs, staring at her in that disturbing way that made her palms ache. "If you hadn't turned off your phone, I wouldn't have had to come all this distance to ask for your cooperation."

Her cheeks went hot.

"I'd like to think we can return him to Leon in good shape. Of course if another day away from Virginia jeopardizes your chances of being promoted, then I'll call for a taxi to drive you to the consulate. The decision is up to you."

Another twenty-four hours with Andreas... Unlike Leon with Thea, Andreas hadn't proposed they spend a night of passion together and then go their separate ways. Otherwise he wouldn't have brought the baby with him.

To Gabi's shame, *she* was the only person who couldn't be trusted in this situation. Andreas had asked her to help him take care of Nikos as a favor to his brother, nothing more. Tears stung her eyelids. Gabi loved Andreas desperately, but he didn't love her.

She nestled Nikos closer. What this all added up to was that Andreas had a kind streak, stronger than most people's. He'd known she would have adopted the children if things hadn't worked out. This last twenty-four hours had been offered as a gift before he let her go back to where she came from.

Clearing her throat, she said, "I didn't bring anything with me except my purse."

"That's not a problem," came his deep voice. "Your cabin has cosmetics. There's a robe and extra swimsuits for guests. You really won't need anything else."

She was dressed in her linen pants and blouse. Since they weren't going to do anything but be on the cruiser, she supposed he was right and could feel herself weakening. She hated her weakness.

"I'll have to phone my parents and my old boss." She also needed to change her plane reservation.

Andreas reached for the baby. "While you do that, I'll feed this little guy. It's after seven. He's starting to look around for his bottle."

She waited until he'd gone below deck before phoning her family. After three rings her mother answered. Gabi explained she was still with Andreas, but her mom sounded upset when she told her about his plans.

"Darling? You're a grown woman capable of making your own decisions, but for what it's worth, I don't think this is a good idea. You have to look after yourself now. You're going back home with a broken heart. Do you really think it's wise to prolong the inevitable?"

"No."

"Of course you want extra time with Nikos, but Andreas doesn't need you to help him tend the baby."

"I know."

"I can tell I've said too much. Forgive me. All I want is your happiness, and there hasn't been a lot of that since you flew to Greece after Thea became so ill."

She gripped the phone tighter. "You haven't said anything I haven't been telling myself since I first met him. Thanks for being my mom." Her voice caught. "When I hang up, I'll give Nikos a kiss and come home. See you in a little while."

CHAPTER NINE

A BRUSH through her curls and a fresh coat of lipstick helped Gabi pretend she was in control before she went down the companionway to say a final goodbye. Midway to her destination she could hear the sounds of bossa nova music playing quietly in the background.

Before she stepped onto the floor of the main salon, a slight gasp escaped her throat to see an elegantly decorated table with candles and fresh pink roses. Their sweet scent filled the room.

As she looked around her gaze caught sight of Andreas coming out of the galley with two plates of food. Her heart thumped loud enough for him to hear. "Where's Nikos?"

Andreas put the plates on the table. "Good evening, Gabriella Turner. I'm glad you could make it. Nikos fell asleep after his bottle waiting for you. I put him in my stateroom, but left the door open in case he wakes up for some reason."

The next thing she knew he held out a chair for her. "Please sit down and we'll take advantage of this wonderful Brazilian meal Stavros has prepared for us. It's a specialty of his due to his part-Brazilian nationality." She didn't know that. "He's really outdone himself tonight."

No one in the world had charm like Andreas. Now more than ever she needed to keep her wits about her. The romantic ambience was too much. "I agree everything's lovely, but—"

"No buts or you'll hurt his feelings. He's grown very fond of you and the twins. So have I. Since you first came to my office, all you've done is sacrifice for me and Leon, not to mention our entire family. It's time you were waited on for a change. With this meal, please accept the gratitude of the Simonides clan."

Gratitude?

Suffering another heartsick pang, she sat down across from him. When the meal was over she would thank him and Stavros. Following that, she would leave the cruiser without tiptoeing in the other room to give Nikos one last kiss.

The fabulous *churrasco*, a beef barbecue served on skewers, made a wonderful change from the Greek food she'd enjoyed for the last four months, yet she had to force herself to eat. To her chagrin she'd lost her appetite knowing she wouldn't be seeing Andreas again. His keen eyes couldn't help but notice.

He lifted his wineglass and took a sip, eyeing her over the rim. The candlelight flickered in his eyes, bringing out the flecks of silver that made them so beautiful. "Who would have dreamed when you swept into my office, things would turn out the way they have?"

She wiped the corner of her mouth with a napkin. "We can only hope Deline's decision to go back to Leon is permanent."

Andreas breathed in sharply. "He's a changed man. By the time baby three comes along, he ought to be an expert in fatherhood. That ought to be good for something."

Gabi heard the concern in his voice and wanted to comfort him. "Since Thea isn't alive, I'd like to think it will be easier for Deline to love the babies for themselves, especially after she's had their baby."

"Let's hold that thought," he said in a purring voice. "More wine?"

She shook her head. "I haven't even finished what I have." Her gaze happened to flick to the half-full glass. She noticed the liquid moving.

It suddenly dawned on her she could hear the motor of the cruiser. They were skimming the placid water at full speed!

Only now and then did she feel the vibration from another boat's wake. Gabi had been so deep in thought about Deline and Leon, she hadn't noticed.

"We've left the port—" she cried in panic.

He nodded, not acting in the least perturbed. "Why are you so surprised?"

Her hand went to her throat in a nervous gesture. "Because I'd decided to go home after dinner. You don't need me to help take care of Nikos. I realize you only did this to let me have a little more time with our nephew, but the gesture wasn't necessary."

Though he didn't move, if she weren't mistaken his eyes darkened with some unnamed emotion. "We're at least a third of the way to Milos, but if you want Stavros to turn back, I'll tell him."

"No—" She rubbed her temples where she could feel the beginnings of a tension headache coming on. "Since we're that far out to sea, I'm not going to ask you to change your plans now." She was such a little fool.

"You look pale. What's wrong?"

"Probably nothing a walk up on deck in

the night air won't cure. Please excuse me. The dinner was outstanding. I'll be sure to let Stavros know."

She pushed herself away from the table and rushed up the stairs. When she reached the rear cockpit, she could still hear the Latin music. Her blood throbbed with the beat. The urge to dance right into Andreas's arms was becoming a violent need.

Out here on the water there was a stark beauty to the seascape. It provided another haunting memory to take home with her.

"Feeling better?"

She hadn't realized he'd come up on deck. Andreas moved with the quiet stealth of a gorgeous black leopard. Swallowing hard, she said, "Much, thank you."

"I checked on Nikos. He's in a deep sleep."

"That's good." He stood too close to her. She moved to the leather bench and sat down to look out of the windows.

"Aside from missing your parents and the twins, are you looking forward to going home to the States?"

"Yes," she lied. "I love the work I do."

"They'll be lucky to get you back. If you ever need a reference, I'll vouch for you in the most glowing terms."

"Thank you." Unable to sit still, she stood up again. "If you'll excuse me, I'm going to go to bed."

"It's not that late. There's going to be a moon like the kind you don't see very often."

"I'm sure that's true." She clasped her hands together. "But I'm afraid I won't be able to stay awake. It's been a long day, and the wine has made me sleepy."

He rubbed the pad of his thumb along his lower lip. "You only drank half a glass."

Nothing escaped him. "It doesn't take much for me. Goodnight." She made it as far as the entry when he called her name. She swung around and looked back at him. His hooded gaze disguised any emotions he was feeling. "Yes?"

"I'm curious about something. How did working for me compare to the work you do for your boss?"

Gabi couldn't understand why he'd asked her that. "They're both very challenging in their own ways." If she stayed on deck any longer, he'd break her down and get the truth out of her. Then she'd really want to sink in a hole and hide from him. "Where will we be docking in the morning?"

"Why?" he demanded with an edge to

his tone. "Are you hoping it will be at the villa so you can fly back to Heraklion in my helicopter?"

"Only if it won't put you out."

"How could it do that?"

His mood had changed. She'd angered him when it was the last thing she'd wanted to do. "I think you're tired, too. The strain of Kris's surgery has caught up with both of us. Get a good sleep, Andreas. I'll see you in the morning."

Without waiting for a response, she went down to her cabin. Once she'd checked on the baby to make sure he was still sleeping comfortably, she showered and went to bed using the guest robe hanging on the bathroom door. Surprisingly, she slept until Nikos woke her up at six wanting to be fed.

After dressing in the same outfit she'd worn last evening, she took off his diaper and bathed him. He loved the water and wanted to play. Finally she dressed him and put him in his carry-cot. On the way to the cockpit, she got his bottle out of the fridge in the galley and carried him up on deck to feed him.

To her surprise the cruiser was moored at a pier along a stretch of beach she'd never seen before. Because it was dawn, the layers of hills in the light above the sand took on lavender to purple hues with each receding line.

At the top of the first hill a small, white cycladic church was silhouetted against the sky. The sheer beauty of it stood out and drew her gaze. She realized she was looking at a sight quite out of this world. A glimpse of Olympus?

"This is my favorite spot on Milos in the early morning," came the familiar male voice she loved. "Before you went home I wanted you to see it at first light."

She cast him a sideward glance. "I can see why. It would be impossible to describe this to anyone and do it justice. This is something you have to experience for yourself."

Andreas lounged against the entry, focusing his gaze on the church. "I was a boy when my parents first brought me here. I thought it had to be the home of the gods."

"Would you believe I thought the same thing when I came up here just now?"

His eyes found hers. They seemed to be asking something of her. "How would you like to go up there? It's a bit of a climb, but not difficult and won't take long. Stavros will watch Nikos for us."

All the warning bells were going off telling Gabi not to go, but she sensed this was too important to Andreas to turn him down. He wanted her to see a place that had deep meaning for him. She knew he didn't show this private side of him to very many people.

She felt honored. Even if she could never have this man's love, she had garnered his respect and that was something to treasure. "I'd like that."

Andreas pulled out his cell phone and told Stavros they were going ashore for a little while. Within seconds the older man arrived at the cockpit with a smile.

"I'll take good care of the little one."

Gabi thanked him for the lovely dinner and his willingness to tend Nikos. "We won't be long," she assured him.

"Shall we go?" Andreas led the way off the boat and along the pier. This morning he was wearing white pants and a sport shirt in a dusky blue silk. She couldn't take her eyes off him.

As he ambled up the path she could imagine him as a boy. She ached to think she'd only known him a short time. All those years when she'd missed the in-between part were gone. She would never know the rest of the years yet to come...

A debilitating stab of pain took the wind out of her. She had to stop halfway up the path in order to gather her strength so she could keep moving. Finally they reached the top. From this vantage point she had an incredible view of the Aegean a thousand feet below.

Andreas turned to her with those penetrating eyes. "What do you think?"

"You didn't really need to ask me that."

A smile broke out on his face so beautiful, she had trouble breathing. "Years ago couples wound their way up from the village on the other side to be married here, but the tradition dwindled out because the guests weren't up to it."

She laughed, still out of breath herself. "Nowadays it would have to be the rare couple who…" The rest of the sentence didn't come out. Why did he mention that subject? Bringing Gabi here was too cruel. She knew he hadn't meant to be, but she couldn't take anymore.

"I—I think we'd better get back to Nikos."

"We just got here." His unflappable manner was starting to unnerve her. He moved closer. "I want to take you inside. The priest came early and opened it especially for us. He's anxious to meet you."

Gabi blinked. "I don't understand."

"Maybe this will help." In the next breath he pulled her into his arms and lowered his compelling mouth to hers in a kiss of such intense desire, he set off a conflagration inside her. It went on and on, deeper and longer and so thrilling, her legs shook.

"With every breath in my body, I love you, Gabi Turner. I want you for my wife and have asked the priest to marry us. Everything's been arranged."

"But I thought—"

"You think too much. I've wanted this since the moment you came into my life."

His electrifying tone and the fire in his eyes caused her to tremble. She could hear him talking, but she couldn't believe any of this was really happening.

"Little did I know that the minute Kris survived his operation, you would try to get away from me. You do love me, don't you? Say it— I've been dying for you to admit it."

"I would have said it weeks ago," she cried, throwing her arms around his neck so she could cover his face with kisses. "I'm in love with you, darling. I don't know if you're in my dream, or I'm in yours, but it doesn't matter because I've needed this forever."

His mouth sought hers again and they clung in a rapture that swept her away. He cupped her face in his hands. "Tell me I'm the man you were talking about," he demanded almost savagely. "Admit it," he cried.

"You *know* you are," she said with her heart in her eyes reflecting the lavender light. "I love you so desperately you can't imagine, Andreas." Now that he'd kissed her again, she was addicted to his mouth, seeking it over and over in an explosion of need, yet the terrible hunger they had for each other kept on growing.

At last he drew in a harsh breath. "There's no way I would ever let you go. I'm in love with you, Gabi. The kind I didn't think would ever happen to me. The way I feel about you, we have to get married *now*."

Gabi needed no urging. He grasped her hand and led her inside the small, seventeenth-century church where he'd come as a boy. The robed priest was waiting for them. She felt as if she were floating in a dream, but it seemed real enough by the time he'd pronounced them husband and wife.

Andreas turned to her with a look of eager, tremulous joy. "Let's go, Mrs. Simonides."

Like happy children let out of school, they ran down the path to the waiting cruiser far below. When they reached the bottom, Andreas swept her in his arms. "I've been wanting to do this for weeks."

"Congratulations on your marriage," Stavros called out while her husband was kissing her senseless. "Don't worry about Nikos. He's up in the cockpit with me learning the ropes."

"Have I worn you out yet?" Andreas whispered against her throat. It was already early evening. Only temporarily sated, they were wrapped together on their sides, still unwilling to let each other go, even to sit up.

She stared into his adoring eyes. "I'm ashamed to admit that will never happen. I can't remember when I wasn't in love with you."

"The evening you stood at the elevator in my office fighting for our nephews' lives, I found out what the meaning of real love was all about. It hit me so hard and fast, I'll never be the same."

Her eyes misted over. "I knew how deeply I loved you when I saw you interact with the twins. The kind of caring you showed them and your brother told me this was a man above the rest and the woman lucky enough to win his love would be the happiest woman alive."

She caressed the side of his firm jaw. "I'm that woman, Andreas. You make me so happy, I'm frightened."

His expression sobered. "So am I. Joy really

does exist for some. We have to guard it with our lives, *agape mou*."

She nodded, pressing her mouth to his, loving the taste and feel of him. "It's so sad that Thea never found it."

He pulled her on top of him. "My poor brother came too close to losing it. I swear I'll love you till the day I die."

The second his hungry mouth closed over hers, Gabi let out an ecstatic sigh, needing her husband's possession. How had she lived this many years without him? Time didn't exist as they gave each other pleasure almost beyond bearing.

"Uh-oh," she whispered into his hair some time later. "I think I heard a little cherub who's been ignored too long."

Andreas bit her earlobe playfully. "I'll get him."

In half a minute he'd brought the baby to bed with them. He lay him on top of his chest, a position Nikos didn't like as well as on his back.

"Oh, Andreas...isn't he the most adorable child you ever saw?"

"Thea and Leon did good work, didn't they?"

"Yes," she admitted with a gentle laugh.

His smoldering gaze found hers. "I can do good work, too."

Emotion made her voice husky. "I already know that."

"Will you be disappointed if our first baby isn't a twin? I'm not unaware you'd planned to adopt these two."

"That was the original plan." She kissed Andreas's shoulder. "But when I saw Leon with them in Apollonia, the ache for them passed because another ache had taken over. I discovered I wanted my own babies with you."

"*Gabi…*"

Somehow they got lost in another kiss, but Nikos didn't like being caught between them and made his discomfort known.

"It's okay, little guy." Andreas lifted him in the air and got to his feet. "Estelle's waiting to take care of you tonight." He put him in his carry-cot and got dressed.

Gabi sat up in the bed, taking the sheet with her. "She is?"

"Since we're on our honeymoon, she insists. When we get back in the morning, we'll fly to Athens with Nikos and tell everyone our news, then we'll head straight to Crete. In the meantime, I want you to stay in that bed and wait for me. I won't be long."

"You'd better not be. I already miss you."

He shot her a sizzling glance. "You don't know the half of it, but you're going to find out."

A thrill ran through her body. She ached with love for him. The moment he disappeared with her precious Nikos, she got out of bed and threw on her robe. Her purse was in her cabin. She padded out of the stateroom to get her phone and call her parents, who were delighted with the happy news.

"Well, we'll see you tomorrow, then, darling," her dad said, clearing his throat. "Tell Andreas welcome to the family."

She already had...in ways that would make her blush over the years.

"I will. See you tomorrow. Love you."

No sooner had she hung up than she could hear Andreas calling to her. "I'm in my cabin!"

He came to the door out of breath, his eyes alive. "What are you doing in here?"

"I was just letting Mom and Dad know our news. They're thrilled out of their minds."

"So am I," he murmured, taking her down on the bed with him. "I told Stavros to head for Papafragas beach. If no one's around, I want to make love to you there. It's one of my many fantasies since you blew into my life."

She kissed his eyes and nose. "That's twice you've used that expression."

"Because you're like a fragrant breeze that blows across the island, filling me with wants and needs beyond my ability to express."

"I love you so much I'm in pain, Andreas."

"So am I, and plan to do something about it right now. We can either swim in like we did before, or we can take the shortcut down the steps to the sand from the other side."

She let out a squeal. "There's a shortcut?"

He burst into deep laughter, the kind that rumbled out of him. "So I *have* worn you out."

"Never. But right now I'd rather reserve all my energy for loving you. How long before we get there?"

Andreas undid the sash on her robe. "Long enough, my love."

CHAPTER TEN

AFTER making love over and over again, they lay entwined on the sand until it gave up all its heat. By the middle of the night, Andreas had to throw a light blanket over them.

"Look at those stars, darling. With the walls on either side of us, it's like viewing the heavens through a telescope."

"I *am* looking," he answered her. "They're in your eyes." He couldn't believe he was actually holding his wife, his lover, his best friend. His *life*.

She gave him that special smile he felt wrap right around his heart. He needed to love her all over again. "When we bring our children here one day, we can never tell them…well, you know."

Gabi could be bold one minute, shy the next. Always the giver. There was so much to learn about her. Thank heaven this was only the beginning.

"You mean how we consecrated this spot for our own?" he whispered against her throat.

"Yes."

"I came close to ravishing you on this sand before."

"I came even closer to letting you," she confessed. "You'll never know how much I wanted you that night."

He expelled a sigh. "I wasn't sure of you then. Irena told me that when she saw us together, she felt this energy radiating from us like a fire had been lit."

"Andreas—" She clasped him tighter. "Here I am with you—all of you—I have you totally to myself—and I still want more. Maybe there's something wrong with me to love you this much."

He kissed her trembling lower lip. "If there is, I don't ever want you to get well."

"This night is enchanted. I wish we could hold back the morning. It's going to be here before we know it."

"The morning will always have its enchantment, Gabi. That's because, no matter where we are, we'll always wake up to each other."

"Promise me," she cried urgently.

His adorable wife loved him as much as he loved her. Before the joy of it gave him a heart attack, he proceeded to convince her that this was only the beginning.

Those Matchmaking BABIES

MARIE FERRARELLA

Prolific romance author **Marie Ferrarella** swears she was born writing, 'which must have made the delivery especially hard for my mother.' Born in West Germany of Polish parents, she came to America when she was four years of age. Marie was only fourteen when she first laid eyes on her future husband, Charles Ferrarella. After receiving her English degree, specialising in Shakespearean comedy, Marie and her family moved to Southern California, where she still resides today. Ever practical, Marie was married in a wash-and-wear wedding dress that she sewed herself, appliqués and all.

Marie has one goal: to entertain, to make people laugh and feel good. 'That's what makes me happy,' she confesses. 'That, and a really good romantic evening with my husband.' She's keeping her fingers crossed that you enjoy reading her books as much as she's enjoyed writing them!

Visit her website, www.marieferrarella.com.

Prologue

The babies were crying again.

Crying and sapping her strength bit by bit.

The buzzing in her head increased, fueling the desperation that was threatening to wash right over her.

She loved them, truly loved the babies. But she wanted to be free. Wanted once more to taste and touch the freedom of being responsible only for herself, not two small lives. Wanted the freedom of waking up in the morning after a long night's sleep, knowing that any decision she made that day would affect her and only her.

Freedom. It whispered enticingly to her, its song riding the waves of the wind.

She slouched behind the steering wheel of the ancient vehicle, driving slowly now through the streets of a town whimsically renamed Storkville, weighed down by the responsibility she shouldered alone. Yes, there was her sister to help, and to worry, but the bottom line was the babies were hers. Hers to raise, hers to feed. Hers to account for and to.

Tears welled up in her eyes as she bit her lower lip. She couldn't take it anymore. She was too young to feel this old, this hopeless, this hemmed in.

If only there was a way...

She saw the building then.

At first glance, it looked like a house lifted from another era, when things were simpler. When men who created babies stayed to see them grow to maturity rather than disavowing any connection to them, disappearing forever from their lives. A stately Victorian house, prim and proper in its appearance, yet somehow warm and inviting, like a maiden aunt who baked wonderful cookies.

She stared at it, slowing the old car even more.

The sign before the house proclaimed it to be a daycare center.

A daycare center in a town known for its love of babies. For its love of children of all ages.

She looked back at the two tiny infants with identical faces if not identical genders who sat strapped in their car seats behind her. Their cries had quieted, but the noise still echoed in her head. They would start again soon—the cries, the demands.

She sighed, looking at the building. In a moment, the daycare center would be behind her. Just like the rest of her life.

Her eyes widened as the idea came to her.

And suddenly, there was a way....

She sat up straight, no longer slouching, no longer hopeless.

She knew what she had to do.

Chapter One

"**H**annah! Hannah, you've gotta come, like, quick!"

Standing in her front room, Hannah Brady's heart somersaulted into her throat. Those were not exactly the kind of words the owner of a newly established daycare center wanted to hear.

"Wait here." The unnecessary instruction was issued to the eighteen-month-old Hannah deposited into a wide playpen a second before she hurried to see what was going on.

The high-pitched entreaty had come from Penny Sue Lipton, her fifteen-year-old part-time volunteer. Stuck halfway between the childhood of her past and the inviting promise of the adulthood in her future, for Penny Sue, fifty percent of life was pure excitement, the other fifty percent was pure boredom. Hannah tried to calm herself with that knowledge as she rushed to the rear of the Victorian building she had inherited from her Great-Aunt Jane just at what had felt like the eleventh hour of her life.

But when she heard Gertie, who everyone knew as Aunt Gertie and who was well into her sixties and as stable as the day was long, call out, "Oh my dear lord, Hannah, come quickly. You're just not going to believe this," Hannah had a sinking feeling that this wasn't just Penny Sue overreacting. She had trouble.

As far as she knew, all the occupants of the daycare center, tiny and otherwise, were accounted for. That meant that none of them had gotten into any sort of mischief that would throw two of her volunteers into what amounted to a dither.

Reaching the back of the building Hannah discovered that none of her small charges were in trouble...but there certainly was trouble. Trouble with a capital T.

Hannah's mouth dropped open as she came to a skidding stop beside the two volunteers—and two babies, neither of whom she recognized. Aunt Gertie was holding one of the two infants in her arms, cooing to it to get it to stop its fussing. Penny Sue was squatting down beside her, scooping up the other child. The babies had on identical clothes and seemed to have emerged out of identical infant seats.

Penny Sue turned toward Hannah, grinning broadly. Her green eyes were dancing. What Penny Sue lacked in experience, she made up in enthusiasm. The young girl clearly loved babies.

The one she was holding had a firm grip on her curly, reddish hair. "Hey wow, like, isn't this cool, Hannah? They were like, there, on the doorstep when I opened the back door. Foundlings." She held the

MARIE FERRARELLA 11

baby up a little higher, as if presenting it for show and tell. "Just like in those old movies."

Hannah had a feeling that, unlike in the old movies, the babies wouldn't go back to their rightful owner at the end of two hours, right before the second feature. She pressed her lips together.

"All we need is the sound of violins and snow falling. Speaking of which," she said, glancing out at the darkening sky with its smell of rain in the air, "we'd better get them inside before they get sick."

As the two women withdrew into the warm kitchen scented with freshly baked sugar cookies, courtesy of Aunt Gertie, Hannah grasped an infant seat with each hand and dragged both into the house. She placed the seats just inside the door, then picking up the lone diaper bag that had been beside the seats, she shut the door behind her.

And the morning had got off to such a good start, she thought. She'd gotten two new charges with the promise of three more next week. Business was picking up and it was beginning to look as if she was finally going to be able to compensate Gertie and Penny Sue for their time.

So much for that happy, satisfied feeling. She turned to look at Penny Sue, hoping against hope for answers. "Where did they come from?"

Smitten by the baby she was holding, Penny Sue didn't bother looking up. Instead, she lifted a shoulder haphazardly and let it drop. "Beats me."

Gertie, her own arms filled with baby, was standing closer to Hannah. Curious, Hannah ran the back of her hand against the baby's cheek. Bright blue eyes looked at her and the child cooed. There wasn't the hint of cold about the soft skin.

"Well, they weren't out there for long," Hannah judged. She looked at Penny Sue. "What made you open the door when you did?"

Very carefully, Penny Sue separated a thick strand of her hair from small, pudgy fingers. "I just walked into the kitchen—I smelled Aunt Gertie's cookies which were, like to die for." She flashed Gertie a grin, then saw Hannah's look urging her on. "And then I thought I heard somebody knock."

If someone knocked, that meant that someone had to have been there. Maybe just turning away when Penny Sue came to the door. Maybe the teenager had caught a glimpse of whoever had abandoned the children without realizing it.

"Did you see anyone?" Hannah's voice was eager.

Penny Sue shook her head. "I saw the babies first because they were making this noise, you know? And then I, like, called you to, like, come quick." Hannah tried not to look impatient. Penny Sue must have realized what she was doing because she said, "I know, I know, stop using the word *like*. I'm, like, trying—" Chagrined, she bit her lip. "I mean—"

Hannah held up her hand. This wasn't the time to play Professor Higgins to Penny Sue's Eliza Doolittle. "Right now, I just want to know if you saw who knocked on the door."

Suddenly, Penny Sue's eyes brightened. "Yeah, I did see someone. I saw some lady running off."

"What lady?" Hannah asked.

"I don't know. I never saw her before," Penny Sue

replied, looking at Hannah. "I mean, like, she was hurrying away and—"

Coming to Penny Sue's rescue, Gertie held up a crumpled piece of paper. "Hannah, look, there's a note. I just found it inside the baby's sweater."

Taking the yellow piece of paper from Gertie, Hannah looked at it. The edges were jagged and torn, as if it'd been hastily yanked off a pad or out of a notebook.

"What's it say, what's it say?" Penny Sue breathlessly demanded, coming closer to Hannah. Shifting the baby to her other side, she tried to peer over Hannah's shoulder to read it.

"Not much." Disappointed, Hannah read it out loud. "'I know you can take care of my babies better than I can.'"

The single line was written, not typed, which meant that this could have been an impulse abandonment, she reasoned.

Hand to the back of the baby's head, Gertie placed the infant against her shoulder, nodding thoughtfully as she looked at the yellow paper. "Must be someone from town if they know that," she speculated.

"Or they, like, said that to throw you off the trail," Penny Sue said excitedly. "Maybe these are kidnapped babies, or, like, maybe—"

Hannah sighed. She didn't need this. Trying to steer carefully through the narrow waters and sharp turns of the situation facing her, she dropped one hand onto Penny Sue's shoulder.

"Or, like, maybe," Hannah suggested fondly, a smile lifting the corners of her mouth, "we'd better call in Sheriff Malone before you get any more carried away.''

Sheriff Tucker Malone flipped closed the small spiral pad he'd been using to take down notes and tucked it into the pocket of his bomber jacket. He looked from Penny Sue to Hannah. ''And that's all any of you can tell me?''

Hannah exchanged looks with the young girl beside her. It was obvious that Penny Sue felt nervous, but Hannah knew it was the demeanor of the sheriff himself and not any secret she was hiding that made the teenager fidgety.

''That's all any of us know, Tucker,'' Hannah told him. ''Whoever left those babies looked like a stranger.''

''To Penny Sue,'' Tucker qualified, glancing at the young girl. It was obvious that he didn't set much store by anything Penny Sue had said.

''But I—'' Distressed, Penny Sue began to protest in defense of herself. Hannah gently cut her short.

''Why don't you go help Aunt Gertie with the children?'' she urged kindly. ''I'm sure she's got her hands full right about now. The afternoon snack is way overdue.''

''Sure thing, Hannah.''

Resolutely, Penny Sue nodded and withdrew from the formal living room where Hannah and Tucker were sitting opposite one another.

The babies were in their seats on the floor before them, waving their hands and kicking their feet—two pieces of animated evidence. Beside them were all the worldly things they appeared to have: a diaper bag with two feeding bottles, two chewed plush toys and a delicately ornate baby rattle that had all the appearance of being an heirloom. Hannah knew Tucker was hoping that the latter might be traceable, but he had expressed his doubts.

The babies were carbon copies of one another, with reddish-brown hair and large blue eyes. Each baby was wearing a sweater with a name embroidered on it: Steffie and Sammy. As to what their last name was, that was anyone's guess.

"One of each," Tucker murmured, looking down at the babies. He raised his eyes to Hannah. "Any thoughts on the matter?"

"Other than being stunned?" She shook her head. The babies had been all she'd thought about since she'd placed the call to the sheriff's office. "No."

Steely eyes held hers captive. Tucker always knew when he was being lied to, although he didn't see the reason for it now. "Any particular reason the mother picked you to leave them with?"

She didn't care for where this was going. "We don't know it's a mother," Hannah pointed out. "Just because Penny Sue saw a woman hurrying away in the distance—"

"True enough," he interrupted. "Know anyone who'd leave them with you?"

"If I knew the person who'd leave them, then I'd know the babies," Hannah pointed out. "And I don't." She looked down at the two round, shiny faces. "It's as much a mystery to me as it is you. That's why I called you."

And it was true. If she had known the troubled parent who had chosen to leave these adorable children with her, she would have done everything in her power to talk them out of it before ever bringing Tucker into the picture. Tucker Malone, as everyone knew, was a good man, an honest man, but he believed in adhering to the letter of the law and compassion was not among the qualities she would have attributed to him right off the bat.

Compassion, she felt, was what was needed here. For everyone involved.

"How about that anonymous donation you were supposed to have received when you opened the center? The one to help you keep things operating smoothly."

She looked at him sharply. "How did you know about that?"

He pushed his Stetson back on his head with his thumb. "Word gets around here, you know that, Hannah. Think that whoever gave you the donation did it for a reason?"

She didn't follow him. "Such as?"

"Such as a down payment on having you take the babies. Conscience money," he clarified.

She looked at the babies, stunned by the thought. "No." She found her voice and it grew stronger. "I don't believe that."

"Just a thought." Tucker rose, careful to sidestep the infant seat. "Well, I'll see what I can do about this." He picked up the rattle from the sofa, slipping it into his front pocket as well. "In the meantime, we're not really set up for this kind of thing." He looked at Hannah, who had stood up next to him. "Why don't I get Health and Human Services to appoint you temporary guardian of these two until I can find something more to go on? After all, you're a licensed foster parent.''

Caught off guard, Hannah looked down at the twins. She hadn't really thought much beyond reporting the incident to the sheriff. Being responsible for the children on a twenty-four-hour basis was something she hadn't even considered, despite being a certified daycare administrator.

''You mean keep them?''

''Not keep them,'' he amended. ''Just have them on loan. They wouldn't look too good in the county jail and I don't have any place else to put them. What better place for them than in a daycare center?''

Pointing out that the key part of the word was *day* seemed somehow futile from where she was standing. Reluctantly, she had to admit that Tucker was right. Where else could the babies go?

Besides, in the last half hour, waiting for Tucker to arrive, Hannah had found herself already falling in love with the small foundlings.

There was no point in putting up an argument. ''Okay, I guess you're right.''

Tucker nodded. ''I'm the sheriff, I'm supposed to be.'' He pulled the brim of his hat down and turned toward the doorway. One of the babies began to fuss. ''I'll see myself out.'' Pausing at the threshold, he told her, ''I'll let you know if I find out anything.'' Tucker's eyes met hers just before he left. ''You do the same.''

Hannah stooped to pick up the fussing baby. Holding Sammy against her shoulder, she patted his small back. ''Count on it.''

* * *

She'd been torn about the next step, knowing it had to be taken, yet hesitating to take it. Not because of any doubts in her mind as to the competence of the man she was about to call, but because of doubts Hannah had as to her own reaction. Her own ability to stoically withstand a meeting face-to-face, with him. With Jackson.

But there was no getting around it. The babies had to be checked out by a competent pediatrician. Storkville now had one. Five months ago, because of his own failing health, Dr. Gregory Bowen had retired after practicing in Storkville for thirty years. Four months ago, Dr. Jackson Caldwell, Jr., newly returned to town to bury his father, Jackson Sr., took over Dr. Bowen's practice.

It had taken Jackson very little time to reclaim his place in the community he'd abruptly left behind three years ago. After a while, it was as if he had never really left.

Hannah hesitated calling him because she was afraid that the same thing would happen with the place Jackson had once occupied in her heart. A secret place she had never told anyone about. Especially since she'd married his best friend.

But she'd placed the call, knowing that there was no other choice open to her, telling herself that she was an adult now and it was time for her to behave like one. At least outwardly.

After four months of waltzing around and carefully avoiding him, she'd invited Jackson into her home and stood now silently watching him as he examined the babies in one of her late great aunt's guest rooms.

It was a bedroom out of another era, when ladies' bedrooms were more feminine and ladies themselves held their tongues rather than let their true feelings be known.

Maybe things hadn't changed all that much after all, she thought, waiting for his prognosis.

She hadn't had a chance to redecorate the bedroom. There'd been so much to do with preparing to open the new daycare center that all she'd had time to do was air the room out. She wished she'd picked the living room for the exam to take place in, instead of here. With the sky dark and pregnant with fat rain clouds just outside the window, it felt as if there were ghosts looming inside the room. Not the least of which were ghosts from her own past, a past she'd wanted but had never really had with Jackson.

Jackson returned his stethoscope to his neck and smiled at a twin. Sammy looked as if he returned the smile, his eyes crinkling. Jackson was slower raising his eyes to Hannah.

"Except for Steffie's runny nose and sniffles, both babies appear to be in perfect health. Whoever left them on your doorstep certainly didn't abuse them."

"Other than depriving them of love and dumping them on a stranger's doorstep." Hannah bit back the bitterness she knew he could hear in her voice.

Moving to the side, she busied herself with slipping a fresh diaper on Sammy and deliberately avoided looking at Jackson.

Slowly, he slipped the stethoscope into his bag. He'd been surprised, to say the least, to get the call from Hannah this afternoon. He'd also been more pleased than he'd wanted to be to hear her voice on the other end of the line. He'd been back for over four months now and had only managed to catch fleeting glimpses of her in and around town.

He was avoiding her as much as she was avoiding him, he supposed.

But bumping into one another had been inevitable. After all, the town was not all that large. Jackson just hadn't expected their first meeting after so long to be this dramatic.

In his heart, he supposed he was relieved he hadn't been called out to examine one of Hannah's own children. A child created out of her and Ethan's love. It had surprised him to learn that Ethan and Hannah had had no children. But then, they had only been married a little more than two years before Ethan had died in that car crash.

That, he recalled, had been over a year ago.

Jackson glanced at Hannah. How had she handled the pain of Ethan's death, and did she still love her late husband?

With effort, he blocked out the thought, pushing it away. He had no business wondering about that. No business being anything but a pediatrician. And perhaps, if she'd still have him, Hannah's friend. Present or absent, he'd always been Hannah's friend. And never more of one than when he had left town.

The silence was making Hannah crazy. She grasped at the first half thought that crossed her mind. ''It was good of you to come.''

Goodness, did that sound as hopelessly stilted to him as it did to her? But what do you say to a man you once loved with all your heart, a man who'd never loved you at all? Who had gone out of his way to urge you into the arms of his best friend just to be rid of you? Or so it had seemed at the time.

She'd thought once that they were friends, and hoped for more. She'd come away with far less and learned a valuable lesson as well. Never bet your heart on anything but a sure thing. Neither Jackson, nor Ethan, it eventually became apparent to her, had been a sure thing.

She raised her eyes to Jackson's. "I would have gone to your office, you know." She'd expected to do that when she called for the appointment. Getting him on the line, instead of his nurse, had caused her to falter and act like a fourth-grade schoolgirl, forgetting her lines in the school play.

"It would have been far too much for you to handle," he told her, snapping his medical bag shut. "And you obviously had a lot to deal with."

Jackson knew he should go. But he couldn't quite make his feet take the steps that would lead him from the room and to the stairs. There were questions knocking around in his mind, questions that were begetting more questions even as he stood here.

So instead of leaving, Jackson looked around, seeing far more than the lacy room they were in. "It's a nice place."

"My great-aunt left it to me when she died. It has, as they say, possibilities," she said, pride evident in her voice.

It was the first time since he'd entered the house that he'd seen her smile. It took him back over years of memories he hardly admitted to himself he had. "Why a daycare center?"

It seemed so natural to her, she was surprised that he'd ask. "I've always loved children."

"Yeah, me too."

She laughed softly, unaware of the sound. "I've noticed." With Steffie already in her arms, she moved to pick up Sammy. "I'll take these two," she murmured. Then seeing the bemused expression on his face she added, "They're small."

"Not that small," he countered. Putting down his bag, he took Sammy from her. "Here, let me help. You can't do everything yourself, you know."

Her eyes held his for just a fleeting moment. She told herself that she felt nothing, that her stomach tightened only because it was trying to remind her that she'd had nothing to eat except one of Aunt Gertie's sugar cookies since the babies had turned up on her doorstep. "Why not? I have until now."

She was a strong, resilient woman. Funny, he didn't remember her being this resilient. With the bag in one hand, holding Sammy against him with the other, he led the way out of the room. "You've done well for yourself. Ethan would have been very proud of you."

Hannah followed him out.

She sincerely doubted that.

Chapter Two

"So, how are they, handsome?"

Caught off guard, Jackson discovered that Aunt Gertie was standing right outside the bedroom door. Knowing the woman the way he did, he realized he shouldn't have been surprised by her appearance. Hannah had left her downstairs to handle the parents who were coming to collect their children at the end of the day. He should have known she would be here the moment her job was completed.

The woman was the picture of eagerness as she looked at him over the rim of her glasses now, waiting for an answer. The tension he'd felt the moment he'd entered Hannah's new home lifted as he grinned at Gertie. "They're fine, although Steffie seems to be getting over a cold."

"Small wonder, being left out on a doorstep like that," Gertie said. Without waiting for an invitation, she took Sammy from Jackson, tucking the baby against her. Her countenance radiated warmth as she looked down at the small face. "Poor lamb," she cooed.

His sentiments exactly, Jackson thought. The situation still struck him as highly unusual. Child abandonment was something that you expected to hear about taking place in large cities, where, fairly or not, the citizens were thought to be colder, prone toward being disinterested even in their own children. The same sentiments seemed inconceivable here in a town known for its love of children.

Bemused, he turned to Hannah. "And you have no idea who left these babies on your doorstep?"

Hannah shook her head. "None whatsoever."

She had a feeling she was going to be saying that a lot in the next few days. Storkville was not the most exciting town on the map, and any deviation from the norm instantly turned into a source of entertainment and provided the populace with the opportunity to speculate to their heart's content. Given that the town was more or less two thousand strong, that could translate into a great deal of speculation.

"You know," Aunt Gertie murmured thoughtfully, still looking at Sammy's face, "in this light, Sammy kind of looks like you, Jackson. It's almost spooky. There was a photograph on your mother's dresser that looked just like this."

His curiosity piqued, Jackson leaned over Gertie's shoulder and studied the small, sleeping face. He didn't really see it. "You think so?"

Hannah's eyes darted to the other baby, then fleetingly passed over Jackson's face. She saw nothing more than Gertie's very active imagination at work.

"All babies tend to look like someone's baby pictures," Hannah said dismissively, hoping to put an end to that particular tempest in a teapot before it began. "I'm surprised at you, Gertie. Being practically the town's resident baby-sitter, you above all people should know that."

Gertie pursed her lips together, studying Sammy. The baby stirred, the pucker disappearing. The resemblance faded.

"Yes, I suppose you're right." Gertie raised her eyes to Jackson's. "If these babies *were* Jackson's, I know he'd do the right thing and step forward, marrying the babies' momma. Wouldn't you, Jackson?"

It suddenly dawned on Jackson what the older woman had to be thinking. As if this wasn't enough of a mystery to deal with, Gertie was tossing in another curve. He could just hear the rumors starting now: *Storkville's Dr. Caldwell providing his own patients.* He had to nip this in the bud, now.

"Don't look at me with those eyes of yours, Gertie." He glanced at Hannah. Did she share Gertie's suspicions? "I was nowhere near Storkville when those babies were conceived."

"What makes you think they're Storkville babies?" Gertie challenged. "Hannah thinks they were left by someone just passing through, don't you, Hannah?"

Curious, Jackson looked at Hannah for an explanation. *Did* she think the babies might be his?

Uncomfortable with the penetrating look she saw in Jackson's eyes, she looked away, her attention seemingly taken by the baby in her arms.

"Makes sense. The town's not that big. We know

everyone by sight if not by name. Nobody we know had twins ten, twelve months ago. It's not the kind of thing you can hide around here.''

There were times when your life was almost painfully an open book, she thought. Like hers had been with Ethan. The funny thing was, she'd been the last to know. Everyone except for her, she had the feeling, had known about her husband's roving ways almost from the start.

And then again, maybe she had just chosen to be blind, she thought.

''Maybe it's someone who left town,'' Jackson suggested.

Gertie looked at him beneath hooded eyes, her mouth amused. ''Which brings us back to you.''

''This seems to be where I came in.'' Jackson began rolling down his sleeves, then buttoned them. ''So I think I'd better leave.'' He looked at Hannah. ''I'll stop by tomorrow after my hours to see how Steffie's cold is doing.''

Like her brother, Steffie was sleeping. Was it her imagination, or did Steffie's breathing sound just a tad labored? Feeling a little uncertain, Hannah looked at Jackson. ''So you don't think I need a prescription or anything?''

He knew that look. It was the panicky one new mothers got the first time their baby was sick. He was surprised at the depth of Hannah's concern, but then, he shouldn't have been, he thought. He'd always known how big her heart was.

He tried to sound as assuring as he could. ''Not that I can see. These things clear themselves up. If you have any questions, just call. I'm staying at the house until I figure out what to do with it.''

Hannah noticed that Jackson had said ''house,'' not ''home'' and wondered if that was telling or just a thoughtless slip on his part.

Gertie snorted again and they both looked in her direction.

''I'll tell you what to do with it, Jackson.'' Her eyes slid over Hannah before continuing, her implication clear. ''You can marry yourself a good woman, have her redecorate the place and then have yourself lots of babies, that's what you can do with it.''

Handsome to a fault, the way his father had been before him, Jackson'd had had an endless parade of people try to match him up ever since he'd passed through puberty. He took Gertie's heavy-handed suggestion in stride.

''I have lots of babies,'' he pointed out to her, humor curving his generous mouth. ''They troop into my office eight hours a day.'' He glanced at the baby she was holding. ''Sometimes longer.''

One of Gertie's gray brows rose as she gave the man whose bottom she'd diapered more than once a penetrating look. ''Of your own, doctor-boy, of your own.''

Jackson said nothing, though the smile on his lips became a little less animated, a little more forced. There would never be any babies of his own, because there would never be a wife in his life. There was no way he would ever risk making a mistake like that, the mistake of following his heart and ignoring his mind. Ignoring reality. Unlike his father, to Jackson marriage was not an institution he was going to defile by making a mockery of it.

More than that, he would never hurt the heart of someone who loved him. Of someone he loved…

He looked at Hannah and abruptly tabled his thoughts. There was no reason to allow them flow in that direction. The best way to handle futile situations was to avoid them, not explore them.

"Maybe someday," he said to Gertie, knowing that was the safest response he could make.

Any attempt at the truth, or even alluding to the fact that he intended to remain alone for the remainder of his life, would only get Gertie going. It would be tantamount to waving a proverbial red flag in front of a bull. Gertie took full credit for beginning the movement that had had the town council rechristening the town with its unusual moniker. It had all come about because of a rash of births that took place nine months after a blanketing power failure had hit the entire area. Even before that, Gertie had always behaved as if it were her preordained duty to couple together all the unattached citizens of Storkville. She'd tried her hand with him once or twice with no luck. He'd hoped that in his self-imposed exile she might have mellowed, but he should have known better. Leopards didn't change their spots and Gertie, if anything, had only gotten more determined with each year that passed by.

"Someday you'll be pushing up daisies, doctor-boy. The time to look to your future is now, in the present," Gertie commented.

He finished buttoning his second sleeve. "I'll keep that in mind."

"Why don't I see about settling these two in?" As easily as she had taken the first baby, Gertie now commandeered the second one from Hannah. Her eyes moved from Jackson to Hannah. "You can see Jackson to the door."

He was already on the head of the stairs, hoping to forge a path of retreat. "I know where the door is, Gertie. I came through it."

Hannah slipped her arm through his before she realized what she was doing, the gesture coming naturally to her from a time when she hadn't had to rethink every move, reexamine every word in order not to give away any clues to her actual feelings. For a second, she thought of pulling it away again, but that would only call more attention to the situation than she wanted. So she made the best of it, pretending that they were still at a point in time when there was so much of life in front of them, so much promise for them. Before she had become disillusioned by both Jackson and Ethan.

"Let's go while the getting's good," she urged him in a conspiratorial whisper, "before she launches into another full-scale assault."

"I think you might be right," he whispered back. Fascinated, he watched as his breath ruffled the stray hair along her temple. His stomach tightened.

It felt good to have Hannah beside him, her arm linked with his as they walked down the stairs.

Maybe it felt a little too good, he cautioned himself. He'd hoped that time would take a toll, on her if not on his affections. But all three years had done was make her that much more beautiful to him, that much more stirring.

Her perfume drifted along the air, just the faintest scent that aroused him and caused fragments of memories to dance through his mind, reminding him of how much he actually had missed her. Missed her even though she had lingered on his mind like a lyric that was just out of reach, a melody that refused to solidify itself into a full chorus. All it would have taken was a trip back to set that longing to rest, and there were times when he had almost given in to the temptation.

But he hadn't.

He hadn't left Storkville in the first place just to come sneaking back. No matter how much he'd wanted to return. He'd left town back then for his own good. And hers. And Ethan's if he thought about it, although to be honest, Ethan had not figured into the mix very prominently for Jackson. Other than Ethan being the better man for Hannah than he was.

Reaching the bottom of the stairs, he turned to say good-bye. The words wouldn't form into audible sounds. He just wanted to look at her. So they stood in the foyer, the hurricane lamp on the nearly table dimly outlining their bodies, throwing silhouettes onto the wall that were freer to move than they were.

She was more beautiful than ever, he thought again. The young girl he'd loved and had kept locked away in his heart had blossomed into a hauntingly beautiful woman in the years he had been away. But there was a sadness in her eyes that the smile on her lips couldn't negate or erase.

It made him ache just to look at her. And he wondered how he'd managed to stay away as long as he had. Stayed away even when he should have returned, if only as a sign of respect.

He owed her an apology, if not an explanation. Before he knew what he was doing, he took her hands in his. "I'm sorry I didn't come back for Ethan's funeral."

She lifted a slender shoulder, letting the incident, and the apology carelessly pass. She'd looked for him that day, and called herself weak for it.

"That's all right, there was really nothing you could do anyway."

Nothing but hold me, let me talk to you the way I used to. Did you know that all I wanted from Ethan for my first anniversary was a divorce? That I used to pray you'd come back to rescue me from the mistake I'd made. The mistake you encouraged me to make? No, I guess you wouldn't know that. You had your life and it was one you'd chosen to live—without me, she thought.

His hands tightened on hers, encasing them. He had the oddest feeling that he'd failed her somehow, that she'd needed him and he hadn't been there. "Hannah, what is it?"

Rousing herself, she squared her shoulders. Her look was studied innocence. "What's what?"

"There was something in your eyes just then—"

He'd been her friend once. Her friend always, in reality. And sometimes friends had to be cruel instead of kind. But the look he had seen just now undid him, melting away all his noble intentions and making him want to just hold her in his arms until whatever it was that bothered her passed.

"Just the lighting," she passed off with a laugh.

She drew her hands away, breaking the link between them. Hannah gestured around. "The house looks a great deal darker than it should in the evening. Great-Aunt Jane never had enough lamps or light fixtures in this place. It's something I'm planning on fixing, once I get a little ahead."

She was babbling, she realized and forced herself to stop. But he made her uncomfortable. Her *feelings* for him made her uncomfortable.

Her words had him reaching for his jacket and the checkbook in his pocket. Money, at least, had never been a problem in his life. If he couldn't give her what he wanted, at least he could help in this minor way. "How much do you need?"

"Oh, I don't know, maybe—" Hannah stopped abruptly when she realized what he was up to. Her hand covered his as if she were keeping him from drawing a weapon. "I'm not going to start that."

He looked at her, puzzled. When she kept her hand on his, he stopped trying to get his checkbook out. "Start what?"

"Taking money from my friends."

She'd always been headstrong, he thought. Apparently some things hadn't changed. "Don't call it taking, call it borrowing."

But she still shook her head. "It wouldn't matter if I called it Jacob, it would still amount to the same thing." There was no way she was going to take his charity. "I made it this far on my own, I intend to make it the rest of the way on the same path." And then she paused, debating, searching his face for her answer. "Several weeks ago, someone sent me an anonymous donation to help get the center started. That wasn't you, was it?''

This was the first he'd heard of it. ''No, it wasn't me.'' Although he wished it was. He'd known people with far more than Hannah who would have welcomed a no-strings loan. He let his hand drop. Only then did she withdraw hers.

Jackson smiled. He couldn't help the admiration that came into his voice. ''I don't remember you being this rigid.''

''People change.''

He shook his head again. What was that line, the more things changed, the more they stayed the same? ''Not you, Hannah, not ever you. You started out being sweeter than honey and you'll go on that way.''

She would have believed him once, believed he meant what he said. Now she merely shrugged it off. After glancing out the wndow, she looked at him. ''Well, I'd better not keep you. It looks like a nasty storm is coming. I wouldn't want to see you caught in it. The creek still has a habit of overflowing at the worst possible times.''

Was she nervous? Why? It couldn't be because of him. He'd never made her nervous before. He smiled at her words. ''Is there a good time for the creek to overflow?''

''Don't get smart—although you always were the smart one. Ethan always used to say that.''

He looked at her for a long moment. ''The smart one, huh?'' From where he was standing, he wasn't the smart one at all. ''Oh, I don't know about that.'' The wind, making its displeasure known, began to howl. He knew he really had to be leaving. "I'd better go. It was great seeing you again."

She let the smile come then. Unguarded. "It was nice seeing you, too."

Impulse prompted the words that came next. He spoke before he could stop himself. "Listen, maybe if you're not doing anything later this week—"

Self-preservation leaped up within her, bringing another quip to her lips. "I'll be doing a lot of things."

He took it as a rebuff, one he knew he deserved. It was better this way, he told himself. "Right. Sure. Well, I'll stop by to look in on Steffie. You—"

Jackson moved to pick up his medical bag and froze. He had no idea if it was the lighting in the foyer, or if it was seeing her after so many years of just thinking about her. His hands found their way to her hair, framing her face a second before his lips touched hers.

He told himself that what he was doing was meant in friendship, but he was a lousy liar, especially when it came to himself.

He kissed her because he needed to, because he wanted to and because he couldn't find enough strength to walk away from the moment and the temptation. The light had fallen along her lips and all he wanted to do was seal it in permanently while sampling a taste. Just a single taste. Just this one time.

Her breath evaporated a second before she felt the pressure of his mouth on hers. The exact second when she realized what he was about to do.

She'd kissed him once before, at her twenty-first birthday party. They'd both been a little bit intoxicated, and a little less inhibited. He'd kissed her in the garden while they had made a wish on a firefly, thinking it was a shooting star falling to earth.

The power of that kiss had remained indelibly marked on her soul all these years.

It paled now in comparison and fell silently away in the wake of this one.

Her head began to spin wildly. It felt as if she had consumed an entire bottle of wine in a few seconds on an empty stomach. The force of his kiss rushed through her. He was being gentle: as gentle as snowflakes at the beginning of the season's first snowfall.

The impact was all the greater for it.

She would have said that as gentle as it was, there was a wealth of passion in his kiss. But how could the man be passionate when he'd removed himself so entirely from her life? When he hadn't taken the trouble to even come to see her after he returned to town?

It made no sense at all.

But it was hard to make sense when lightning was igniting her whole body. When the stillness around her only magnified the sound of her pounding heart.

She had been waiting ten years for him to kiss her again.

There were some things that time, with its misty powers, enhanced, playing a mischievous trick that made you believe that something was actually better than it had been. But time had played no such tricks here. If anything, time had muted the impact, leaving the sweetness but deleting the power.

It all came back to Hannah now as she wound her arms around his neck and leaned into the kiss.

There was absolutely no doubt left lingering in her mind.

It had been worth the wait.

Chapter Three

It wasn't enough.

Like a single, teasing drop of water to a thirsty man, the kiss only made him want more. Crave more. Jackson struggled not to weaken any more than he already had, but it was like sinking into quicksand. The more he struggled, the deeper he sank.

Damn it, he was a man, not a boy, he wasn't supposed to be given to a boy's careless disregard of danger this way. And Hannah was that. Danger with a capital D because he'd realized that being with her for even a short amount of time made him forget all his well-ordered promises to himself, made him forget his noble ideals and effectively reduced him to a mound of needs and desires, all vying for control of him. His mind had been lost somewhere in the fray.

But somehow, though he wanted only to wrap his arms tighter around her, to deepen the kiss even more, he managed to pull himself away from the center of the vortex that had almost succeeded in sucking him in.

More shaken than he'd thought possible, he took a deep breath before he trusted himself to look into her eyes. "I'm sorry, I shouldn't have done that." Belatedly, he realized he was still holding her and abruptly dropped his hands to his sides.

Hannah felt as if something had caved in inside of her. What do you say when a man tells you he regrets kissing you?

You agree, if for no other reason than to save your pride. So she did. Pulling herself together as best she could, she raised her head with the grace of a princess facing an attacking enemy.

"No, you shouldn't have."

Why, when she was agreeing with him, did her words feel as if they were all sharpened daggers, slashing at him? Why did the look in her eyes make him feel so guilty, as if he'd just done something horrible?

Maybe he had. Jackson hurried to make what amends he could. "It's just that—"

"Just what?" she asked coolly, while her mind demanded hotly, *Talk to me, Jackson, let me know that you're not just being cruel. Give me a reason to keep my hope burning, damn it.*

Talking would only make things worse, Jackson realized. He'd never had the gift of gab. That had been Ethan's forte. Ethan had always been the one who knew what to say and when to say it. How to charm the husk right off a cob of corn. Jackson had only the truth and the truth wasn't allowed to come forth.

Picking up his bag, he did the only thing he could. He made his retreat.

"It's late, I'll—I'll see you." Jackson pulled the door shut behind him. And cursed himself for the mistake he'd just committed.

Hannah stood perfectly still, in direct contrast to the turmoil going on inside her. What had just happened here?

Was she going out of her mind? He'd just kissed her as if he'd wanted nothing more than to be with her tonight, then hurried away as if he wanted nothing more than never to see her again.

Confused, she gave up trying to make sense of any of it.

"Was that the door?"

Startled, Hannah jerked her head up and turned to see Gertie standing at the top of the stairs.

Coming down to join her, Gertie looked around and saw that there were just the two of them now. She sighed, obviously disappointed. "I was hoping he'd stay for breakfast."

There were toys to put away and a front room to straighten, neither of which were going to take care of themselves. Picking up a discarded truck, Hannah got started.

"Breakfast? You mean dinner, don't you?" Hannah asked.

Gertie followed in her wake. "I'm over half a century old, Hannah, I know what I mean. If I say breakfast, I mean breakfast." With another, even more heartfelt sigh, she shook her head. "Maybe it's too soon."

Dropping the two toys she was holding into the

large, colorful toybox, Hannah turned around and looked at Gertie suspiciously. "Too soon for what?"

The grin that took over Gertie's face was positively bawdy. "You know." She winked instead of answering specifically. "I always did think you two made a nice couple."

Hannah frowned as she threw another toy a little too hard into the toybox. "Well then, you'd be the only one."

"Oh, I don't know about that. Didn't feel the heat coming from that man's eyes when he was looking at you?" Gertie questioned.

She didn't need this right now. Hannah threw in another toy, a rabbit that bounced out as soon as he landed against the growing pile. Biting off a choice word, she picked the stuffed animal up again and this time placed it inside the toybox.

"There was no heat, Gertie." There was a warning note in her voice.

"Have it your way," Gertie sniffed. "As I recall, you always were a stubborn child."

Hannah stopped returning toys to their container and glanced toward the doorway and the stairs beyond. "Speaking of children—"

"They're asleep," Gertie assured her. "I put them both down in the nursery. They look right at home there in that big, old canopied crib."

In her redecorating plans, Hannah had sentimentally left that room just as it was. The nursery was where all seven of her great-aunt's children had slept as infants. None had reached old age. Other than being cleaned, the room had not been changed in over three-quarters of a century.

Hannah dropped the last of the toys into the toybox. "Maybe I'd better look in on them." She had a great deal of affection for Gertie, but right now, she wanted to get away from the woman's one-track conversation.

"I think you'd do better to look in on yourself," Gertie said softly just as Hannah passed her. "You're still a young girl, Hannah."

Stopping, Hannah shook her head. It had been a long time since she'd felt like a young girl. Losing her parents, her illusions and then her aunt had seen to that. "I'm thirty-one."

"That's young in my book." Gertie's chuckle sounded more like a cackle. "Heck, to an octogenarian, you're hardly more than a baby yourself."

She was being too edgy, Hannah told herself. Gertie was merely trying to be helpful. She placed her hands on the woman's shoulders. "Gertie, I know you mean well, but let it alone."

"Fine with me if you want that fine specimen of a man to be snapped up by someone else."

Gertie's remark caught Hannah's attention. Telling herself that Gertie was doing this on purpose didn't help. "Who?"

A pleased, knowing look highlighted the older woman's expression. "Jealous, are we?"

"No, I—"

Damn, she was putting her foot into it, wasn't she? But she couldn't help the curiosity that came over her. *Was* there someone in Jackson's life? Was that why she hadn't seen him since he'd returned? The town was small and gossip was the major local pastime, but she rarely had time to listen.

Gertie patted her arm. "Rest easy, there's no one else right now. I was just speaking figuratively, but mark my words, a man like Jackson won't stay on the market indefinitely."

"I'm not in the market. I've got my hands full right now." Hannah looked around the semi-straightened room. "Fuller than I bargained for."

"Well, I can stay the night, help you get your feet wet, so to speak," Gertie said.

Hannah wasn't about to impose. More than that, she wasn't going to be able to feel as if she was standing on her own two feet if she kept leaning. "I can handle it."

Gertie laughed shortly. "No woman alive can handle twins by herself the first night. Stop being so stubborn, Hannah, and let someone help you once in a while."

Hannah's affection for Gertie got the better of her. "Yes, ma'am."

"Much better." Pleased, Gertie slipped her arm around the younger woman's shoulders. "You'll take some work yet, girl, but you'll do."

By morning, the twins had given new meaning to the word *demanding*.

Hannah'd had no idea that two babies could be so difficult to manage. They didn't sleep at the same time, they slept in tandem. No sooner was Sammy asleep than Steffie was awake, her little nose dripping and her small, pitiful cries wrapping themselves around Hannah's heart.

There were hardly two winks to be rubbed together all night.

Babies or no, Hannah seriously doubted if she could have slept very much anyway. Every time there was a second in which she could close her eyes, she found herself reliving the kiss she'd experienced. She couldn't seem to remember a single kiss, a single moment of lovemaking with Ethan, but Jackson's kiss had branded her. Recalling it, her body would grow rosy, then hot and all sleep was banished indefinitely.

By morning she'd felt like death warmed over and was in no condition to face a squadron of children and their parents. Rallying, she took a cold shower and drank a hot cup of coffee. It helped. Some.

For once, the children proved to be less demanding than their parents. Word, as Hannah had suspected, had spread faster than a prairie fire. Everyone wanted to know about the babies on her doorstep. Themes and variations of the same questions were asked over and over again until her head felt like it was going to come off. Her temper was getting progressively more frayed. That, she knew, was a result of the sleepless night.

She was going to have to find a way to manage without harboring the spirit of a wounded bear, she thought, closing the front door as the last parent left that morning. It was almost noon.

Hannah sighed, closing her eyes as she leaned against the door. It took effort not to slide down to the floor against it. What she needed, she decided, was more coffee. More liquid stimulation and less of the emotional kind.

It was a moment before she sensed she wasn't alone. Hannah opened her eyes again.

Gertie, one of the twins in her arms and Angie, a

little girl of three, hanging onto the edge of her smock, stood eyeing her. Hannah straightened, squaring her shoulders.

"You look awful, girl," Gertie clucked sympathetically. "Did you get *any* sleep last night?"

"Some," Hannah lied. There was no point in discussing the whys and wherefores of her sleepless night. With luck, it was just a fluke and tonight would be better, with a return to normalcy.

Given that the babies would still be here, she sincerely doubted her own cheery prognosis.

"Yeah, right," Gertie said. "You should have woken me up. I sleep like a rock, but if you shake my shoulder, you can rouse me."

The last thing Hannah wanted was for Gertie to upbraid herself on her account. "Gertie, you're wonderful. You're already helping me out here, putting in all these hours without any pay. I just can't keep taking advantage of you like this."

The older woman's face softened into a warm smile. "It's only called taking advantage if I do it against my will. This isn't against my will, girl, I love it. Playing with these babies and caring for them is a lot more rewarding for me than sitting around, crocheting things for relatives who, when they receive them, will only wind up throwing the things away or stuffing them into boxes they'll never open."

Hannah was quickly discovering how futile it was to argue with the woman about anything. "Well, if you put it that way...."

Gertie leveled a satisfied look at her over the rim of her glasses. "I do."

The doorbell rang.

The effect of Gertie's warm assurance faded, and Hannah stiffened. She took a quick mental inventory of all the children beneath her roof. Everyone currently in her care was accounted for, including Heather Riley, whose mother had called to say the toddler would be out for the week with chicken pox.

That meant that whoever was at her door most definitely had no business being here.

Probably someone from the newspaper, Hannah thought glumly, here to do a story on the twins. She hadn't had to face that yet, but she knew it was coming just as surely as November followed October.

"I'll get that," Gertie declared.

Hannah caught her arm, stopping her. "That's all right, Gertie, I can answer my own door." A sense of acute relief flooded through her when she saw that it was Tucker on her doorstep and not some reporter from the newspaper.

Hope took anxiety's place. "Oh, Tucker, did you find the twins' mother already?"

Tucker pushed his Stetson back on his head with the edge of his thumb. "No, but I did find your mystery lady. Or rather, Penny Sue's." As he stepped out of the way, Hannah saw for the first time that Tucker wasn't alone. Recognition was instantaneous. The rest of the sheriff's words were unnecessary. "She says she's a cousin of yours, Hannah."

Caught between being stunned and overjoyed, Hannah found herself momentarily speechless. What she lacked in words she made up for in gestures. She threw her arms around the woman before her and gave her a fierce hug—as best she could. The other woman's swollen belly got in the way.

Releasing her, Hannah stepped back and drew her very pregnant cousin into the house. "Gwen, my God, Gwen, just look at you." Her eyes swept over Gwen's ripened form. "When did all this happen?"

Instinctively, Gwen placed a protective hand over her belly. "Seven months ago."

Expecting to see Gwen's husband somewhere in the near vicinity, Hannah peered out. But there was no one there.

Puzzled, she looked at Gwen. "Where's—?"

"Where he should be," Gwen said, cutting her off. "Back home."

The finality in Gwen's tone told Hannah she was treading on very sensitive terrain. Sympathy poured through her. Maybe Gwen was here waiting for some huge argument to blow over. "Is there anything I can get you?"

Gwen smiled at her cousin. "Yes, the address of a place that's renting—cheap if possible."

A small breath escaped Hannah's lips. "That final?"

Gwen nodded. "That final." She left no room for discussion.

Hannah knew what it felt like, to have a marriage die right before your eyes. To see it slip away through no fault of your own. To cover the awkwardness she knew Gwen had to be feeling right at this moment, she changed the subject. "Why were you at the back door earlier? Why not the front? And back or front, why didn't you come in?"

Gwen's smile was rueful. "I guess I was working up my courage to face you. It isn't easy coming back, letting people know things have gone wrong in your life. Besides, I wasn't at the back door. My courage petered out before I got within ten feet of your place."

"Then it wasn't you who knocked." Hannah looked at Tucker. "It must have been the twins' mother," she guessed. Hannah slipped a comforting arm around her cousin's shoulder. "Did you happen to see anyone else around just before you lost your courage? Somebody dropped off two bundles of joy on our back steps…"

Again, Gwen shook her head. "The sheriff already asked me that when he found me in the diner. I was too preoccupied with my own problems to really see anything, I'm afraid."

Behind her, Gertie cleared her throat rather loudly, drawing Hannah's attention to her own oversight.

"Where are my manners? Gertie, I'd like you to meet my cousin, Gwenyth Parker. Gwen, this is Gertie Anderson. And this," still a little flustered, Hannah turned toward Tucker, "is Sheriff Tucker Malone."

Something akin to an amused look flittered across Tucker's face. He nodded toward Gwen. "We've already met."

"Right, sorry." Hannah flashed an apologetic smile in his direction before turning toward her cousin. "I guess it's just that you caught me off balance, what with your visit and being pregnant and all."

"The word," Gwen corrected kindly, "is *divorced*. I remembered what you always said about Storkville, and I thought I'd try to start a new life for myself and the baby in a place that's warm and forgiving."

"Well then, you've certainly come to the right

place. We're warm and forgiving all right," Gertie assured her, taking Gwen's hand in hers and, for all intents and purposes, taking her under her wing as well.

"Thank you, Mrs. Anderson, that's very comforting to know."

Gertie waved away the formality. "Everyone calls me Aunt Gertie and I think I might know just the place for you. There's a little house, not far from here." Gertie glanced at the sheriff. "You know the one I'm talking about, Tucker. The cottage on Ben Crowe's ranch. He's looking to sell it, but he might be interested in renting, you never know. It's been empty for a while."

Familiar with the house Gertie was describing, Tucker nodded. "Right."

After everything she'd been through, this was almost too easy. Trying to contain her excitement, Gwen looked from Gertie to Hannah. "When could I see it?"

"Well, I'm a little busy here, helping with the babies and all," Gertie said. "Maybe Tucker here could run you up there."

Gwen hated imposing, but she was really eager to find a place of her own to settle into. She turned toward the sheriff hopefully. "If it wouldn't be too much trouble..."

Jumping in, Gertie curtailed any possibility of Tucker saying no. "Trouble?" she snorted. Temporarily handing off the baby to Hannah, she took Gwen's hand. "The man doesn't know the meaning of the word trouble. Mark my words, little mother, this is the most trouble-free town ever created. Probably the most neighborly, too. Am I right, Tucker?''

"You're right, Gertie," he agreed, amused.

The picture was not as pure as Gertie was painting it, but he saw no reason to contradict her outright. Besides, it was probably futile anyway. The woman enjoyed being right. And in getting her way. Cornered, Tucker had no choice but to go along with the silent request he saw in the pregnant woman's eyes.

Stepping forward, Tucker addressed Gwen politely. "Sure. If you want to see the place, I'll take you."

"Thank you, Sheriff. All of you," she added, looking at the two women. And then she hesitated. "Would you mind if I stayed with you until all this is settled?" she asked Hannah.

"Mind?" Hannah echoed. "I insist on it."

"You're the best, Hannah," Gwen enthused.

Hannah carefully slipped Steffie back to Gertie and hugged Gwen again. "We're family. We have to stick together. You're always welcome in my home, no matter what." She knew Gwen was eager to see the house, but she had a feeling that Gwen needed reassuring more than she needed a roof over her head at the moment. Besides, if for some reason renting didn't pan out, Gwen could always stay with her indefinitely. The house was certainly big enough. "Tucker, could you put off taking Gwen to see that house for a few minutes or so? I think maybe a little tea and conversation is in order here." She looked pointedly at Gwen.

"Well, I'm not much on conversation," Tucker said, "and I'll pass on the tea, but if you have coffee—"

"Coffee it is." Hannah slipped her arm around Gwen and ushered her into the kitchen, leaving Gertie to bring up Tucker and the rear. She heard the older woman chattering away at Tucker about babies and tried not to laugh.

Half an hour later, Tucker and Gwen were at the front door, ready to leave. Just as Tucker reached for the doorknob, the doorbell rang. He noticed that Hannah, so animated only a moment ago, froze at the sound.

"Anyone been giving you trouble lately?" he wanted to know.

"No." This time, it had to be a reporter. "Just anticipating the worst."

"Woman after my own heart," Tucker said with a laugh as he pulled open the door for her.

The sound of a man's laugh registered at exactly the same moment as Jackson's excuse came tumbling from his lips. "Hannah, I thought I'd drop by during my lunch hour instead—oh."

Had he walked in on anything? Was Hannah seeing someone? That there might be a man to share her laughter, her secrets and perhaps her love, had never crossed his mind.

It did now.

Chapter Four

It took Jackson a minute to collect himself. "Sorry. I didn't mean to interrupt anything."

Tucker nodded a brusque greeting at Jackson. "You're not. We were just on our way out." His hand on the small of Gwen's back, Tucker paused in the doorway to look at Hannah. "I'll let you know if I find out anything about the twins."

Hannah nodded. "Thank you. And Gwen, after you look at the house, we need to have a proper, long visit."

"I'd like that," Gwen said, smiling.

"Me, too," Hannah assured her just before Tucker pulled the door closed behind them.

"Well, I'll just go see to the children," Gertie announced cheerfully. "Here," as an afterthought, she handed Steffie to Hannah, "you'll be needing this if you're going to take advantage of doctor-boy's kind presence here."

Aiming a triumphant smile at Jackson that left him completely mystified, Gertie took the hand of the little girl beside her and disappeared into the front room, leaving the two of them standing in the foyer, the baby between them.

Feeling awkward again, Hannah cleared her throat. "This way." This time, she led him into another room, one where she had several cribs set up for the infants she anticipated would eventually be placed in her care during the day while their parents worked. Right now, the twins were her youngest charges by a good six months.

She felt that it was her responsibility to remain in the room while he performed the quick, routine examination on Steffie, but inside, Hannah was restless, like someone who didn't know quite what to do with herself.

Jackson retired his stethoscope, placing it into his bag. "Steffie's doing about the same. Her nose is still runny, but there's no fever. How was she during the night?"

Thinking back, Hannah tried to be accurate. "She didn't cry any more than Sammy did."

That certainly sounded positive, Jackson thought. Which was more than he could say for Hannah. There was an edge to her today that hadn't been there yesterday. And she looked a little harried.

"Well, she looks pretty good, despite her runny nose." He laughed shortly, unable to refrain from commenting. "She looks better than you do."

That was something she didn't need to hear. Elbowing him out of her way, Hannah reached into the crib and began putting a fresh diaper on the baby. "You always did have a way with words."

Now he'd gone and hurt her feelings, he upbraided himself. That hadn't been his intent. Why couldn't he talk to her? He used to be able to talk to her for hours at a time.

"I didn't mean that as an insult, I was just making an observation—as a doctor."

Hannah spared him a glance over her shoulder as she powdered a freshly cleaned bottom. "Broadening your practice?"

Jackson wasn't sure if that was sarcasm or not. Once he would have known. Once, Hannah didn't have a sarcastic bone in her body, but a lot had happened since those days. He shrugged carelessly.

"It's a small town, things tend to overlap. A doctor can't afford to be rigid in his views about where his boundaries stop."

She wanted to shut the words away. They came anyway. "What about a man? Does the same rule apply?"

He studied her face for a moment, at a loss. "If this is about yesterday…I already apologized."

His answer only succeeded in getting her more agitated. She could feel her anger, so long repressed, so long banked down, beginning to flare. Slipping the romper back on the baby, she left Steffie in the crib and turned to face Jackson.

"Yes, this is about yesterday and I was wondering why you felt you had to apologize. You've done some things in your life that you should apologize for, but that really wasn't one of them."

The accusation was impossible to miss. "Oh? And what things should I have apologized for?"

She moved over to the door, closing it. She didn't want Gertie or anyone else overhearing.

"Disappearing the way you did, for one. You played Cupid, practically pushed me into Ethan's arms, and then when I married him, you didn't even stay for the reception."

"I came." He'd been best man despite his protests. He'd had no choice but to attend.

"But you didn't stay," she reminded him. He'd remained long enough to make the traditional toast. When she'd looked for him later, her mother had told her that he'd left abruptly.

"I had a plane to catch." He'd made his decision to leave town the day that Ethan had told him about the wedding. Though he had pushed them together by stepping out of the running when Ethan had confessed his feelings for Hannah to him, he knew he couldn't remain to watch the love between Ethan and Hannah blossom and bear fruit. He wasn't strong enough for that no matter how much he wished he was. A man knew his limits. "My life was taking me in other directions."

Yes, she thought, directions he purposely mapped out away from Storkville. Away from his friends and everyone who cared about him. Away from her.

But if he'd done that, why had he returned? "And now that direction has made a 180-degree about-face?"

He said the obvious, the one thing that had finally brought him back to the small town he'd promised himself he'd left behind forever. "My father died."

She knew he'd returned because of that. It had been the first thing she'd thought of when she'd heard of Jackson's death. Which was why, when Jackson had made no effort to see her after he'd come back, the sting had been almost too much for her to bear.

"That was four months ago."

"What is it you want from me, Hannah?" Jackson asked.

"An explanation. The truth. I don't know." Restless, she began to pace about the small room. "Maybe I'm just mad. Damn mad." Even as she made the admission, she could feel herself growing angrier at his abandonment. Whatever his reasons were, right now, they weren't good enough.

Her eyes blazed as she turned on him. "I could have used a friend, Jackson. When everything was falling apart around me, I could have used a friend."

He wanted to reach out and take her into his arms. He wanted to hold her and tell her he was sorry. But all he could safely do was give her his reasons, and not even much of that.

With a sigh, he shoved his hands into his pockets. "I thought I was being one by staying away."

She stared at him incredulously. Did he actually believe what he was saying?

"That's the stupidest thing I ever heard. I needed someone to talk to, to lean on. Maybe I shouldn't have, but I did—damn it," she said throwing up her hands in exasperation. "I don't even know why I'm saying this now, except that I haven't had enough sleep to keep a gnat moving, and I've got all these responsibilities in the next room." She waved in the general direction of the front room, where most of the

But he was faced with evidence of the contrary almost every time he turned around. The apple never fell far from the tree, and the tree he had come from had roots that were rotten.

"Maybe I was afraid that Ethan would be jealous of that. He was my best friend, I didn't want to give him any cause for jealousy. Besides, things change when you get married." He thought of his own parents, of how his mother had told him how attentive his father had been to her until they had gotten married. And of all the women who had come along in the wake of those vows.

"Yes," she agreed quietly, "they do." And Ethan had changed after their vows had been exchanged. Not at first. In those early months, with the excitement of the adventure they faced still fresh, he'd been every bit the loving husband. Or so he had seemed.

But slowly, the freshness had faded and, with it, Ethan's attentions.

This wasn't the time to dwell on that. She didn't want Jackson reading things in her expression, didn't want to mar the image he carried in his mind of his best friend.

"So," she asked brightly, "do I have anything to be concerned about with Steffie?"

"Not really. I'd just watch her. Continue doing what you were doing. I'd say keep her away from her brother until her sniffles are gone, but it's probably too late for that."

She couldn't resist picking Steffie up and holding her for a moment. There was something so soft, so endearing about the small bundle. "You mean because they came in together?"

He nodded. She looked good like that, he thought. Natural. Someone like Hannah should have a brood of kids all around her. Her own kids. He felt a pang at the thought.

"The time they're really contagious is during the incubation time, which means that if he's going to come down with anything, he's already caught it."

Hannah thought of Sammy. There'd been no indication that he was congested or even harboring anything. "He seemed fine during the night and this morning."

"Could be he gave it to her, or maybe her cold will bypass him. Just because they share space doesn't necessarily mean they'll share the germs." He couldn't help grinning at the bemused expression on her face. She seemed overwhelmed, but if he knew Hannah, she'd manage. She always did. "That's what keeps it interesting," he confided. "I wouldn't worry about it. They both seem like very healthy babies."

She couldn't help looking down at the face of the baby against her breast. "Makes you wonder why someone would just toss them away like that, doesn't it?"

If they had been hers, there was no way she would have ever allowed herself to be separated from them, let alone willingly leave them. What kind of a mother did something like that?

"They didn't toss them away," he pointed out. "They gave them to you to care for." He followed her out into the hall.

He made it sound almost like a selfless action, but she had her doubts about that.

"I have a feeling that whoever left them had no

idea who they were leaving them with. They were just hoping someone would feel sorry for the twins and take are of them.''

''A stranger?'' he guessed. Hannah nodded. Jackson rolled the thought around in his mind, deciding it was more than possible. ''Well, Storkville does have a reputation.''

''Penny Sue,'' she called. ''Could you take Steffie for me? It's time for her lunch. Ask Gertie to help you with Sammy.''

Appearing, Penny Sue tossed her hair over her shoulders proudly. ''I can take care of them, it's just a little feeding.''

''Famous last words,'' Gertie declared, eyeing the young girl as she came up next to her. ''I'll handle things here,'' Gertie assured Hannah. ''You just take care of the good doctor here.'' She all but shooed her out of the room. ''C'mon, children,'' she declared to the other nine children, ''we're going to play a game called Watch Gertie Feed the Babies.''

''She's a good woman,'' Hannah said. ''I don't know what I would do without her. But I really wish Gertie had come up with a better name when she started her little legend about Storkville. Makes us sound like something out of a storybook.''

The notion made Jackson smile. ''Maybe sometimes you are.''

''Oh? What kind of a storybook?'' She realized that she was flirting with him—and that it felt good. ''Something to do with princesses and dragons?''

He pretended to let that sink in. ''Yes, I could see you as a princess.'' And if truth be told, he already had. More than once. An unattainable princess he could never hope to possess.

She laughed softly. It was good to talk like this, teasingly, the way they had in the old days.

"Thanks, I really needed that." And then a hint of mischief curved her mouth. "You realize that if you'd said you could see me as the dragon, I would have had to kill you."

When she looked at him like that, with laughter shimmering in her eyes, all he could think of was kissing her again and somehow sharing in that laughter, having it filter into his own soul. "No danger there. You're not the one I see as a dragon in this story."

He sounded so serious just then, it was almost as if they hadn't regained old ground at all. "Then who?"

He waved away her question and his own slip of the tongue. "Doesn't matter, the dragon's gone." It was just his legacy that lived on, Jackson added silently.

He was being awfully mysterious, Hannah thought, but there was something in Jackson's eyes that kept her from asking who he was talking about. She told herself that it was enough that they had dropped some of their armor, that she had managed to clear the air and that they were slowly getting back on the footing they'd once held.

She glanced back into the front room. Gertie and Penny Sue seemed to have things under control. Silently, she blessed them, then looked at Jackson.

"You said you were on your lunch hour. Can I fix you something to eat?"

He glanced at his watch. It was getting late and he had a two o'clock appointment coming in. "No, I'd better be getting back. I'm cutting it short as it is."

"Business that good?"

"This is the town for babies," he reminded her.

He was rushing away from her. Yesterday, she would have let him leave. But she'd glimpsed the way things had once been between them and it gave her hope that they could be that way again. So she stalled a little.

"Sure I can't tempt you with anything?"

That was just the problem, she could and he wasn't sure just how up he was to resisting that temptation, no matter how much he knew that he should. "No, that's okay."

He'd given up his lunch hour to look in on Steffie. The least she could do was feed him, Hannah thought. "How about a sandwich to go?" She saw him wavering. Jackson probably hadn't eaten anything all day. She remembered how he used to forget to eat when he got involved in something. "I make a mean peanut butter and jelly sandwich."

He laughed. "I haven't had one of those since—" he looked at her, bits and pieces of memories coming back to him "—we used to play house together."

"It wasn't house," she corrected him primly, though her eyes were dancing. "It was club." She slipped her arm through his, subtly directing him toward the kitchen. "You and Ethan were very specific about that. You didn't want any of your friends seeing you doing anything the least bit unmanly. I guess manhood was a big deal for a ten-year-old."

That took him back. If he closed his eyes, he could

still see their clubhouse. They'd built it themselves, the three of them, out of discarded wood left over from a guest house Ethan's father had built on the property. They'd had the devil's own time, dragging the planks up into the tree. In the end, it had been Hannah who had managed better than they. She'd gloried in showing them up, a scrawny girl pitted against two boys.

The memory pleased him. "You climbed better than any boy I ever knew."

Something lit up inside Hannah. She liked seeing him smile. "The treehouse is still up, you know."

He didn't know. He'd expected it, like all things from childhood, to have been taken down long ago. "You're kidding."

Hannah shook her head. "Nope." The clubhouse had been constructed on Ethan's parents' property. She and Ethan had lived at the house after his parents moved to Denver. "Ethan wanted to have the tree removed. He said it was in the way." She'd been upset when she discovered him talking to a gardening service, pricing the cost of the removal. She felt as if the last bastion of her childhood was under attack. "Some grand plans for a huge pool, but I argued for the treehouse."

"And you won." As he recalled, she always could argue better than either one of them.

Hannah slipped her arm from his. She shrugged carelessly, not wanting to get into that. "It never really got resolved. Ethan was killed in that car accident that same weekend."

"I'm sorry I wasn't here." He'd said that already, yesterday, but noble reasons or not, he should have come, Jackson thought. He should have attended the services. But he was afraid of what the sight of Hannah weeping at Ethan's grave would do to him. And what it might make him do, or say to her.

"I could have used you," she told him truthfully. "But there really wasn't anything you could have done. I handled the arrangements and made the best of it." It almost seemed as if all that had happened in another lifetime, to another woman. "Life goes on, right?"

"Yeah, it's been known to."

"Anyway, let me fix you that sandwich. By the way, what do house calls go for these days? I forgot to ask yesterday." She opened the cupboard and took out a jar of raspberry jam and a jar of peanut butter. "I remember my grandmother said she used to pay the doctor three dollars when he stopped by the house, but that was before house calls went out of style." A loaf of bread plucked out of the refrigerator joined the jars on the counter.

He watched her hands as she worked. It was safer than looking at her eyes. "One peanut butter sandwich should take care of it—as long as you put in extra peanut butter."

Laughing, she dipped the knife back into the jar. "Extra peanut butter it is."

Tucker returned with Gwen shortly after Jackson left. Gwen had tentatively rented the house, but it wouldn't be ready to move in to for a couple of weeks and it was agreed that she would stay with Hannah until then. Since Hannah refused any form of payment, Gwen insisted on helping her at the daycare center. Counting Rebecca Fielding, the new ob/gyn who sporadically dropped by the center to volunteer her services, Hannah had almost more volunteers than she knew what to do with. It was a nice feeling.

Tucker surprised her by returning a third time just after parents began arriving to pick up their children. Hannah left Gertie to the task of ushering off the children, knowing there was nothing the woman enjoyed better than visiting with their parents, while she took Tucker into the small parlor.

"Just thought you'd want to know that your initial instincts that the twins' mother might be from out of town were right on the money," he told her, running the rim of his Stetson through his hands. "I asked around and Penny Sue's father recalls seeing a woman driving a beat-up old pickup on the outskirts of town, heading west. Being Penny Sue's father, he couldn't help jotting down the license plate. But he only got part of it down. Doesn't correspond to any vehicle from around here."

"Was it an out-of-state license?" If it was, she thought, that made the search that much more difficult.

"No, as a matter of fact, the license was issued in Nebraska. I'm going to put in a call to the DMV in Omaha. Got a friend working there. See if he can come up with anything."

"On just a partial plate? They can do that?"

"You'd be surprised what they can do," he'd said, moving toward the foyer. "It'll take time, but right now, that's the only thing we've got to go on. We're not making much headway with the rattle." He'd almost forgotten. Reaching into his jacket, he took out a legal envelope from his pocket. "In the meantime, I got the court order from the judge, making this official." He handed the envelope to her. "The twins are now legally in your custody until we can get this all resolved."

Accepting the envelope, she held it for a moment without opening it. "I hope nobody's going to regret this."

At the front door, Tucker covered the knob with his hand. "Give yourself a little credit, Hannah. The rest of us have all got faith in you."

"Well, I always wanted to be a mother, I guess this'll show me if I'm cut out for the job."

"No doubt in my mind," he told her, leaving.

Yes, she thought, but there was certainly doubt in hers.

Chapter Five

Hannah wasn't sure exactly what drew her to it, only that she had a sudden, irresistible urge to visit the old tree house that stood on her late husband's property. Standing in the moonlight at the foot of the old oak, looking up at the square structure nestled in its branches, a wave of sentimentality washed over Hannah so completely, it was difficult for her to draw a deep breath.

She had no idea why she felt tears stinging her eyes. It was silly. Maybe she was developing allergies. Or getting Steffie's cold. Sniffing, she blinked the tears back.

Maybe it was seeing Jackson again that had drawn her here, or maybe it was just an overwhelming urge to revisit a time when there were no responsibilities, no hurt feelings and life had held the promise of an endless, joyful surprise. Whatever it was, she just couldn't help herself. She had had to come back to see it again.

So, after the daycare center was officially closed for the day and Penny Sue had left, she'd asked Gertie if she'd mind staying and watching the twins for about half an hour. Just long enough for her to spend a few minutes here. She didn't want to leave Gwenyth alone to cope with everything her first evening.

Gertie had taken Hannah's sweater off the coat rack, shoved it into her hands and all but pushed her out the door. She had looked well pleased that Hannah was getting out of the house and told her to take her time.

She, Ethan and Jackson had built their beloved tree house in the oak tree that was located in the middle of the backyard. It was sufficiently far away from the house to allow the three young building partners to pretend they were off on their own, yet close enough for their parents to be able to look out and make sure that everything was all right.

At least Ethan's parents had looked, as had her own from the house next door. Jackson's parents, as she recalled, had never come looking for him or wondered where he was.

Thinking about it now, she remembered that the Caldwells had never given any indication that Jackson had any rules restricting him. She and Ethan had curfews, but not Jackson. Jackson could stay out as long as he liked, stay away as long as he wanted. No one seemed to care.

She supposed that was why he'd seemed so dark and attractive to her. He was the very image of the young, brooding rebel. A rebel with kind eyes.

Ethan had envied Jackson his freedom, but she hadn't. Not really. In her heart, though she'd never admitted it, she'd felt sorry for Jackson. She felt that there was something lacking in a life where you didn't have your parents to fall back on. A life where you couldn't be certain that they would be there to catch you if you fell and hold you if you hurt. She'd never gotten anything but a sense of there being distance between Jackson and his parents and it made her sad for him.

But Jackson had acted as if it didn't bother him at all, as if the freedom Ethan envied him was the greatest thing in the world.

Some had considered him wild in those days. She'd just thought of him as untamed and thrilling to be with.

Certainly nobody who knew Jackson Caldwell Jr. had ever expected him to grow up to become a doctor, let alone a pediatrician. Pediatricians had to have an affinity for children, and no one had thought that Jackson could have feelings like that.

Mostly, she supposed, the town had figured he'd grow up to be a spoiled rich kid coming to no good, the way so many others had before him.

A soft smile curved her mouth. She'd known better, even then. She'd known that the person who existed just beneath the carefully crafted facade was someone entirely different. It was that person she'd spent hours talking to. That person who she felt had become her very best friend. And he had been—then. Oh, she'd told people that it was Ethan because of course you were supposed to say the man were going to marry was your best friend, but even when they had shared the initial intimacy of marriage, Ethan had never been as close to her soul as Jackson had been.

Which was why when Jackson had left town so abruptly, she'd felt like a piece of her had been permanently ripped away. An irretrievable piece she was never going to be able to recover or replace.

Her loss had only intensified when Ethan began coming home late, began making up excuses for missing occasions and forgetting about important dates—like their second anniversary. They'd made reservations for dinner at the restaurant where he had proposed to her. She'd dined alone. He'd been incredibly repentant immediately thereafter, inundating her with flowers and a beautiful gold pin she never wore. The gifts meant nothing because the sentiment wasn't real. The Ethan she'd thought she loved wasn't real. And the real Ethan didn't change.

After a while, she'd felt completely adrift, betrayed by the very ideals she'd clung to so tightly while she'd been growing up.

But she hadn't come here to think about lost ideals, she'd come to try, for a moment, to recapture a happier time. A time when she had loved everything and everyone and been so full of hope.

She wanted that feeling back, if only for a little while.

Testing the wooden slats she vividly remembered hammering into the tree with Ethan and Jackson, Hannah slowly climbed up. The tree house seemed smaller, but the climb felt steeper. One of the slats creaked ominously, but it held, as did the others.

Carefully, she made her way inside what was little more than a wooden box with a doorway and two windows carved out. She couldn't help the smile that came to her lips. If anyone had happened by, they'd have probably thought she'd lost her mind.

But she was hungry for a tiny piece of the past.

Maybe, like everything else, revisiting this faraway portion of her life would prove disappointing. Everyone said you couldn't go home again. She wondered if that meant to tree houses as well.

There was debris on the wooden floor, swept inside by more than seventeen years of storms that had come and gone since the last time she had been here. As she found a space for herself on the floor, a spider quickly scurried out of the way.

"Don't worry," she murmured to it, "I'm not moving in. Just visiting."

Very slowly, she looked around. It was so much smaller than she remembered. But then, the last time they had all sat here, they'd been fourteen, on the cusp of entering high school and a whole different world had been beckoning to them. The tree house had seemed hopelessly childish then. A remnant of their past. Right now, it seemed only incredibly sweet, if somewhat cramped.

Ethan had wanted to give it a Viking burial back then, she recalled. One last hurrah before they entered high school. It had been Jackson who'd pointed out the danger in that flashy act. She'd always wondered if he'd opposed Ethan because he'd actually had a practical side to him, or because he's seen how upset she'd been at the thought of destroying something that had been such a large part of their lives. To her, the tree house had symbolized a bond that had been forged between the three of them.

She supposed she'd never know what Jackson's reasons were for stopping Ethan. Either way, Ethan had reluctantly agreed, though lamenting that it would have made a wondrous sight, visible to the whole town—before the fire department could come to put it out. That day, Ethan had been the reckless one while Jackson had been the voice of practicality. Hannah should have picked up on that.

The boards beneath her creaked unexpectedly even though she hadn't shifted. She didn't weigh all that much more than she had at fourteen, but time and weather had taken their toll on the tree house and she wondered if she was taking unnecessary chances, being here. What if the planks broke and she fell? She certainly couldn't afford to get hurt now.

Daycare center owner foolishly climbed into her old tree house and fell through the rotting floor. Stay tuned to your local news. Film at eleven.

Biting back a grin, she decided to stay a few more minutes before going back to her house. She couldn't remain here for long, anyway. Gertie had to go home. It wouldn't be fair to make her stay another night, no matter how much she protested that she enjoyed helping out with the twins.

The twins were her responsibility, not Gertie's or Gwenyth's.

Moonlight winked in through the window that faced the back of the yard. Looking through it now, if she tried very hard, she could even catch a glimpse of Jackson's house. Located further up on the winding hill, the Caldwell estate looked down on the rest of them like a feudal lord looking down on the surrounding peasants who made up his fiefdom. When she'd been a lot younger, she'd secretly thought of Jackson as a prince, a dark, brooding prince who'd someday come galloping into her chambers and rescue her. From what, she wasn't sure. The very act would have been sufficient to win her tender heart.

Funny how he'd commented about her being a princess earlier today. Maybe, she mused, they were still in tune to one another a little bit after all.

Hannah sighed. She'd indulged herself long enough. It was time to go back before Gertie thought she'd abandoned her.

Getting up on her knees, she made her way to the opening, taking care not to move too fast and tempt fate in the form of a loose board.

Then she gasped. Rocking back on her heels, she stared at the person blocking her way out of the tree house.

Jackson.

Automatically she placed a hand over the heart that was even now racing madly. "What are you doing here?"

He was as stunned to see her as she was to see him. Finding Hannah here had been the furthest thing from his mind. He'd heard she'd rented out the house where she and Ethan had lived, but that the people were away on an end-of-summer vacation. Hannah was supposed to be at her own home now, not here.

Pleasure spilled out through him and he grinned at her question. "The peanut butter sandwich you gave me for lunch made me nostalgic. Can I come in? I forgot the password."

"Passwords," she corrected, backing up so he could make his way inside. "Passwords. One for all,

all for one.'' That had been her idea, conceived right after she'd read *The Three Musketeers*. It had seemed so very romantic and dashing to her, though she hadn't said as much. She didn't want Ethan and Jackson to laugh at her. Especially not Jackson.

''Right.'' It came back to him. The floor felt rough and dirty beneath his hands as he made his way in. ''I should have remembered that.''

Why should he? He hadn't remembered to live the credo, she thought. The rebuke was hot on her tongue, but she let it go. What was the point?

Their faces inches away from one another, he tried to put temptation out of his mind. Instead, he watched her catch her lower lip in her teeth as Hannah look around at the tree house uncertainly. ''I'm not sure this can support both of us.''

For once, it looked as if he had more faith than she did, Jackson thought. ''Sure it can. Don't you remember how handy we were? We built this tree house to last forever.''

''We built it to last forever for three skinny kids,'' she reminded him.

Still on all fours, he let his eyes sweep over her quickly, trying his best to seem detached and professional. If he pulled that off, he was probably a better actor than he gave himself credit for, he thought.

''Well, by the looks of you, you haven't gained very much in all that time and I don't think I weigh more than Ethan and I did put together back then. It'll hold up for at least a quick visit.''

Jackson sat down in the center, crossing his legs before him. Listening for any telltale groans, Hannah followed suit, facing him. She told herself she was having trouble breathing because of the dust in the air, not because she was sitting here in the moonlight with a man she had loved for more than half her life.

Looking around, Jackson shook his head, marveling. "What did we do in here for all those hours?"

"Lots of things," she told him, pretending to take umbrage that he could have so easily forgotten something so precious. "We talked, read comics, made plans. Thought about the future. Remember how there were times when we thought it would never come? That we were going to stay ten years old forever?"

"Yeah, but by the time we hit fourteen, the future was just right outside, reaching out to us and we couldn't wait to get to it."

He remembered making plans even back then to leave home and the shame that never seemed to be that far away from him. That was when he'd still believed he could outrun his heritage, that it was possible to distance himself from what haunted him.

She shrugged. She had never been as eager as either Ethan or Jackson had been to forge ahead. Maybe it was because she'd never wanted things to change. "I don't know. Right now, the past looks better."

He thought she was referring to Ethan's sudden death. "I can understand that." Jackson had no idea how to convey his sympathy to her. The news of Ethan's accident had hit him very hard as well. "I know it had to hurt a great deal, losing Ethan like that."

Hannah pressed her lips together. What was the sense of telling him that the pain of losing Ethan had come long before Tucker had walked into her house that muggy summer afternoon, and told her Ethan had died instantly in a head-on collision with a truck whose driver had lost control of the wheel. Because he was kind, Tucker had tried to keep from her the fact that there was someone else in the car with Ethan. Another woman. The last in a long line. But she'd found out soon enough.

It wasn't anything she hadn't come to expect.

But Jackson obviously wasn't aware of any of this, or of Ethan's insatiable quest for women. What was the point in shattering any illusions Jackson might still have about his former best friend? "Yeah," was all she said.

There were spaces now between the boards they had nailed together so diligently, spaces that allowed the wind to come whistling through. "Wind's picking up," Jackson noted. "Maybe we'd better take this trip down memory lane somewhere where it's warmer. Can't have you getting sick."

For her part, she wouldn't have minded staying here a little longer and absorbing the memories. But he was right, they should be getting back.

She smiled. "If I do, I know a great doctor."

About to get up, he stopped. She was looking at him strangely. "What?"

"Nothing." But his look urged her on. "Okay, I have to admit it. I'm still having a little trouble picturing Storkville's bad boy being a pediatrician."

He grinned. At times, it surprised him, too. But it was all part of his desire to be as different a man from his father as he could. "Well, I did go to medical school. That should have given you some kind of clue I was serious about being a doctor."

She offered no apologies. "I thought maybe you

were doing it because it was easier going to school than trying to be respectable.''

He supposed that was to be expected. Because his father was the kind of womanizer he was, because Jackson himself had gone out of his way to break rules and stir up trouble, he could see why his final career choice would be such a surprise for not only her but for the rest of the town.

''I wasn't that bad. A few harmless pranks, my father always made restitution.'' And exacted payment out of his hide for it in private twice over, Jackson remembered. But that wasn't anything he'd ever shared with anyone, not even Hannah.

Thinking back now, as he looked at her, he remembered that it was Hannah more than Ethan who had shared the thoughts he had been willing to impart. Hannah who had kept his counsel and his secrets. Always Hannah.

And Hannah had married Ethan. With not only his blessings, but his urgings, he reminded himself.

''It wasn't the pranks that made you the town's bad boy, Jackson.''

''Oh, then what?'' he asked.

Hannah closed her eyes for a second, going back in time. When she opened them again, she realized that the journey hadn't been necessary. This, at least, hadn't really changed. It still made her heart race just to look at him.

''There was something in your eyes, something about you. That air of danger.'' And it was still there, she thought. Just beneath the surface. That edgy danger that made a woman's skin tingle just to be near it.

Jackson laughed, shaking his head. "You're romanticizing."

The romantic in her had faded away almost three years ago. "I'm remembering," she corrected. And then she smiled at him again. "That's what I always liked about you, you never knew the effect you had on the girls around you. Or the women. You never had a swelled head."

Unlike Ethan, she added silently. Ethan had known exactly the kind of power he had over women. And had known just how to use it. Her mistake, now that she looked back, was that she'd never realized it.

He waved away the words. She was letting their friendship color her judgment. Yes, there had been girls, lots of them. And though he had enjoyed them, he had known exactly what they were after at the time.

"They were attracted to the Caldwell name. And the Caldwell money." He realized that had to sound bitter to her and he tempered his voice. "You and Ethan were probably my only real friends."

Closest, maybe, she allowed. Certainly no one had cared about him more than she had. And Ethan had always stuck up for Jackson, that much she could say about him. But she laughed at the poor-little-rich-boy image that came to mind.

"Nobody would have ever guessed, seeing you. You could have had your pick of girls. They were always around." And she knew he had slept with some of them. Knowing that had kept her awake nights, hurting. Wishing he would notice her that way. But he never did. "Why didn't you ever marry anyone?"

He hadn't expected that question coming from her. He shrugged carelessly.

"Because I never found anyone genuine enough." Jackson looked at her. *And because I was already in love with you.* What would she say if he said that to her? Would she think he was teasing her? Or would she draw away, upset that her husband's best friend had had feelings for her? "I guess some men are just confirmed bachelors."

"And some men are five feet three, but you're neither."

She said it with such conviction. Had he done something to give himself away, to make her suspect the depth of the feelings he'd always had for her? He'd kissed her, but she had to have had a great many other men do that.

"What makes you think so?"

"I know you too well. Confirmed bachelors fall into two camps," she said. "The ones in the first camp are womanizers who just want to have their fun and move on. The ones in the second camp are woman haters and want to have nothing to do with the fairer sex." She looked at him pointedly. "Neither description fits you."

There was something about her, sitting here with the moon highlighting her, that twisted his gut with longing for things that could have been, had he been anyone but who he was. "You're absolutely sure of that?"

"Absolutely," she whispered. He looked as if he was going to kiss her. *Oh please, let him kiss me.*

But instead, he drew back. "You always could argue for hours."

She tried not to sound as disappointed as she felt. "Everyone needs a hobby."

It was time to go, before he gave in to the temptations ravaging him right now and took her, here and now, in the place where their innocence had been maintained so well.

"Mine's making sure people don't get sick. Sitting in tree houses when the temperature's dropping isn't part of that." He nodded toward the doorway. "Want to go first, or should I lead the way?"

She swallowed, giving up the moment, telling herself she'd only been imagining things anyway. "You go first, I'll follow."

As it turned out, it proved to be a good plan, because otherwise, she might have broken her ankle or something equally as vital. Just as Hannah was on the third to the last board on the tree, it finally gave way, cracking beneath her foot. A tiny gasp escaped her lips as she felt herself falling.

The next moment, she felt Jackson's arms closing around her, pulling her to him. Saving her.

Chapter Six

The air left her lungs as if it had been sucked out by some huge, old fashioned blacksmith bellows. It was the proximity of the man, not the fall itself that had done it.

Grasping his arms to steady herself, Hannah could have sworn she felt Jackson's heart beating just above hers. And just as quickly.

"As the closest doctor in the immediate vicinity, I prescribe that you not go climbing into tree houses anymore." A hint of a smile moved across his lips. "Or at least not until they can be retro-fitted for safety," Jackson said, loosening his arms and holding her away from him.

She didn't want to back away just yet. She knew she should, but she just couldn't seem to back away. Cocking her head, she looked up at him, memorizing every plane, every contour of his face. As if it wasn't already branded in her mind and in her heart. "Have anyone in mind to do the retro-fitting?"

He willed his hands to release her, and found only disobedience. "I'm still pretty handy with a hammer and nails."

A vision of Jackson, his shirt off and sweat glistening on his skin, came to her. It took a second for her to find her tongue. "Do you come cheap? I can't afford to pay much."

As if he could ever take money from her, even if he had needed it. He'd heard that Ethan had left her with a mountain of debts to pay off. Her great-aunt had left the house, and a way out for her, just in time.

"We can work something out."

Work something out. God, how desperately she wanted to work something out. "Promise?"

The smile softened the features of his face, making him seem almost boyish instead of a man in his third decade of life. "No promises, remember? If you don't make promises, then you can't accidentally break them."

But you can, she thought. You can make promises with your eyes. The way he had with her. But whether he said them aloud or not, he had always been there for her. Until her wedding day.

Hannah struggled against a wave of bittersweet feelings. She lost.

Before she could dig in again, she found herself being swept away. Not being able to stem the tide, she went with her feelings, with her instincts.

With her needs.

Rising up on her toes so that her mouth was level with his, she pressed her lips to Jackson's. She couldn't have said what possessed her to do it, to turn soft banter into softer intimacy, except that every fiber of her being had wanted it. Begged for it.

She needed to kiss him, to have his lips against hers again. She needed to feel that wild, intoxicated emotion surging through her, taking her prisoner as it went on a wild and all-too-fleeting ride.

Jackson had been struggling with himself, struggling not to kiss her. Struggling to do the right thing. Suddenly, the decision was taken out of his hands.

All his noble intentions turned to ashes. With the taste of her mouth against his, her sweetness robbed him of his ability to think, leaving him only to react. He lost his train of thought and took advantage of the moment and the opportunity.

Tightening his arms around her slender form again, he felt her body pressed against his as he deepened the kiss and fell head long into it.

All his life, things had come easily to him—except the one thing he'd wanted. Hannah. He wanted to discover all her secrets, worshipping every inch of her body here under the dusky blanket of twilight.

And then what? his mind silently demanded. Wait for the other shoe to drop? Wait until something made him move on, made him leave her? Made him hurt Hannah the way his father had hurt his mother? It was only a matter of time.

He was too much his father's son to discount the reality of that. Whenever he looked into the mirror, he saw his father's eyes looking back at him. His father's face. While he'd been growing up, everyone had always been quick to point out how much he resembled his father, how many similarities there were between them, whether in athletic prowess or in the way that women would flock to them both.

Jackson didn't want to be his father. He couldn't change his looks or his abilities, but he could do something about the detractions. He could be selfless and rein in his own desires to keep the inevitable from transpiring.

That meant not allowing his feelings to get in the way of what he knew was the right thing to do.

But it was so damn hard when he was standing in the moonlight like this, holding Hannah in his arms. Wanting her. When he could feel her, warm and pliant and willing, against him. When he could taste her hunger and it matched his own.

Damn him, he thought, he was taking advantage of her vulnerability. What kind of a man was he?

Hannah could feel him withdrawing, could pinpoint the instant Jackson's thoughts intruded into what had been, only a second before, a glorious physical moment.

He left her. Left her as surely as if he'd taken the actual steps away from her.

Shaken, she drew back. A woman had her pride, even if there wasn't much of it left.

She looked down, avoiding his eyes. "Sorry, I guess my lips must have tripped, too."

Passing his palm along her cheek, he raised her head until she was forced to meet his gaze. "Don't ever be sorry, Hannah. You have nothing to be sorry for. It's me who should be apologizing to you."

Did he have any idea how much that stung? It took effort to keep her voice steady, to keep her emotion from flowing into it. "For what?"

"For kissing you. Before and now." He regretted it, sorely, regretted sampling what he shouldn't, what he couldn't have.

Why? her mind screamed. Why did it seem so wrong to him to have feelings for her? She interpreted it the only way she knew how.

"Is this because of some loyalty you feel you owe Ethan?" she asked. When Jackson made no response, she took it for agreement. Anger at the unfairness of the burden of the secret she had to bear broke through. "Maybe if you'd stayed around to get to know Ethan, you wouldn't feel so badly about what just happened."

"I did know Ethan. What are you saying?"

"Nothing." What was the sense of dragging up the things that went on between a husband and wife? Of the disillusion that was the hallmark of her marriage? Maybe if he knew, Jackson would even put the blame on her for what had happened. And maybe part of it *was* her fault. How many nights had she lain awake, thinking that if only she'd be more of a woman she could hold on to her man? There were far too many to count.

She shook her head, regretting the slip. "I'm tired, Jackson." She tried to get past him but he caught her arm.

His eyes searched her face, looking for a clue, for something more to go on. But her expression was impassive, her eyes flat. "Is there something I should know, Hannah?" he pressed.

Her temper flared again. "Yeah, in your heart. Right there," she poked at his chest with her finger, "that's where you should know." And then she caught herself. What was the matter with her? Mustering a contrite smile, she shook her head again. "Never mind. Forget what I just said. It's just exhaustion talking. I'm going home now. I suggest you do the same." Hannah walked by him, her perfume lingering in the air in her wake. "Good night, Jackson. It was nice reminiscing with you."

He stood looking at her go, knowing that if he went after her, one of them would regret it. He couldn't afford for it to be her.

She'd been waiting for him. Knowing she shouldn't, she still did.

Throughout the next morning, no matter what Hannah was doing, whether it was taking care of the twins, or playing with the children, or talking to the parents who came to drop them off, Hannah kept listening for the doorbell to ring just one more time. Although she knew she shouldn't, she was waiting for Jackson. Waiting to hear his familiar footfall on her front step.

All the while she was calling herself an idiot. By noon she had graduated to a hopeless idiot.

But when Jackson finally did arrive, all her self-deprecating upbraidings went out the window the second she opened the door. They blew away when she saw the flowers in his hand. Not flowers neatly swaddled in a long box and lying on a bed of green tissue paper, but flowers from the bushes that surrounded his house. He'd picked red roses for her. Her very favorite.

It took a second to clear away the lump in her

throat. She raised her eyes to his, hoping she wouldn't do something stupid, like cry.

"You remembered."

Jackson walked into the foyer and she closed the door behind him. "Hard not to remember, you used to steal them all the time when you were younger," he said.

Hannah sniffed. He would remember that. "I didn't steal them."

His eyes crinkled slightly. "What do you call cutting them off and taking them away?"

"Borrowing." She grinned, taking the bouquet into her hands. "I just never got around to returning them."

The look of pure pleasure on her face was worth more than the most priceless jewels. "Am I forgiven?"

"You're forgiven." She laughed, turning the bouquet around. The next moment she winced. "Ow."

"What?" His eyes immediately lowered to her hands. "I shaved off all the thorns." He'd taken extra care, just as he'd seen the gardener do for his mother when he'd been a boy.

"Well, I think you missed one." She held up her finger as proof. A single drop of blood oozed from the fresh wound. "No harm done."

She was about to pop the finger into her mouth, the way she might have with any minor cut, when he took her hand in his. Her heart flipped over as she watched him do exactly what she'd intended, slipping the wounded finger between his own lips.

Her eyes held his as a wide sliver of excitement shimmied all through her.

"Very doctor-like of you," she teased. Teased because if she didn't, she was going to throw herself into his arms again and embarrass both of them.

His smile went right to her inner core, setting it on fire. "Some time-honored traditions a doctor knows not to tamper with. Maybe I'd better go take a look to see how Steffie and Sammy are doing," he suggested.

Struggling with the hot, pink blush that was fighting to overtake all of her, Hannah dropped her hand to her side. "Maybe."

"You know," Gertie murmured to Hannah, taking the topic out of the blue as she was wont to do whenever the whim moved her, "for a man with a thriving practice and hardly much time to breathe, Jackson Caldwell certainly does seem to come around here often enough." She took a large tray of hot oatmeal chocolate chip cookies out of the oven and slid it onto the stove top.

It'd been more than a week since the babies had appeared on Hannah's doorstep. More than a week with no more leads than had initially been discovered. And Jackson had made it a point to stop by each day, either during his lunch break or after office hours to look in on the twins, monitoring their progress.

Though she tried not to, telling herself she was just setting herself up for a fall, Hannah looked forward to the visits. Waited for them.

But she tried to look nonchalant as she defended Jackson's actions. "He comes here as a favor to me, to check the babies out."

"Uh-huh." Wiping her hands on her apron, Gertie

gave her a knowing look. "That's not all he's checking out."

With Penny Sue and Gwenyth in the front room with the children, Hannah began to prepare a plate of cookies to take to them for their afternoon snack. "Maybe he's afraid they might be harboring something or coming down with something."

Gertie dismissed the excuse with a short laugh. "Ask me, it's the good doctor who's finally come down with something—and it's high time, too." Hannah stopped piling cookies and gave Gertie a warning look. "Don't give me that look, Hannah Dawson. I've got eyes."

The last thing she wanted was Gertie spreading rumors. Friendly, outgoing and everyone's grandmother, the woman was on a first-name basis with the entire town. "Well, they obviously need to be rechecked, and it's Hannah Brady, not Hannah Dawson, remember?"

"That was just a temporary aberration." Taking out the second tray and resting it beside the first, Gertie took a deep breath, growing serious. "You married the wrong man, Hannah."

She knew that now, maybe knew that then, but being told so frayed her temper. "I married the man who asked me, Gertie. The man who said he loved me and wanted to make me his wife." And Jackson hadn't. Ever.

Gertie saw the distress in Hannah's eyes. "Sorry. Didn't mean to get you upset." Momentarily contrite, Gertie looked away. "Sometimes I just run off at the mouth when I shouldn't."

Nothing like a retraction to stir up her guilt, Hannah thought. She laid a hand on Gertie's arm, her voice softening. "And I didn't mean to snap at you, Gertie. It's just that, well, things feel all mixed up to me right now." Picking up the heaping plate of cookies, she began to head out to the front room.

"Love'll do that to you," Gertie murmured under her breath.

Hannah stopped in the doorway, turning her head. "What did you say?"

"Not enough sleep'll do that to you," Gertie replied innocently. Picking up the second platter Hannah had prepared, Gertie followed her out. "Tonight, why not let me stay here and you go to my house? Nice and peaceful there," she promised. "Nobody'll disturb you—unless you want them to, of course."

Gertie placed the platter on the table against the wall, leaving it to Penny Sue to distribute the cookies. Squeals and pleas immediately abounded from the pint-sized citizenry.

Moving aside, Hannah lowered her voice as she inclined her head next to Gertie's ear. "I don't see what you're doing, volunteering in a daycare center, Gertie. You should be running a matchmaking service."

Gertie pursed her lips together, eyeing Hannah purposely. "Don't seem to be having much luck in that department right now."

She looked at the slender young blond doctor in the front room, who, along with Penny Sue and Gwenyth, was suddenly inundated by a sea of little hands, all raised for hand-outs. New to Storkville, the woman had offered her services to the center in the last few weeks, despite a full-time career and home.

"I'm hoping for better luck with my lemonade. Well, not me, exactly." Gertie lowered her voice to a whisper. "But Dr. Becky. Made up a batch just for her this morning. That don't do the trick, I'm afraid nothing will."

Hannah looked at the woman they were talking about. Dr. Becky was Dr. Rebecca Fielding who, together with her husband, Dr. Mike Fielding, worked at Storkville General Hospital. Rebecca had been attempting to become pregnant for over a year now. The irony of it was that Rebecca was an ob/gyn, up on the latest fertility breakthroughs.

Frustrated and desperate at not finding herself in the family way each month, it looked as if she was about to subscribe to Aunt Gertie's theory that her "special, top-secret lemonade"—which Gertie had announced was "patent pending"—would do the trick where science and the machinations of simple human nature had failed.

Maybe Becky was merely humoring Gertie, Hannah thought. "Has she had any yet?"

"She says she's thinking about it, but I think she's weakening. Poor lamb, I can see it in her eyes every time she comes here." Gertie sighed, watching Becky distribute cookies to gleeful takers. "She wants babies something awful." Gertie glanced at Hannah. "Seems to be a lot of that going on lately."

Hannah took no offense at Gertie's implication. Here, at least, the older woman was right. "Well, for all intents and purposes, I have babies. Two babies." She looked toward where the twins were sitting in their infant seats jabbering away to one another in babyspeak. She could have watched them for hours.

"Indefinitely if their mother or father doesn't come back to claim them."

And right now, that wasn't looking like such a bad thing, Hannah thought. It did no good to try to distance herself from the twins in case Tucker was successful in his efforts to track down their mother. The twosome had already bagged her heart as a trophy. To pretend otherwise would have been a useless lie.

"Even if they do, it'll be a while before they can take custody of the twins," Gertie pointed out. "Mom and/or dad will be facing jail time."

If this were one of the larger cities, there would be no question of that. But people tended to be more forgiving in Storkville, Hannah thought.

"Oh, I've got a feeling Tucker might find a way around that if they turn out to be really contrite."

Gertie shook her head. "I don't know about that. Tucker's pretty hard on things like abandonment. It's no secret he believes that people should face up to their responsibilities. He's got a lot in common with Jackson there."

There was no need to praise Jackson to her. Hannah already thought of him as being in the same realm as a white knight. But she didn't quite grasp what Gertie was trying to say. "How so?"

To keep from being overheard, Gertie stepped out into the foyer. "Well, he came back, didn't he? To take care of his daddy's funeral. The way that boy lit out of town when he left, I didn't think he was ever coming back."

Hannah stared at the older woman. She'd never had any details about that day, only that somewhere during the course of the reception, Jackson had taken off.

It was only later that evening, as she and Ethan were leaving on their honeymoon, that she'd heard Jackson had not just left the reception, but the town as well.

"You saw him leave?"

"Yes, I saw him leave. Nearly ran me down with that car of his. Of course, I don't think he saw me. But I saw him, just for a second when the car drove by. He looked really upset." Gertie sighed and shook her head. "I always figured he and his daddy had had some kind of a major falling-out. Things were never the same between those two after his Momma died of a heart attack."

Hannah remembered how distraught Jackson had been. She'd never seen him that way before. There had been only a momentary break in the strong front he always presented to the world, but she had seen it. Seen the tears brimming in Jackson's eyes. Though he hadn't seemed particularly close to his mother, her death had hit him hard. Anna Caldwell had died alone in her room. Rumor had it that her husband was out on the town. Jackson had been the one to discover her when he came in to say good-night.

Hannah had done her best to comfort him, had been by his side at the funeral but there'd been no reaching Jackson. He'd gone off into that place he went to whenever he wanted to distance himself from what was going on around him.

She'd ached for him that day. And later.

"But he came back to tie up all the loose ends, make whatever amends he had to," Gertie concluded. "That makes him a big man in my book."

Hannah didn't understand. "Amends?"

"For his daddy. That man was always tomcatting

around. Those two might have shared a name, but they're nothing alike. Jackson's daddy was a charmer and as shallow as a one-inch pool. Our doctor-boy might not smile much, but he runs deep. And he's got a good heart.'' She looked at Hannah pointedly. ''Remember that.''

Hannah saw no reason for the advice. ''I do.''

''Good.'' Gertie suddenly smiled broadly. ''Because it looks like he's back.'' She pointed to the front door.

Chapter Seven

Still holding the platter of cookies, Hannah turned around to open the door with her free hand, then stepped back to allow Jackson to come in. The grandfather clock in the study chimed the hour. It was two. He was late.

"I thought maybe you weren't coming today," she told him as she closed the door.

"I almost didn't."

Gertie's words rang in her ear. He'd realized that there was no further need to keep coming this way and was about to tell her this was the last time. She braced herself. "Oh?"

"There was an emergency at the office. At least, Mrs. Donovan thought it was an emergency. Her son Teddy decided he liked pussy willows so much, he stuck them up his nose to keep them close forever. According to Mrs. Donovan, he started screaming almost immediately.'' Jackson shook his head. ''Tucker escorted her and Teddy into the office.''

''Why?'' Hannah wouldn't have thought that pussy willows would readily come under the heading of a 911 call for the sheriff.

''Seems Mrs. Donovan ran every light from her house to my office, thinking Teddy was going to choke to death.'' The woman was lucky to have made it to his office without causing an accident, he thought.

Acquainted with the two, Hannah could just envision it. Jackson, in the eye of a hurricane, trying to calmly go about his work while Mrs. Donovan wrung her hands, lamenting, and her son screamed blue murder. ''So I take it that you successfully separated Teddy from the pussy willows?''

''Not without much protest.'' He tugged on his ear. ''My ears are still ringing. I tell you, if that kid doesn't become either an opera singer or an umpire, then it'll be a great loss to one world or the other.'' For the first time, he became aware of the plate she was holding. Oatmeal chocolate chip had always been his favorite and time had done nothing to alter that fact. He could feel his taste buds go into high gear. ''Anyway, can I convince you to give me one of those?''

The way he looked at the cookies on the plate had her suddenly wishing she was one, too. ''You're in luck. I'm highly bribable today.''

The smile that curved his lips was nothing short of powerfully sexy. ''What'll you take in trade?''

Silently, she offered one to him, and he made it his own immediately. Hannah watched as he bit into the cookie with the relish of a small boy who'd managed to break into a secret hiding place and appropriated the booty. There was contented pleasure in Jackson's expression.

Was it possible to be envious of a cookie? she wondered.

"A little adult conversation that doesn't have 'like' appearing twice in every sentence, or that ends in some thinly veiled innuendo that I should start thinking about becoming the nineties, updated version of The Merry Widow. That's an operetta," she added in case he missed the reference.

The last of the large cookie disappeared between his lips. He eyed her. "Hannah Dawson, are you talking down to me?"

Dawson. He was the second person to call her that today. Hannah realized that hearing her maiden name seemed far more appropriate to her than hearing her married one. Funny, now that she thought of it, but she felt far more like Hannah Dawson these days than Hannah Brady. She wasn't even sure just how Hannah Brady would feel anymore. It was almost a relief to put Hannah Brady behind her now.

"Talk down to you?" she echoed. "I wouldn't dream of it. It's just that most men aren't familiar enough with operettas and old musicals to even recognize their names."

He pinched a second cookie, his eyes shining. "I recognize it. And if that's your way of saying I'm unique. I'll accept it."

Leaning against the wall, she knew she could stand like this with him forever. They were talking almost like the old days. Days she missed acutely. "Fishing for a compliment, are we?"

Since she seemed to be in a good mood, he availed himself of one more cookie. After all, lunch had come and gone and his stomach was still empty.

"It's been a hard morning. Dana Hewitt brought her triplets in for their check ups. Unfortunately, the visit also included boosters." There were times when being a pediatrician was a challenge. This had been one of those times. He'd needed the extra hands of not only the triplet's mother, but of his nurse as well. "You think twins are a handful, take it from me, they've got nothing on triplets. That woman deserves a medal."

If the last week was any indication of what Dana Hewitt's life was like, Hannah had another take on the assessment. "I'm sure she'd enjoy a mini-vacation instead."

"You're probably right," he agreed. "These are good." Jackson held up the tiny piece he had left of his third cookie. "You make them?"

She shook her head, straightening. "Wish I could take the credit. No, that's just one the talents that Gertie brings with her to the place."

Moving slightly back, she caught sight of Gertie: she was playing a board game with three of the older children. A fond smile slipped over Hannah's lips as she watched for a moment.

"She gossips like a supermarket tabloid at times, but her heart's in the right place and I know I'd be lost without her. We've only been open for a few weeks and she's already indispensable to me." Hannah sighed, grappling with reality. "I just wish I could pay her."

"Oh, I think she's getting compensated," he assured Hannah, observing the older woman. Judging by the wide grin, Gertie was having the time of her life. "Kids might run you ragged, but they keep you young and moving."

A rubber ball came flying at them out of nowhere. Hannah's hand whipped out, making the catch before the ball could hit her.

"Yeah, to avoid being a target." Pulling her face into a serious expression, purely to get her point across, she looked at the two culprits who had come running up to her for their ball. Rather than surrendering it, she rhythmically tossed it up in the air and then caught it. "Boys, what did I tell you about playing ball in the house?"

"Don't," they both chimed in together.

"Right. Take it outside." She handed the ball to the child closest to her, a tow-headed boy of four named Neil. "And you," she said, looking at Jackson, "why don't you take it inside?"

Frowning, he looked about elaborately. "I thought I was inside."

"I mean into the parlor." She nodded toward the room where her great-aunt used to entertain suitors as a young woman under her father's watchful eye. "Sit down a few minutes, take a deep breath." She looked at what he was still holding in his hand. "Enjoy your cookie."

Her words amused him. "Trying your hand at playing doctor?"

"No, just being head of a daycare center. Giving

orders seems to come with the territory." So did having eyes in the back of your head, she thought. Turning, she made eye contact with Ricky Fellows and shook her head. He let go of Lily Allen's braid, a contrite expression on his young face. Lily ran off.

She did have a way about her, Jackson thought. She was far more authoritative than he'd ever thought her capable of being. "I notice that no one seems to mind listening to you."

"Being taller than all of them has its advantages." She laughed to herself. "I can remember when I thought being tall was the most awful thing that could have happened to me." Feelings vividly replayed themselves in her mind. "I felt like such a beanpole."

He'd never thought of her as awkward or gangly. "You were striking."

The euphemism made her laugh softly. "Yeah, easy for you to say now. Where were you when I could have used someone to back me up?"

To him, Hannah had always been able to handle herself. He could never have played Lancelot to her damsel in distress. She wouldn't have expected it or tolerated it. "I don't recall you ever needing any backup."

A lot he knew. She'd been teased a great deal, but she had pretended to have a tough skin. Eventually, the teasing had stopped. Blossoming the way she had hadn't hurt, either.

"That was because you were too surrounded with sweet, young, overly nubile things to be able to see past the tight circle they formed around you."

When had she learned to exaggerate? "Funny, I don't seem to recall your imagination being so creative.'' He looked down at the plate she was still holding. When had he managed to eat so many cookies? ''I seem to have depleted your supply.''

''There's more in the front room, if you want to risk venturing in.'' He raised his brow, puzzled. ''The kids have all had their naps and, thanks to Gertie, their afternoon sugar high,'' Hannah explained. ''They should be fairly ready to bounce off all the walls by now.''

''The way around that,'' he told her, walking into the room and straight for the other plate, ''is to get them into some calm group activity. Read them a story.''

That was all the rabble had to hear, Hannah thought, looking at them fondly. Prior activities and even the cookies were forgotten at the mention of their favorite word.

''A story?'' Jonathan, a tiny, freckled boy piped up, excitement lacing his high voice.

Suddenly, the cry of ''Story, story,'' went up all over the room. Before he knew what was happening, Jackson found himself beset by almost a dozen upturned faces, all eagerly looking at him.

From the center of the pint-sized ring, Jackson turned toward Hannah. He could hear Penny Sue and Becky laughing on the sidelines. ''I take it that's the wrong word to use around here.''

''Depends on who you are.'' Hannah stepped forward to rescue him. ''Maybe you'd better pocket a few more cookies and make your escape while you can. I'll take it from here. The babies are in the next room, still down for their naps.''

But Jackson was in no hurry to get away. He enjoyed reading to children. "That's okay, I've got a little time before I have to get back. My next two appointments canceled. I can read a story as long as it's not too long."

There were children's books of all lengths, thanks to the library Hannah's great-aunt had maintained. She looked through a few that were on the table. "How are you with Dr. Seuss?"

Jackson held out his hand for the book. "Just my speed."

She sincerely doubted that. The man went far beyond the elementary and endearing words found between the covers of the children's favorite author. Selecting one of the late writer's more popular books, she gave it to Jackson then sat back and waited to hear him read.

Pleasant surprise arrived almost instantly.

It was hard to reconcile the wild, brooding bad boy she'd once secretly pressed to her heart with the dark-haired man who now sat cross-legged on the floor, surrounded by an enthralled audience hanging on his every word, even though those words had been all but memorized by the same audience.

He'd chosen the right profession, Hannah thought, watching him. Children were intuitive, they could sense who liked them and who was only pretending. There was no pretense with Jackson Caldwell. Anyone could see that he liked children; liked not only the idea of children, but the reality of them as well: the demands children could make so easily on his time and patience.

Jackson read to them with gusto and feeling, his

voice taking on the nature of the characters in the book.

He didn't merely read, he performed, Hannah noted. And the children ate it up with glee.

"More," they cried almost in unison when he closed the book, adding a heart twisting "pleeease," before he could turn them down.

Rising, Jackson looked to her for help. The single telegraphed plea went right through her, warming Hannah. She liked the fact that for this single instant, she and Jackson were a team.

"Dr. Caldwell has to go back to his office right now, kids. But I'm sure he'll be back again very soon if you all behave yourselves." Grasping him by the wrist, Hannah extricated him from his admirers, then accompanied him out to the foyer.

"Nicely done, especially that behave part." He found himself smiling into her eyes when she turned to face him at the door. Smiling into them and getting lost there. "Don't miss a trick, do you?"

She wouldn't have quite put it that way, but she was glad that he had. "I might be taller, but they definitely outnumber me. I can't afford to let them get the upper hand."

He was almost to the door when he remembered why he'd come in the first place. "I almost forgot, how are the twins today?"

There was really no need for him to examine either of the two. They were healthy and thriving. "Getting cuter every day. Steffie's over her cold and Sammy's not showing any signs that he's coming down with it. I don't think he caught it." A wave of sadness washed over her. Hannah hid it, slipping her hands into her pockets. "I guess that means you won't have to be stopping by anymore."

When she looked like that, she almost seemed vulnerable. "I didn't just come by to look in on the twins."

"Oh, really?" She knew she shouldn't be holding her breath. But she was.

"Really," he echoed. "I needed to spend some time with an old friend."

She told herself this wasn't ever going to go past this stage and that it should be enough. "Watch the old part. I'm sensitive."

"You're also as far from being old as I am from being a leprechaun."

"Well, that's because they have a height requirement."

He snapped his fingers. "There you go, dashing my hopes again."

"Again?" She thought she saw a fleeting, wary look in his eyes when she asked. But the next moment, it was gone and she told herself she'd just imagined it.

"Poetic license. Listen, can you get a sitter for the twins tonight?"

She thought of Gwenyth, but her cousin was busy going between her house and the one Gwenyth was about to rent, getting it ready. She didn't want to impose on her. "There's Gertie. She keeps volunteering to stay with them. Why? What did you have in mind?"

"Nothing much, just a sudden whim for dinner away from the madding crowd. Maybe catch a movie. The way we did in the old days."

In the old days, she recalled, there were three of them doing things together. Even after she and Ethan had gotten engaged.

"You're on," she told him.

He almost called twice to cancel, upbraiding himself in the confines of his own mind all afternoon and on the drive back to his house. It was a mistake to go through with this. Seeing her at the daycare center with a score or so of children and adults within several inches of them at any given time was one thing, an intimate table for two was quite another.

"What the hell were you thinking of?" he asked himself.

What he'd been thinking of was having dinner with a beautiful woman. Of isolating an evening and pretending, just for a while, that actions had no consequences, no ripple effects, and that he had no shadows cast over him, no heritage weighing heavily on him.

Would it be so hard, he wondered, to let himself pretend? Just this once?

He was still carrying on the terse, if silent argument as he drove over to Hannah's home.

Time to stop arguing, he told himself, turning the ignition off. He was here.

Jackson took a deep breath, then opened his door and got out.

This was ridiculous. He didn't recall ever being nervous about taking a woman out before. But then, he'd never taken Hannah out before, at least, not alone. Oh, there had been long, one-on-one talks and evenings spent in each other's company, but then there had usually been a schoolbook in between them, sparking the initial reason for the get-together.

Never, in all those years, had he approached her door with the intention of taking her out for the evening without Ethan being somewhere very close by.

Confidence was a wonderful thing, he thought as he walked away from his car. You only realized how much you needed it when it was absent.

Calling himself an idiot, Jackson made himself go up the front steps before he changed his mind and chalked the whole venture up to a bad idea that should have never been executed.

Even if he went through with it, there certainly was no future to it beyond tonight.

He wasn't sure if that knowledge relieved him, or made him sad.

This was Hannah, he told himself. Hannah, whose company he enjoyed. Hannah, who had been a part of everything in his life that had been good and clean and decent. When the ugliness in his own home had threatened to overwhelm him, when he couldn't bear to be privy to the lies, the deceit that went on behind the walls of the Caldwell estate, he would seek out Hannah, Hannah and her parents, who had both been so normal, so warm. Being part of their lives had reminded him that the world wasn't completely bathed in dark hues, that there were good people around and that men could stay faithful to wives who loved them.

She was part of the light and he was part of the dark, he thought as he rang the doorbell, listening to the soft chimes. There could be no future because he wouldn't allow himself to taint that light. But for to-night, there could be a present.

He strained to hear approaching footsteps from somewhere beyond the other side of the door.

Hearing the doorbell, Gertie went to the foot of the stairs and called up, "Jackson's here. Don't keep him waiting, dear."

Nerves suddenly popped out, as huge as stealth bombers and moving just as swiftly through Hannah.

Could you will the flu? Or a fever? Hannah wondered, looking herself over in the full length mirror and seeing only disaster.

Because if she could will herself instantly ill, she wanted to. Desperately. Every outfit she owned had been tried on and discarded, deemed all wrong for the occasion. She literally had nothing to wear and she didn't want to go.

Didn't want to be disappointed.

Get on with it, Hannah, she ordered herself.

Hurriedly Hannah slipped into shoes that matched her dress and grabbed her purse off her bed.

The walk to the head of the stairs felt as if she were taking the last mile. Gertie was down there, waiting. The doorbell rang again and Gertie looked up at her expectantly.

Hannah took a deep breath and then let it out again before coming down. "I thought in your generation you were supposed to keep a man waiting."

Gertie snorted. "My generation had a few things backwards. And besides, you've already kept him waiting for a long time, wouldn't you say?"

"What I'd say," Hannah told her, stopping to kiss

the wrinkled pink cheek for luck as well as out of affection, "is that you've been inhaling too much talcum powder lately and it's made your thinking fuzzy. Jackson and I are just friends."

Gertie nodded, stopping a second to fuss with a tendril at Hannah's temple. "Friendship is a very important ingredient in the mix and a good place to start. Well, go on," Gertie waved her to the door, "let him in."

Hannah felt as if she were using someone else's legs as she crossed to the door and finally opened it. Someone else's voice came out of her mouth. "Hi."

He'd begun to think he'd gotten his nights mixed up and that she wasn't home. Seeing her now froze all thoughts in his head. She was wearing a simple electric-blue sheath that caressed every curve on her body.

And made him want to do the same.

There was barely enough saliva in his mouth for him to offer a single word in reply. "Wow."

She couldn't read his expression. "Is that a good wow or a bad wow?"

"A good wow. Definitely a very good wow." He raised his eyes to her face, then tilted his head. "What have you done to your hair?"

She *knew* she should have left it down. "You don't like it?" She was already grasping at a pin. "I can take it down—"

Jackson caught her wrist gently in his hand. "No, I like it. I like it very much."

There was something in the way he looked at her that made her body feel warm all over.

Hannah nearly melted as Jackson took her wrap from her and slid it up along her arms.

Finding her voice, she turned to look at Gertie. "Thanks for watching the twins. I'll be home early."

"I won't hold you to that," Gertie called after her. "Have a good time!"

"We will," Jackson tossed over his shoulder, slipping his arm around Hannah's as he ushered her down the porch steps.

Embarrassment harnessed her. Could Gertie have been any more obvious?

"Are my cheeks red?" Hannah asked him.

Stopping at the passenger side of his vehicle, he pretended to take a closer look at her face, then laughed. "Only very pleasantly so."

The sound of his laugh helped quell the uneasiness in her stomach.

But not much.

Chapter Eight

Hannah felt his eyes on her. When she raised her own to his, she realized that he wasn't looking at her, he was looking at her plate.

Jackson frowned. She'd hardly touched anything. "I don't remember you eating like a bird."

It wasn't that the food wasn't good, it was just that the knot in her stomach wouldn't loosen enough to let her enjoy it. Telling herself that she was acting like an idiot didn't help.

She grasped at diversion. "Actually, that's a misconception. Depending on the bird, they can eat up to three or four times their weight a day."

Taking a sip of his wine, Jackson laughed, shaking his head. "That part I remember."

Just to the right of them, the band began to play a low, bluesy number and she began tapping her foot to the rhythm. "What? About the birds?"

"No, about you correcting me. You did that a lot

when we were growing up.'' She'd been fearless like that, he remembered, never allowing him to labor under a misconception when she could help it. He grinned. ''I guess your mother never told you that correcting a guy when he's wrong might damage his ego.''

She raised her own glass and took a small sip of wine. It felt as if it was going straight to her head. Or was that him? ''From where I sit, your ego's fine, and my mother taught me to be myself.''

He wouldn't have had it any other way. It was what had always made Hannah so unique to him. She'd always had the courage of her convictions, never standing on ceremony, but doing and saying what she thought was right.

''Smart lady, your mother. I always liked your parents.'' They had died six months apart and he'd missed both their funerals, not having heard about their deaths until it had been far too late even to send condolences. He leaned forward over the table. ''How have you held up since they…?''

A vague shrug rippled along her shoulders. Losing them had been far harder for her to deal with than Ethan's death. ''As well as can be expected. Not a day goes by when I don't miss them.''

He could well understand that. ''At least you had them.''

''You had yours, too.''

He set his mouth grimly. ''Not the same thing.'' He'd never been close to his parents, not even his mother, whom he'd loved. There'd never been a feeling of unity, as he'd observed in hers. ''My parents weren't like yours. Yours were warm-hearted people.''

She knew his parents was a sore topic for him so she left it alone. ''They liked you, too.''

He warmed to the memories, letting them in. He'd hung around her house so much, the Dawsons had all but adopted him as the son they'd never had. He supposed, looking back, he'd sought emotional asylum with them.

''What I liked most about your parents was that they were honest and real. There were no pretenses, no hidden secrets. Every time your father looked at your mother, I knew he was in love with her.'' How many times had he wished Hannah's father had been his own? Too many to begin to remember. ''That's a very rare quality in a man.''

She thought of Ethan. ''I know. At least in some men.''

He looked at her for a long moment, wondering if she was thinking of him when she said that. Jackson nodded at her neglected plate. ''Well, since you're not eating, would you like to dance?''

She stopped tapping her toe and stared at Jackson. ''Now?''

He grinned at the surprise in her eyes. ''Since the band's here and they're playing I thought that now might not be a bad time, yes.''

In all the time she'd known him, he'd never asked her to dance. Not that she hadn't fantasized about it countless times. But right now, she wasn't sure that she could. ''You're asking me to dance with you?''

''Am I not speaking English?'' he asked with a laugh.

She shook her head as if to clear it, not as if she were giving him a silent answer.

"I'm sorry, it's just that—" She stopped, collecting herself. Since he liked honesty so much, she decided to give it a try and tell him why she was stuttering like some confused, adolescent schoolgirl. "You have no idea how many times I used to imagine that you'd ask me to dance."

"Used to?"

In for a penny, in for a pound, wasn't that what her great-aunt used to say? Hannah nodded. "Yes."

"When?"

Lowering her eyes, she looked at the way the light was squeezing itself through the wine in her glass and twinkling over the surface. "When we were growing up. You want me to give you inclusive dates?"

Was she serious? How could he have missed that? Missed the implication behind it? "No, it's just that I had no idea…"

She raised her eyes. "You didn't have an idea about a lot of things."

Just how far did this lead? he wondered. Had she cared for him once as something more than just a friend? "Such as?"

"Such as the way girls felt about you." Hannah bit her lip, then let the words free. "And the way I felt about you."

"You."

"Me."

He still couldn't get himself to believe it. Hannah had to mean something else, there had to be something qualifying her words to keep them from meaning what he thought they meant. "And that was…?"

She'd just reached the end of her embarrassment tether. Nervous, she forced herself to stop twirling the stem of her wine glass between her fingers. "What is this, you buy a girl a little dinner, ply her with wine and then expect her to give you all her secrets?"

He didn't want her to feel as if he were probing, pushing her. She probably thought he was doing it to have his vanity stroked when nothing could have been further from the truth. To spare her, despite his desire to know, he withdrew. "I didn't mean—"

Hannah moved back her chair and let him guide her to the dance floor. She couldn't leave him wondering, but she could couch it in the past, saving her own face. "Well, all right, I guess you're entitled to know. You would have known if you'd only been paying attention. I had the biggest secret crush on you."

Crush, Hannah figured, was a far safer word than *love,* though the latter was much closer to the truth than the former.

And still is, a voice whispered across her mind.

"You did." It was more of a stunned repetition than a question.

He looked, she thought, as if he could be knocked over with the proverbial feather. Or maybe he'd just gone into shock. She didn't know whether to be amused or hurt. "I did."

He didn't know what to think, what to say. "And was it?"

She didn't follow. "Was it what?"

"A secret?" Or had she told someone? Had she shared her feelings with someone else and made it seem as if he were some heartless idiot who ignored her? God, but he wished he had known, had some inkling.

Was he worried that she might have embarrassed him by sharing her feelings for him with a girlfriend? ''I never told anyone how I felt, if that's what you mean.'' The smile that found its way to her lips never reached her eyes. ''Only my diary knew.''

Something else he didn't know about her, he thought. How much more was there that had eluded him? ''You kept a diary?''

''Sure.'' She'd kept one faithfully during her teen years and into her twenties. She'd stopped the day before she married Ethan. Looking back, she wondered if that had been some sort of sign she'd ignored. ''I had to get my feelings out somehow—or bust.''

The conversation was getting serious, and awkward. He made an attempt to lighten it for both their sakes. ''I thought you always took your feelings out on Ethan and me—but I guess I was wrong.''

She looked at him for a long moment. ''Yeah, you were. About a lot of things.''

When he'd opened the door with what he'd thought was a harmless question, he hadn't been prepared for the flood of revelations that came his way. But he couldn't help asking, ''Meaning?''

She might as well clear the air about as much as she could. But she would keep back the most important part. ''Leaving town like that, in the middle of our wedding. Gertie seemed to think that it was because of some argument you had with your father. Was it?''

He had no idea how Gertie could have had an opinion about his departure, one way or another. Gossip, he supposed. But gossip wasn't what he wanted Hannah to know. "No, by then my father and I weren't really speaking. He was into his own thing and hardly knew that I was alive. I don't think he even realized I'd left for several weeks." By then he'd long since moved out of the house and taken a place near the hospital. "It wasn't as if we ran into each other a lot. He was busy elsewhere."

Tom-catting around, Gertie had called it, Hannah thought. But she wasn't about to open up wounds that might not have completely healed. "All right, if you didn't leave because of your father, why did you leave?"

He didn't want to go into that. Not yet, perhaps not ever. He nodded toward the band. "The music's stopped."

But she remained where she was for a moment, looking at him. "So have the answers."

"Let it alone, Hannah." Placing his hand to the small of her back, he ushered her back to their table. "It doesn't concern you."

Stunned and momentarily speechless she blew out an angry breath as she sank down in her seat again. "Well, I guess that certainly puts me in my place, doesn't it?"

Words had never been his best method of communication. "Hey, I didn't mean—"

Hannah cut him off, not wanting to hear any lies. "Didn't you? You tell me that we're friends, and then you tell me to butt out. Is there some kind of tier arrangement you have for your friends, a caste system I wasn't aware of?"

Telling her the truth might kill the very friendship she was throwing in his face. "Hannah—"

Living with Ethan had taught her how to withdraw into her shell. "Sorry, maybe I expected too much. Maybe I just expected you to be honest with me." A flood of emotions threatened to drown her. She could feel them welling up inside. "But if Ethan couldn't be, why should you? You owe me less than he did."

The conversation was swiftly going in directions he didn't follow. "Ethan? What are you talking about? What wasn't Ethan honest about?"

She'd said too much, alluded to too much and she could feel tears beginning to sting her eyes. She wanted to leave before he could see them. Taking her purse, she rose abruptly. "Look, it's been a lovely evening, but I really have to go."

Before he could say anything, she hurried away.

He caught up to Hannah in the parking lot. There was no way he was going to let her leave like this, with so much hanging unspoken between them. Catching her by the arm, he turned her around to face him, fighting to curb the flash of temper he felt. "Just where do you think you're going?"

Stubbornly, she tried to pull her arm away, but he had a firm hold on it. "Home."

His eyes narrowed. "On foot?"

Hannah tossed her head. "We still have buses here. We're not entirely backward, no matter what you might think."

"Nobody ever said you were backward."

"Then why treat me that way?" Hannah demanded, finally managing to pull herself free. "Why not answer me?"

"Because you might not like the answers."

Some of the anger left her voice, softening it. "Why don't you let me decide that?"

He couldn't risk it. Couldn't tear away the one good, decent thing that had been part of his life. That was why he had left to begin with, because he was afraid that jealousy would get the better of him, outweighing his friendship.

"Because it wouldn't be fair to you. It's bad enough that…"

She waited for him to continue, but he didn't. "That what?"

He only shook his head. Confession was not always good for the soul. Sometimes, it hurt more than it healed. "Never mind."

She knew defeat when she faced it and her frustration was hard to contain. "There you go again, keeping things from me. Is it a thing with you men?"

She was still talking in riddles, riddles he intended to solve. If there was something troubling her, he wanted to know. No one was more important to him than Hannah. "What are you talking about? And what was it about Ethan you wouldn't tell me back there?"

He noticed that they were garnering curious glances from a couple just leaving their car. Taking her by the arm, he began to walk to the edge of the parking lot, as calmly as if they were out for a stroll instead of trying to resolve something between them.

She looked for words that wouldn't come. "I don't want to tell you because you and Ethan were friends and because…because I couldn't stand it if you thought there was nothing wrong with it." What if he took Ethan's side? What if he told her that all men cheated on their wives and that it was something to turn a blind eye to?

He was more lost than ever—and more determined to find his way. "Start at the beginning."

Where was the beginning? Did she even remember anymore? Hannah thought. "I can't. I don't know when the beginning was. It just sort of started."

They had left the restaurant lot and were walking along the block, the way they used to. Except the topics had never been so serious then. "What just sort of started?"

"Ethan's stepping out on me."

Jackson stopped walking and looked at her. "What?"

"Stepping out on me. Seeing other women. Betraying our vows. I don't know how else to say it. I don't want to say it," she cried. "It tastes too bitter on my tongue to have to talk about it."

Of all the things she could have said, this was something he wouldn't have guessed. Ethan had been crazy about Hannah. It was one of the reasons Jackson had stepped away, because he was so certain that Ethan would love her the way she deserved to be loved. The way her father had loved her mother.

Jackson felt a sense of betrayal, for her as well as for his own beliefs. "Ethan saw other women?"

She laughed shortly and began walking again. "I see you still have that razor-sharp mind of yours."

"When?" Jackson still couldn't make himself believe it. "When was he seeing other women?" Maybe it had only been her imagination, he thought. But he had never known her to be the suspicious type.

"When wasn't he? I'd like to think that the honeymoon was free of other women, but I can't really swear to that. I suppose he might have caught a lady or two on the side even then. Hawaii was full of beautiful women and I was too busy getting used to the idea that it was only the two of us from there on in.'' Hannah glanced at him pointedly, the streetlight illuminating the sadness in her eyes.

It still seemed so unreal to him. "Ethan? Ethan cheated on you?''

Why couldn't he accept it? She had. And then the fear began to form within her again. Was he going to blame her for Ethan's indiscretions? Was he going ask if she drove him to it? If she wasn't woman enough for Ethan?

She couldn't help the sarcasm that entered her voice. ''With every breath he took, I eventually discovered. I tried to pretend it wasn't happening, tried to act like the good little wife and make him happy but it seemed that what really made Ethan happy was variety.''

Words couldn't begin to explain how angry he felt for her. ''Oh God, Hannah, I'm so sorry.''

''Yeah, me, too,'' she said softly. ''Did you know that when he died there was someone else in the car with him? He'd told me he was going out of town on business. Tucker tried to hide it from me. I guess he figured I was going through enough without having that tidbit thrown at me. But I found out.'' She pushed the hurt away as best she could. ''The wife always finds out, you know. And usually sooner than later.''

Because he had no words to tell her how sorry he was, no words to express how truly surprised he was, Jackson said nothing. But he took Hannah into his arms and just held her. Held her as a friend, not as someone who had loved her in silence.

He blamed himself for what she'd gone through. The irony of it twisted through him like a sharp knife. He'd tried to spare her and because he had pushed her into Ethan's arms, Hannah had endured the very thing he'd been trying to prevent.

"I'm getting your jacket all wet," she said.

"It'll dry."

He took out a handkerchief from his pocket and slowly dried her eyes with it. She held very still.

"I really needed you back then," Hannah whispered. "I needed someone to talk to. I wished you had left me a number, an address, something."

Pocketing the handkerchief again, he threaded his fingers through hers. They started to walk again. "I'm sorry, so very sorry, Hannah."

"I know." She did. She just needed to hear him say it. "No point in dredging up the past this way. It's done and gone."

They'd walked full circle, coming back to the restaurant's parking lot. He nodded toward it. "Want to go back and finish our meal?"

"You think it's still there?" They'd been walking for at least fifteen minutes. "They've probably cleared the table by now."

"Only one way to find out." Jackson put his hand out to her.

After a moment's hesitation, Hannah placed her hand into it. "I guess I'm game if you are."

The table, they discovered, was still just as they left it. Their server had obviously thought they were still on the dance floor. When they walked past him from the direction of the front entrance, he looked at them oddly. Waiting until they were seated, he approached and asked if they wanted something else instead.

"Just dessert," Jackson said, then looked at Hannah. "Unless you—"

The knot that had been in her stomach had shrunk some. Enough to slide in a rich piece of cake, or at least ice cream.

"Dessert sounds fine." She gave the server her order, then waited until he retreated after writing down Jackson's choice. "You still have that sweet tooth?"

"What?" He laughed. When he was a kid, he'd always felt that meals should begin with dessert and if there was any room left over, then something healthy should be added. As a doctor, he was forced, at least in theory, to reverse his preference. "Eating Gertie's cookies didn't convince you?"

"I guess you do at that." She thought of the unexpected afternoon treat. "The kids loved having you there today, reading to them. I'd forgotten how much patience you had."

The server returned with a giant slice of cake that would have confounded a lesser man. Jackson merely looked at it with relish. "What do you mean?"

She raised her long spoon and began diminishing the sundae that had been placed before her. "That semester you tried to teach me calculus."

"Oh, yeah. As I remember it, I didn't try. I succeeded."

"Only after long, harrowing hours." Perhaps a little longer than was truly necessary, but she had looked forward to their sessions. "Ethan gave up on me, but you didn't."

"I thought of it as a challenge. And you needed to pass the course."

What she had needed, Hannah remembered, was him. She'd actually learned the concepts a great deal faster than she'd let on. But she'd enjoyed being tutored by him, enjoyed knowing that Jackson was coming over for a couple of hours to try to drum calculus theory into her head.

"Well I did, thanks to you." Hannah looked at him over her spoon, debating, then plunging forward. "Where did you go when you left?"

"New York."

"Wow." The large city was a completely different world from Storkville. "You really did want to get lost, didn't you?"

"I wanted to be busy," he corrected. "And I had been offered a position at one of the teaching hospitals there."

He'd never told her. "To teach?"

He laughed. Obviously she had more regard for his abilities than he'd had. "To learn. And I did. I learned a great deal."

"Well, we can certainly use all that knowledge right here in Storkville. It looks like we're going to have a fresh flock of babies here, soon. Not the least of which is my cousin Gwenyth's."

"So she's staying on?"

Hannah nodded. "She's determined. Gertie helped her find her own place. It's right next to Ben Crowe's ranch. I promised to help her move in on the weekend, not that there's going to be a lot to move in."

"Need help?"

"Always."

He inclined his head. "Count me in."

Her smile was wide, drawing him in. "I was hoping you'd say that."

He stopped sampling his dessert. "So we're officially friends again?"

"I never stopped being your friend, Jackson. Even when I thought you'd stopped being mine."

He believed her. It made grappling with his feelings that much harder.

Chapter Nine

Jackson wasn't quite sure how he had got himself roped into this. One minute, he was dropping by the daycare center as had become his habit, the next minute, he was knee-deep in strange party favors, lopsided cardboard cartoon characters, and enough red-white-and-blue crepe paper ribbon to cordon off Central Park from the rest of New York City.

Hannah, it became rapidly apparent, was in the middle of getting ready for the first birthday party to be held at the daycare center, and it was obviously going to be a major event.

It had been after hours when he'd arrived and she had pulled him into the front room immediately. He'd thought there was some sort of an emergency until he saw all the disassembled party decorations. She put him to work cutting out an endless parade of dancing elves who were, eventually, going to find their way along the walls.

Sitting at the coffee table, he paused to look at her beside him. She was cutting out a squadron of forest animals. The party boy, she'd informed him, loved animals. And Hannah always aimed to please.

Her hair kept falling into her face as she concentrated, and she kept pushing it back, only to have it fall again. An odd feeling was shimmering through him. He realized that it was contentment. "You know, I'd forgotten about this."

She spared him a quick glance, then looked back at what she was doing. She'd already nicked three fingers and didn't want to make it a complete set if she could help it. "Forgotten about what?"

He laughed. The entire area was covered with party crafts. Until half an hour ago when the last of the children had gone home with their parents, she'd had all her charges engaged in what looked like a cottage industry about to take off. They'd been excited about it, too. Because she had been.

He leaned over and pushed back the wayward strand behind her ear. "About how overboard you can get when it comes to holidays and birthdays."

"I do not go overboard," she sniffed. Then honesty had her adding, "Exactly."

"Yeah, you do," he told her fondly, finishing another nimble-footed elf. He took a second to admire his work before starting on the next one. "Don't you think this is a bit much for pre-schoolers?"

"This is exactly right for pre-schoolers. I can't wait for Halloween to come. Then I'll show you overboard."

He bet she would, too. "I repeat, don't you think it's a bit much for pre-schoolers?"

"No," she protested. "They're the ones who enjoy it most of all, who are still into the magic of it."

He raised a brow as he glanced her way. "Aren't you getting Halloween confused with Christmas?"

She laughed. To her, it was all magic because children were magic. And because each holiday was filled with the magic of warm memories. "Nope. Believe me, I get nothing confused with Christmas." She grinned impishly. "Maybe you should brace yourself."

He looked at her, wondering what she was up to. "For what?"

"For Christmas—and to be utterly overwhelmed." She went all out for Christmas, starting at the very beginning of the month and leaving all the decorations up until after New Year's. Ethan had always said that she did too much, but when he'd said it, it had sounded far more like complaining than when Jackson had said it just now.

Overwhelmed. That would be the word for it, he thought, trying not to look as if he was staring at her. "That happened the first time you ever walked into my life."

He was teasing her now, she thought. "We went to elementary school together."

"Yeah, I know." Carefully, he completed the elf's feet before going on to easier details.

She stopped cutting, mystified. "How could you possibility remember back that far?"

"I remember." Then, because he sensed she didn't believe him, he went on to prove it to her. "You had on a pink dress and a pink bow in your hair. I remember looking at you and thinking that you looked twice as sweet as cotton candy.''

Now she knew he was teasing her. ''Five-year-old boys don't think like that.''

''How would you know?'' He sent her a smug look. ''Ever been a five-year-old boy?''

''No.'' That had nothing to do with it. She'd been around them enough, volunteering her time at the hospital children's ward before she'd ever had the opportunity to have her own daycare center.

''Then don't pretend to know what they're thinking. Besides,'' he added, ''it was a harmless enough thought then.''

''Then?'' she echoed. As in the difference between then and now? Hannah looked at him more closely, the cut-outs temporarily forgotten. ''Does that mean it's not harmless now?''

That had been a slip. Jackson laughed at her quick uptake. ''You know, for a daycare center owner, you ask questions like an interrogating district attorney. There. Done,'' he pronounced, retiring his scissors.

He did nice work, she thought, surveying the long chain of elves. Reaching over to the three rolls of crepe paper closest to her, she presented them to him. ''Right, now the D.A. would like you to start hanging streamers.'' She pointed vaguely around the room, leaving it up to his imagination where to place them.

Jackson looked down at the rolls dubiously. ''I hope you don't mean all over the house.'' He looked around. ''This is one big house, Hannah.''

She grinned. ''Afraid of a little work?''

''No...but this is one big house,'' he repeated.

''Just do the first floor and the banister, that'll be

enough. I'll do the outside of the house tomorrow morning.'' There was a sign she'd stayed up making last night that she knew would gladden Anthony's heart. The little boy had lost his mother this year and his father was really worried about his son facing the first birthday without her. Hannah was determined to do whatever she could to make it a happy occasion for the six-year-old.

"You know," Jackson said, twisting the three strands together awkwardly, "this isn't exactly a major holiday." Two of the rolls fell from his hand, unraveling as they went.

Hannah stooped to retrieve them. Holding one, she quickly rewound the other, making her way to Jackson as she went. "That all depends."

"On what?" he wanted to know.

"On whether it's your birthday or not." She thrust the red roll into his hands and began rewinding the white one.

"If it were my birthday, I wouldn't want any fuss."

She raised her eyes to his. "Yes, I remember." And then a smile curved her mouth. "Now tell me if I ever listened."

The question evoked warm memories. It had been Hannah who had always made him feel special. "No, I can't say you ever did." He surveyed the room, trying to envision how she could outdo herself when Halloween came along. "You really going to do more for Halloween?"

"You bet. I plan to start decorating in the middle of October—"

"Why, in heaven's name?" he asked, cutting her

off. "You're not the local department store, you don't have to sell anyone on anything."

She stared at him. What did that have to do with anything? "It's not about selling, it's about festivities."

He snorted. "Halloween is about candy and getting sick on it. And doing what you shouldn't."

He had her there. "That one you're going to have to explain."

Reunited with the second runaway roll of crepe paper, he began twisting the chain again. "Think about it. All year long, you tell kids not to talk to strangers, not to take candy from people, and then one night a year, you tell them that it's okay to go out and collect as much as they can carry, blackmailing people while they're at it."

Hannah looked at him uncertainly. "Blackmailing?"

"Sure." His fingers were getting red and blue from the crepe paper. Jackson wiped them on his jeans and continued twisting the strands. "What else would you call yelling out 'trick or treat?'"

Someone had siphoned all the fun out of the Jackson she had known. "Boy, you must be a regular joy to be around when Christmas comes, Ebenezer. Tell me, what did the big city do to you?"

Living in New York had only honed his attitude. It was living in a home with no joy that had initially forged the feelings he now had. Although, for a little while, when he had interacted with Hannah and her family, that attitude had been placed on temporary hold.

"Opened my eyes up a little more," he told her.

She shook her head, taking the crepe paper rolls from him. He was creating tight curls rather than festive chains. Quickly, she began to braid the three strands together. Long chains began to fall from her fast moving fingers. "I don't know about your eyes, but it certainly sucked out your soul."

No, he thought. My soul I left behind me when I left Storkville.

Suddenly, she wanted to make him smile, to wipe away that serious look from his eyes. "Guess it's my sworn duty to get it back for you. Here." Quickly, she dipped into the candy bowl on the coffee table and peeled away the wrappings on a miniature candy bar. Then, as he began to protest, she popped it into his mouth. "Something to start the process and sweeten you up."

Jackson removed the chocolate from between his lips, holding it in his fingers. "I don't need sweetening. Guys aren't supposed to be sweet."

"Says who?" She stopped braiding and looked at the candy bar in his fingers. "Now look, it's melting in your hand. Eat it." With a small salute, he returned it to his mouth and consumed it—then froze as she playfully took hold of his wrist and proceeded to lick the melted chocolate from his two fingers. "There, now you won't get chocolate on anything."

When she raised her eyes to his, the playful expression slipped away from her face. In its place, as sudden as a twister rising from nowhere, was an urgent longing that wound all through her. What she saw in his eyes was desire. The same kind of desire she felt rattling the bars of her restraint.

"Except, maybe you," he murmured, bringing his mouth down to hers.

She could taste the chocolate. Taste, too, the wild, sharp tang of passion mixed with desire on his mouth. The chain she had been braiding so swiftly fell from her lax fingers, sinking to the floor in a partially unraveled heap. It was the furthest thing from her mind as she wound her arms around Jackson's neck, wound her thoughts completely around the man who had occupied her mind and her heart for all these years.

Jackson deepened the kiss, tightened the embrace. Did she have any idea what she did to him? Any inkling of how crazy she made him, standing there before him, all pure and tempting?

"I thought we were decorating for Anthony's birthday, not Valentine's Day," Gertie quipped as she walked in, carrying a box of more cute little stuffed forest creatures she'd unearthed in her own basement. Her children had played with them in their day. Amazingly enough, they were still in pretty good shape. She plunked the box down on the sofa beside the coffee table. "Thought you might want these." Her eyes twinkled with approval behind her glasses. "Didn't realize you were testing each other's lips for future apple-dunking contests."

Flustered, running her hand through her hair, Hannah shot her a warning look. "Gertie—"

The older woman held up her hand in front of her, as if to shield her eyes. "Sorry, the light's too bright in here for me to stay. I'll just go and see about feeding the twins."

The twins. How could she have forgotten that it was their dinnertime? Chagrined, she quickly stepped away from Jackson and crossed to the portable play-pen where the twins were playing. "I should be doing that."

Following her, Gertie shook her head. She glanced over her shoulder at Jackson. "I'd say you had your hands pretty full, Hannah. Not that I can blame you."

If her cheeks got any redder, she was going to spontaneously combust, Hannah thought ruefully. "That's all right, Gertie. Why don't you see about helping out with the birthday decorations instead? I like feeding the babies."

"She has a weakness for strained carrots in her hair," Gertie confided to Jackson.

Taking an interest, and welcoming the chance to change the topic and make a quick getaway from the decorations, he joined Hannah at the playpen. He looked down at the twins. Today, he hadn't even bothered going through the charade of examining them. The twins were healthy and doing well.

"They're not eating well?"

"They're eating," Hannah replied, bending over to pick up Sammy. The little boy smiled gleefully as she took him into her arms. "Like typical babies. Half goes into their stomachs, half they wear. It's a trade-off."

Jackson pretended to look skeptical. "As their doctor, I should take part in their feeding at least once, make sure that they're getting their proper nutrition."

She welcomed his company. Too much, she knew, but she'd deal with that at another time. Right now, she just wanted to enjoy having Jackson near her.

There was no denying how much she cared about him. Words hadn't passed between them about that, at least not about how she felt about him at the present moment. She'd only confessed to having had a crush on him in the past. They probably never would talk about the present, which was fine with her. It was far less embarrassing that way.

But that didn't alter the facts any. And the fact was that she loved him. And always would.

If Jackson wasn't sleepwalking through his life, he'd realize that, she thought. But it was better this way, because if they talked about it, if one of them said the words out loud, then Jackson might feel compelled to tell her something noble, like he was very flattered, but—

That awful word: *but*. Positive that he would use it, Hannah wasn't sure if she was up to hearing it. What she couldn't cope with was better left alone.

Turning, she handed Sammy to him then picked up Steffie. "Okay, just remember you asked for this," she warned.

Yes, he thought, following her into the kitchen, he had.

"So, what's on the menu tonight?" he asked, looking around.

There were two high chairs at the table where two chairs had once been. The latter were now standing against the far wall, two retired sentries still at attention, still waiting to be pressed into duty. The table, like the house, was from another era and looked out of place beside the high chairs—and the profusion of decorations that seemed to be everywhere in the room.

Jackson's eyes widened as he turned to look at Hannah. "My God, you've struck here, too."

"Strained lamb stew and yes, I did," Hannah replied, answering both his question and his statement as she slid Steffie into her high chair and snapped the belt around her middle, securing her in place. Jackson echoed her movements with Sammy. "Anthony might walk in here. I just wanted to make sure that the whole house looked festive to him. It's the least I can do."

"Least?" he echoed.

"Because he's facing this without his mother for the first time. His father told me she always used to make a fuss." She gave a small half shrug, awkward with having to explain herself. "I just want him to be happy."

She really was something else, he thought. "You want the whole world to be happy."

Her eyes met his. "Nothing wrong with that."

"No," he agreed. "Nothing wrong with that." It was just impossible, that was all, he added silently.

She moved to the stove to check on the two jars that Gertie had left warming. "I just wish I had a little more time to clean the place up properly, but I've been so busy. Do you realize that I haven't even made a dent in the attic?"

To him, attics were for storing, not for cleaning. "Why don't you just leave the door closed and forget about it?"

She looked at him over her shoulder. "Forget about it? I'm looking forward to it. There're some old trunks up there I haven't had a chance to open up yet. I'm saving that for a special treat."

"Treat?" Jackson didn't think of rifling through old, musty trunks as something to look forward to.

"Sure, they're probably full of old memories." Turning the burner off, she gingerly removed the jars then tested the contents of both by spooning a drop from each onto the inside of her wrist. Satisfied with the temperature, she brought the jars over to the table. "Maybe Aunt Jane even kept diaries."

Jackson took the spoon Hannah handed him and picked up one of the jars from the table. "Isn't that an invasion of privacy?"

"Only if my great-aunt were alive. Now that she's gone, it's just like sharing the important parts of her life with her."

The workings of her mind left him in bemused awe. Coaxing the spoon between Sammy's lips, Jackson could only shake his head. "Like I said, you should have been a lawyer. You're completely wasted as a daycare center owner."

Steffie's appetite was in rare form tonight, she noted. Hannah could hardly get the spoon to the baby fast enough. "Oh, I don't know. I find working with the children pretty fulfilling. As well as exhausting."

He smiled as Sammy finally opened his mouth wider. "You do seem to have a flair for it. Praise for you is running pretty high."

"Oh?" She looked at him. What had he heard? "Whose?"

"The mothers of some of the children in your center." More than a few had gone out of their way to tell him how much happier their children seemed to be now that they were attending the daycare center. "They can't say enough about you."

Hannah beamed. It was nice hearing that her efforts were appreciated. "Really?"

"Really." He glanced in her direction, seeing her smile. "You had to know you were doing a good job."

"Well, yes, I knew," she admitted. "But it's nice to know that it's appreciated. And that what I'm doing is making a difference in someone's life."

That, he would have thought, went without saying. The Hannah he knew was bright enough to intuit that. "Just knowing that they can leave their children in the care of someone who they trust, who they know is responsible and loving lifts a great weight off their shoulders."

Using the bib she'd tied on Steffie, she cleaned the little girl's very messy chin. "That's me, the weight lifter." He laughed and she looked at him. "What?"

"Nothing, I just thought that might be a good costume."

"Costume?" She was immediately interested. "For what?"

Jackson saw the alert look in her eyes and, too late, realized his mistake. "Never mind."

"Tell me," she prodded. "I won't make you put up any more streamers."

"You always did have a flair for bribery." She'd probably hear about it anyway, he reasoned. "The hospital's throwing a costume party next week to welcome the new director to the staff."

"Costume party? What are you going as?"

The whole thing was pure foolishness and he didn't have time for it. "The invisible man."

Her eyes narrowed. "You're not going."

Jackson inclined his head. "Good guess."

"But you have to go," she insisted. "You don't want to insult the new director, do you?"

Jackson didn't particularly care about the director one way or another as long as the man didn't interfere with his relationship with his patients. "What I don't want is to feel like an idiot."

She grinned. "You won't. Just leave everything to me."

Jackson sighed. "Oh, all right."

That, he realized later, was his first mistake.

Chapter Ten

"Aren't pirates supposed to have a wooden leg, a patch over one eye and a parrot on their shoulder?"

Feeling decidedly uncomfortable, Jackson walked out of the guest room where he'd gone to put on the costume that Hannah had got for him for the party. He was on the verge of phoning in his apologies, or simply taking his chances being branded a no-show. It wasn't as if his career depended on attending.

Anything seemed better than walking around outside like this.

And then he saw her, and his thoughts about attending began to change radically. He hadn't realized that while he was struggling with his sense of values and putting on his costume, she'd be putting on hers.

Jackson contracted a severe case of dry mouth as he surveyed the way her blouse dipped low with every breath she exhaled. Walking over hot coals would be worth seeing her like this.

He looked nothing short of fantastic. She'd known he would the moment she'd seen the pirate's costume in the shop. The part suited him far better than that of a knight in shining armor, the costume she'd been considering until she saw this one. There was something very roguish about Jackson that this brought out in spades.

"Not my pirates." Tucking her tambourine under her arm, Hannah adjusted the sword at his hip. "My pirates have twenty-twenty vision in their mesmerizing blue eyes and two feet, not one. And as for the parrot, it would definitely interfere when they stopped to kiss the woman they rescued from another pirate king's ship." She grinned mischievously, adding, "A pirate king who had a patch over his eye, a wooden leg and a parrot."

He laughed shortly, looking himself over critically in the mirror that hung above the carved table in the hall. He supposed he didn't look like a complete fool—and if nothing else, his going to this function did seem to make Hannah happy.

"Sounds more like a Hollywood version than something out of Robert Louis Stevenson."

Hannah shrugged nonchalantly. She was trying very hard not to stare, but his pirate's shirt was open almost to his waist, and the view from where she stood was disarming, to put it mildly. "You have your fantasies, I'll have mine."

He looked at her standing beside him in the mirror. "Is that what this is?" Jackson turned toward her, a warm smile on his lips. "A fantasy of yours? To be attending a hospital function with a man wearing wide pants, high-heeled boots and a shirt with sleeves big enough to hide three or four of his patients in?''

''Sure,'' she answered glibly, turning her face up to his, ''what's yours?''

His eyes washed over her. With her wrists and neck laden down with thin golden chains, her chestnut hair swirling about her like a wayward autumn breeze, Hannah looked every inch the gypsy. He could almost hear her reading fortunes. He knew what he'd like his to be.

''To be attending a hospital function with a woman dressed in a swirling red skirt and a gaily colored scarf jauntily tied at her waist.''

In reply, Hannah raised the tambourine she was holding and hit it rhythmically with the heel of her hand. She shook it so that the tiny cymbals all along its perimeter chimed in. ''Then I'm happy to be able to fulfill your wish.''

If only, he thought.

Dragging himself out of his mental revelry, Jackson looked down at the costume and wondered if the sword was going to trip him up during the evening. Or if he'd wind up hitting someone with the scabbard. ''My real wish is to get out of these clothes.''

Her grin widened as her eyes began to sparkle with humor. ''Careful, doctor, you have a reputation to maintain.''

When she looked at him like that, he nearly swallowed his tongue. Pretending to be oblivious was next to impossible so he didn't even try. ''Just when did you get this damn sexy?''

Hannah shrugged, sending her peasant blouse slipping seductively off her shoulder. As she moved it back into place, the look in his eyes registered, pleasing her beyond words. The compliment he'd just paid her, after the years of self doubts she'd endured, did her far more good than he could ever begin to guess.

Her laugh was low and seductive as she went to get the long fringed shawl that she'd chosen to go with the costume. "Maybe it's the full moon that brings it out of me."

Opening the front door, Jackson pointed toward the sky. "That's a crescent moon."

"So it is." Undaunted, Hannah laughed. "You should see me when it gets full."

He resisted the urge to kiss her, knowing that if he gave in, they might never make it through the front door. Certainly not to the party. "You're really something else, you know that?"

He was stalling. She placed both hands to his back and pushed him through the doorway. "And you are going to make us late if we stand here talking any longer."

So much for the best laid plans of mice and men, he thought with an inward sigh. "You know, I really don't want to go."

What she knew was that this function was important and that there were certain rules of protocol to follow, even for a former rebel like Jackson Caldwell. She figured that since he'd told her about the invitation, that meant that deep down at least part of him wanted her to talk him into going. Hannah had never shirked a duty, and she wasn't about to begin now with Jackson.

Calling out a final good night to Gertie, who'd volunteered to remain with Gwenyth to baby-sit and was upstairs bathing the twins, Hannah slipped her arm through Jackson's. "You really don't want to offend the new director right off the bat, do you? Besides, it'll be fun."

Jackson frowned. "Not my definition of fun."

But, oddly enough, it was.

On the whole, he'd never really cared for any kind of formal parties. He'd seen far too many of them in his parents' house. People milling around, pretending to have fun while making empty conversation as they held cocktail glasses they were constantly refilling. People who came with one person while trying to arrange a tryst with another. He preferred dealing with people on a one-to-one basis. If it were up to him, parties in general would have been outlawed. And the first on the list would have been costume parties.

And yet, he was having a good time, almost against his will.

There was just something about experiencing the evening through Hannah's eyes that consequently, no matter how much he resisted it at first, made him enjoy himself.

In a way, it was as if he was truly seeing her for the first time. People seemed to gravitate toward her because she shone so brightly. She took an avid interest in everything and everyone. Being near her just naturally seemed to make everything better. His mood included.

He watched as she danced with the new director and Jackson suddenly found himself growing jealous of a balding, fifty-seven-year-old, out-of-shape man in a Robin Hood costume because Hannah was laughing at something he had just said to her.

If anyone had been privy to his mind, they would have said he was in love, Jackson mused. He had to do something about that.

But not tonight.

"You certainly know how to work a room," he murmured to Hannah as he came up next to her. The director's attention had been temporarily commandeered by the head nurse dressed as a duchess. The woman whisked the breathless Robin Hood away. Jackson handed Hannah a cup of punch.

She took the cup in both hands and held it first before sipping. "What do you mean?"

"Everywhere I turn, I hear people mentioning your name." He nodded at the man who had just relinquished her. "The director thinks you'd be wonderful at fund-raising. He's about this far," Jackson held his thumb and forefinger a half-inch apart, "from offering you a position with the hospital."

That was flattering, but she shook her head. "Not interested."

Jackson played devil's advocate. "You never know. The offer might come with a lucrative benefits package, not to mention a tempting salary."

"I don't need a lucrative benefits package, I'm young and alone," she pointed out, trying not to dwell on the deep holes those words dug within her, "and there are far more important things in life than a salary, tempting or otherwise." She heard Jackson laugh as she brought the cup to her lips. "What?"

Her answer had pleased him a great deal. "You would have been a revelation to my father. He felt that there was nothing more important than money.'' His mouth hardened as he thought of the countless affairs that had littered his father's life—and stained his mother's. Jackson looked off into space. "Not even momentary lapses into recreational fields.''

Lost, Hannah tugged on his sleeve until he looked at her again. "How's that again?''

"Nothing,'' he said, waving his thoughts away. This was no time to be talking about his father. "So, that's it?'' He studied her face, looking for some indication whether she was serious or strictly making conversation. "You're going to be running a daycare center for the rest of your life?''

She finished her punch, but continued to hold the cup in her hands. Maybe it was the punch that made her hear it, but she didn't like his implication. "You make it sound insignificant.''

He hadn't meant to offend her, he'd just thought that her goals were loftier. "Not insignificant, just not, well, big,'' he said for lack of a better word.

Cocking her head, she looked at him, the empty cup dangling from her fingertips. "Influencing children's lives, giving them a warm, solid base, that isn't big to you?''

It looked as if he was treading on sacred territory. Jackson backtracked. "I didn't mean that.''

"I should hope not.'' She managed to say it before the smile slipped out, betraying her. Jackson knew he was off the hook.

Because the strongest thing Hannah ever drank was an occasional glass of very weak wine, the punch was having more of an effect on her than it should have. Too late she discovered that the fruity taste that had tantalized her tongue was not all due to fruit obtained in the produce section of her local grocery store. A warm glow lit in her stomach in response to the look Jackson was giving her.

Her eyes teased his. "Dance with me, Jackson." She lifted her hands to his, waiting. "Make me feel as pretty as you made me sound earlier tonight."

He gladly took her into his arms. Holding her here, in front of all these people, was safe. He couldn't do anything that might lead to something else, not here. And if holding her close to him like this constituted sweet agony, so be it. At least he was holding her.

"You don't need a press agent for that, Hannah. You are pretty." And then, mid-sentence, he changed his mind. "No, I take it back. You're not pretty."

The tune coming from the orchestra comprised predominantly of high-school seniors in music class barely registered. "I'm not?"

"No, you're not. Wild flowers are pretty." He leaned his face into hers, whispering against her ear. "Roses are beautiful. And you, Hannah Dawson Brady, are definitely a rose."

She could feel her eyes stinging. No one had ever said anything that lovely to her before. Not even Ethan when he was trying to flatter her. "Now you're going to make me cry."

She wasn't kidding, he realized. He wished he had a handkerchief, but his costume hadn't come with pockets. "Don't do that. I'll have fourteen people in the immediate vicinity pummel me to the ground if they see you crying while you're dancing with me."

The entreaty had done the trick, lightening the mood. She laughed. "You say the silliest things."

He smiled into her eyes. "Must be the company I keep." Jackson pressed his cheek against her hair, for a moment just steeping himself in the scent and feel of her. He felt his senses becoming intoxicated. "What's that you're wearing?"

Nestled within the warmth of his embrace, she felt as if she was dancing in a dream. "Clothes."

He almost laughed and without thinking, kissed her hair. "No, I mean what's that scent?"

Ripples of pleasure undulated through her. She could feel his breath on her skin. "Punch?"

She could taste it, feel it, every time she exhaled. Or was that simply her being intoxicated by him? She wasn't sure, but she was more than willing to carry out experiments to find out.

She was slightly tipsy, he thought, and all the more adorable for it. "No, I mean the perfume you're wearing. What is it?"

She thought for a second, taking mental inventory. "Maybe that's the herbal shampoo," she guessed, looking up at him. "I'm not wearing any perfume."

And maybe, he thought, it was just the essence of her that filled his senses. Maybe it was just the smell of her skin, of her hair, of her, that was making him crazy.

He held her closer as they danced.

The trip back to her house seemed to end before it had begun. Hannah had no sooner sat back, leaning against the headrest, her eyes slipping closed, than she was opening them again. It was time to get out of the car.

She tried not to be too obvious as she stretched,

getting the kinks out of her shoulders. She turned to Jackson. "Now, aren't you glad I made you go?"

He pretended to hold on to the lie, knowing she knew better. "No."

"Your nose is growing." She touched it as she made the announcement, leaning over the emergency brake, causing emergencies of her own in his blood as he looked at her and her receding blouse.

This had to be some kind of a celestial test he decided, and if he wasn't careful, he was going to be flunking. Big time.

"Okay." Getting out, he rounded the hood and opened her door for her. "I'm glad you made me go." Still, he wanted her clear on why he was glad he'd gone. "But it was only a good time because you were there."

"Good." Taking his hand, she allowed him to help her out. "Perfect thing to say." She rose to her feet, then remained where she stood for a second. "Especially to a woman who's having trouble feeling her legs."

"Did we dance too much?" he asked.

She shook her head. "No, you can never dance too much. But on the subject of too much, I think maybe I did have too much punch."

Surprised, he looked at her incredulously. Up until now, he'd assumed she was just tired. "Two glasses over the course of an entire evening is hardly too much to drink."

She pointed toward the front porch and the legion of steps that had formed in her absence. "Then why did the stairs suddenly get steeper and taller?"

He looked at them and then laughed, playing along.

"Maybe it's the lighting." Then, in the spirit of the evening and the costume he was wearing, he went with an impulse. "But I tell you what, there's a perfectly simple solution to this navigation problem you seem to think you have."

"Oh?" She raised her eyes to look at him, trying to keep the buzzing in her head at a minimum. "What?"

"This."

The next moment, Hannah found herself being scooped up in his arms. A thrill ricocheted through her before she thought to protest. "Wait, you'll hurt your back."

He mustered a wounded look. "Are you trying to insult my manhood?"

"Never," she breathed. Settling in, she twined her arms around his neck and sighed in contentment as he carried her up the porch steps.

"Good, because a ten-year-old, out-of-shape weakling could carry you up the stairs, Hannah. I've got paperweights that weigh more than you do."

"You must have a lot of paper on your desk," she murmured, her breath warm against his chest as she rested her head there.

She closed her eyes, absorbing the sweet sensation of feeling him carry her up the stairs to her front door. Of the rhythmic beating of his heart. With a sigh, she waited for him to set her down.

When he didn't she opened her eyes to look at him. "What?"

He wanted to go on holding her just a little longer. "Just thinking."

He sounded so serious. "What?"

If he told her, the moment would end. Maybe she'd even be annoyed with him. He wouldn't blame her if she were. "Thoughts I shouldn't be."

"Maybe you shouldn't be thinking them," she told him quietly as he set her down and her feet touched the porch. Feeling oddly confident, she took out her key. "Maybe you should be doing something about them instead."

The key that he took from her nearly slipped through his fingers as he heard her say words he fervently wished he could obey. Jackson turned his back to her as he unlocked her door.

"You don't know what you're saying, Hannah." Unlocking the door, he stood back to let her enter first.

"I think I do." She walked into the foyer. There was only one lone lamp on, casting a dim pool of light on the Oriental rug. Her heart began to pound. "I haven't had that much punch, if that's what you're thinking."

When she looked at him like that, he felt himself sinking into her eyes. "What I'm thinking is that I want you, Hannah. And I shouldn't."

"Why?" The word hung in the air between them as she turned her face up to his. "Is wanting me such a terrible thing?"

"Yes." He was losing, damn it. Losing the struggle with honor, with decency. "No."

She swallowed, silently willing him to make love with her. To take her now and put an end to the ache in her soul. "Which is it?"

"Depends on who you are," he told her softly, his fingers tangling in her hair. "Me. Or you."

"I'm me," she told him, her voice hardly above an inviting whisper. "And for me, having you want me isn't a terrible thing." She drew the only conclusion she could. And prayed he'd tell her that she was wrong. "That means it must be a terrible thing for you."

"Hannah, this isn't a game."

She'd never believed that, not for a moment. The stakes were far too high for it to be a game to her. Her eyes searched his face for a clue as to what he was thinking. "But there will be winners and losers, won't there?"

"Yes." Jackson framed her face, wanting her more than he wanted to wake up the next morning. "There will be winners and losers. And I don't want you to be a loser."

She wouldn't be, not if he made love with her. Not if she could, just once, feel that he was hers. She had been his for so very long.

"Put your money where your mouth is," she coaxed, her lips a fraction away from his.

He surrendered. "I'd rather put my mouth where your mouth is."

"That, too," she whispered.

Rising up on her toes, Hannah ended the internal debate for him by sealing her mouth to his.

The instant she did, Jackson pulled her urgently into his arms, unleashing the wild, erotic emotions that had been beating their wings so wildly within him.

More than anything in the world, he wanted to make love with her. To take her and make her his once and for all, the way he already had a hundred, no, a thousand times in his mind. Since before the days when Ethan had had any claim to her. Since before the days when he knew he couldn't taint her this way.

But tonight, there was something about her, about the uninhibited look in her eyes. Something about the feel of her body as she'd held it against his while they were dancing.

Something about her.

Jackson was helpless to fight off the urgent demands of his own body when faced with the warm, open invitation of hers.

Standing in the darkened foyer, he felt himself getting lost in the taste of her mouth, the sweetness of her breath, the softness of her body as it molded itself to his.

He kissed her over and over again, his blood rushing, his mind swimming. Caressing the curves and swells that had so sorely tempted him all this time, he fought to keep from pulling her costume away from her. He wanted tonight to be memorable for her, not something to be filed away as a result of unchecked passion that had gotten out of hand. Above all, he wanted to pleasure her.

The sound of crying pierced the disjointed thoughts racing through his mind.

Gasping for air, Hannah drew her head back. How could she have forgotten? ''The twins.''

They weren't alone. The entreaties that were battering their souls and their bodies echoed off into the night, fading.

Chapter Eleven

The realization of what she had almost let herself do penetrated. She had completely forgotten herself. Completely forgotten her obligations and had been a heartbeat away from giving in to needs that had been her daily companion for as long as she could remember—longer—at the expense of two small babies who were helpless without her.

"I'd—I'd better tell Gertie she's free to go," Hannah stammered.

"Speaking of going, I guess I should be doing the same," Jackson murmured.

Why was it, when he was with this woman, he forgot everything he had ever promised himself to abide by? Why did he constantly put himself into situations with her that made him yearn to turn his back on everything he knew he couldn't in good conscience forsake?

Unable to answer his own questions, Jackson began to cross to the door.

It shouldn't end like this, on such an awkward note. She didn't want him to think she was rejecting him or what had almost happened between them. What she was rejecting was the timing. Her hand on the banister, she paused. "Can I interest you in a cup of coffee?"

She could interest him in a great many things, coffee only being at the end of the long list, he thought. He shook his head. Jackson had to admit, at least to himself, that he was in far deeper than he'd ever imagined he would be. Resisting Hannah was becoming increasingly more difficult each time he was faced with the temptation.

This time the babies had come to his rescue, so to speak. The next time, there might not be a wake-up call coming to the aid of his lax conscience at the eleventh hour. The next time, he might give in and make love with Hannah.

And become hopelessly caught in a tender, tempting trap he had absolutely no business being in.

Jackson sighed inwardly. Once he was with Hannah, it seemed almost impossible to do the right thing. Heaven knew, it was almost humanly impossible to keep her at arms' length.

Maybe then, a small voice within him whispered, you shouldn't be around Hannah.

"Coffee sounds great, but it'll only keep me awake and it's getting late," he said opening the door. "And I've got to be at the hospital early tomorrow morning."

It was a lie, but it was the best he could do with

his brain scrambled this way. He wasn't accustomed to lying, especially not to her.

Hannah looked at him in silence. He was lying. She could feel it even if she couldn't understand why. Was she that unappealing to him? Why did he always stop himself at the last moment, as if he were suddenly thinking better of what he was about to do? As if he realized that he'd almost done something stupid?

The thought hurt and she put it out of her mind. But the feeling lingered. She hadn't been woman enough for Ethan to keep him from looking elsewhere for company and sensual pleasure. Was the same true with Jackson? Didn't he find her attractive enough at least to try to make her change her mind? To try to get her to go to bed with him? If one of the babies hadn't cried, if Gertie hadn't been here, would she have wound up being embarrassed anyway, not by what she'd wanted to do, but by what Jackson didn't want to do?

"Wouldn't want to interfere with your hours," she agreed woodenly. She suddenly realized that he was still wearing the pirate costume she'd rented for him. "Um, you can bring the costume back tomorrow if you like—or whenever you want to stop by," she added, afraid that he might think she was taking his presence in her life for granted.

Because she was.

Not for granted, never for granted, but she'd come to expect it and look forward to it the way someone looked forward to being in the presence of a secret treasure that came into their lives every so often.

Jackson looked down at himself, chagrined at the oversight. How the hell could a man forget he was wearing a billowing shirt and wide trousers? Unless, he thought, that man had just kissed Hannah.

There was no sense in going home like this, not when his clothes were here. Shrugging out of the shirt, he began walking toward the guest room where he'd left his clothes. ''No, I might as well get this over with now. I'll just go into the other bedroom and take the rest of this off—''

The sharp intake of breath had them both looking up the stairs to the source. Their eyes locked with Gertie's. Even at this distance, it was easy to see that Gertie's were filled with amused, unabashed pleasure.

She waved them both back to what she presumed they were about to do. ''Sorry, didn't mean to walk in on anything.''

It didn't take a clairvoyant to know what Gertie was thinking. ''You didn't,'' Hannah told her quickly, eager to clear up the misunderstanding before it got out of hand. ''It's not what you're thinking.''

''Thinking?'' Gertie covered her bosom with clasped hands, the soul of innocence. ''Why I'm not thinking anything except that I can take the twins over to my place. Ask Gwenyth to come along, too.'' The gleam in her eye, so guileless a second ago, turned positively wicked. ''Give you and Jackson time to really play doctor and patient.''

''Gertie!'' Almost speechless, her throat drier than the summer desert at noon, Hannah could only manage to squeak her protest.

Gertie looked at her impatiently. ''Well, if I said 'make love together,' you'd get all flustered and pink.'' She gestured at Hannah's face. ''Just the way you are right now. Honestly, Hannah, you really are old enough to be doing this, you know." She looked meaningfully at Jackson, who, for his part, was torn between being amused and feeling sympathetic for what Hannah was going through.

"We're not *doing* anything," Hannah insisted. "Jackson's only taking off the costume so he can give it to me to take back to the rental shop tomorrow, along with mine."

A quick look at both their faces confirmed the explanation. Gertie shook her head in disappointment as she came down the stairs. "I just don't know what this new generation is coming to. If everyone were like you two, the town council'd have to change the name of this town again, this time to Dullsville."

Tired, upset and at a loss as to how to cope with all the emotions that had been let loose to run rampant through her, Hannah just kissed her soft cheek as Gertie came to the bottom of the stairs. "Thank you for watching the twins, but I could really do without the running commentary."

"No," Gertie pronounced astutely, looking at Hannah sternly before turning her condemning gaze on Jackson, "you can't."

The woman never saw him coming.

So preoccupied with her own thoughts, her own concerns, she never saw the man coming at her until it was too late. One minute she was making her way to the bed and breakfast inn just on the other side of the narrow street, the next minute he was coming at her.

A scream echoed in her throat as he plowed right into her, knocking her down.

He had no face.

Something black was wrapped around it, obscuring it from her vision. She thought she saw two dark eyes boring into her, but she couldn't be sure. It might have just been the sudden flare of panic burning into her.

And then the growing pain in her head blotted out everything before that, too, faded away.

"Can you hear me?" a voice asked.

She felt someone patting her hand and she struggled to open her eyes. When she did, she found herself looking up into the face of a woman she had never seen before. An older woman with short gray hair and a kindly, concerned smile that widened now with relief. The woman's eyes, bright and alert, seemed to be searching her face for something.

"Are you all right, my dear?"

Holding tightly to the woman's hand, she raised herself up. The immediate world refused to come into focus, spinning around her.

"I don't know," she answered hoarsely. Fear and confusion fought a duel with tiny, pointy straight pins, jabbing at her as she tried to pull her thoughts together.

And found that there were none to pull.

Panic superseded pain.

Eyes widening, she stared at the woman. Her voice shook when she asked, "Where am I?"

"This is Storkville, dear," the woman told her kindly. "And some horrible creature just bashed you over the head with some object he was holding and stole your purse and the overnight satchel you were carrying. I saw the whole thing," she volunteered, then added with a note of frustration, "but I couldn't stop him." She shook her head. "I don't even know who he was, he was wearing some kind of a stocking over his head like in those movies about bank robbers." The older woman shook her head again, lamenting. "Nothing like this has ever happened in Storkville before."

"Storkville?" she echoed, trying to sneak words past the excruciating pain in her head.

The name meant nothing to her. The details the other woman had just recited meant nothing to her. She didn't remember anyone hitting her, anyone taking something from her.

She couldn't remember anything.

"Yes, Storkville," the other woman repeated patiently. "Storkville, Nebraska, the most fertile city in the union, per capita, bar none." So saying, she beamed for a moment, then the smile faded as she bent closer to look her over. "I don't live far from here, dear. I was just out for my evening walk," she explained. "Why don't I take you home, make you a nice cup of hot tea? Unless you have a reservation at the bed and breakfast over there." She nodded vaguely over her shoulder at the street just beyond.

"No, I don't have a reservation," she answered hoarsely. At least, she didn't think she had one. She didn't know.

"Do you think you can walk, Emma?"

She looked up sharply at the woman. Did they know one another? Was the woman someone to her? "Why did you call me that?"

Looking perplexed, the woman touched something

at the base of her throat. A moment later, the sensation registered. Metal. She was wearing a gold chain necklace with a small oval medallion in the center.

"That's what it says engraved right there. 'Emma,'" the older woman read, then raised her eyes to her face. "That's your name, isn't it?"

The young woman looked at her blankly. "I don't know."

"I do declare, I haven't seen such a spate of excitement in this town since—can't remember when." Bustling into Jackson's office, Gertie commandeered the chair closest to his desk and settled in. "Thanks for seeing me, I brought you these." She took a small bag of cookies out of her purse and placed them on his desk. "Still a little warm," she said proudly. "I know how much you like them."

Jackson felt himself about to be steamrolled. This was the first time he'd seen Gertie since the night of the costume party when he and Hannah had almost made love. He'd made his decision on the way home that night. He'd been coming over too much, that had to stop for both their sakes.

No one could have been more surprised at Gertie's sudden appearance in his waiting room, requesting a private moment. He wondered if it had to do with Hannah.

He looked at the bag. "You really shouldn't have gone to the trouble."

"No trouble at all. I like baking. Like knowing what's going on, too," she added craftily. "Which is why I'd hate to be Tucker right now. That young man's still got his hands full, trying to find the twins' rightful parents and now he's got to deal with a mugger, too.'' Not standing on ceremony, she reached over and opened the bag she'd brought, taking out a cookie for herself. ''And I wasn't much help to him.''

He'd heard all about that. It was hard living in Storkville and not hearing local gossip making the rounds. The day after the mugging had happened, it had been the topic of conversation both in his office and at the hospital where the young woman had been brought. The poor woman had been diagnosed with temporary amnesia that, so far, gave no indication of fading.

''You gave him a description,'' Jackson pointed out.

Gertie snorted. ''Some description. A medium-sized, average-looking man with a nylon stocking on his head. If the streetlight hadn't hit that belt buckle of his with the deer head on it, there would have been nothing to set him apart from scores of other men.''

Jackson took a bite of one of Gertie's offerings and felt himself softening to the invasion. ''Not too many men running around out there with stockings pulled over their faces,'' he quipped. And then he leaned back in his chair and studied Gertie's face. ''But you didn't come just to talk to me about this mysterious woman. What's the real reason you came here, Gertie?''

Gertie purposely avoided his eyes. ''I wanted to ask your advice about my granddaughter.''

He was aware that she had several grandchildren. ''How old is she?''

Gertie waved her hand vaguely in the air. ''Young.'' And then she looked at him, leaning closer over the desk. "It's about her heart, Jackson." She took a deep breath. "It's in pain."

He paused, trying to remember the name of the pediatric cardiologist who was on staff at the hospital. "Dr. Campbell's the cardiac specialist, maybe you should be talking about this to him."

Gertie frowned. "It's not that kind of pain."

For a talkative woman, Gertie certainly did take a long time in getting to the point, Jackson thought. "Oh?"

Proceeding cautiously, Gertie nodded. "She's in love with someone."

If that was the case, he had no idea why Gertie was bringing this to his attention or what she thought he could do about it. "She told you?"

Gertie shrugged vaguely. "Some things, you just know. Anyway, she's in love with this really wonderful guy, but for some reason, they just can't seem to get together." She looked at him pointedly. "I don't think he's getting the message."

Obviously they weren't talking about adolescents. In which case this really was none of his business. "Maybe he doesn't have feelings for her."

"Oh, he has feelings," Gertie assured him firmly. "I know he has feelings. But the fact of the matter is, he didn't have the greatest relationship with his own family. Certainly not with his father and I don't think he thinks he knows how to have a relationship with a woman. Meanwhile, she—my granddaughter—" Gertie emphasized "—is just pining away in silence." Her eyes pinned him. "What can I do to help them?"

Okay, so this was about him. It had taken Jackson

a minute there, probably because he was dumb-founded that Gertie had taken it upon herself to act like some kind of go-between. He sincerely doubted that Hannah had put her up to this. Hannah would probably be mortified if she knew.

"Nothing," he told her firmly, returning her look. "There is nothing you can do. You might not have all the facts at your disposal."

She knew a runaway when she saw one. And Jackson, for whatever reason, was running from what could, no, what was, she amended, the best part of his life. "Oh, I think I do."

"No," he countered, his eyes holding hers, "you don't."

She continued with the charade though she knew that they were now both aware she wasn't talking about her granddaughter, but Hannah. "I know his father was no good, but that doesn't mean anything. Trouble is, he seems to think it does. There's no other reason for him to be holding back."

That she was right on target astounded him. But the subject was painful and he didn't want to talk about it. Jackson was perfectly aware that what his father had been was not a secret in Storkville, but that still didn't make the memory any easier to deal with.

With a terse movement, he closed the bag of cookies, silently turning down the offering. "Could be he's right."

Gertie frowned. "If that were the case, then every child of every criminal would be a criminal. You don't believe that, do you?"

She was twisting things. "That's different."

"Only if you make yourself believe that." Gertie

shook her head. "I'm not talking about my grand-daughter."

Jackson laughed shortly. "I didn't think so."

"Hannah's in love with you." Gertie knew Hannah would be furious with her if Hannah knew she was here, talking to Jackson like this, but it had to be done. Someone had to take the initiative and it looked as if neither one of them was going to do it. "She's never said a word, but I can tell." Gertie leveled her gaze at him. "And you're in love with her."

His patience wearing thin, Jackson rose from his seat. He'd heard enough. "Gertie, I don't have time to argue about this or tell you how wrong you are, I've got a patient coming in in a few minutes."

"You can argue all you want, still doesn't change anything. About either one of you," Gertie said. "Ever read the poem Evangeline?"

"No," he replied.

"Well, I did. Had to," she added matter-of-factly. "Teacher forced us. Anyway, it was set a long time ago." She could see his growing impatience, so she stepped up her pace. "When doesn't matter. The point is, there were these two young people in it. Crazy about each other. They were just about to get married when suddenly, through no fault of their own, they were separated. The rest of their lives, they kept looking for each other and missing one another over and over again. Sometimes they were only a few feet apart, but they didn't look in the right direction. Reading that poem, I wanted to scream at them, saying, 'Look, you idiot, before it's too late. She's standing right over there.'" Gertie shrugged. "'Course I couldn't then, but I can now." She rose majestically from her seat as she looked Jackson squarely in the eye, "Look, you idiot, before it's too late. She's standing right over there." Then, her head held high, Gertie crossed to the door. "All right, I've said my piece. The next step is up to you. It'd better be the right one, doctor-boy."

And with that, she swept out of the office, leaving him staring at the vacant doorway.

Jackson scrubbed his hand over his face. It was worse than he thought, and he was going to have to do something about it.

Chapter Twelve

She'd tried to be patient, she really had. Once she'd heard the rumor that he was leaving, Hannah had gone through an entire gamut of feelings: surprise, anger, numbness, and then endured them in reverse order. All without hearing a word from Jackson to either confirm or deny, or even to say hello.

The silence made her edgy. By the end of the day, Hannah figured she'd lasted as long as she could. Asking Gertie to stay with the twins and usher off the last of the parents, Hannah had driven over to Jackson's office in the small single-story complex that stood across the street from Storkville General Hospital.

Sailing into the outer office, she passed Jackson's last patient, barely nodded at the woman holding on to the little girl's hand. She hadn't come to exchange pleasantries.

Karen, Jackson's nurse, looked surprised to see her,

even more surprised that she had come without either twin. "Is he in his office, Karen?"

"Yes."

"Alone?"

Karen looked confused and slightly concerned. "Yes, but—"

That was all she needed. "Good." Hannah shot past her and walked into Jackson's office.

Busy writing up the chart of the child he had just examined and diagnosed, Jackson didn't look up immediately. He assumed it was Karen, coming to say good night before she left for the day.

His assumption faded when he heard Hannah's voice. "Is it true?"

Jackson looked up. Surprise melted. Something had told him she would come. Still, he pretended not to know what she was talking about, buying himself a little time that wouldn't matter in the long run. "Hannah, what are you doing here?"

"Is it true?" she repeated, struggling to keep the fury she felt from shaking her voice. "Are you leaving Storkville?

Giving up at least a piece of the charade, Jackson laid his pen down. "Yes, as soon as I can find a replacement." He hadn't wanted her to know, not until everything was finalized. He didn't want her to look at him with those eyes of hers and turn his selfless plans to dust. "How did you find out?"

For less than two cents, she would have punched his lights out for hurting her so.

"Rebecca mentioned to Gertie she'd heard a rumor that you were leaving and Gertie told me." Her temper began to slip out of the reins around it. "What difference does it make how I heard? What matters is that it didn't come from you. And you weren't going to tell me again, were you?"

Why did doing something right make him feel so guilty? "I was going to get around to it."

"When?" she demanded hotly. "After you'd been gone a week? A month? A year? But then, disappearing is your style, isn't it? I'm surprised you stayed this long."

He wanted to go to her, to hold her. To tell her that it wasn't his choice, but it was the one he had to make.

He remained where he was, because touching her would negate everything. Would make him stay when he needed to go. "It'll be better for everyone all around if I left."

"Everyone?" she echoed incredulously. "Who's everyone? It can't be the kids, because the whole town thinks you're the best pediatrician they've ever seen. And it certainly can't be me because I never wanted you to leave in the first place."

He felt so damn weary. With all his heart, he cursed his father's soul. "That's just it, I am doing this for you."

Hannah stared at him, stunned. "Me? How are you doing it for me?" Suddenly aware that she was shouting, she lowered her voice. "Did I ask you to go?"

If anything, everything about her had asked him to remain. But it didn't change the fact that he couldn't stay. Shouldn't stay. "It's better this way, you'll see."

How could he say that? How could he possibly *think* that? "No, I won't."

Allowing himself a single contact, he reached for her hand, but she pulled it away. He sought her eyes instead. "Trust me."

That was just it, she had. She'd sworn to herself that she wouldn't, not after the last time, after he'd disappeared on her like that, but she had. She had trusted him with her heart and now look where it had gotten her.

She shook her head, her voice as hollow as her soul felt right at this moment. "I doubt if I can. Ever again. I was beginning to, but now that's gone." Her eyes were accusing. "Just like you'll be."

Why was she making this so hard for him? Didn't she know how he felt about her? How he'd always felt? Couldn't she sense it? "Didn't you hear me? I'm doing this for you."

He was insulting her with a lie. Hannah fisted her hands in her lap. "Oh please, spare me. Spare me that at least. That old chestnut's as overused as—" her voice took on a martyr-like quality as she rolled her eyes heavenward "—'If it would have been anyone, it would have been you.'"

His face was somber as he looked at her. "It would have been. Is." If he could have taken that leap of faith for anyone, he would have taken it for her. Because he'd never loved anyone but her.

She didn't know whether to laugh or cry. "Words, Jackson, just empty words."

Unable to remain calm any longer, Jackson rose to his feet. "Damn it, do you think it's easy for me, leaving you?"

"Well, it must be, because you're doing it," she

shot back. "As fast as that expensive car of yours can go."

Jackson dug his knuckles into the blotter on his desk as he leaned over it, his face inches away from hers. "I'm doing it, damn it, because if I stayed, then I might do something stupid."

She rose too, facing him down. "Like what, Jackson? Like make love with me? Is that what you think is stupid?" She wanted to know. "Or are you afraid of suddenly feeling—what?" She thought of Ethan, of why he had gone out of his way to find and bed other women. Because she had disappointed him in bed. There was no other explanation for it. She couldn't find fault in any other part of the life they shared. It had to be that. "Noble intentions mingled with acute disappointment? Is that what has you running out of town?"

"What the hell are you talking about?" he asked.

"I'm talking about you running from me."

How much could he tell her without telling her everything? She had to be made to understand that the choice wasn't his to make. It had been preordained—if she were going to be happy. And above all, he wanted her to be happy.

"Don't you understand? I'm running from you because I can't stop thinking about you, because every time I see you, I want you. Because I want to make you my wife."

No, she didn't understand, she thought. And she was understanding less with each passing moment. "And this is what...repulsive to you?" Hannah fought back tears. "You think you're insane for wanting me?"

Helpless, he took her hands in his, then dropped them as if they were both on fire. He began to pace the room. "I'm insane *from* wanting you. Don't you understand? I can't do that to you."

"Now I'm the one completely lost. Do what to me?" Hannah asked.

Exasperation filled his voice. "Marry you."

She waited, but nothing more came in the wake of the declaration. "I'm still lost."

He said it as simply as he could. "I don't want to hurt you."

"And you think leaving isn't going to accomplish that?"

Jackson shook his head sadly. "Not as much as staying. As marrying you."

"Jackson, what are you talking about?" She wasn't going to leave here, she swore to herself, without getting this cleared up at least to her satisfaction. If she was going to be rejected a second time in her life, she was damn well going to know why. "Why would marrying you hurt me? Do you turn into a werewolf at the first sign of a full moon? I promise I won't arm myself with silver bullets," she said, sarcastically.

"What I would turn into," he said quietly, "would be something a great deal worse than a werewolf."

Now he was scaring her. Not with hints at creatures, but at what he believed existed inside of him. "What?" she wanted to know. "What could you possibly turn into that's worse than a werewolf?"

Turning away, he closed his eyes and gave her the rest of it. "I could turn into my father."

She stared at his back, waiting for him to turn

around. When he didn't, she moved around him until she was facing Jackson. "Excuse me?"

"My father," he repeated. "Jackson Caldwell, Sr., a man who was dedicated to the constant quest of conquering the next beautiful woman who came down the pike, all the while breaking the heart of a woman whose feet he wasn't fit to kiss."

She remembered what Gertie had told her, but couldn't see the connection between father and son, other than blood. They were nothing alike. Searching Jackson's face, she saw that he seemed to believe otherwise. "You're serious. You're leaving town, leaving me, because you think you're going to turn into a lecher?" It didn't make sense to her.

"Not a lecher, my father." He laughed shortly. "Although the two are synonymous."

How could he possibly believe what he was saying? Unless he was leading some double life she knew nothing about, and that simply wasn't possible in Storkville, there was no evidence for him to even begin to think he could be anything like his father.

"My God, Jackson, is that why—why—wow." She sank down in the chair, stunned by the revelation of what had been going on in his head all this time. "Is that what you think? That after a lifetime of being a good, kind and decent human being, you were suddenly going to grow fangs, bay at the moon and go tomcatting around, as Gertie likes to put it?" It stole her breath away. Pieces were beginning to fall together. "And here I thought—I thought—"

Jackson looked at her. "Thought what?"

She blinked, attempting to reconcile things in her

mind. "I thought that you pushed me toward Ethan because you didn't want me."

He laughed at the absurdity of that. "I pushed you toward Ethan because I wanted you, but I thought he could be everything for you that I couldn't be."

And that was the irony of it, she thought. "He was. He was fast, loose and as shallow as a two-year-old's wading pool. And completely engaged in making adultery his full-time hobby. Everything you weren't."

He was his father's son and the roots ran deep. "How can you be so sure?"

Pity filled her for what he had lived with. And anger with it for what he had made them both live. "Because I apparently know you a great deal better than you know yourself. Do you think this is genetic? Something that suddenly kicks in at a certain age?" She couldn't hold back the anger even though she tried. So many years wasted. So much misunderstanding. "Or maybe there's a switch inside that just turns on after you say 'I do' and then you don't want to? That was your father's style and Ethan's, not yours, Jackson."

His eyes told her she wasn't getting through. Her frustration mounted. "Look at you, look at your life. Everything your father was, you're not, other than good-looking and rich. Your father was ruthless, you're selfless." She jabbed a finger at his chest, at his heart. "Right there, that's the proof. You were always monogamous in your relationships." She drew a deep breath, remembering. "All of which I was incredibly jealous of."

He remembered going through the motions, trying

to deny his feelings for her, to sublimate them and scatter them to the winds by seeing other girls. It hadn't worked. "There was no reason to be. Those women meant nothing to me."

She was glad to hear it, even now. "That reinforces my point even more. You didn't care about them, and you still only dated one at a time."

He shoved his hands into his pockets, looking away. "I was trying not to be like my father."

"Well, guess what? You succeeded." Hannah stared at his back which was so stiff, so formal. She felt him drifting away from her and there was nothing she could do. The frustration clawed at her. "What makes you think that you can't continue not being your father?"

"The stakes are too high to risk finding out," he said.

And that would be her, Hannah thought. "Why don't you leave that for the stakes to decide?"

Jackson shook his head. "I won't risk it," he repeated.

Hannah looked at him in silence for a long moment. The emptiness within her grew to astounding portions. "You might not be like your father, but you're just like Ethan. Neither one of you thought I was good enough to stay with."

"That's not true." He reached for her, but she backed away, her eyes accusing.

"Isn't it?" she demanded hotly. "Ethan was always looking for something better, never giving me a chance to be that something better for him. And you, you're even worse, you won't even sample the goods before making up your mind."

His eyes were as dark as his soul felt. He was sending away the only thing in his life that mattered. "It's not about sex, Hannah."

Hannah pressed her lips together, fighting for control. "Well, it certainly isn't about love, is it? Because people who love each other try anything and everything they can to save what they have and more importantly, what could be." Something tore within her. She'd had enough. "You know what? You can just pack up your shingle and go, I don't care anymore. I'm through caring."

She crossed quickly to the door, then stopped, her hand on the knob. Hannah looked at him over her shoulder. "And I was wrong. You are like your father. Not because you'd be unfaithful but because you're completely heartless."

The door slammed in her wake.

The next few days were wrapped in a thick haze, moving around her like heavy smog. Hannah went through the motions, doing what was required of her, pushing ahead because it was the only thing that convinced her she was still alive, still breathing.

It amazed her how long a person could keep moving after their heart had been reduced to shattered pieces.

The others at the center noticed and tried their best not to appear as if they had. It was impossible not to detect that the spirit had left her voice, the zest had left her eyes. But she was trying. Trying very hard.

And for their parts, Gertie, Penny Sue and Gwenyth were incredibly cheerful, mentioning no topics heavier than the selection of the afternoon snack. She blessed them for it, blessed them for not asking, not trying to help a situation that was beyond mending.

The only thing that would do any good was time. And she would have plenty of that. Alone, she mused as she stood in the room she'd converted to the downstairs nursery, changing Steffie.

"Don't get mixed up with men, Steffie," she told the small, round face beaming up at her. "It's not worth the hassle."

"You're right."

Startled, she looked up and saw Jackson standing in her doorway. Something pulled within her stomach, tight and hard. He hadn't been by, on any pretext, for the last few days. She hadn't attempted to see him, steeling herself for a time when she wouldn't be able to see him.

He's come to say good-bye, she thought.

Closing the diaper, she picked Steffie up and tried to act as if her heart wasn't about to beat right out of her chest. "Which part?"

There were hints of circles under her eyes. She hadn't been sleeping. That made two of them, he thought.

Like a man testing icy waters, he slowly entered the room. "Take your pick."

"I'm through picking, through hoping."

He tried to get a better view of her face, to read her expression. "God, I hope not."

She placed Steffie back in the playpen in the next room. It was after hours. Penny Sue and Rebecca were gone, as were the children. Gertie had already said good-bye. Hannah assumed she must have let

Jackson in on her way out. Gwenyth was at her new place for the night.

"Why?" With effort, she kept her voice sufficiently without emotion. "What do you care?" The front room looked as if a tornado had gone through it. Because she had to keep busy, Hannah began picking up toys and putting them away. "Have you found a replacement yet?"

Getting down on his knees beside her, he started picking up pieces of a puzzle, placing them back into their frame. "I stopped looking."

She froze and looked at him. "Does that mean you're going to stay?"

His eyes met hers. Was it too late, he wondered. "Depends."

Don't, don't start hoping, Hannah, you know what happens when you start hoping. "On what?"

Tossing the puzzle piece he was holding aside, Jackson took her hands in his and slowly rose to his feet, bringing her up with him. "On whether I can get you to forgive me."

A smile flirted with her lips. "Which part?" she repeated.

He hadn't even been able to practice this. There was no right way to say it, so he just plunged in. "All of it. I've been a jerk..."

The smile became an easy grin. "Go on, so far we're in agreement."

He began to hope that it was going to be all right. That it wasn't too late to make amends and start over. "I've been running scared from my father's shadow for so long, I was doing exactly the very thing I didn't want to do. I was hurting you. I sent you into Ethan's arms and let him hurt you.''

The anger in her heart left as if it had never been there. "It's not as if you had a crystal ball."

She'd always been quick to forgive, he thought, but he wasn't. Not when it came to himself. "No, but maybe if I'd had a little more faith in the man I could be…"

Her eyes smiled at him. "I had faith enough for the two of us."

"Had." He caught the single world that could wound him. "Does that mean—?"

Because her heart was moved, she kissed his cheek. "It means I made a reference to the past and used correct grammar. It doesn't mean that the feeling, or the faith, is gone."

He took the plunge. "So would you be willing to marry me?"

Her mouth dropped open, but recovery was quick. "Only one way to find out."

He held his breath. "And that is?"

She was trying very hard to keep a straight face when everything inside her was cheering. "Ask me."

Taking her hands in his again, he looked into her eyes. "Hannah, will you marry me?"

She drew her hands away, placing one on her heart. She fluttered her lashes. "Oh Jackson, this is so sudden. I'm going to have to think about it." She turned away. The next second, she'd gone a full 360 degrees and was facing him again. "I've thought about it. The answer's yes." Relief and joy flooded her as she threw her arms around him. "It's always been yes."

Sammy's babbling grew louder, drawing her attention away from Jackson momentarily. She still had responsibilities to think of. "What about the twins? I've gotten very attached to them. I can't just give them up unless we find their parents. You'd be taking on a wife and a ready-made family."

"Couldn't be better." His eyes washed over her face as he allowed the love he felt for her to finally emerge unshackled and unrestrained. "I don't deserve you."

She grinned. "True, but we'll work on that."

His arms closed around her as he drew her close to him. "Got a schedule worked out?"

"I thought we'd start immediately."

"Sounds good to me." How had he ever thought he could walk away from her again? Once had been hard enough, twice would have been impossible. "I love you Hannah."

She closed her eyes, savoring the sound. "Say it again."

"I love you, Hannah," he whispered. "I love you. I'll say it as often as you like and as often as it takes to convince you."

Mischief rose in her eyes. "You know what they say."

He laughed. "No, what do they say?"

She cocked her head. "Actions speak louder than words."

"I can do action," he murmured, his lips a scant inch from hers.

"I was counting on it." It was the last thing she said for quite some time.

* * * * *

Babies in the
BARGAIN

VICTORIA PADE

Victoria Pade is a bestselling author of both historical and contemporary romance fiction, and mother of two energetic daughters, Cori and Erin. Although she enjoys her chosen career as a novelist, she occasionally laments that she has never travelled farther from her Colorado home than Disneyland, instead spending all her spare time plugging away at her computer. She takes breaks from writing by indulging in her favourite hobby—eating chocolate.

Chapter One

Darkness hadn't completely fallen when Kira Wentworth drove from farm-and-ranch land into the city proper of Northbridge, Montana, on Wednesday night. Still, most of the stores and shops that lined the small college town's main thoroughfare were closed. Even the gas station was being locked up as she pulled into the lot.

"Excuse me," Kira said from the window of her rental car to the attendant as he removed the key from the door and pocketed it. "Can I bother you for directions?"

"Nothin's hard to find in Northbridge," the teenage boy informed her as if she was asking a dumb question.

He did come to the side of her car, though.

"I'm looking for one-o-four Jellison Street," she informed him.

The freckle-faced teenager didn't have to think about it before he said, "That's the Grant place. Officer Grant is laid up with a broken ankle so he should be there."

The teenager gave her brief instructions. Then, without another word, he rounded her car to go to the single island and padlock the nozzle on the only gas pump.

"Thank you," Kira called after him.

"Sure," he answered, taking off on foot and leaving her behind without a second glance.

Kira rolled up the car window again and turned the air conditioner higher. Just the thought that she was within three blocks of her destination increased her stress level and made her hotter than even the mid-July temperature warranted.

Hoping the heat and the drive through the open countryside hadn't made her look too much the worse for wear, she glanced at herself in the rearview mirror before heading out of the gas station.

Her mascara hadn't left smudges around her blue eyes, and light mauve lipstick still stained lips that weren't too thin or too thick. But despite the fact that she'd reapplied blush in the Billings Airport when she'd landed, her skin looked pale again.

"It might not even be the same guy," she reminded her reflection. "This could still be a wild-goose chase."

But the reminder didn't help much. She continued

to feel as if she had butterflies in the pit of her stomach, and if the pallor of her skin wasn't enough, there was further proof of her nervousness in the fact that somewhere during the drive from Billings she'd tucked her hair behind her ears—a habit her father had detested.

She hurriedly took a comb from her purse—as if Tom Wentworth might appear at any moment to punish her for the infraction—running it through the precision-cut, shoulder-length, straight honey-blond hair until every strand was right where it belonged.

Then she replaced the comb, reapplied blush to her high cheekbones, tugged at the collar of her white blouse to make sure it was exactly centered at her throat and plucked a single string from the right leg of her navy-blue slacks.

Not perfect, she judged as she took another look at herself in the mirror, but at least she was presentable and it was the best she could do under the circumstances.

She noticed then that the clock on the dashboard read five minutes after nine and it occurred to her that she probably shouldn't waste any more time. She didn't know much about small-town life, but if even the gas station was closed already, maybe everyone went to bed early, too. And she didn't want to risk having to wait another day to find out what she'd come to find out.

She put the sedan back into gear and pulled out of the station, taking a right at the only stoplight, and then a quick left after that onto Jellison.

What she found there was a nice neighborhood shaded with tall elm, oak and maple trees lining the street on both sides. Beyond the trees at the curb were medium-size frame houses that looked as if they'd all been pressed through the same cookie cutter in 1950.

The two-story, wedding-cake-shaped houses with the covered front porches were distinguished from one another only by the different earth-tone colors they'd been painted, the outside shutters and flower boxes that had been added to several of them, and the yards—some with elaborate landscaping and others with only well-tended lawns.

The address she was looking for came into view on the fourth house from the corner—that one had tan siding, white shutters and a wooden swing hanging from chains on the left side of the porch.

There was a black-and-white SUV parked in the driveway with Northbridge Police stenciled on the sides and back. There weren't any cars parked in front, though, so Kira pulled to a stop at the curb.

Before she turned off the engine she took the manila folder from the passenger seat and opened it. Inside was the newspaper article from Sunday's *Denver Post* that she'd cut out and laminated.

It was a small piece about two Montana men—one an off-duty police officer and the other a Northbridge business owner—who had rushed into a burning house to rescue a family trapped inside. The two men had saved the family and then had gone back in for the pets only to have a beam knock Addison Walker unconscious and break Cutler Grant's ankle. Still, Officer Grant had managed to drag the unconscious businessman to safety.

The name Addison Walker meant nothing to Kira.

But Cutler Grant—that was something else. Kira knew—sort of—a *Cutty* Grant.

There wasn't much information about the two men in the pictureless piece, but it did say that Cutler Grant was a widower with eighteen-month-old twin daughters.

That was a surprise. The *Cutty* Grant Kira knew had married her older sister and they'd had a son. A son who would be twelve years old by now.

So maybe this really was a wild-goose chase and the Cutler Grant in the newspaper wasn't the same Cutty Grant she knew.

But what she was hoping was that this *was* the same man. That she'd find out that the wife who had left him a widower with eighteen-month-old twins was his second wife. And that he would be able to tell Kira where to find Marla and their twelve-year-old son.

Kira put the slip of paper neatly back into the folder and replaced it on the passenger seat.

Then she turned off the car.

Ignoring the tension that tightened her shoulders, Kira picked up her leather purse and took it with her as she got out.

The scent of honeysuckle was in the air as she headed for the door. Light shone through the windows of the lower floor and the front door was open—probably to let in the cooler evening air—so apparently the occupants of 104 Jellison Street were still awake.

She climbed five cement steps to the porch. As she approached the door she could see through the screen. There was a man sitting on an antique chair, talking on the phone.

He caught sight of her, and without missing a beat, he motioned for her to come inside.

Who did he think she was? Kira wondered, staying rooted to that spot, unsure whether or not to actually go inside.

Although his looks had matured, she could tell that this man was the Cutty Grant she was looking for. But she knew there was no way he recognized her. The one and only time he'd seen her had lasted a total of ten minutes before she'd been dispatched to her room. Besides, she looked completely different than she had then.

But when she remained on the porch, he motioned to her even more insistently, and she didn't know what to do but oblige him. So she opened the screen and went in.

"Betty, we'll be okay," he was saying into the phone. "Family comes first. You have to take care of your mother."

Kira didn't want to appear to be listening so she kept her eyes on the floor. The floor where he had one foot stretched out in front of him. One big, bare foot with a white cast cupping his heel and disappearing under the leg of a pair of time-aged blue jeans that hugged a thigh thick enough to be noteworthy.

She tried to keep control of her eyes but they seemed to have a mind of their own and continued up to the plain white crew-neck T-shirt that fit him like a second skin and left no doubt that he was in good enough shape to have dragged a full-grown man out of a burning building. His chest and shoulders were that substantial, bulging with toned muscles. And his biceps were so big they stretched the short sleeves of the T-shirt to the limit.

"No, don't do that."

For a split-second Kira thought he might be talking to her, and she glanced quickly to his face.

But he was still talking into the phone. "You can't take care of things here and take care of your mom, too," he said.

In fact he wasn't even looking in Kira's direction. His focus really was on the floor where hers had begun, and he didn't seem aware that Kira's gaze was on his face now. Somehow that made it more difficult to lower her eyes and instead she was left studying the changes in him.

The seventeen-year-old boy she remembered had been cute enough to make her jealous of her older sister. Yet the boy was nothing compared to the man.

The grown-up Cutty Grant had the same sable-colored hair only now he wore it short all over and messy on top rather than long and shaggy.

It wasn't only his haircut that had changed. His face had gone from boyishly appealing to ruggedly striking. His very square forehead had become strong. His distinctive jawline and straight, slightly longish nose were more defined, and every angle and plane of his face seemed more sharply cut.

His upper lip was still narrow above a fuller bottom lip, and when he smiled at something the person on the other end of the phone said, two grooves bracketed either side of that mouth, which had gained a certain suppleness. And an indescribable sexiness, too.

His deep-set eyes hadn't undergone any alteration with age—they were still a remarkable shade of green unlike any other eyes Kira had ever seen. Dark green, the color of Christmas trees. Evergreen trees. And all in all, Kira thought that she'd never even met a man as head-turningly handsome as the adult Cutty Grant.

"Yes, the place is a mess, but Lucinda had no business reporting that to you," he said then.

Kira needed an excuse to tear her eyes away from him and that gave it to her. She forced herself to look from him into the living room.

She didn't know about the rest of the place but that room was definitely in disarray. There were toys on the floor, on the end tables, on the brown tweed sofa, even on the desk in the corner. There were children's clothes strewn here and there, including one tiny pair of pink shorts hanging over the lampshade of a pole lamp in the corner. There were unused diapers spilling from a sack on top of the television in the entertainment center. There was a plate with the crusts of a sandwich left on it, a half-empty glass of milk, and another smaller glass overturned in a puddle of orange juice on the oak coffee table. And there was just an overall air of clutter everywhere that sparked an urge in the meticulous Kira to put it all in order.

But of course she resisted that urge.

"I mean it, Betty. Forget about us until she's better. The girls and I will manage."

Kira noticed then that there was even debris on the stairs—more toys, more baby clothes, a sock that must have belonged to Cutty, and it occurred to her that no matter what he was telling the person he was talking to, he wasn't managing very well.

But in spite of that he insisted, "Really, you don't have to come by here in the morning before you pick up your mom from the hospital—"

There was a pause while the person on the other end interrupted him to say something, and whatever it was it apparently convinced him because he sighed and said, "Okay, but then that's it. An hour tomorrow morning. After that, I don't want to see you around here until your mom is a hundred percent better. If nothing else I'll get Ad over to help."

Whoever he was talking to said something that made Cutty Grant laugh a deep, throaty laugh that sounded so good it was almost sinful.

Then he said, "Yeah, I know, Ad isn't any more domestic than I am, but he can get more done with a bump on the head than I can with a bum ankle that's supposed to be elevated all the time. Just don't worry about it. Now I have to go. I have company. I'll see you in the morning. But only for an hour," he added, slowly enunciating each word for emphasis before he said goodbye.

The minute he hung up he turned his attention to Kira. "Sorry about that. That was the woman who usually helps me out around here with the babies and the housekeeping. Her mother herniated a disc in her back and she's fretting about leaving me in the lurch. She knows I'm not good for much when I'm supposed to stay off the foot," he said, pointing to his injured ankle.

Kira watched him stand and take a cane that was braced against the wall beside him.

Even leaning his weight on the cane he still stood at least six foot two and if Kira had thought his physique was impressive when he was sitting down, it was even more impressive when he was upright. There was definitely nothing boyish in that big, powerful tower of a man and it left Kira slightly dumbstruck.

Not that he seemed to notice as he continued. "So. Here you are. I could have sworn we said Thursday night between eight and nine to make sure the babies were asleep or I wouldn't have returned Betty's phone call."

That brought Kira to her senses. "Who do you think I am?"

"The journalism student from the college who's doing the article on Ad and me. Isn't that who you are?"

That explained why he'd waved her in.

Kira shook her head. "I'm not from the college," she said. "I'm Kira Wentworth. Marla's sister."

That sobered him instantly. In fact, it pulled his

amazing face into a frown that put two vertical creases between his eyebrows.

"Oh."

All the animation had drained from his voice and he didn't say anything for so long that Kira felt inclined to fill the silence with the reason for her sudden appearance on his doorstep.

"The Denver newspaper ran a little article about you and the other man saving a family from their burning house. It was the first time I had any clue about where Marla might be since the two of you left thirteen years ago. I'm here looking for her."

Cutty Grant closed his green eyes and Kira saw his jaw tense before he opened them again and sighed a sigh that sounded resigned but not happy.

He pointed toward the living room and said, "Let's go in there and sit."

Solemn. Kira knew whatever he was going to tell her couldn't be good, and her grip on her purse turned white-knuckle as she did as he'd suggested and went into the living room that looked as if a cyclone had hit it.

"Please. Sit," he repeated when she went on standing even then.

Kira conceded, passing up the littered sofa to remove a rag doll from the Bentley rocking chair that was at a forty-five-degree angle to the couch. She kept hold of the doll with her arms wrapped tightly around it, hugging it close as Cutty Grant joined her, sitting on the only clear spot on the sofa and raising his casted foot to a pillow on the coffee table in front of it.

For what seemed like an eternity he didn't speak, though. Or even look at her. Instead he kept his eyes on the cane, balancing it across his legs like a bridge.

And in the silence it occurred to Kira that although she'd seen signs of infants and of Cutty himself, she hadn't seen anything that would lead her to think her sister or her nephew were a part of the equation here. But she still hoped against hope that Cutty Grant was going to tell her he and Marla had divorced, that Marla had taken their son somewhere else, that he was a widower with two daughters because his second wife had died....

But the minute he said, "I'm sorry," Kira knew better and her heart sank. There was just something so ominous in his voice.

"Marla and I had a little boy," he told her then. "Your parents knew that so you must have, too."

"I knew you'd had a boy, yes," Kira confirmed tentatively, as if, if she hedged, it might not make the worst true.

"Then you probably knew he was autistic."

That surprised her. "No, I didn't know that. I only knew Marla had had a son because I overheard my mother telling my father when the baby was born. They never told me directly—she was so thoroughly disowned that I wasn't even to mention her name— and after that I never heard them talk about her or the baby again."

"There was an *after that*—" Disgust rang in his

tone but he seemed to reconsider what he'd been about to say and changed course. "Anthony. We named him Anthony."

It was unabashed pain that Kira heard in Cutty's voice then. Pain that etched his handsome face.

"I'm really hoping this isn't as bad as it seems," she said when he let another long silence pass.

Cutty Grant took a deep breath and shook his head to let her know in advance that her hopes were to no avail. "Seventeen months ago, it was February but we were having springlike weather, so Marla took Anthony into the front yard to get some fresh air. I don't really know why, but for some reason Anthony ran between two cars that were parked at the curb. There was a truck coming. Going faster than it should have been. The driver didn't see Anthony. Or Marla running after him…"

It was difficult for Cutty to say what he was saying, and after another pause he finally finished. "The truck hit them both."

Kira hadn't been prepared to hear that. Intellectually she'd realized that it was possible it was her sister who had left Cutty Grant a widower, but she hadn't really believed it was true.

"Marla is dead?" she whispered.

"I'm sorry."

"And Anthony?"

"He was killed instantly."

Through the tears that sprang to her eyes, Kira saw moisture gathering in those of the man across from her, too. But still she couldn't help the accusing tone when she said, "And you didn't let us know?"

A flash of anger dried his eyes and when he answered her it was barely contained in his own voice. "Marla lived a few hours after the accident and one of the few things she said to me during the time she was conscious was that she didn't want me to call her father. That she didn't want him here. Even if she didn't make it. I respected her wishes." And it was clear that he'd had no desire himself to bring Tom Wentworth into the picture.

"But *I* would have wanted to know," Kira said quietly as she lost the battle to hold back her own tears and they began to trail down her face.

Cutty Grant got up and limped out of the room, returning with a box of tissues that he held out for her.

Kira accepted one, thanking him perfunctorily and wiping her eyes as she struggled with the complex emotions running through her.

"I'm sorry," he repeated, setting the tissue box on the coffee table and sitting down once more. "If it's any consolation, not seeing you again after we eloped was the one thing Marla regretted."

It wasn't much consolation. It didn't take away all the years of missing Marla. Of wondering where she was. Of wishing she would call or write. Of longing to see her again, to be sisters again. It didn't take away all the time since Kira had grown up and been out on her own when she'd wanted so badly to have

Marla in her life and not had any way of knowing where she was.

"I tried to find her," Kira said through her tears, not really understanding why it was suddenly important to her that he know. "My parents said they didn't have any idea where she was—"

"That was a lie."

Kira had suspected as much but she couldn't force them to tell her.

She didn't say that to Cutty, though. She just continued. "I went to three private investigators but I couldn't afford their fees. I even tried different things on the Internet. But no matter what I did, I came up empty." As empty as she'd felt so much of the time after Marla had left. "I know we weren't related by blood, but she was still my sister. We shared a room from the time I was three years old. And, I don't know, I guess rather than being rivals or fighting with each other, we sort of banded together..." Kira's voice trailed off before she said too much.

But Cutty picked up the ball where she'd dropped it and said, "Does your father know you're here now?"

Kira finally managed to stop the flow of tears and dabbed at her face with the tissue. "He and my mom were killed a year ago in a freak accident. They were coming home from a day in the mountains when there was a rock slide onto the road. They were hit by a boulder that came right down on the car. They both died instantly."

"I'm sorry," he said once more. "Your mother was a nice enough woman."

That was true. It was just that *nice* hadn't had any potency against the strong will of the man she'd married. The man who had adopted her three-year-old daughter.

But that seemed beside the point now. Kira had come here hoping to find the sister she'd so desperately wanted to reconnect with. Hoping to find family. And it suddenly struck her that the only chance of that might be in Cutty Grant's twins.

"The article said you have eighteen-month-old daughters," she said then.

"Upstairs asleep as we speak," he confirmed, a brighter note edging his voice at the mere mention of them.

"Marla's babies?"

"Yes. They were barely three weeks old when the accident happened."

"My nieces," Kira said, trying it on for size because blood or no blood, if they were Marla's babies, Kira felt a connection to them.

"I guess so," Cutty conceded.

"I'd like to meet them. Get to know them. Would you let me?" she said impulsively and without any idea how she might go about that.

Cutty's frown from earlier reappeared and he didn't jump at the idea. Instead he said, "Like I said, they're asleep."

"I know. But…"

And that was when, completely out of the blue, the

mess in the room caught her attention again and an idea popped into her head.

"What if I took the place of that woman you were talking to on the phone a few minutes ago?" she said before the notion had even had a chance to ferment.

"Betty? What if you took Betty's place?" He sounded confused and leery at the same time.

"You said she took care of the twins and helped around the house, and without her—and with you needing to stay off your ankle—you're obviously in a bind. So what if I did it? I'd like to help and that way I could get to know the babies. Bond with them."

The more Kira considered this, the better it sounded to her.

But from the look on Cutty's face it wasn't having the same effect on him.

"Don't you have a job or a husband or a boyfriend or something you need to get back to?"

"No, I don't. In May I finished my Ph.D. in microbiology. I'm going to start teaching at the University of Colorado for the fall semester, but that doesn't begin until the last week in August. I wasn't really sure what I was going to do with myself until then but that means I'm free."

"No husband or boyfriend, either?" he asked, and Kira couldn't tell if he was looking for an out for himself or satisfying his own curiosity.

"No, no husband or boyfriend. I have one really close friend—Kit—but she can get along without me.

Plus she'll bring in my mail and water my plants for me, so it won't be any problem for me to stay.''

"You really want to spend your summer vacation picking up after us? Changing diapers?'' Cutty asked skeptically.

"I really do,'' she said, hating that she sounded as desperate as she felt. "I admit that I don't have any experience with kids,'' she confessed because it seemed only fair to let him know what he was getting into. "But when it comes to cleaning—''

"You're Tom Wentworth's daughter,'' Cutty supplied. "I don't know, I like things casual.''

"Casual is good. I can be casual.'' Although she wasn't quite sure what *casual* housekeeping and child care meant.

But still he didn't look convinced. In fact, he looked downright dubious and as if he was on the verge of saying thanks, but no thanks.

Why would he, though? It was clear he needed help and she was offering it.

Unless maybe he still harbored resentment toward her family for the way things had played out that night thirteen years ago when he'd come with Marla to tell their parents that he'd gotten their seventeen-year-old daughter pregnant.

"You know,'' Kira ventured, "I didn't have anything to do with what went on between you and my father. I know how ugly it got. He sent me to my room but I was hiding on the stairs, listening to what went on. He was a difficult man—''

"That's an understatement. He was a tyrant.''

Kira didn't dispute that. "But nobody can change the past and now he's gone and so is Marla. But there are your twins. And me. I lost all these years that I could have had with Marla, with Anthony, and I can't get them back. But I could have a future with the twins. If you'll just let me."

She hated the note of pleading that had somehow slipped into her tone.

And Cutty Grant must not have liked it much, either, because she saw his jaw clench suddenly and his voice turned tight. "I'm really not the bastard your father thought I was. The kind of bastard who would keep you from knowing your nieces."

"I didn't—I *don't*—think you're that. I just know there have to be hard feelings—"

"Harder than you'll ever know. But I'm well aware of the fact that you were only a kid, that you didn't have anything to do with it."

"Then will you let me stay?"

Again he didn't answer readily, and she knew he wasn't eager to agree even if he did need the help.

But in the end she thought that he might have wanted to prove he wasn't a bad guy, that he wasn't punishing her for something she'd had nothing to do with, because he said, "I suppose we can give it a try."

Kira was so happy to hear his decision that she couldn't help grinning. "Shall I start right now?" she asked with a glance at the clutter all around them.

"It'll all wait for tomorrow."

In that case Kira thought it was probably better to get out of there before he changed his mind.

"Then if you'll tell me where I can find a hotel or a motel I'll get a room and be back first thing in the morning."

Again he let silence reign as he seemed to consider something before he answered.

"If you aren't particular about the ambience you can stay out back. Where Marla and I lived when we first got here."

"No, I don't care about the ambience. And it's probably better if I'm close by."

He didn't look convinced of that but he didn't rescind the offer.

"Do you have a suitcase somewhere?" he asked instead.

"Out in the rental car."

"Why don't you go get it and I'll show you the accommodations?"

Kira didn't waste any time complying. She hurried out to the car, retrieved her bag from the trunk and went back inside.

Cutty didn't get to his feet until she was there. Then he did, leading the way from the living room through an open archway into a kitchen that was a disaster all its own.

He held the back door open for her, and she stepped into the small yard ahead of him, coming face-to-face with what looked to have been a garage once upon a time.

"This whole place belonged to my uncle Paulie.

He converted the garage into an apartment for Marla and me, and added another garage to the side of the house later on.''

"So this is where you lived after you eloped?" Kira asked as they crossed the few feet of lawn and Cutty opened that door for her, too.

"Until my uncle died and left it all to us. Then we moved into the house. It's been fixed up and refurnished. Ordinarily I rent it to students from the college. But since it's summer vacation it's empty.''

Cutty reached in and flipped a switch. Three lamps went on at once, illuminating an open space arranged as a studio apartment.

There were no walls, so only the furnishings determined what each area was used for. A double bed and an armoire delineated the bedroom. A small sofa and matching armchair, a coffee table and a television designated the living room. And some kitchen cupboards, a sink, a two-burner stove with a tiny oven, a refrigerator and a small table with two chairs made up the kitchen.

"That door alongside the armoire will put you into the bathroom," Cutty explained without going farther than the doorway. "There's a tub with a shower in it but the water heater is pretty small so if you do a lot of dishes you'll want to wait half an hour before you take a bath.''

"I'm sure it'll be fine.''

What she *wasn't* sure of was why he had that dubious look on his face again, as if he was having second thoughts about this whole arrangement.

But if he was, he didn't say it.

Instead he said, "The girls are usually awake by seven."

"Seven. I'll be over before that," Kira said enthusiastically.

Cutty nodded his head. "There are towels in the bathroom. Sheets in the armoire. If you need anything before the morning—"

"I'll be fine."

He nodded again, which bothered Kira. If he didn't want to go ahead with this, why didn't he say something?

But all he said was, "Good night, then."

"See you first thing in the morning," Kira assured, moving to the door to see him out.

He turned to go without another word, leaving her with a view of his backside.

And although, as a rule, men's rear ends were not something she took notice of, it only required one glance to recognize that his was a great one.

A great rear end to go with the rest of his great body and his great face and his great hair.

Not that any of that mattered, because it didn't, she was quick to tell herself. She was only staying there for the babies, and anything about Cutty Grant was purely incidental.

Except that, incidental or not, she went on taking notice until Cutty Grant disappeared inside his house.

Chapter Two

Cutty had a hell of a time falling asleep Wednesday night and when he woke up before dawn Thursday morning it was aggravating to find his mind instantly on the mental treadmill that had kept him from sleeping in the first place. The treadmill Kira Wentworth's appearance on his doorstep had caused.

She'd really shaken things up for him, and as he rolled onto his back and tried to fall asleep again, he didn't feel any more sure of his decision to let her stick around.

He'd never expected to see any Wentworth again. Not after so many years and not when he was persona non grata in the extreme with Tom Wentworth.

Tom Wentworth who was the only Wentworth he ever really thought about when he thought about the family Marla had been estranged from. But then her adopted mother and adopted sister were just specks in the shadow Tom Wentworth cast, so it wasn't surprising that they wouldn't be uppermost on his mind for the last thirteen years.

Cutty opened his eyes and looked at the clock on his nightstand.

It was just after 5 a.m.

He doubted he would be able to sleep anymore but he didn't want to get up, either, so he cupped his hands under his head and stared at the ceiling.

He still couldn't believe that Kira Wentworth had shown up.

Marla's sister.

He'd only seen her once before. Actually, he'd only met her mother and father one time, too. But while Tom Wentworth's face was one Cutty would never forget, he had barely glanced at Kira before her adoptive father had ordered her to her room that night thirteen years ago. So there was no way Cutty had recognized her. If he had he might not have been so willing to let her come into his home. Her or anyone connected to Tom Wentworth.

Tom Wentworth.

Yeah, meeting him just once had been enough. More than enough, Cutty thought.

Marla's father hadn't wanted Marla to date in high school so she'd only seen Cutty on the sly. They'd made arrangements through friends; they'd met at the movies or the shopping mall; they'd seen each other at school functions. And always they'd had to keep an eye out for anyone who might report back to the controlling father, who ran his household with an iron fist.

But six months into dating, Marla had realized she was pregnant.

Cutty didn't think he'd ever seen anyone as afraid of anything as she'd been to tell her father.

Two seventeen-year-olds facing a nearly three-hundred-pound mountain of mean—the memory was still fresh in Cutty's mind.

To say it had been an ugly scene was an understatement. Tom Wentworth hadn't even wanted Cutty in the house. He'd hit the ceiling at just the sight of a boy there with his daughter. But Marla had insisted that they all needed to talk. Then she'd told her father what they'd come to tell him.

And all hell had broken loose.

Cutty still couldn't believe the way Tom Wentworth had exploded. It was as if a bomb had gone off in that living room. He'd screamed that Marla was a whore. A tramp. A good-for-nothing slut. And worse.

There hadn't been much Cutty could do during the tirade. Nothing much anyone could do but sit under the rain of hurtful, hateful words. But when Tom Wentworth had begun to demand that Marla have an abortion, Cutty had stood up to him. He'd told Tom Wentworth that Marla didn't want to have an abortion.

And Tom Wentworth had nearly beaten him to a pulp.

A few good punches of his own had saved Cutty,

but after that he'd been afraid to leave Marla there alone with her enraged bull of a father. So Cutty had taken Marla with him and left, not having any idea what he was going to do with her.

And a baby.

The sun began to make its rosy entrance through Cutty's bedroom curtains, and for a while he watched it, trying not to relive those early emotions that could still creep up on him every now and then. He'd been just a kid himself. A scared kid. With no one close by to turn to. He'd felt responsible. Overwhelmed. Terrified. He hadn't known what the hell he was going to do....

Lying there wasn't getting him anywhere, he decided suddenly and swung his legs over the side of the bed. He sat up on the edge, gripping the mattress and let his head drop forward.

Tom Wentworth had washed his hands of Marla—that's what he'd told her when she'd tried to call him the next day in hopes that he might have cooled off. She was on her own. He didn't care what happened to her.

Her adoptive mother had packed some of her clothes and sneaked them out to her because her father had said she wasn't even entitled to those.

And that had been that.

At least for a couple of years until Marla had gone behind Cutty's back. But that had been that in terms of Cutty and the Wentworths.

Until now.

Now when Kira Wentworth had shown up on his doorstep.

He really had thought she was the journalism student when he'd first caught sight of her coming up his porch steps. The journalism student had already interviewed his friend Ad, and Ad had told him she was slightly older than the average college student. That she was thin. Pretty. Blond.

Kira Wentworth fit that description. Although the minute he'd laid eyes on her he'd thought that he wouldn't say she was merely pretty. Kira Wentworth was beautiful. And her hair wasn't just blond. It was the color of honey shot through with sunlight. Plus she had skin like alabaster. And the softest mouth he'd ever seen. And a small, streamlined nose. And those eyes! They were the blue of a summer sky on a cloudless day. Not to mention that for a petite woman she had a body that wouldn't quit....

So, okay, he couldn't deny that that first sight of her had stirred things inside him that hadn't been stirred for a long, long time. But how confusing was it that the first person he'd been attracted to, since he seemed to have gotten his head together again after Marla's and Anthony's deaths, was a Wentworth?

Incredibly confusing, that's how confusing it was.

Rationally, Cutty knew there was no reason to hold a grudge against Kira Wentworth. But that had been his reaction when she'd told him who she was. In spite of his initial attraction to her. He'd been tempted to kick her out of his house. What had gone through his mind was that he didn't want any Wentworth anywhere near him because with any Wentworth came the potential for contact with Tom Wentworth. Or the effects of having been raised by him.

But Cutty hadn't wanted to be a hard-ass, so he'd tried to curb the feelings.

And apparently he'd been pretty successful, since only a few minutes later his heart had gone out to Kira when he'd told her about Marla and Anthony and witnessed the blow that struck.

He'd been so successful at curbing his negative feelings that he'd even been tempted to comfort her with a hug.

Well, more than a hug. What he'd really been inclined to do was take her in his arms, learn what it would feel like to have her head pressed to his chest, her body against his….

But she's a Wentworth, he'd reminded himself to chase away that urge.

Or at least to resist it. The urge hadn't exactly gone away, he just hadn't acted on it.

In fact, he'd still been struggling with it when she'd offered to come in and care for the twins. And him.

He hadn't expected that and once more his emotions had taken a swing toward the negative. He'd instantly imagined another Wentworth in his house. He'd flashed on the way things had been. On the way they could be again.

Cutty closed his eyes and shook his head as if that would get rid of the thoughts that he felt guilty for having had the night before and again now. Thoughts of Marla. Of life with Marla.

But guilty or not, the bottom line had been he really hadn't been thrilled with the prospect of Kira stepping in for Betty.

After all, she'd been raised by the same man Marla had. And there she'd been, with the ink barely dry on her Ph.D. as a clue to the likelihood that she was an overachiever, not a hair out of place, not a wrinkle in her clothes, her makeup flawless, her posture perfect, and Cutty hadn't had a doubt she was cut from the same cloth Marla was.

So no, he hadn't wanted Kira's help.

Only she'd made him feel like a heel for denying, not only the help she was offering, but for denying her the chance to meet the twins. To get to know them. To be a part of their lives.

They were her nieces, after all, and Cutty had known that if Marla had been there she would have welcomed Kira with open arms—both for herself and for the girls. He'd known that Marla would have wanted her younger sister to know her daughters.

So he'd caved.

Cutty opened his eyes and sighed, disgusted with himself. Just when he'd thought his life was finally settling down, here he was in a muddle of conflicting thoughts, conflicting feelings again. And for about the tenth time, he asked himself if he'd really accepted her help as temporary nanny and housekeeper because it was what Marla would have wanted, or if he'd had some kind of attraction to her. In spite of himself.

He hoped he'd only accepted her help because it was what Marla would have wanted.

Sure he'd told Ad a couple of weeks ago that he thought he was finally ready to get back into the swing of things again. But slowly. Cautiously. With great care and consideration given to exactly who—and what—he let into his life again.

And a pair of blue eyes—no matter how incredible a blue they were—didn't change that.

He grabbed his cane from where it rested against the nightstand and got to his feet.

Kira would do the same job Betty did, and he would make sure his relationship with her was no different than the relationship he had with Betty—purely friendly.

And that was all there was to it.

Because while he might have finally made it over the hump of grief and been ready to restart his life, it wouldn't be with Kira Wentworth.

What he was ready for was an ordinary, everyday woman who took things in stride, who knew when to put on the full-court press and when not to, who knew the value of people over the value of appearances, who stopped long enough to smell the flowers.

And he didn't think for a minute that Dr. Overachiever Microbiologist Kira Wentworth was that woman.

After a restless night, Kira was awake before her alarm went off. The moment she remembered where she was and what she was slated to do today, she was too antsy to linger in bed. She got up and went into the bathroom for a quick shower.

The sun was just dawning when she came out of the bathroom and stood in front of the armoire to survey the clothes she'd brought with her. She didn't have the slightest idea what was involved in taking care of eighteen-month-old babies, which meant she wasn't sure what to wear. But she was sure that she wanted it to be just right.

Not that she thought her nieces would even notice what she had on, but she so desperately wanted them to like her that every detail of this first meeting seemed important.

Maybe something bright, she thought, taking out a red silk shirt.

Or was that *too* bright? Would it scare them?

Maybe.

She replaced the shirt in the armoire and continued the search.

Definitely not the black high-necked blouse, she decided when that was the next thing that caught her eye. Black was too austere. It might send the message that she wasn't accessible and the last thing she wanted was for her nieces to see her as standoffish.

And white might make her look too washed out, so she decided against the white rayon cap shirt, too.

Kira was tempted to wear the flowered sundress with the full skirt but she wasn't sure if that was practical. Although she did give it a second look when it also occurred to her that this was essentially her first day on a new job and making a good impression was probably not a bad idea.

But the impression she was thinking of making

with the dress was on Cutty and the moment she realized that was what was dancing on the edges of her mind she shied away from the sundress for sure.

She wasn't in Northbridge to impress Cutty. Her goal was connecting with the babies—*only* with the babies—and she wouldn't let herself be distracted from that. Not even by a pair of deep, dark green eyes that had longer, thicker lashes than any man should be entitled to.

No, she wasn't even going to think about him. Wasn't that what she'd told herself the night before when she'd had so much trouble getting to sleep because every time she'd closed her eyes he was there, in her thoughts? There was one reason and only one reason she'd come to Montana and that was to try to have what remained of her family in her life again. And what remained of her family were the twins. Cutty was merely incidental. To her at least. He was just the person she had to go through to get to her nieces.

So what was she going to wear? she asked herself.

She forced herself to focus on the clothes in the armoire. To concentrate.

What about the linen slacks and the short-sleeved yellow silk blouse with the banded collar?

Comfortable but not sloppy. A little color but not too much. Sort of casual—because Cutty had made that odd comment about how he liked things casual— whatever that meant. So, okay, the linen slacks and the yellow blouse it was, she decided.

The slacks that made her rear end look good.

Not that that was a factor in her choosing them, she swore to herself. It was just a coincidence.

She took the pants and the shirt to the bed and laid them out before she turned to the small dressing table to do her hair and makeup.

Although she would ordinarily have worn her hair loose on the first day of a new job, for this particular job she thought it should probably be kept under control. That meant pulling it away from her face. A French knot seemed too stiff and formal, but she thought that a ponytail might be just the ticket. So she brushed her hair, pulling it tightly back and tying a pale yellow scarf around it to keep it there.

Once she was finished with her hair she applied a little blush, mascara and lipstick. Then she returned to the bed to put on the clothes she'd chosen before pulling on trouser socks and loafers, and concluding that she was ready to face the day and this new undertaking.

Ready and eager.

"To meet the twins," she said out loud, as if someone had accused her of being eager for more than meeting her nieces.

And that wasn't the case. She wasn't eager to see Cutty again, she tried to convince herself. How could she be eager to see the person who would no doubt be watching her every move, judging her, comparing her to Marla?

Of course she wasn't looking forward to that. Even if the person doing the judging *had* turned into a staggeringly handsome man.

Aunt Kira, I'm just here to be Aunt Kira.

Aunt Kira.

And Marla had been Mom...

That seemed so strange.

Whenever Kira thought of her sister she thought of the age Marla had been the last time Kira had seen her—seventeen. Just a teenager.

But Marla had grown up. She'd been a wife. A mother.

And now she wasn't just out in the world somewhere where Kira had hope of finding her again. Now she was lost to Kira forever. Tears flooded her eyes. Tears for her lost sister, for her lost nephew.

Kira knew there was nothing she could do to bring back either of them and reminded herself that there were still the twins. Marla's twins. And if she couldn't have Marla, if she couldn't ever know Anthony, at least she could maintain her connection with her sister through those babies.

Which was exactly what she intended to do, she vowed as she left the dressing table to make the bed, fighting the longing that things had been different. That her family hadn't ended up the way it had.

And not just because it would have been nice to have had Marla and Anthony in her life. If things had been different and Marla hadn't been estranged from them all it might have also been easier for Kira to think of Cutty Grant as her sister's husband, as someone who was off-limits.

As it was, she didn't have any sense of him as family. Maybe that was part of why it was so difficult to get past how attractive he was. So difficult not to notice it. Not to be affected by it the way any woman would be affected by it.

She was determined not to be, though, Kira told herself forcefully. She was going to have with the twins what she'd missed with Anthony. To be Aunt Kira now, even if she hadn't been before.

Aunt Kira, she thought, moving into the tiny bathroom to straighten it. *Nothing but Aunt Kira.*

And she meant it, too.

It was just that it would have been so much easier just to be Aunt Kira if Cutty wasn't going to be right there with her every minute. Right there where all she would have to do was look up to see his face. Those eyes. That big, hard body...

But she wasn't going to let herself be affected by it. She wasn't. She really wasn't.

She was going to do the best she could to take care of the twins, to get to know them, to earn their love, and in the process she was also going to keep their father nothing more than a sidebar to her relationship with them.

She was going to make sure of that if it was the last thing she ever did.

It was just that it might not only be the *last* thing she ever did.

It also might be the hardest...

Kira left the apartment at 6:45.

As she crossed the yard she wondered if Cutty would be awake yet or if he stayed in bed until the twins woke him. If that was the case and she couldn't get into the house, she had every intention of waiting outside the back door on one of the patio chairs just to make sure that she was there the minute she was needed.

But when she got to the house the back door was open and through the screen she could smell bacon frying and see Cutty sitting at the kitchen table—his foot propped on a second kitchen chair. There were also two babies in matching high chairs on the other side of the table, and a short, plump, older woman who was setting bowls on the high chairs' trays.

Kira felt a sinking feeling at the thought that she was already late. That someone else had had to come in to do the job she'd volunteered for.

But she didn't want to make it any worse by wasting time standing there looking in from outside, so she knocked on the screen door's frame.

Cutty looked away from the twins and that first glance of those evergreen eyes sent the oddest sensation through Kira. It was like a tiny jolt that skittered across the surface of her skin.

"Come on in," Cutty encouraged.

Kira opened the screen and went in, apologizing as she did. "I'm sorry if I'm late. I thought you said seven was early enough to get here and it's not even that yet."

"I did say seven was early enough," Cutty responded. "But Betty—this is Betty Cunningham," he interrupted himself to do the introductions. "Betty, this is Kira, Marla's sister. Anyway, Betty came over early on her way to the hospital to get her mother, and I dropped the cane coming down the stairs and woke the girls, so here we are.''

Betty had waited for him to finish, but just barely before she came to stand directly in front of Kira to wrap her arms around her and give her an unexpected hug. ''It's so nice to meet our Marla's sister.''

Kira tried not to stiffen up at the physical contact from the stranger. ''Thank you,'' she said. ''It's nice to meet you, too.''

Betty released her and turned toward the table, extending one hand in the direction of the twins as if they were the prize on a game show. ''And these are our darlings. Cutty said you didn't get to see them last night.''

And that was when Kira got her first real look at her nieces.

She'd never been an easy crier before, and she didn't know what was wrong with her now, but yet again quick tears filled her eyes at that initial glimpse of the two babies, who were paying no attention to her whatsoever.

There wasn't any question that they were Cutty's children but there was enough of Marla in them to cause Kira's tears. Identical, they both had Cutty's sable-colored hair in tight caps of curls that were just like Marla's. They had big green eyes slightly lighter than Cutty's, chubby cheeks and rosebud mouths like Marla, and the cutest turned-up noses Kira thought she'd ever seen.

''This is Mandy,'' Cutty said, pointing to the baby

on the right. "And this is Mel—short for Melanie. About the only way any of us can tell them apart is that Mel has that tiny mole above her left eye. We're hoping Mandy doesn't get one like it or we'll have to go back to guessing which of them is which."

Fighting the tears because she was afraid Cutty and Betty would think she was crazy if they saw them and because she didn't want to alarm the babies, Kira went to the table and leaned across it.

"Hi, Mandy. Hi, Mel."

They were doing more playing with their oatmeal than eating it—Mel had a handful she was squishing through her fingers and Mandy was taking spoonfuls and placing them meticulously on the tray around the bowl—but they finally looked up from what they were doing.

Kira didn't know what she'd expected, but it wasn't what she got. Mel immediately held out her arms to Betty as if to save her from Kira, and Mandy's adorable little face screwed up into a look of great alarm before she let out a wail.

That made Kira *really* want to cry.

"Oh, no, it's all right. I'm your aunt," she said as if that would make any difference.

It didn't.

Betty hurried to the high chairs, standing behind them and wrapping a comforting arm around each of the babies as she bent over between them to pull their cheeks to hers.

"Poor little dears," she cooed to them. "They're usually so good with strangers."

"It's okay, girls," Cutty assured his daughters. "Kira's a nice lady."

Mandy had cut short her wail, but both babies still stared at Kira as if she were some kind of alien life-form.

"Just give them a little time. They'll warm up to you," Betty said.

"Sure they will," Cutty chimed in.

It didn't make Kira feel any better.

And it wasn't much help when Cutty said, "Betty, why don't you show Kira the ropes around here so the girls will eat?"

Kira didn't think it was a good sign that she had to be removed from her nieces' sight in order for them to relax enough to have their breakfast. But there was nothing she could do except comply and hope the twins would warm up to her. Eventually.

Disheartened, Kira followed Betty out of the kitchen.

"Really, they'll be okay after a while," the older woman said confidently.

"I hope you're right."

That seemed to put an end to the subject then, because Betty said, "Let's start in the nursery," and led Kira down the hallway that ran alongside the staircase and up the steps.

The second floor of the house was as much of a disaster as the first. On the way to the nursery Betty picked up a few things, but it didn't make a dent in the mess.

The nursery itself was painted white and trimmed

in mauve, with one wall papered in a print where cartoonish jungle animals all played happily in a rain forest.

There were two cribs, two dressers, two toy boxes, but only one changing table.

"That's Mel's bed. That's Mandy's," Betty began, pointing out which was which. "But sometimes if one or the other of the girls is fussy they sleep better if you put them in the same crib."

The older woman crossed to Mandy's bed and began to strip off the sheet. "I probably have enough time to help you with these beds. Marla always changed the bedding every day. I've tried to go on doing things like she did because I know that's what she would have wanted."

There was a strong message implied that Kira should do things as Marla would have wanted, too.

Kira went to the other crib and began to strip the sheet from it. "You must have known Marla well."

"Northbridge is a small town—everyone knows everyone well. And then I helped out three days a week after the twins were born so I got to know her even better. Not that Marla really needed any help, because believe you me, she didn't. It was Cutty who brought me in but I mostly just fed the babies bottles and tried to play with Anthony while Marla did the real work. She was just a marvel as a mother and housekeeper. Actually I can't think of anything she wasn't a marvel at."

Unlike her younger sister, Kira thought, as she lost her grip on the crib sheet three times before she finally succeeded in getting it stretched over all four corners of the mattress.

But at least the other woman didn't notice. Betty just continued talking. "You should have seen Marla with Anthony. He was a sweet boy but he was a handful. It never fazed your sister, though. She was devoted to him. She was like a saint, that girl."

Kira didn't know what to say to that, especially since what Betty was saying was making Kira worry about how she was going to accomplish all Marla apparently had.

Betty then hurried out of the room with the sheets in her arms, saying as she did, "You can do the rest of the room later. In the meantime we can put these sheets right into the washer. Marla always did at least one load of laundry a day, and I'm sure you'll want to, too."

Kira watched the plump older lady stuff the sheets into the washing machine in the closetlike space that opened off the hall, hoping it and the dryer operated the same way the machines in her apartment laundry room did so she wouldn't have to ask for instructions.

"Cutty told me this morning that he's not having you do anything in his room. He says he'll take care of it himself," Betty informed her, bypassing the closed door across the hall from the nursery and moving into the bathroom where towels, washcloths, baby clothes, tub toys and various soaps, shampoos and lotions littered the space. There was also a ring around the tub and stains all over the sink and countertop.

"Baths everyday," Betty instructed. "In the evenings before bed. That was how Marla did it. And she would never have left the bathtub dirty. Or a speck of dust anywhere or the floors unvacuumed or—well, or anything less than immaculate. I'm telling you, she was amazing."

"She always was," Kira said, trying to do a little in the way of straightening up the bathroom.

"Oh, honey, no. Marla kept that soap dispenser on the right side of the sink and that's where it belongs."

Kira put the pump bottle where she'd been told to.

Betty adjusted it to just the right spot, explaining as she did, "Marla liked everything exactly so. But I don't have much time, and you can get this done later. Let's go back downstairs so I can show you a few things there."

The older woman led the way out of the bathroom and Kira followed.

There was another closed door on the other side of the bathroom and Betty nodded in that direction as they went by it.

"That was Anthony's room," she whispered as if it were a secret. "There's nothing in there. Even when Anthony was here he could only have a mattress on the floor, and at the start of the summer Cutty finally got rid of it. He gave away his own bed and bedroom furniture, too. It was a clean sweep. He bought all new things for himself, but of course there was no reason to get anything for Anthony's old room. Besides, there's work that needs to be done in there and until it is... Well, no sense furnishing it."

Kira glanced in the direction of the closed door, curious about what kind of work the room needed and why. But she didn't feel comfortable asking so she merely followed Betty down the stairs as the woman continued her nonstop chatter.

"It was good for Cutty to make some changes, though. We all thought it meant he was ready to get on with his life, and we were glad to see it. For his sake and for Mandy's and Mel's. A person can't grieve forever. That's just not healthy. Would you look at this mess?" Betty said, changing subjects as they reached the living room but not taking so much as a breath to let Kira know she was suddenly talking about something else. "Two days I've been gone, and I just can't believe what a shambles this place is in. You came at the right time, that's for sure. Now I can take care of my mother and know everything here will be all right. If poor Marla saw a mess like this she'd have had a fit. Never a thing out of order—that was Marla."

Betty went on to point out the box in the corner of the room where the downstairs toys could be put away, as well as outlining how often Marla had washed windows. And turned mattresses. And scrubbed walls. And wiped down baseboards. And polished furniture and silver. And made hot meals and home-baked cakes and cookies and her own bread.

The list seemed to go on and on until Kira began to think she might have a panic attack if she heard one more word.

Maybe Betty saw it on her face because she

stopped suddenly and said, ''Oh, not that you have to do all Marla did. I don't know if anyone could do all Marla did. I'll just be happy if you can keep everybody clean and fed and the house picked up until I can get back here.''

''I'll do my best,'' Kira said, realizing that Marla had left her a very high standard to live up to.

''I'm sure you'll be fine,'' Betty said. ''Now let me give you a quick tour of the kitchen and tell you about the babies' schedule before I let you get to work.''

Kira followed the plump woman back to the kitchen where Cutty was trying to coax his daughters to eat.

The reappearance of Kira didn't aid that cause because this time when she walked into the room they watched her warily and paid no attention to what their father wanted of them.

''After breakfast I get the darlings cleaned up and dressed for the day,'' Betty was saying, oblivious to the twins' continuing disenchantment with Kira. ''Some mornings they'll watch *Sesame Street* while I get to work on the house, or they'll play—''

''Those are the good mornings,'' Cutty contributed wryly, leaving Kira to guess what happened on the bad mornings.

Betty didn't address it, though, she just went on. ''They're ready for lunch around noon and then I let them digest their food for about half an hour before I put them down for their naps. That's the best time to catch up. They'll be awake again about three or so. We try to have dinner around six. Then there are baths and hair washing. They like to look at books before bedtime—they won't sit still if you try to read to them but if you point to the pictures and tell them what they are, they like that. I put them to bed for the night about eight or eight-thirty, and that's the day.''

Kira felt winded just listening to it.

But she wasn't going to let either Betty or Cutty know that and decided she would look at it all as a challenge. A challenge she was confident she could meet just the way she'd always met every other challenge in her life. After all, she'd been well-trained in meeting standards set by someone else. Plus she kept her own apartment pristinely clean. How much more difficult could it be to take care of two little girls on top of doing the housework around here?

''Okay,'' she said simply enough.

''You'll do fine,'' Betty insisted, looking at her watch. ''I'd better leave you to it so I can get Mom out of that hospital before she tries hitchhiking home. She warned me to be there first thing this morning or else. But if you all need me—''

''Don't worry about us. We'll manage,'' Cutty said.

''What's this *we* business?'' Betty countered. ''Remember, you're supposed to stay off that ankle. You just let Kira do everything. After all, she's Marla's sister. She'll be able to handle anything.''

Kira didn't refute that because she knew she would bend over backward to do every bit as well as Marla had. As always.

"Okay, I'm off," Betty announced.

She kissed the babies on the top of their curly heads as Cutty said, "Tell your Mom hi and that we hope she feels better."

"I will," Betty answered before bustling out amidst her goodbyes.

And then there Kira was, alone with Cutty and that incredible face that looked amused at something, and two babies who both eyed her warily.

"Are you sure you're up for this?" Cutty asked then.

"Absolutely," she said.

And she honestly thought she was.

Even as she glanced around at the stacks of dirty dishes, at the babies who seemed to hate her, and thought about all she suddenly found herself in charge of.

Marla had done it. And done it well.

She would, too.

"You were on your ankle too much, weren't you?"

It was nine o'clock that night before Cutty got the twins to bed and, coming down the stairs after putting laundry in the dryer, Kira saw him flinch as he sat on the couch and raised his foot onto the throw pillow on the coffee table.

"It's okay," he said, looking embarrassed to have been caught showing pain.

But it was Kira who was really embarrassed. She'd been much more hindrance than help today and she knew it. She had only to look around at the chaos that had grown rather than diminished to realize just what a detriment she'd been.

"Why don't you sit down so we can talk?" Cutty said then.

"That sounds bad. You're going to fire me, aren't you?"

He laughed. A deep rumble of a laugh that sounded better than it should have to Kira. "You just look like you need to sit down," he said.

She caught sight of her reflection in the living room's picture window and was nearly startled by what she saw. Her blouse was partially hanging out of the waistband of slacks stained with Mandy's chicken-noodle soup from lunch, half of her hair had slipped from the scarf-tied ponytail and the other half was bulging out of it more on one side of her head than the other, and all in all she looked as if she'd just been through the wringer. In fact, she was more of a wreck than the house was.

"Oh," she said, reaching up to snatch the yellow scarf so her hair could fall free. She stuffed the scarf into her pocket and then finger-combed her hair into some sort of order.

"Come on. Sit a minute," Cutty urged.

She did, perching like a schoolgirl on the edge of the easy chair to his left.

Cutty's dark green eyes studied her, and it occurred to Kira that even though they'd basically been together all day and evening she'd been so enmeshed in one thing after another that she'd hardly glanced at him.

He didn't look any the worse for wear, though. The gray workout pants that stretched across his massive thighs and the muscle-hugging white T-shirt he wore were still clean. Even the five o'clock shadow that darkened the lower half of his striking face only gave him a scruffiness that was very sexy.

But the last thing Kira needed was to notice *that* now.

To avoid it she forced herself to stare at the applesauce caked on her shoe. "I'm so sorry about…" She shrugged helplessly. "Everything today. Really, I swear I'm usually the most organized, efficient person anyone knows. And believe it or not, my apartment is always spotless."

"I don't doubt it," he said. "But add a couple of busy, mischievous eighteen-month-olds to the equation and it tends to throw everything off."

Why did he seem to think her failure today was funny?

"Even when my focus was on school and I was under a lot of pressure to get grades as high as Marla always had, I could still juggle all my work at home with all my classwork and even my research. My room at home and my apartment after I left home never looked like this…" Kira motioned to the even bigger mess all around them. "I was sure if Marla was a whiz at all of it the way Betty said she was, that I would be, too."

"Marla wasn't *always* a whiz at it. She started out having trouble taking care of a baby—*one* baby—and everything else, too. We both did. But as time went on—''

''I'll get better,'' Kira promised before he could finish what he was saying. ''I mean it. I'll come over here at four tomorrow morning before you or the girls are awake and—''

''Whoa!'' Cutty said with a shake of his head and a big hand held up palm outward. ''I didn't want to talk to you about trying harder—''

''So you *are* firing me.''

''I never hired you, how could I fire you? You're just helping out and all I wanted to talk to you about was relaxing.''

''Relaxing?'' Kira repeated as if the word wasn't in her vocabulary.

''I think you're trying too hard and getting in your own way.''

Trying too hard? Was there such a thing?

''It's making you kind of fumble fingered.''

''I know I seemed to drop and spill everything I touched today, and I spent all my time cleaning up my own messes rather than making any headway with the ones that were already here. I'm not usually that clumsy.''

''And when it comes to the girls—''

''They still don't like me.''

''You're just unfamiliar to them, and they're missing Betty—she's like a grandmother to them. They'll get used to you but you can't force it. They can be pretty contrary when you try.''

And Kira had the soiled clothes and shoes to show for it.

Still she knew he was right. The way she'd handled the twins certainly hadn't been the recipe for success, since all they'd wanted to do was escape from her overly cloying attentions—frequently by displays of temper—and Cutty had ended up having to step in to do everything.

"I'm sorry," Kira said again. Then, with another glance at the debris all around them, she added, "Maybe I can get some things done now."

"I think what you should do now is go soak in a bubble bath," Cutty said. "And we'll start over tomorrow. Maybe *without* so much concern about how Marla did things."

Kira had spent an inordinate amount of time asking how her sister did everything. "Betty said—"

"I can imagine what Betty said. But Betty isn't here and neither is Marla, and we just need to get things taken care of regardless of what Betty said or how Marla did things."

"Okay," Kira agreed, thinking that that was a nice way of saying she just needed to get *something—anything*—done.

But then he managed to raise her sinking spirits with a simple, winning smile. "You know, I appreciate that you're here and willing to help out. And I'm glad you want to get to know the girls. I just think things will run more smoothly if you can go with the flow. Like I said, *relax.* Have a little fun, get a little done. There's no right way. There's no wrong way. There's no big deals.''

Kira nodded. "I'll try." But the truth was, she'd been taught that there was *always* a right way and that was how she had to do everything. She wasn't too sure she could ignore that now.

Cutty took his foot off the pillow and stood then. ''Come on. Let me give you a key to the back door so you can get in whenever you want, and then you can go have that long soak in the tub. Tomorrow will be a better day.''

Kira thought he was probably figuring it couldn't be a worse one.

But still, the idea of sinking into a bath full of bubbles was too tempting to pass up and she stood, too, following Cutty to the kitchen and feeling guilty for the sight of him limping even more than he had been the night before.

''I really am sorry,'' she told him yet again as they reached the kitchen.

''I'll let it go this time but another day like today and I'll have to dock your pay,'' he joked.

He took a key from the hook beside the door and turned around, giving her a full view of a mischievous smile that put those creases on either side of his mouth and made an unexpected warmth wash through her.

''Before this is over I might end up having to pay you,'' Kira said, making a joke of her own. ''In fact you can probably start a tab with those two dishes and the coffee mug I broke.''

Cutty just laughed and again she liked the sound of it. "You are kind of a bull in a china shop," he said as if it were a compliment.

"Not usually," she assured. "Honestly, no one who knows me would have believed this today."

He didn't say anything to that. He merely gave her the key.

But as she accepted it their hands brushed. Only briefly. And Kira found herself oddly aware of it. Of the heat of his skin. Of the little shards of electricity that seemed to shoot up her arm from the point of contact.

It was just silly, she told herself.

Although, she also thought when Cutty spoke again that his voice might have dropped an octave, and she had to wonder if he'd felt it, too.

But if he did, he didn't indicate it in *what* he was saying.

"And don't even think about coming over here at four tomorrow morning. Seven is plenty early enough. You'll probably have to wait half an hour or so for the girls to wake up even at that. But maybe if you're the first person they see instead of Betty, it'll start things off more in your favor."

"Like ducks bonding to the first thing they see when they hatch?"

He grinned. "Something like that, yeah."

"I'll hope for the best."

There was a moment then when their eyes met and held. Kira didn't understand why or what was in the air between them when it happened. But there was definitely *something* in the air between them. Something that seemed more than just the camaraderie of being in the trenches together.

But then it passed and Cutty opened the screen for her, holding it while she went out.

"See you in the morning," he said then.

"Good night," she responded.

But even as Kira walked across the yard to the garage apartment she could still feel the remnants of that change that had hung in the air for that single moment.

What had that been about? she wondered.

She honestly didn't know.

But she did know that even after the fact, it left her feeling all tingly inside.

Chapter Three

"It was the weirdest damn thing. There was this minute when I actually thought about *kissing* her."

Cutty was sitting in the kitchen of Ad Walker's apartment at seven-fifteen the next morning with his ankle propped on one of Ad's chairs.

Ad was Cutty's best friend and after Cutty had suggested to Kira that he leave her alone with the twins this morning, he'd done just that. His police-issue SUV had an automatic transmission, and since it didn't have a clutch and it was his left foot that was out of commission, he could drive even if he wasn't supposed to walk any more than necessary.

He'd taken advantage of that fact and driven to the restaurant-bar Ad owned on Main Street. There were two apartments above Adz, one in which Ad lived.

Cutty had had to hop on one foot to get up the outside stairs but once he had he'd pounded on Ad's apartment door until Ad woke up to let him in.

A bleary-eyed Ad had made coffee, and it was over two cups of that strong, black brew that Cutty had told him about the appearance of Kira Wentworth on his doorstep and her insistence on staying to help out.

Cutty had also told Ad what had been on his mind since Kira had walked through his door, culminating in that moment when he and Kira had been saying good-night the evening before and the air all around them had seemed charged.

"So you just *thought* about kissing her? You didn't do it?" Ad asked, sitting across the table from Cutty in the same position—with his legs propped on the remaining chair even though they weren't in need of elevation.

"No, I didn't do it," Cutty answered as if the question was ridiculous.

"I think you should have."

"Come on," Cutty said as if his friend had to be kidding.

"Why not? A beautiful woman shows up out of the blue—the first woman I've ever heard you say that about, by the way. You have trouble keeping your eyes off her all day long—especially when she's bending over," Ad said, summarizing what Cutty had already told him. "You felt sparks—even though you don't understand it. Who's to say she didn't feel them, too?"

"Come on," Cutty repeated, this time with a groan.

But Ad wasn't fazed. "You said yourself that it was time you got back on the horse—so to speak. I don't see anything wrong with going for it."

"She's Marla's *sister*," Cutty reminded.

"Well, sure, technically. But she's Marla's *adopted* sister. They weren't related by blood. Plus, they only shared a roof when they were kids and not even for their whole childhoods. If Marla were alive and they passed each other on the street they might not have even recognized each other. And no matter what their relationship was a lifetime ago, the bottom line is that to you, this woman is just a woman. No different than if she was a newcomer to Northbridge who you met at church."

"Still," Cutty persisted with his coffee cup poised at his lips so he could take a drink after the word left his mouth.

"Good argument," Ad countered sardonically. "And the reason you don't *have* a good argument is that this woman being Marla's *adopted* sister is absolutely no reason you couldn't have a thing with her."

"You have to admit it's a little—"

"It's a little nothing. I can't see where there would be a single thing wrong with it. Two separate women. Mostly unrelated to each other. It's not freaky so stop even thinking that it might be."

Cutty gave him a mock salute, pretending to take the order.

"There is a bigger issue here, though," Ad went on. "Is this Kira like Marla?"

There weren't many people who had known the real Marla. But Ad had. He was also the only person Cutty felt free to talk to honestly because he was the only person Cutty had ever confided in about his late wife and marriage.

"That's not just a bigger issue," Cutty said. "It's a huge issue."

"So she *is* like Marla?"

Cutty shrugged. "I don't know. Maybe. Maybe not. She was raised by Marla's father—that's not much of an endorsement. I don't think he would have let anybody get away with being less than a shining monument to him. She has a Ph.D. in microbiology—that can't mean she's a slacker. And since she didn't get enough done yesterday she was downstairs trying to clean the kitchen at six this morning even though I told her point-blank to come around seven when the girls usually wake up."

Ad's eyebrows rose. "Not good signs," he agreed.

"On the other hand," Cutty said, and he couldn't help laughing when he did, "she hit my place like a second tornado. So far she's been all thumbs. She's broken dishes. Spilled cereal. Made a mess of every-thing she's touched. And even though she swears she's usually a great housekeeper and it's just trying to keep up with the twins that's causing it, I may not find my house still standing when I get back."

"And you liked that she made mistakes," Ad accused.

"I wouldn't say I *liked* it. I need help around there, somebody to take Betty's place, and I'm sure as hell not getting that with Kira. I was on this ankle so much yesterday and last night that I had to take a pain pill to get the throbbing to quit so I could sleep. I haven't had to do that in three days.''

''Okay, so while it might indicate that she's different from Marla, it's not doing you much good right now,'' Ad amended. ''How is she with the girls?''

''Oh, so bad. I'm liable to have to arrest myself for being a neglectful parent because I left them alone with her this morning.''

''They'll be fine. They've survived my baby-sitting in a pinch.''

''And Kira's about as bad at it as you are. Although it's also possible that the twins might hurt her,'' Cutty added with another laugh. ''They don't like her yet, that's for sure. I'm hoping if she gets them up this morning and neither Betty or I are anywhere around, they'll have to let her take care of them and maybe that'll break some of the ice. But as it stands now, she is definitely not their favorite person.''

''None of this makes her sound much like Marla,'' Ad observed.

Cutty sobered again and Ad caught it and said, ''But something about her is like Marla. What?''

''She *wants* to do it all the way Marla did. She doesn't know how to accomplish it—yet—but I can tell that's how high she's set the bar.''

Ad didn't have anything to say to that right away. Instead he took a drink of his coffee and then stared at the cup even after he'd set it back on the table.

''I can't get into that…that whole perfection thing

again, you know?'' Cutty said then, his voice quiet, solemn, determined. And reluctant, too. Reluctant to even allude to anything that spoke badly of his late wife.

"Yeah," Ad agreed the same way.

"I'm not even going to take the chance."

"So you didn't kiss her."

Cutty shook his head.

"But you wanted to," Ad said on a more upbeat note. "At least that means you really are back in the land of the living."

"Or that I'm just a glutton for punishment," Cutty countered wryly.

"That, too," Ad confirmed with a laugh. Then he said, "Maybe I should come by and meet her. Give you my expert opinion."

"You just want to check her out."

"That, too," Ad repeated with another laugh.

"Okay. But you'd better be on your best behavior."

"Nothing less."

"Any chance you could make it over tonight? When I saw how things were going yesterday I had to call that journalism student and reschedule my half of the interview for tonight. Only tonight she has to be there at seven, which means the twins will still be up. Maybe you could help Kira keep the girls out of the way while I talk to the reporter."

"Sure."

"Great. And will you do me a favor? Will you run

by my office later today when your brother starts his shift and get that paperwork from him?''

One of Ad's brothers was Cutty's partner on North-bridge's police force.

"You're supposed to be recuperating, not working," Ad reminded.

"Paperwork doesn't put any weight on my ankle, and at least I'll feel like I'm doing something to earn my paycheck."

"Uh-huh. And I guess it's a good idea to have something to keep you from watching your new housekeeper bending over."

"Oh, yeah," Cutty agreed.

The problem was, he doubted that paperwork would do the trick any more than anything he'd tried the day before.

There was just something about Kira that had his eyes wandering to her like heat-seeking missiles every time she was in sight.

Whether she was bending over or not.

Kira felt as if she were walking to the guillotine as she climbed the stairs at 7:45 that morning. She was on her own. Cutty was gone. There was no chance of Betty bustling in to rescue her. And one of the twins was calling, "Da...Da..." from the nursery.

It was a cute, pleasant little summons of Cutty. Kira hoped that meant that at least one of the girls was in a more receptive mood than yesterday. But even if one or both of the twins was happy now, that didn't necessarily mean the high spirits would last when Kira showed her face in the room.

"Just be positive and upbeat," she advised herself as she reached the nursery door. "Positive and upbeat and don't try too hard," she added, recalling what Cutty had said the night before.

She closed her eyes and willed the tension out of her shoulders. But it didn't help much and when the next, "Da!" was more insistent, she decided keeping the twins waiting too long was not going to get the day started on the right foot, either.

So she opened her eyes and the nursery door and went in.

"Good morning," she said cheerily. Probably too cheerily.

Mel and Mandy were both standing up in their respective cribs, grasping the railings for balance. Cutty had told her that in the summer heat he let them sleep in only their diapers. But Mel had taken off even that. And neither of them was glad to see Kira.

"Da?" Mel queried, her tiny forehead wrinkled into a frown that threatened tears.

"Your daddy isn't home this morning. He's at work," Kira lied, hoping their daddy being at work was something that registered as routine for them.

Maybe she was right because although Mel's bottom lip came out in an elaborate pout, she didn't cry.

"Down," Mandy demanded then.

"We have to get a diaper on Mel before she has an accident," Kira answered.

"Down!" Mandy insisted.

Wanting to please her, Kira went to Mandy's crib. "Okay, I'll put you down to play with your toys while I get a diaper on Mel. Then it's your turn."

Kira lifted Mandy out of her crib and set her on the floor before picking up Mel and taking her to the changing table.

Within moments of setting Mel on the changing table, Mandy toddled out of the nursery.

"No! Mandy, come back here!"

Mandy didn't so much as pause in her flight.

But there was Mel, already on the changing table, stark naked, and Kira couldn't leave her.

"Let's do this fast," she muttered to herself, reaching for a fresh disposable diaper.

But she was only partway through putting it on when she heard a loud, crashing thunk and an ensuing, "Oh-oh…"

"Mandy? Are you all right?" Kira shouted, her tension turning to panic just that quick.

Of course the baby didn't answer.

With Mel's diaper half on, half off, Kira snatched her up and ran out of the nursery in search of Mel.

She found the other baby in the bathroom, gleefully splashing the water out of the toilet, clearly remorseless about having knocked the tissue box from the back of the toilet tank into the bathtub, taking with it a bottle of shampoo that was now running down the drain.

"No, Mandy, that's icky," Kira groaned.

She stood Mel on her own two feet to haphazardly

fasten her diaper and then snatched Mandy away from the toilet to wash her hands in the sink.

"You noddy," Mandy decreed during the process.

"Right. I'm the naughty one. The naughty one isn't the stinker who ran away to play in the toilet."

"You sinker," Mandy countered. "Wan Beh-ee."

"Betty isn't here, either," Kira said, feeling disheartened at the reminder that she was not on the list of people the twins wanted taking care of them.

Still, she dried Mandy's hands and arms, trying to believe that the babies would come to like her eventually.

"Okay, now let's change your diaper," she said when she'd finished, as if they were embarking on a great adventure.

But that particular adventure couldn't begin immediately because then she realized that Mel wasn't where she'd set her only moments before. Mel was no longer in the bathroom at all.

"Oh, no," Kira said, thinking that they were like scurrying little mice—the minute their feet hit the floor they took off.

Why hadn't this happened the day before when Cutty had taken care of them? she asked herself.

Then she recalled that whenever he'd had to concentrate on them one at a time, he'd put the other one in the playpen downstairs. Or in a high chair, or in one of the cribs. Or he'd closed the nursery door.

"Containment—that's the first lesson of the day," she said.

Ignoring Mandy's demand to be put down and her

attempt to wiggle out of Kira's arms, Kira took her to search for Mel.

"Da? Da?"

Kira followed the sound of the tiny voice to Cutty's bedroom. Mel was apparently looking there for her father.

"He's not here, honey," Kira informed the little girl from the doorway.

Kira didn't want to go into Cutty's room with it's mahogany furniture and the king-size bed he'd already made up for the day and covered with a plain blue spread. It was his *bedroom* after all. Where he changed his clothes. Where he slept. Where he put on that clean-smelling aftershave that reminded Kira of the ocean and still lingered in the air. It just seemed too intimate a place for her to trespass.

But of course Mel wouldn't come out when Kira asked her to and Kira was left with no choice but to go all the way into the room and catch the baby who made a dash for Cutty's bathroom when she saw Kira coming.

With Mandy in her arms and Mel by the hand, Kira hurried out of the bedroom and back to the nursery for Mandy's diaper change.

This time Kira closed the nursery door, locking herself in with both girls protesting just the way they had the day before anytime she'd tried to take care of them.

"So much for bonding with me when there's no one else around," she muttered to herself.

Fully aware that this was only the beginning of the day.

And that she hadn't miraculously gotten any better at baby wrangling overnight.

"Oh, no, Mandy, how did you get up there?"

Kira's whisper was a lament as she turned in response to the thud she heard behind her.

After an entire day of more mishaps with the twins, the fact that Mandy had climbed from one of the kitchen chairs onto the table and knocked over a gallon of milk was one more rung on the ladder of frustration that evening.

Kira made a dive for the milk carton and for the baby, but by the time she'd righted the container, a good portion of it had flooded out onto the table, run over the side and was dripping onto the floor.

But Kira could hardly get mad at the baby since it was her own fault. She'd been putting Mel in one of the high chairs—a task which ordinarily would only have taken a minute. Only rather than doing it quickly, before Mandy could get into mischief, Kira's attention had wandered—along with her eyes— through the archway that connected the kitchen to the living room.

The living room where Cutty was with the Northbridge College newspaper reporter who had come to interview him. And Kira was having trouble keeping herself from being nosy about it even though she was supposed to be giving the twins crackers and milk to occupy them.

Now she had no choice but to focus on the girls. And the latest mess that had left the kitchen looking every bit as bad as it had before she'd cleaned it spotlessly at dawn this morning.

With Mandy in tow, Kira grabbed a dish towel and tried to staunch the flow of milk onto the floor, leaving it like a dam on the table while she put Mandy into the second high chair.

As she did she couldn't keep her gaze from drifting once more out to the living room where Cutty sat on the couch and the very attractive graduate student was half interviewing him, half flirting with him.

Of course Kira knew it shouldn't make the slightest bit of difference to her. So what if some woman was flirting with him? So what if the woman was tall and thin enough to be a model, or had full, wavy platinum-blond hair that fell to the middle of her back, and breasts at least two cup sizes bigger than hers? It meant nothing to Kira. She was only here for the twins. What Cutty did was Cutty's business. She just hoped he could see through that phony little giggle. And that overly rapt interest.

Who did that woman think she was fooling with those coy glances from under her lashes? And that slow smile with all those ultrabright white teeth?

"I'll bet she practiced that in the mirror for weeks before she had it just right," Kira muttered.

Was Cutty buying it?

He was smiling back. Laughing at something she'd said. That laugh Kira liked so much.

He'd spruced himself up in anticipation of this—

that didn't sit well with her, either. He'd gone upstairs after dinner and put on a clean, pale blue sport shirt with his jeans. He'd shaved, too. And come back down smelling of aftershave.

Kira wished she'd been able to do that. Well, not shave and splash on aftershave. But she wished she'd been able to change out of the wrinkled linen slacks and equally creased camp shirt she'd had on since five-thirty this morning.

Yes, she'd managed to keep from having food spilled on her today, but that was the best she could say about her appearance. Even if she'd made sure her hair would stay in the ponytail at her crown by putting a rubber band on it rather than merely tying it up with a scarf, it would still have been nice to have had the chance to smooth it a little.

Plus, what harm could there have been in refreshing her blush? Or applying some lipstick for the evening? But no, there she was, bare lipped, probably pale, dressed in wilting clothes, while the other woman looked as if she'd just come from a spa.

And wasn't she using it all to good effect? Flipping that remarkable platinum hair around. Bending over to brace her elbows on her knees as if she was so fascinated with Cutty's every word. Showing eye-popping cleavage from the scoop neck of her tank top.

"We don't like her," Kira whispered to the girls as she finally broke a graham cracker in half and gave one to each of them.

"Mik," Mandy reminded then, and only then did Kira recall the spilled milk.

It had soaked through the dish towel and continued to run down the table leg onto the floor. It had also spread to the center of the table and dripped through the crack where the table separated to accommodate a leaf, adding a second puddle underneath, too.

Kira sighed. "She's out there being Miss Wonderful, and I'm in here just messing up again."

"Who's being Miss Wonderful?"

Kira nearly jumped out of her skin.

She spun around and discovered the source of her fright—there was a man standing on the other side of the back screen door.

"You scared me to death," she said.

Apparently feeling at home here, the man opened the screen and came in without an invitation. "Sorry."

He was a tall, good-looking son of a gun with a blinding smile that said he wasn't all *that* sorry.

He held out his hand to her to shake and said, "Ad Walker. I promised Cutty I'd stop by tonight to help you keep the twins corralled."

Kira accepted his hand and replied, "Kira Wentworth."

"Marla's sister. I know."

She knew who Ad Walker was, too. He was the man who had rushed into the burning house with Cutty. The man who Cutty had dragged from the inferno after Ad had been knocked unconscious.

"It's nice to meet you," Kira said. Then, to let him know she was aware of who he was, she added, "I read about you and Cutty in a Denver newspaper. I'm glad to see you don't have any lingering effects of the fire."

"No, no broken bones. Just a bump on the head," he said as if he'd taken it in stride when Kira knew he'd spent two days in the hospital.

He pointed his chin in the direction of the living room then. "I did my part of this interview a few days ago so I recognized Sherry when I saw her through the front window. I came around back so I wouldn't interrupt them."

"Ah."

There was something about the way he was looking at her that convinced Kira he was comparing her to Marla. And just that quick she was once again the geeky, awkward younger sister with braces on her teeth.

Trying to escape feeling inferior, she turned away to pour the babies two sippy-cups of milk.

That seemed to draw Ad Walker's attention away from her, to the milk mess, and then to the rest of the kitchen.

"Holy smoke. I thought Cutty said you were in here early this morning cleaning this place?"

"I was. And I had it in good shape, too. Believe it or not." It was just that then the twins had been turned loose for the day and breakfast, lunch and dinner dishes had ended up stacked in the sink and on the counters because Kira had been so overwhelmed once again by her young charges. And now the milk had spilled, so it didn't seem as if she'd done anything.

But Kira was less interested in explaining all that than in the fact that Cutty had talked to his friend about her.

"So why would Cutty tell you I was here early this morning?" she said as she wiped off the milk container and put it back in the fridge.

"He just mentioned it in passing."

Kira had been hoping to learn what exactly Cutty had said about her—if he'd said she didn't compare to Marla in the housekeeping department—and why he'd been talking about her at all.

But Ad Walker didn't seem inclined to say any more. Instead he turned to Mel and Mandy and greeted them with an affectionate and enthusiastic, "How're my girls?"

Both babies tilted their heads back so he could bend over and give them each a kiss on the cheek.

It was cute and funny and it made Kira laugh. "Have you trained them or have they trained you?"

"What can I say? They're just two little flirts," he responded.

As he pretended to taste the soggy cracker Mel offered him a bite of, Kira began working on the spilled milk.

Whether to escape or merely to help out, he excused himself from the twins, left them to their snack and pitched in.

"How long has Sherry been here?" he asked in the process.

"Only about fifteen minutes," Kira answered.

"And already you think she's Miss Wonderful?"

Back to that.

But Kira could tell he was teasing her and she wasn't about to let him get the best of her.

"Well, from a man's point of view, isn't she?" she countered with a nod toward the living room.

Ad craned his neck for another look. "I don't know if wonderful is the word."

"What word would you use? Hot? Gorgeous? Built like a brick house? Or just stacked?"

Why had she said that?

It was his turn to laugh. "You sound a little jealous."

"Me? That's crazy."

"Uh-huh," he said as if he knew better. "You can relax. She isn't his type."

"Whose type?" Kira asked, pretending she didn't know he was referring to Cutty.

"Our boy out there."

"It wouldn't make any difference to me if she was," she said, careful to make it sound as if she meant it.

But Ad Walker didn't seem convinced. He just said another knowing, "Uh-huh."

"Really. I'm not jealous. I just hate to see Cutty sucked in by someone who obviously has more on her agenda than an article for a college newspaper."

For the third time Ad Walker repeated, "Uh-huh."

Kira decided it was easier to change the subject than to fight this.

"I think we better move the table so I can clean

under the leg. If I only clean around it, it's going to stick to the floor.''

Ad obliged her, tipping the table so she could also wash the leg itself and under the center where the milk had dripped through.

Then he moved the table completely out of the way so she had free access to both puddles on the floor.

When she was finished she helped him slide the table back where she thought it had been originally.

''Marla said it had to be exactly under the overhead light,'' Ad explained, adjusting it from two angles before he was satisfied.

Kira thought it would leave more room if it was centered in the room rather than under the light but she didn't say anything. Marla's house. Marla's things. Marla's way.

''More cacker,'' Mandy demanded then.

Kira gave her one half of a second cracker and gave Mel the other half.

''How long does this interview take?'' she asked her assistant.

He shrugged a shoulder and went to the sink to rinse some of the dishes piled high there. ''I was with Sherry for about an hour and a half but I guess it depends on how deep into Cutty's background she wants to go. He might have more to tell. He's an interesting guy, you know.''

Kira opened the dishwasher and began to load the rinsed dishes. ''Actually, I don't know anything about him. Marla didn't bring him around or even confide in me. The first time I knew he existed was the night they both came to the house to tell our parents she was pregnant. Then they eloped and from that point on my father referred to him as the…person…who had ruined Marla.''

"Person?" Ad repeated. "I'm guessing you deleted the expletive?"

"Many," Kira admitted. "The nicest thing he ever called Cutty was trash."

"Cutty is anything but trash," Ad defended as if he couldn't believe anyone had ever thought such a thing about his friend.

"I know. But to my father—"

"Things happen, that's what makes us all human," Ad interrupted, still in Cutty's defense. "I didn't know him before he was seventeen but since then the Cutty I've known is a guy who's worked hard—under circumstances that might have broken anyone else— to make the best of himself and tough situations."

"I don't doubt it," Kira assured him, meaning it. From what little she'd seen of Cutty in the short time she'd been in Northbridge she already knew he wasn't the depraved degenerate her father had always made him out to be.

But still Ad seemed to feel the need to convince her. "For my money, you won't find a better man anywhere. People around here give most of the credit to Marla for everything but the truth is, if it hadn't been for Cutty—"

Ad cut himself off this time, as if he might be on

the verge of saying something he'd had second thoughts about.

Then, instead, he said, "I don't want to tell tales out of school. Let's just say that Marla and Cutty had a rough go of it, but Cutty had a rough go of it even before he met Marla."

"He did?" Kira said with uncamouflaged surprise as it struck her for the first time that not only didn't she know anything but the basics about Marla and Cutty after they'd eloped, she also knew absolutely nothing about Cutty before that. About his family or where they'd stood on the whole teenage pregnancy issue or if they were still in his life.

And she suddenly realized she wanted to.

But it didn't look as if she was going to be filled in by Ad because just then Mel shouted, "Wan down," and held out her arms to the big man.

"I think I'm being paged," he said in response. "How about if I take them into the yard to play for a few minutes and then we'll get them to bed?"

"Wanna pay," Mandy chimed in to make sure he knew she wouldn't stand for being left out.

"Sure," Kira agreed.

She helped him take the twins from their high chairs and watched as he herded them outside, pleased to see that despite the fact that they obviously liked Ad, they didn't want any more of his assistance than they did of hers, that they were just independent little things.

But once Kira was alone in the kitchen she again began to wonder about Cutty.

Particularly about why he'd had a *rough go of it* even before he'd met Marla.

And out of that was born a determination to have her curiosity satisfied.

Ad helped Kira get the twins to bed but that was too big a task to allow for any opportunity to question him about what he knew of Cutty. And once the girls were snugly tucked in for the night, he said he had to get back to his restaurant and he left the way he'd come in—through the kitchen door.

Kira could have slipped out, too, and gone to the garage apartment for what remained of the evening. But that was about the last thing she wanted to do because it meant that the few words she'd exchanged with Cutty during the day, the little time she'd had with him, would be all she ended up with.

Not to mention it would also mean that she would have no chance of learning more about Cutty and that she would be leaving him alone with Miss Wonderful.

So she didn't follow Ad out the back door and go to the garage apartment.

Instead she folded the day's laundry and finished cleaning the kitchen, all the while willing the reporter to leave.

She didn't get her wish until nearly ten o'clock but by then the kitchen was sparkling.

"Wow," Cutty said when he limped in after letting the reporter out the front door. "You worked overtime in here."

Kira could hardly say she'd done it to avoid ending

the day without getting to talk to him, so she didn't acknowledge the comment at all.

In lieu of that she said, "You must be dry after so much talking. Can I get you a glass of iced tea?"

"Only if you'll sit and have one with me."

It pleased her more than she wanted to think about that he'd come from being with the other woman and still seemed to want to be with her.

"Sounds good," she said, taking two glasses from the cupboard and pouring tea from a pitcher in the refrigerator.

"The girls got to bed without too much problem?" Cutty asked then.

"With the help of your friend."

"Ad—yeah, I saw him come and go through here."

"He didn't want to interrupt your interview," Kira said.

"I wish he would have. I think that woman was hitting on me."

"And you wanted to share the joy?"

"No, I could have used the protection," Cutty said with a laugh. "Getting married at seventeen doesn't leave you experienced at this stuff. Besides, I think she was a barracuda."

Okay, so maybe what Kira had been experiencing *was* jealousy, because hearing that Cutty hadn't been taken in by the other woman went a long way in improving her mood. And giving her a surprising sense of relief that she was a little afraid to explore.

She brought the two glasses of tea to the table, pulled out a second chair for Cutty to prop his foot on, and then sat across from him on a third ladder-back chair.

"Mel and Mandy seemed more cooperative today," he observed then.

"I'm still not their favorite person but they seem to be tolerating me."

"Thanks for all the work you did on the living room during their nap this afternoon. The Barracuda never guessed that there hadn't even been a place to sit earlier."

"I'm just glad I actually got some things accomplished today," Kira said, letting her relief over that sound in her voice.

Cutty didn't comment. He merely took a drink of his tea.

Kira did, too, wondering all the while how she was going to get into the subject she really wanted to be talking about.

As she searched for a segue she couldn't help surreptitiously studying him.

The one thing she decided she couldn't fault the reporter for was being attracted to him. He was such an appealing combination—rugged, sexy masculinity and the kind of sensitivity that made him seem accessible and genuinely caring.

Then, too, there was the fact that he was jaw-droppingly handsome with a face of chiseled planes and those long-lashed evergreen eyes....

"So, you and Ad seemed to have a lot to talk about in here tonight," he said then, drawing her out of her reverie.

Was she mistaken or was there an edge of something that almost sounded like jealousy in *his* voice?

She couldn't be sure but just the possibility gave her a whole new lease on life.

"Mainly we were talking about you," she said, seizing the opening his comment gave her rather than playing coy.

"If you were talking about me it must have been a boring conversation."

"As a matter of fact, Ad said he didn't know how long the interview would take because you're an interesting person."

"I think he was putting you on."

"I don't think so. But it did occur to me when he said it that I don't really know much about you."

Cutty shrugged, conceding that point. "There's not much reason you *would* know anything about me."

"I'd like to, though," Kira said, jumping in with both feet.

Cutty's mouth slid into a crooked smile that looked pleased to hear it. "You would?"

"I would. Ad said that you had a rough go of it— his words—even before you met Marla. Is that true?" Kira asked.

"I didn't have a storybook childhood, if that's what he was referring to," Cutty admitted, but without a hint of self-pity.

"What kind of childhood *did* you have?"

"In a nutshell, my mother walked out when I was a baby, so I never knew her. And my father was an alcoholic. Not a functional, social-drinker kind of alcoholic. We're talking the town-drunk kind of alcoholic.''

"Really? Was he like that before your mother left or did his drinking come after that?"

"I don't know to tell you the truth. I only know that from my earliest memories he spent more time drunk than sober."

"Did he hold down a job?"

"Off and on. He'd dry out—to him that meant he only drank at night and on the weekends. When he was doing that he'd get whatever job he could. But it would only last a few weeks, a month maybe, before the Friday night binge didn't end on Sunday. Then he'd lose the job. Disappear for days on end—"

"Disappear?"

"He wouldn't come home and I wouldn't know where he was," Cutty explained.

"But he'd leave you with someone, right?"

The question made Cutty laugh a humorless laugh. "Until I was six we rented an attic room in an old house in Denver from a woman named Mabel Brown. Mabel was pretty old but she looked after me, made sure I always had something to eat, a lunch to take to school. But if you're asking if there were formal baby-sitting arrangements made, no, there weren't. Mabel just sort of stepped in when my dad didn't come home."

"But only until you were six?"

"That's when Mabel died. She hadn't owned the house, she'd been renting, too, and using what my father paid her—*when* he paid her—to make her own rent. The owner wasn't happy to discover that and kicked us out. That was when an old army buddy of my dad's let us move into the two rooms above his gas station. Jack was the army buddy and he sort of took over where Mabel had left off. Home-baked cookies were replaced by Vienna sausages," Cutty finished with a laugh.

Suddenly Kira's own home life and her harsh father didn't seem so bad.

"Why didn't anyone call Social Services and have you put into a nice home?" she asked.

"Jack would never have turned my father in for anything. Besides, he lived right behind the station. He just told me whenever my father didn't show up, to knock on his door and I could stay with him. So that's what I did."

"What about school? Didn't a teacher ever realize what you were going home to?"

"I didn't tell anybody. I was afraid of getting my dad into trouble. Besides, in a lot of ways, it was just how I lived. What I was used to. I didn't really know any different. And if I needed a parent to show up for something at school and my dad wasn't in one of his dry phases, Jack came and told them he was my uncle."

"What about that—an uncle, I mean. Didn't you say something about an Uncle Paulie?"

"Right. Uncle Paulie. Actually he was my *great*-uncle. But he lived here, in Northbridge and his health wasn't terrific so he never came to visit. He just sent Christmas and birthday cards, and money when my father asked him for loans. He always let me know I was welcome if I ever wanted to move in with him, but he never turned my dad in or anything. You have to understand, as bad as this sounds, my pop was the nicest guy in the world. He was a happy guy, drunk or sober, he was warm and kind and good-hearted. Everybody—including me—loved him. He just had a problem.''

''And you never considered going to stay with your uncle?''

''I had to stick around to take care of my dad,'' Cutty said as if it should have been evident.

''No, your dad should have been taking care of you,'' Kira corrected. ''What about food and clothes? Did he provide those?''

''He'd come home with a sack of groceries whenever he thought of it but they didn't last until the next time it occurred to him so when I'd run out I'd eat with Jack. Plus Jack let me work in the station. I'd sweep up. Stack cans of oil. Keep the counter stocked with gum and candy bars—whatever I could do as a little kid. He'd pay me and I'd stash the cash and use it for stuff to eat here and there.''

''And clothes?''

''Once a year, the day before school started, Jack would take me to the Army Surplus store. He'd buy me two shirts, two pairs of jeans, a package of socks, a package of undershorts, a pair of work boots and a coat if I needed a new one. It was like my employee bonus,'' Cutty said with another laugh.

This story was breaking Kira's heart but Cutty told it as if it was no big deal.

"As I got older," he continued, "Jack taught me how to work on cars and I got to be a pretty good mechanic. So by the time I was a teenager I was making fair money for that. Then I bought my own clothes."

"What happened to your father?" Kira asked then, assuming he was no longer living since Cutty had referred to him in the past tense.

"He died the day before I turned seventeen," Cutty said sadly despite the fact that the man had obviously not been much of a parent to him. "He was drunk, of course, in an alley in downtown Denver. He either passed out or just went to sleep, and froze to death during the night."

Kira didn't know whether to say she was sorry or not. It had been so long ago, that didn't seem called for, so instead she said, "When you were seventeen— did you know Marla then?"

"We were in school together, so I knew her, sure. But we didn't start dating until about a month later. We were put into the same group to do a project in a physics class."

"Were you still living over the gas station?"

"Living and working there," Cutty confirmed.

"So at seventeen you essentially had your own apartment to take a date to," Kira said as one piece fell into place.

"The recipe for disaster," he said, guessing what she was thinking.

But she wasn't only thinking that things might have been different if he and Marla hadn't had quite so much privacy. She was also thinking that she was getting a fuller picture of the young Cutty. A picture that explained some things.

"So from when you were just a little kid you not only had to take care of yourself, but of your father, too," she summarized then. "And even when you had the chance to leave you didn't because you felt like you had to take care of your dad. That sense of responsibility must have played a big part when Marla got pregnant."

Again Cutty shrugged as if that was just a given. "Her being pregnant was my doing," he said.

"And when Marla didn't want to have an abortion, you eloped. Then did you guys both live over the gas station?" Kira asked because she honestly didn't know what had happened to them after that.

"We only stayed at the gas station for a few days. It wasn't a good place for Marla. That was when I finally took Uncle Paulie up on his offer and we came to Northbridge."

He said that with a note of finality in his tone that Kira took to mean he didn't want to talk about what happened then. So even though her curiosity was only partially satisfied, she didn't push it.

Instead it was her turn to say, "Wow."

"Like I said, not a storybook beginning all the way around."

"That's an understatement." And no wonder his friend had been so defensive on his behalf. It was amazing that after growing up the way he had, Cutty was the man he was.

And what a man he was sitting across from her, calm, strong, confident. And so attractive. Even more attractive—if that were possible—now that she knew all he'd gone through, all he'd overcome and risen above.

"I should probably go," she said suddenly when she realized that their eyes had been locked together for a few minutes for no reason she could explain.

Cutty didn't say anything. He merely went on watching her.

Kira stood and took both of their empty glasses to the sink to rinse and put in the dishwasher.

When she turned again he was standing, bracing part of his weight on his cane, tall and straight, with those broad shoulders and that slightly disheveled hair and those eyes still on her.

"Tomorrow I'd like to use nap time to get myself some more practical clothes," she said then, in a hurry to inject something mundane into what suddenly seemed charged and somehow sensual. "Jeans. T-shirts. I didn't pack with the twins in mind."

Cutty was slow to pick up the ball but after another moment of feeling as if his gaze was caressing her, he seemed to concede and said, "There are a couple of small stores on the main drag and one department store near the college. I'll give you directions."

"Okay. Thanks."

Kira knew she needed to leave but it wasn't easy to force her feet to take her to the door.

"I guess I'll see you in the morning then," she said, hoping to give herself more impetus.

"And you can sleep in a little since the kitchen and living room are clean," Cutty pointed out as he followed her to the screen.

"Right," she agreed. "Except the place could use some dusting and vacuuming and mopping. And I didn't get to the laundry today and—"

They were suddenly standing face-to-face at the door and Cutty had raised a single index finger to her lips to stop the flow of her lengthening to-do list.

He was studying her intently, his green eyes holding her so mesmerized that even when he took his finger away, she still didn't go on.

"I'm just grateful for what you did today," he said in a voice that was deeper, softer, richer than the simple statement seemed to warrant.

Kira forced herself out of the near trance he'd put her into and tried to joke. "I'm just glad I actually *did* something."

He didn't laugh. But then neither did she. Instead they both seemed lost in something Kira didn't quite understand. Something that the touch of that finger to her lips, that look in his eyes, had caused. But whatever it was, from what it was making her feel, she knew she should cut it short before it completely carried her away.

Cutty surprised her then by bending down enough to replace that index finger with his lips, kissing her.

It was quick. There and gone before she so much as closed her eyes. Or kissed him back.

But it was a kiss nonetheless.

"For a job well-done," he said then, making a joke of his own to explain what seemed to have taken him a little by surprise, too.

"Better than a package of socks from Army Surplus," she countered.

It made him laugh, and Kira liked that. And him. More than she thought she should.

So, rather than potentially making a fool of herself, she pushed open the screen door and stepped outside, refusing to look up at that face that had too powerful an effect on her.

"I'll see you tomorrow," she said as she did.

"I'll be here."

He'd clearly only meant that offhandedly but it was enough to make it easier for Kira to leave him and cross the yard to the garage apartment.

Because without the thought that she would get to see him again in only a matter of hours, she might not have been able to make herself go.

Chapter Four

The kiss Cutty had given Kira was the last thing she thought about when she went to bed Friday night and the first thing on her mind when she woke up Saturday morning. She couldn't stop thinking about it. No matter how hard she tried. And she *did* try.

But for some reason, there wasn't a single thing that was capable of distracting her from it. From thinking about that little nothing-of-a-kiss.

Why had he kissed her? she asked herself for the dozenth time as she got out of bed and headed for the shower.

He'd said that it was only a reward for a job well-done and it had sounded like a joke, but maybe it hadn't been. Maybe the kiss really had only been a friendly sort of gesture, she thought as she stepped under the spray of warm water and let it beat down on her. Maybe that nothing-of-a-kiss had genuinely been nothing. Just a thanks for playing temporary nanny and housekeeper. A nothing-of-a-kiss that could as easily have been on the cheek as on the lips.

Except that it *hadn't* been on the cheek.

It had been on the lips.

And Kira didn't honestly believe that it had only been a thank-you kiss. Not when she factored in the way Cutty had been looking at her just before he'd kissed her. Not when she remembered the feeling she'd had of being lost in those eyes.

No, that kiss—no matter how brief—had been more than a thank-you kiss.

Just not *much* more.

Maybe it had been a test-kiss, she thought, still trying to decipher it and what it might have meant.

A test-kiss. Like dipping an elbow in the babies' bathwater before putting them in the tub.

But if that was the case, then what was Cutty testing? Kira wondered.

Her, maybe. Maybe he was seeing what she would do. If she would slap him. Or be horrified. Or kiss him back.

She hadn't slapped him or been horrified. But she hadn't kissed him back, either. She'd just been too surprised to do anything but stand there.

And she shouldn't be regretting that, she told herself as she shampooed her hair. She shouldn't be regretting that she hadn't done anything to encourage him.

She wished she'd kissed him back. She wished that the kiss had lasted longer than it had.

And it was easy to see why. Cutty was beefcake beautiful. He was nice. Kind. Patient. Intelligent. Funny. He was the real deal. The complete package.

Still, that didn't change the fact that she couldn't give in to his appeal, she reminded herself when her shower was finished. It didn't change the fact that she would never allow herself to be merely some replacement—the way her mother had been for Marla's mother.

It was just that it would have helped if there wasn't something there when it came to Cutty, she thought. Something that made her notice every detail about him. Every nuance. That made her extremely aware of every hair on his head. Of every inch of his face. Of every bulge of every muscle.

It would have helped if there wasn't something there that made her know when he came into a room even if she didn't hear or see him. Something that didn't make her heart flutter each time she caught sight of him. Something that had left her whole body aquiver after that nothing-of-a-kiss...

That nothing-of-a-kiss that he should never have begun, she thought as she discarded the towel she'd used to dry off and slipped into her robe.

Not that she wasn't guilty of thinking about what it might be like to have him kiss her. She was. Yes, there had been the odd moment when he was talking on the telephone and his lips were near the mouthpiece and a momentary image flashed through her mind of those same lips pressed to hers.

Yes, there had been more than one occasion when he'd smiled or laughed and her gaze got caught on those agile lips, lingering there while she wondered what that mouth might feel like on hers, what those lips might feel like parting over hers, urging hers to part, too....

But she was only guilty of thinking about it. Simple, fleeting fantasies that she'd pushed aside almost the moment they happened. Flights of fancy. Certainly not anything she would have ever acted on. At least she didn't believe she would ever have acted on them.

But he had.

And she couldn't deny that even just recalling it was enough to send a little rush through her.

"Stop it," she commanded her reflection in the mirror over the sink while she ran a brush through her hair.

But the rush went on undisturbed anyway.

And that worried Kira. It worried her that Cutty had opened a door that should never have been opened. It worried her that she wasn't going to be able to suppress those fantasies if she thought there was any possibility that they might become more than that.

No, no, no. She didn't even know why she'd thought such a thing.

But that was the trouble—now that he'd kissed her, anything was possible.

Except that she wasn't going to *let* anything be possible, she decided. She wasn't going to let anything else happen.

But what did that mean exactly? Was she going to confront him? Tell him flat-out that he'd better never do that again?

That didn't seem like a good idea. She couldn't think of too many things that would make her more uncomfortable than that. And it would make everything that came after it uncomfortable, too. So uncomfortable that Cutty might not even want her help with the twins anymore. And that would defeat her main purpose for being here.

If he ever tried to kiss her again, she would put a stop to it before it actually happened, that's all.

"And I mean it," she said forcefully to herself.

Because when she got involved with a man it would be with a man who wasn't carrying around someone else's shoes for her to fill, and that's all there was to it.

She took a deep, cleansing breath and blew it out, convinced that she'd reached the right conclusion....

Saturday was as chaotic as every other day so far.

That was good in that it kept Kira too busy to dwell much more on the kiss or have any time alone with Cutty to feel awkward.

But it wasn't so good in that when Kira got the twins down for their naps that afternoon the house was so torn apart that she knew she should use the peace and quiet to clean rather than leaving to go shopping.

Cutty insisted, though, that she have that hour to herself, and since she really needed more practical clothes, she forced herself to turn a blind eye to the toys strewn everywhere; to the mud the twins had tracked into the kitchen; to the juice box Mel had dropped, Mandy had stepped on, and Kira had only superficially mopped up; and to the laundry that had yet to be done.

"Okay, but I'll be back before the girls wake up and I'll stay as long as I need to tonight," Kira assured Cutty, concerned that she would still just be doing surface cleaning when she was dying to scrub the place from top to bottom the way she had no doubt Marla would have done by now.

"Take your time," Cutty responded, handing over directions he'd written out for her to the department store near the college.

Kira was actually hoping she wouldn't need to go that far, that between the two boutiques on Main Street she would be able to get what she needed. But she accepted the slip of paper anyway, careful not to touch his hand when she did to avoid the effect any kind of contact had on her.

The first shop stocked mainly gauzy, free-flowing dresses, skirts and vests that weren't any more suitable for chasing the twins than the linens and silks Kira had packed. So that was a complete bust.

But the second shop had a wider selection of just what she was looking for.

She was only at the beginning of her browse when a saleswoman who looked to be Betty the house-keeper's age approached her.

"Am I mistaken or are you Marla Grant's sister?" the woman asked.

Kira stopped sorting through jeans to glance at the tall, slender woman with the gunmetal-gray hair cut short and compensated for with large onyx earrings dangling from her lobes. "Yes, I'm Marla's sister."

"I thought so. I know Betty Cunningham and she told me all about you coming in to help Cutty with the twins. I think that's so nice."

This really was a small town.

"I didn't actually come in to help out," Kira amended.

"But you stayed when you saw the need and that's what counts."

"It's really nothing," Kira demurred.

"We all think you're just a godsend," the woman insisted.

Kira didn't know who *we all* was but she felt guilty for being considered a godsend when she was so bad at the job she'd undertaken. She also hated to think of the talk that would follow when Betty came back to work, discovered how inept she'd been and told *we all.*

"Are you looking for a gift?" the woman asked then, when Kira glanced back at the jeans.

"No, I'm just looking for a few things to supple-ment what I brought with me."

"Well, these are the plus sizes and you're no bigger than a minute. You need the other side of the aisle. Let me show you.''

As Kira followed her, the woman said, ''My name is Carol, by the way. And Betty said you're Kira.''

''Nice to meet you.''

''You know, we just loved your sister,'' Carol informed her as Kira chose two pairs of jeans in her size and moved to a rack of knit tops. ''We all thought she was a saint, pure and simple. The nicest girl in the world and so beautiful on top of it all. Never a hair out of place on that one.''

Kira suddenly wondered if her own hair had slipped out of the rubber band that held it low on her nape today.

But what she said was, ''I loved her, too.''

''We all were just heartsick about her,'' Carol added. ''That accident was a horrible, horrible thing.''

''Yes,'' was all Kira could say. This was not an easy thing for her to talk about, especially with someone she didn't know.

''But we all think Cutty is doing better now and it helps that he has those babies. They just couldn't be cuter,'' the older woman said on a lighter note.

''They are adorable,'' Kira agreed, moving along the rack of T-shirts.

But as she did Marla was less on her mind than was the reporter from the night before. And she found herself drawn to a black tank top that was closer to what the reporter had had on than to anything.

No, that wasn't a good choice, she lectured herself. Especially now, when she was doing so much lifting and carrying and bending over. Definitely not a good choice. She didn't even know why she was considering it. It wasn't as if she ordinarily wore things like that.

So back went the tank top to the rack and she picked up a V-neck with cap sleeves instead.

"I think I would have known you were Marla's sister even if Betty hadn't described you," Carol was saying. "You're every bit as pretty as she was. You girls must have come from good genes."

Kira didn't want to embarrass the woman by telling her she and Marla hadn't been related by blood so she merely thanked her for the compliment.

Then, deciding that the jeans and the four T-shirts she'd picked out were enough, Kira let the saleswoman know she had what she needed.

But as Carol led the way to the cash register, Kira started to think about that tank top again.

She knew she really shouldn't buy it. It would be tight fitting. And low cut.

But it would also be cool…

"Let me get you totaled up," Carol said.

Now or never…

"Oh, just a minute," Kira heard herself say before she realized she was going to.

Then, as if her feet had a will of their own, she made a quick dash to the rack and grabbed that black tank top anyway, bringing it back with her to the counter.

And all the while Carol was ringing her up and continuing to talk about how unbelievable Marla had been, Kira just stood there wondering if the saleswoman was thinking that the tank top was not only not something Marla would have bought, but that it was also something Kira shouldn't be wearing around Cutty.

Or if that was just what Kira was thinking.

The house was quiet when Kira got back. She came in the front door and when she didn't find Cutty in either the living room or the kitchen, she assumed he was upstairs dealing with the end of nap time.

But in case the twins were still sleeping, she didn't call for him. Instead she put the bag that held her new clothes out of Mel's and Mandy's reach on top of the refrigerator and went up the stairs.

When she got to the second floor, though, she didn't find Cutty in the nursery. In fact the nursery door wasn't open at all. But another door was. The door that hadn't been open the entire time Kira had been there. The door Betty had pointed out to her as the door to Anthony's room.

Kira wasn't exactly sure what to do. She was already there and if Cutty had heard her coming it would seem weird now for her to slink back downstairs without saying anything. But she was also worried that if he was in that room, he might not want to be disturbed.

In the end she decided to make a beeline past the open bedroom door to the laundry closet as if doing the wash was the reason she'd come up in the first place. She thought it would give Cutty the opportunity to close the door for privacy if he didn't want to be interrupted.

The trouble was, she couldn't keep herself from sneaking a peek as she neared that room.

Sure enough, Cutty was inside, holding a very raggedy stuffed dog and staring at it so remorsefully that Kira's heart just ached for him. Too much to ignore him and merely do laundry, even if she was disturbing him.

"Are you all right?" she whispered.

He raised his gaze slowly from the stained and soiled toy and gave Kira a sad sort of smile. "Oh, hi. I didn't know you were back."

"I'm sorry. I didn't mean to bother you. I—"

"It's okay. You aren't bothering me. I wasn't really doing anything. I heard one of the girls waking up and I didn't think I should wait to start the climb up the stairs since I'm so slow at it. By the time I got here things were quiet again but you know that won't last long. I didn't want to go all the way down the stairs again and have to come back up them, so I thought I'd take a look at what needs to be done in here while I waited for them to wake up completely."

Kira nodded, understanding that he needed to keep his trips up and down the stairs to a minimum.

"If you'd rather be alone—" she said then.

Cutty shook his head. "No, that's okay. Come on in."

She accepted the invitation and went into the empty room with him, taking a look around.

If someone had said a war had been waged in the

small space she wouldn't have been surprised. There were holes in the walls, pieces of wallboard had been peeled off and scratches and scuff marks marred the paint everywhere.

"Betty told me this was Anthony's room," she said somewhat tentatively because she wasn't sure she should bring it up.

But Cutty didn't seem to mind. "Yep, this was it. Not a pretty picture, is it?"

Kira didn't answer that but he continued anyway. "Anthony was kind of tough on his surroundings," he said, sounding as sad as his smile had looked. "We kept a football helmet on him for when he would bang his head. Steel-toed boots for when he'd be in kicking mode. There was only a mattress on the floor so he wouldn't get hurt. But there wasn't much we could do for the walls or the paint."

"Did he bang his head and kick often?" Kira asked.

"It wasn't unusual," Cutty said.

Neither of them said anything for a moment.

Then Kira confessed, "I wonder about him. What he was like."

"He was...I don't know. He was Anthony. A little boy locked in his own world. A world he didn't like disturbed."

Kira wasn't sure Cutty wanted to talk about this when he paused for a long while so she didn't say more to prompt him.

But then he went on anyway, as if he'd just been

trying to think of other ways to let her know her nephew.

"Anthony never spoke a word. Ever. But he loved music. In fact, he loved it so much that sometimes when he would get into one of his...rages...I'd sing to him and it would calm him down. Of course the flip side of his loving music was that he would get on these humming jags. One song. Every waking hour. For days on end."

"Oh dear."

"Oh dear is right."

"Was the dog his favorite toy?" Kira asked then, nodding at the ratty stuffed animal.

"That's kind of hard to say. Anthony didn't form attachments to much of anything. But repetition is an element of autism. Like the humming, there were things he just did—for no reason—over and over again. One of those things was that he'd sit in the corner and rub the dog back and forth on the floor—like a scrubbing sponge. For Anthony that was as close as it came to being his favorite toy."

"So, if he didn't form attachments to anything, does that mean he didn't form attachments to you or to Marla, either?"

"That's what it means. He didn't like to be touched. Physical contact was one of the things that would set off the self-harm, so we had to keep it strictly to bathing him, washing his hair—only what absolutely had to be done. The music helped there, too, though," Cutty added.

There was a note in his voice when he said it that

told Kira that no matter how difficult it had been to care for Anthony, Cutty had done it lovingly.

"You miss him, don't you? In spite of the bad things," she said then.

"Sure," Cutty said simply. "In spite of everything he was still my boy."

Cutty's voice cracked almost imperceptibly and he turned his back to Kira to set the toy on the window ledge, making sure it was just so—maybe the way Anthony had wanted it. Or Marla.

For a long moment he stayed there, staring at the stuffed dog, and Kira could only hope he had some good memories to help ease the obvious sorrow of his loss.

When he turned back to her again his expression was more serene. "Sounds like the girls are awake."

The soft baby chatter Mel and Mandy sometimes engaged in was coming from the nursery but it hadn't penetrated Kira's thoughts as she'd witnessed Cutty's grief. Now that he'd brought it to her attention, she dragged herself out of her own reverie.

"I'll get them. Go ahead downstairs and get off your ankle."

"I'm a slave to the ankle," he said wryly. "What do you say we break free of our chains for a little while tonight?"

She didn't know what he was suggesting, and her expression must have given her away because he explained.

"If I didn't have this bad foot I'd be playing softball tonight. How about if we pack up the girls and go watch the game? There'll be plenty of hands to help out with them once we get there, and it'll do us all good."

"I shouldn't," Kira said in a hurry.

It wasn't that she didn't want to go. She did. She *really* did. Which was reason enough not to do it because then she'd be giving in to the desire to spend time with Cutty. Plus there was the fact that if she went she wouldn't get her work around the house done and she would have yet another day of housekeeping failure under her belt.

"I was going to get this place cleaned up, remember?" she said. "And maybe even actually dust and vacuum."

"Work instead of play," he summarized, sounding disappointed.

Kira assumed his disappointment was for himself, that he was figuring if she didn't go, he couldn't, either. So she tried to fix that. "That doesn't mean you can't go. I can keep the girls and just clean after they go to bed."

"You'd actually miss a softball game on a beautiful summer night—a *Saturday* night—to *clean?*" he countered as if that were unthinkable.

"The place really needs it. I'm living in fear of someone dropping by and seeing what a bad job I'm doing."

"Everybody needs some recreation," Cutty persisted with all his charm.

Kira wasn't a sports fan by any stretch of the

imagination, but the thought of an evening out in the summer air, with Cutty, *was* pretty appealing.

Still, she repeated, "I shouldn't," and reinforced it with thoughts of Betty and Carol realizing how inferior she was to Marla.

"The messes aren't going anywhere. They'll all be here when you get back," he reminded.

"Exactly."

"Come on," he cajoled in a sort of singsong.

There wasn't a doubt in Kira's mind that Marla wouldn't have gone off to a softball game and left her house in the shape it was in. It was something their father would never have allowed. Something Kira would never have done herself at home. But oh, it was tempting.

"Will you go even if I don't?" she asked.

He grinned as if he'd seen the loophole. "No, I'd stay cooped up here, going stir-crazy. And it would be all your fault."

Kira knew he was teasing her, and that he could very well go without her just the way he'd been able to go on his own to see Ad the day before. She also recognized that going to a softball game with him was hardly in the line of duty for her. That it was almost like a date. And that dating Cutty was the last thing she should be doing.

"Come on," he repeated, "The house will wait. But this is your only chance today to see a game."

There he was, standing so tall and gorgeous and sexy, and he was just so difficult to say no to...

"Okay," she finally conceded. "But if word gets

around that I'm slacking off on the job it's your fault.''

He laughed. ''My lips are sealed.''

And soft and smooth and warm...

But that was definitely not a thought Kira wanted to have so she pushed it aside.

It was bad enough that she'd just agreed to over-look the job she was supposed to be doing for an outing with him. The last thing she needed was to start thinking about that kiss again, too.

''Who's playing this softball game tonight?'' Kira asked Cutty as they worked on opposite sides of the family station wagon to get Mel and Mandy into the car seats in the back seat after dinner that night.

''We're the Northbridge Bruisers,'' he answered with an exaggerated cheerleading quality to his tone.

''Is it Little League?''

That made him laugh. ''No, we're all big boys. There's about twenty of us—all grown-up—who have a sort of league of our own, I guess you could call it. What we do is divide up into two teams by picking names out of a hat—so the teams vary every game to keep it interesting. Then we play softball in the spring and summer, flag football in the autumn and basket-ball during the winter. It's just for fun and exercise.''

''Who are the twenty guys?''

''I'm one. And Ad and his brothers—he has three of them—play. The other fifteen are...well, just Northbridge guys. They run the gamut—we have the younger of our two doctors, our dentist, the local contractor, one guy and his brother who own a ranch outside of town. We're all just—''

''Northbridge guys,'' Kira finished for him.

''Right.''

''And you always only play each other?''

''Most of the time. Every now and then some of the college guys or some of the high-school kids will get together and challenge us to a game. There aren't enough of them at either place to have their own official teams, but they try to give us a run for our money once in a while. For the most part, though, yes, we just compete against each other. Like I said, it's only for fun and exercise.''

Maybe that was what kept him in such good shape, Kira thought, sneaking a peek at him as she clicked Mandy's seat belt into place.

He'd put on a pair of less-faded jeans and a white Henley T-shirt that hugged every muscle of his honed chest, his broad shoulders, his hard biceps. He was clean shaven and smelled heavenly, and Kira knew she was way too happy to be leaving housework behind in favor of spending the evening with him. But she was trying not to dwell on it. Trying to tell herself that there was nothing more to it than a group outing.

''The college must be really small if there aren't sports teams,'' she said when she realized that silence had fallen while she'd been surreptitiously ogling him.

Cutty didn't seem to have noticed. ''Very small. They only have about two hundred students at any given time.''

"That's tiny."

"It's a private college that was founded mainly for people out here in the sticks. First priority for acceptance is given to people who live in the small, rural communities."

With the twins all strapped in, Cutty limped to the driver's side while Kira got into the passenger's seat. Even though she'd ventured out to the two boutiques on Main Street that afternoon, she still hadn't seen much of Northbridge so Cutty had offered to give her the nickel tour before going to the game.

Once they were on their way he began at the end of Main Street where Kira had stopped at the gas station for directions the evening she'd arrived.

As he drove, Cutty pointed out what was what and added a few anecdotes along the way.

Kira listened and took in the sights of the small town.

Most of the buildings on Main Street were built in the early 1900s. Two and three stories tall, they were lined up without any space between them, and with more attention paid to their brick facades than to what was behind those facades.

There was an overhang of some sort from above the first level of almost all the shops, stores and businesses the buildings housed, some with permanent roofing, some with awnings, and some that formed patiolike front pieces that stretched all the way to the street.

The largest building was a four-story redbrick behemoth on the corner of Main Street and Marshall that had originally housed the mercantile. Now it was the medical facility, complete with a five-room hospital.

Northbridge's expansion was obvious as they went farther down Main Street. There the buildings were more boxy than the older models and lacked the character of their predecessors' arches, different-colored-brick outlines and variations in rooflines.

But architecture notwithstanding, the La Brea ice-cream parlor in the glass-fronted shop at the opposite end of Main Street still had a line of customers waiting all the way out the front door.

Main Street ended there in a T. Cutty turned left then, showing Kira the white, tall-steepled church, and, beyond that, the stately blond brick government building that held his office.

The college was farther out, barely on the edges of the city proper. It was a nondescript, flat-walled building that didn't draw much attention from the dormitory that was housed in a stately old mansion that would have done any Ivy League university proud.

Cutty turned the car around in the college parking lot and retraced the T, bypassing Main Street to go east this time. The department store had taken over the corner opposite the ice-cream parlor and past that they drove through small and moderate houses much like the one Cutty owned—all with their own warmth and charm, all at least forty years old, nearly all of them frame with wide porches and homey Victorian touches in their shutters and spindled porch rails.

That took them to the school compound—that's

what Cutty had called it when he'd told her where the softball game was being held.

He'd explained that Northbridge didn't have enough population to sustain separate elementary, junior high and high schools so what had been established instead was a three-building compound that allowed each level a structure of its own to keep the age-groups apart while still sharing a single cafeteria, gymnasium, auditorium, office and combination playground-sports field.

Cutty's own league was allowed use of the gym and the soccer-football-baseball-field-day field for their games.

He parked the car as close as possible to that multipurpose field where the wooden bleachers were already loaded with onlookers.

"You get quite a crowd," Kira observed.

"Friends, family, friends of family—Northbridge is hardly bustling with activities so even small events get a pretty good turnout."

With the engine off and the keys pulled from the ignition, Kira expected that they would be getting out of the car. But instead Cutty angled slightly toward her. And the smile he gave her made it seem as if he knew something she didn't.

"Are you ready for this?" he asked.

Confused, Kira said, "I didn't know there was anything for me to need to be ready for. Do the twins misbehave in public or something?"

"No, they'll be fine. We'll hardly see them. They'll get passed around and spoiled rotten."

"Then what do I need to be ready for?"

"A whole bunch of what you said you ran into today when you went shopping. Everybody's going to want to meet you. And I do mean *everybody*. Northbridge is a lot different than Denver. There aren't any strangers—even with the college in town."

"Today wasn't so bad," Kira said, meaning it even if she had come away feeling inadequate in comparison to Marla again. That just seemed to be her lot in life.

"So you think you can handle it?" Cutty said.

"I think so."

"Okay. Here goes…"

Cutty hadn't been overstating when he'd said that everyone would want to meet her. In the hours that followed getting the twins into their stroller and the slow trek that took them from the parking lot to the field, Kira didn't see much of the softball game. Instead she spent that time meeting and talking to every single person there.

Not that she minded, because she didn't. Everyone was as nice as they could be, and if no one failed to mention Marla and how wonderful, how accomplished, how incredible they thought she was, at least it was good to know that her sister had been so well loved.

It wasn't only Marla who was adored, though, Kira realized as the evening wore on. Or the twins who were fussed over and spoiled. Cutty received more than his share of praise, too.

At first Kira thought it was due to his broken ankle,

but as time went on it became obvious that he was one of Northbridge's fair-haired boys—broken ankle or not. It was almost like being with a celebrity.

When the game was over Cutty declined the invitation to go to Ad's bar and restaurant for the postgame celebration, and he and Kira took the two weary babies home.

It was nearly ten by the time Kira had Mel and Mandy in bed. She headed back downstairs, expecting to find Cutty on the sofa with his ankle elevated on the coffee table. But the living room was empty of all but the toys strewn around it, and the dust and dirt she hadn't yet attended to.

She wondered if he'd gone to bed himself while she'd been busy in the nursery. Although it seemed strange that he might do that without saying goodnight.

Still, the mere possibility dashed hopes she hadn't even realized she'd had. Hopes that the evening might not be quite over.

It was that kiss, she thought as she tried to swallow her dejection. Maybe Cutty was avoiding her. Maybe he was worried she would want him to do it again and he didn't want to. Which was silly because of course she didn't want him to do it again. He didn't have to run and hide to avoid it.

Kira had herself worked up into quite a snit by the time she made it to the kitchen.

Then she found Cutty.

He was standing at the sink, slamming back two

aspirin, oblivious to the course her thoughts had just taken.

And Kira's snit evaporated and her hopes reinflated just that quick.

She tried to ignore those hopes, though, and said, "Is your ankle bothering you?"

"A little," he admitted reluctantly.

"Maybe you should get off of it. I'm going to straighten up a few things in here before I call it a night, but if you want to go up to—"

"How about if I just sit here and keep you company?" he said simply enough.

"Okay," she agreed, wishing she hadn't sounded quite so pleased that he was inclined to stay with her.

She watched as Cutty pulled out two of the kitchen chairs—one to sit on and the other to brace his leg, wondering even as she did why it was that she never seemed to tire of looking at him.

Dishes. Do the dishes, she told herself.

She crossed to where he'd been standing moments before and went to work rinsing what was waiting for her in the sink, ignoring the fact that the African-print skirt and silk blouse she'd changed into to go to the game wasn't a great outfit for dishwashing.

"You're pretty popular around here," she said.

Cutty laughed. "Well, since I have to live and work here I hope at least a few people like me."

"There seems to be more to it than just being well liked," Kira said, recalling the affection that had greeted him at the softball game. "It's as if Marla was the favorite daughter, and you're the favorite son.''

''I know Marla was the favorite daughter,'' he said somewhat under his breath.

''And you are definitely the favorite son,'' she persisted.

''I suppose that's probably not too far off the mark,'' he finally conceded. ''The whole town did sort of take us under their wing.''

''When you first moved here?''

''Soon after. Remember that it's a small town. Everyone knows everyone else's business—sometimes that can be a pain, but other times knowing that business causes folks to pitch in and help.''

''There weren't raised eyebrows over two seventeen-year-olds being married and having a baby?''

''Uncle Paulie set the tone. He didn't look at teenagers having a baby as anything but a part of life. In fact he'd always say it only happened to the living, that the dead didn't have to worry about it.'' Cutty laughed at that. ''I'm not sure how that measures up as words of wisdom go, but after your father acting like we'd just single-handedly destroyed the world, that philosophy was a welcome relief.''

''And the rest of Northbridge followed his lead?''

''Everybody loved Uncle Paulie. Like my dad, he was one of those guys it's hard not to love. He had a big, boisterous laugh to go with his big, round belly, and he gave away as many doughnuts and coffees as he sold. It didn't hurt that he was in full support of us. Then, too, he told anybody who would listen what kind of a life I'd had growing up, and that Marla's father had turned his back on her—that got a lot of sympathy aimed in our direction. We sort of became the town project in a lot of ways that helped us make it.''

''Money?''

''I worked from the second day we got here—in the doughnut shop—so no, not really so much money. But folks gave us old furniture when we turned the garage into an apartment. And there was a communal baby shower to help us get ready for Anthony. But more important there was just acceptance, helping hands in the way of opportunities offered us, baby-sitting so we could finish high school and so I could go to college at night, things like that. Things that were more neighbor helping neighbor, except that for a long time I couldn't reciprocate.''

''But now you do,'' Kira guessed.

''Every chance I get.''

''Every day in your job,'' she pointed out.

She'd finished the dishes and it was too late to mop the whole floor, so she dampened some paper towels and went to work on the mud trail.

The problem was, she was hardly dressed for cleaning the floor and it wasn't easy to do it and keep her skirt out of the way.

She tried, though, hanging on to the billowy cotton with one hand while she crouched down to wield the paper towel with the other.

''If I was to guess,'' she said as she did, ''I'd say that was why you became a police officer—to give back to the community that gave to you when you needed it.''

''That sounds so cliché,'' he said with a hint of a groan.

''So it isn't true?'' she asked, nearly losing her balance and barely keeping herself from falling flat on her face.

She hoped Cutty hadn't seen it. And maybe he hadn't because he just answered her question.

''It's true that I wanted to do something that helped everybody who helped us. Protect and serve—that seemed to fit the bill. But it's not as if I don't like my job, because I do. I wouldn't want to be doing anything else. And to be honest, I think one of the main factors in my choosing to do it was your father.''

That confused Kira. ''My father?'' she repeated, struggling with her skirt every time she moved forward in the odd sort of duckwalk she was doing.

''I hated that he thought I was some lowlife scum. That I was no good. That I'd never make anything of myself. I think in some ways being a cop was the other extreme and maybe that was part of the appeal.''

''Well, no one around here thinks you're anything but terrific,'' she informed him, thinking that she was glad of that, that he deserved it.

Kira duckwalked forward to the dirty spot right beside Cutty's chair and nearly toppled over once more. This time Cutty saw it because he said, ''Why don't you leave that until tomorrow when you aren't in a dress?''

''I'm almost finished,'' she said as she actually did wipe up the last of the mud.

But then she tried to stand.

And in the process she lost her grip on her skirt, stepped on the hem and the next thing she knew, she'd lurched right into big, strong arms that caught her by reflex.

''Oh!'' she cried out in alarm.

After a moment of shock himself, Cutty laughed that deep, rich laugh. ''Hello,'' he said as if she'd intended to end up that way.

Kira tried not to notice the instant wellspring of sparkles that ran all through her at that contact and yanked herself backward, out of his hold.

''I'm sorry,'' she said, sounding as flustered as she felt.

''Are you okay?'' he asked.

''Yes. Are you?''

''As long as you don't count that it's been tough enough keeping my hands off you and you just fell right into my lap.''

Had he really just said he was having trouble keeping his hands off her?

That turned up the wattage on those sparkles.

But Kira pretended that wasn't the case and that he hadn't just said what he'd said. ''You were right, I shouldn't have been cleaning the floor in a skirt. I should have waited. But no, I just had to do it now.

I just couldn't let it go until tomorrow,'' she said, berating herself.

"No harm done," Cutty assured her.

"But there could have been. What if I'd hit your ankle? What if you'd jerked it yourself?"

"My ankle is fine. Besides," he added with a sly, one-sided grin, "How often does a beautiful woman throw herself at me? Let's just say I fell on you last night, and you fell on me tonight, and call it even."

"Does that mean last night was an accident?" she asked before she'd controlled the tone that made her sound disappointed.

Cutty took his foot off the second chair and stood. Leaving his cane propped against the table, he picked up the paper towel she'd dropped, and on his way to throwing it out he paused to lean close to her ear.

"No, last night was not an accident."

He limped to the trash container, leaving Kira lost for a split second in the warm sensation left in his wake.

Once he'd disposed of the paper towel he turned his backside to the edge of the countertop to rest against it, taking his weight off his broken ankle by propping it atop the unbroken one.

"Although," he said then, "I have to admit I didn't put much thought into that little bit of indiscretion beforehand."

"Did you regret it?" That question had just come out on its own, too.

Cutty laughed. "Not hardly. In fact, I've been thinking all day and night about doing it again."

"You have?"

"I have."

"That's probably not a good idea, though?" she countered in a questioning tone that was much too tentative to carry any weight.

"No, it probably isn't," he agreed just as tentatively. "But good idea or not, every time it pops into my head—every time *you* pop into my head—it seems like something apart from everything and everybody else, and not a damn thing I tell myself makes any difference. I just want to kiss you again anyway."

Those sparkles inside her felt as if they had turned into full beams of light that were setting her aglow.

"It does seem like that—something apart from everything and everybody else," she confessed in a quiet voice.

Cutty's smile turned slow and sexy. "Does that mean if I were to kiss you again you wouldn't hit me over the head with the first thing you could grab?"

He would probably be the first thing she'd want to grab.

But she didn't say that. She said, "We shouldn't." Only somehow it came out sounding like an invitation.

"I know," he agreed, bending at the waist and reaching for her, pulling her to stand in front of him and clasping his hands loosely at the base of her spine so that his forearms rode the sides of her waist. "Maybe that's part of what makes it so hard not to."

His dark green eyes searched hers, probing them,

holding them, and even though Kira knew she should pull away, even though she reminded herself of her vow that if he ever tried to kiss her again she would put a stop to it before it happened, she didn't pull away. And she didn't do anything to stop him from kissing her again.

In fact, somehow her palms were pressed to the hard wall of his chest and when he leaned forward, toward her, she did the same until their lips met.

And lingered this time.

Long enough for Kira to savor the heat of his mouth over hers. Long enough for her to kiss him back the way she'd been wishing she had the night before.

It was still only a soft kiss. A starter kiss. With lips just slightly parted. With eyes drifting closed. With the gentle brush of his breath against her cheek and the scent of his aftershave tantalizing her.

But it was kiss enough to make Kira's knees go weak. To wipe away every thought about why they shouldn't be doing it and wonder where it was going to go from there.

That thought gave her a jolt. *Where was it going to go from there?*

It couldn't go anywhere from there. It shouldn't even be there.

It was just that it was so nice…

Then it was over, and she wasn't sure whether she'd ended it or he had. She only knew that, in spite of everything, she wished it hadn't ended.

Still, on the chance that she'd been the one to initiate the break, she tried to make light of it by saying, "Maybe you're just in too much pain to think straight."

Once more he smiled a leisurely, devilish smile. "Actually, I feel pretty good."

But he didn't try to kiss her again, and when she eased out of his grip he let her go.

"You're not supposed to be on that ankle," she reminded.

"I'll survive," he said, staying where he was, watching her.

"It must be getting late," she said then, afraid of what she might do if she didn't retreat. "And I don't suppose the girls sleep in even on Sunday."

"No, they don't."

"So we better rest up for the next onslaught."

Cutty just nodded his handsome head, his eyes never leaving her.

"Is there anything special going on tomorrow? Do you go to church?"

"The girls in church? That's just asking for disaster. I do usually barbecue on Sunday, though. It might take a joint effort, but I think I can stand long enough for that—if you're game."

It was a nice thought—a Sunday at home with a family, Cutty barbecuing, maybe eating outside. So much better than the Sundays Kira frequently spent—long, boring days that ended with solitary TV dinners.

"Barbecuing sounds good," she said. Then, before the urge to kiss him again became any stronger and caused her to actually act on it, she said, "I'll see you in the morning then."

Another nod. "'Night," he said in a husky whisper that only made her want to stay all the more.

And the fact that she *did* want to stay was her cue to go...while she still could.

"Good night," she responded, wasting not even another moment before she forced herself to go out the back door.

But all she really wanted to do was to stay right there in that kitchen with him. With his arms wrapped around her waist the way they'd been. With his mouth against hers and hers against his.

Exploring every possibility of where they might go from there after all!

Chapter Five

"Hi, Kit, it's me," Kira said into her cell phone at 6:45 the next morning when her best friend answered her call.

"I know it's you, your number showed on my caller ID, or I wouldn't have answered," Kit MacIntyre said.

"Because you're up to your elbows in frosting for the cake for the Blumberg wedding. I knew you had to start working on it at dawn this morning so I was safe calling you this early."

"You're almost right. I'm up to my elbows in ganache," Kit corrected. "But I should have the cake finished in time to deliver it by three and still be able to pick you up at the airport at four."

"There's been a change of plans," Kira informed

her. But before she got into that she said, "How was your trip?"

Kit had left Denver the same day Kira had to go to her great-great-aunt's funeral in Iowa.

"It wasn't too bad. As far as that kind of thing goes. My aunt was ninety-six and she outlived so many people that it was a small, quiet send-off. Mostly I'm just kind of bleary-eyed. I didn't get in until one this morning, and I had to be up at five to work on this cake. How about your trip? Why the change of plans?" Kit asked.

Kira had met Kit two years ago when Kira had moved into the apartment across the hall from her. For the first three months that they'd been neighbors they'd only exchanged enough information for Kit to know that Kira was working on her doctorate degree in microbiology, and for Kira to learn that Kit was the Kit of Kit's Cakes—a well-known Denver shop that specialized in special-occasion cakes—primarily for weddings.

But during a snowstorm that had stranded them without electricity for a full weekend they'd shared blankets, candles, food and the stories of their lives, and come out of the experience friends. Kit was the only close friend Kira had had since Marla had left home.

By now Kit knew everything there was to know about Kira, including what had taken her to Montana. What Kit didn't know—since they'd gone in opposite directions on Wednesday and hadn't been able to talk—was what Kira had discovered in Montana.

So Kira told her friend that her worst fears had proven true, that, yes, the Cutler Grant in the article was the Cutler Grant who had eloped with her sister, but that Marla and Anthony had been killed.

"I'm so sorry," Kit said. "I know you were hoping you would find Marla and your nephew, and have a family again. Are you okay?"

"I am. I have some sad times every now and then, but I guess in a lot of ways I mourned the loss of Marla when she left thirteen years ago. And as for having a family again—there are still the twins."

"So they *are* your nieces?"

"They are."

"Tell me about them," Kit urged in a lighter tone. "Are they cute?"

"They're so cute you just wouldn't believe it. But they're so busy you wouldn't believe that, either. They're into everything. They climb like monkeys— if I so much as leave a kitchen chair a few inches from being pushed in they'll be dancing on the table or dumping breakfast cereal all over it and spilling milk and juice into the mix."

Kit laughed. "Are they identical, or can you tell them apart?"

"They look just alike—they both have curly brown hair and big green eyes and cheeks so chubby you just want to kiss them. But one of them has a tiny mole the other one doesn't and I can usually tell them apart by the differences in their personalities. Mel— that's short for Melanie—is all girl, while Mandy seems to have a touch of tomboy in her. She's more adventurous, braver. Mel can be on the timid side, but she loves looking at herself in the mirror. She makes faces and preens—it's hilarious.''

''Do they walk? Talk?''

''They say a few words. *No* is their favorite—it's the first thing they say to everything. They do walk and would rather do that than be carried and—believe me—they get around. It's a full-time job just chasing them. They would also rather feed themselves than be fed, but they don't get much into their mouths so someone has to help. And whatever one of them does, the other one imitates.''

''They sound like so much fun,'' Kit said. ''Make sure you bring home pictures.''

Kira was surprised by the twinge that came out of nowhere at the thought of going home and leaving the twins behind. And Cutty.

But that was the last thing she wanted to think about now and she was glad when Kit provided a distraction by saying, ''So, let me guess—you're having such a good time with your nieces that you decided to spend a few more days with them?''

''Actually, when I got here the woman who usually works as the nanny and housekeeper needed some time off to care for her mother. So I talked Cutty into letting me stay to help him and get to know the girls in the process.''

''Does that mean *you're* the nanny and housekeeper?''

''That's what it means,'' Kira confirmed. ''Informally, anyway. I didn't know what I was going to do with myself until classes start and I just thought why not help out here?''

''I'll bet you've already taken a toothbrush to the bathroom tile, haven't you?''

''As a matter of fact I haven't cleaned the bathrooms hardly at all. You wouldn't believe how bad I am at juggling a house and kids, Kit.''

''You're not bad at anything. And you're especially not bad at cleaning—your apartment is nearly sterile.''

''No, honestly, I'm bad at this. I just can't get on top of things. I mean, I start every day with good intentions, but that's as far as it goes. I get the girls up in the morning and feed them breakfast. Then I pile the dirty dishes in the sink so I can take them upstairs to get them dressed and before I know it the day is over and all I've accomplished is chasing babies from one place—or from one catastrophe—to another, and I've left a trail of more dirty dishes and laundry and diapers and mess and chaos behind me.''

Kit laughed again. ''I get the idea.''

''At first I thought it was because the twins didn't like me and it took so much to get them to cooperate. But now, even though I'm still not who they run to if they want comforting or something, they'll let me take care of them without a fight, and it still doesn't make any difference. Looking after babies ends up the only thing I really get done every single day.''

''That's something,'' her friend pointed out.

''But it's not enough.''

''Says who? The twins' dad?''

"Cutty? Oh, no, it isn't as if Cutty complains. He's great. Which is a problem in itself. Like last night, he talked me into going with him and the girls to a softball game when I should have stayed home and cleaned."

"Cutty is great?" Kit repeated, sounding intrigued by only that portion of Kira's statement.

"He's very nice," Kira amended.

"Is he very *nice looking?*" Kit fished.

"Yes, he's very nice looking."

"And you went to a baseball game with him last night?"

"Softball. It's this sort of informal league a bunch of the men around here belong to," Kira said, purposely expounding on the subject to get her friend off the track she'd been on. "You should have seen these guys, Kit. A few of them were average, but more of them were pretty amazing. It was like a whole bunch of calendar hunks all together at once. I kept getting introduced to one after another of them who were so gorgeous they nearly made my eyes pop out of their sockets. If you were in the market for a man I'd tell you to drop everything and come up here. It must be something in the Montana water."

"What about you? You could be in the market for a man."

Except that, as attractive as so many of the men she'd met the night before were, none of them had appealed to her as much as Cutty had.

But she didn't say that. She said, "Only I'm *not* in the market for a man."

Still, her friend saw through her. "Or maybe you've just already found one. In *Cutty*—whose name, by the way, you say reverently."

"Reverently?" Kira repeated. "You really do need sleep. You're hearing things. What I've found here is a ton of frustration and a challenge I can't measure up to." And she wasn't only talking about the kids and the housework.

"But you're determined to stay until you do—is that why there's been a change of plans?"

Kit said that with a note of innuendo in her voice, as if Cutty was the challenge. But Kira chose to take her friend's words at face value. "I don't know if I'll ever be able to do this as well as Marla did—or even come close—but I promised to help out until the regular lady—Betty—came back, so that's why there's been a change of plans. I switched my plane ticket to one that's open-ended, and I'll just play it by ear."

"Oh-oh," Kit said as if there was a problem with that.

"What's the matter?"

"You don't know if you'll ever be able to do as well as Marla did?" Kit said, paraphrasing that portion of Kira's statement. "Your father isn't there telling you you have to, is he?"

Kira laughed. "No. It's just that you should hear what people around here say about her. Everyone I've met goes on and on about how wonderful and amazing she was. The house was always immaculate. She never had a hair out of place. She was a pillar of the community. She was a saint with Anthony. She was devoted to him. She was…well, from all reports, she was—''

''You're killing yourself trying to be equally as good as your sister again, aren't you?'' Kit guessed.

''I wouldn't say I'm killing myself,'' Kira hedged.

''Oh, Kira,'' Kit said, sounding concerned.

''What?''

''Don't do to yourself what your father did to you for all that time.''

''I'm not.''

''No? Because it sure sounds like you are. He raised the bar higher than you—or anyone else— could ever reach and used Marla as the example of what you had to compete with to try, and, unless I'm hearing things, now you're doing the same thing.''

''*I'm* not using Marla as the example of the way things should be done, everyone else is.''

''And you're still trying to follow that example and feeling like you're not as good or as smart or as fantastic as you should be. Even though, chances are, Marla's greatness is being exaggerated all out of proportion.''

''I don't know, the Marla I knew *was* smart and beautiful and talented and great at everything. Do you think that when she got here she swept the dirt under the rugs or hid the unwashed dishes in the pantry and just fooled everybody?''

''I think,'' Kit said patiently, ''that Marla was *human*. I think she was human enough to sneak around to date a boy her father didn't want her to date and to get pregnant at seventeen. I think that even if her house was clean and she was a good mother, there were probably days when she didn't wash her hair or when the laundry was stacked somewhere out of sight. I think she wasn't some kind of wonder-woman and neither are you, and I hate seeing you falling into even more of a pattern of trying to be and finding fault with yourself for not making it.''

''I don't have to find fault with myself, all I have to do is take one look at this house to know I'm failing,'' Kira said with a humorless laugh.

''See? *Failing.* You *aren't* failing. You're using your own vacation time to help out this guy. No matter what *doesn't* get done, that's still a really good, really generous thing to do. The twins are getting taken care of—which is the main thing, the thing that counts. But all you can say is how much you're *not* doing. From where I'm sitting, Cutty Grant is lucky to have you and should be grateful as all get-out.''

''He's not *un*grateful,'' Kira said. ''He's the one telling me to leave things until the next day or not to worry about what doesn't get done.''

''Then maybe you should take *that* seriously and forget how stupendous Marla may or may not have been.''

Easier said than done…

''Okay, I'll try,'' Kira said anyway, knowing her friend only wanted what was best for her.

''And in the meantime,'' Kit's tone turned sly, ''maybe you can just enjoy your nieces and the very nice-looking *Cutty*.''

Kit sounded like a dreamy-eyed teenager when she said Cutty's name and Kira laughed. "You are bad," she told her friend.

"Try it, you might like it," Kit advised with a lascivious intonation that made Kira laugh again.

"Bad, bad, bad. But will you use your key to my place to go in and water my plants until I get home?"

"You know I will. But only if you swear you'll let your hair down a little with Mr. Very Nice-Looking Montana Man. You deserve some fun, you know?"

"I know—all work and no play makes Kira a very dull girl," Kira repeated what Kit had said to her often since they'd met.

"Play is good for the metabolism—think of it that way," her friend added.

"I'll try," Kira said once more. "I'll also let you get back to your ganache so the Blumbergs can have cake at their reception today."

"Okay. Keep me posted," Kit said before they hung up.

But even as Kira turned off her phone she knew that, despite what she'd told her friend, she didn't need to try to have fun with Cutty. That happened all on its own.

What she did need to work at was trying to improve at everything else.

Because no matter what Kit thought, Kira knew deep down that she just had to be better at the job she'd taken on than she had been.

She just had to.

* * *

"Sim?"

"Sim?" Kira whispered back to Mandy, not understanding the word.

Kira had just gotten the girls up from their naps that afternoon, and Cutty was on the telephone in the kitchen where Kira had taken the twins and given them graham crackers to keep them occupied while she marinated the chicken Cutty was going to barbecue for dinner. But Mandy wasn't interested in the cracker. She was demanding whatever *sim* was.

And now that Mel had heard it, she obviously understood it and wanted it, too, because she began an excited chant, "Sim! Sim!"

"Shh!" Kira said in an attempt to keep the noise level down while Cutty was on the phone. Especially since the questions he was asking the caller were clearly police business. "Can you show me what you want?" she asked the girls as she covered the dish with the chicken and marinade in it and put it in the refrigerator.

"Sim!" Mandy demanded more forcefully now that she had her sister's support.

"I don't know what *sim* is," Kira informed the tiny child, unsure if either twin comprehended what she was trying to get through to them any more than she understood what they were telling her.

"Sim!" Mel shouted.

That prompted Cutty to say into the receiver, "Hang on a minute." Then, with his hand over the mouthpiece, he said to Kira, "*Sim* is swim. They want to swim in the blow-up pool in the backyard."

"Oh," Kira said as light dawned. "Should I let them?"

"It's up to you. You'll have to rinse out the pool, fill it from the hose, bring out a bucket of hot water to heat it and sit with them the whole time."

None of which involved making any headway on the chores Kira was hoping to get to.

Cutty must have seen her indecision because he said, "You can tell them no if you don't want to do it."

Then he went back to his phone conversation and left it up to her.

But by then Mandy had joined Mel in chanting, "Sim! Sim!" and Kira knew she'd be in for a raging tantrum in stereo if she told them they couldn't swim. So she caved.

"Okay, okay, we'll swim. For just a little while, though, because there are so many other things I need to get done today," she said to hush the girls.

"You can put them in the pool in their diapers," Cutty informed her, taking another break from his call as she ushered the twins into the backyard.

Filling the pool with the hose hadn't sounded like a problem, but with Mel and Mandy in tow it was hardly uncomplicated. They didn't have any conception of waiting until Kira had it ready for them. Or them ready for it. Instead, as she was turning on the hose, they got into the small vinyl wading pool, getting their clothes soiled with the dirt that had dried on the bottom from disuse.

"No, we have to rinse it out and fill it before you can get in," Kira told them, setting the hose down on the lawn and going to lift them out.

"Sim!" Mel protested.

"We need water in it to swim," Kira said, putting Mel on the grass and then turning to get Mandy out.

But while she was retrieving Mandy, Mel picked up the hose and aimed it at the pool, dousing Kira and Mandy both, and making Mandy cry.

"Oh, this is not good," Kira muttered to herself, before attempting to comfort Mandy and get the hose from Mel at the same time.

Once she had the hose she put it down again but kept her foot firmly on it as she set Mandy on the lawn beside her sister.

"Can you take off your clothes while I put the water in the pool?" she asked, hoping to distract them, knowing they could undress themselves if they wanted to because they often did it at moments when they weren't supposed to.

But of course they both said, "No."

"Okay, then just sit there while I fill the pool."

Another *no* was the answer to that, but Kira ignored it, snatched up the hose and took it to the pool.

She managed to rinse it and dump out the dingy water but as she finally began to fill it the girls returned.

"Sim!" Mel said.

By then Kira knew better than to expect any patience from them, so she put the hose between her knees to hold it still aimed at the pool and, with her hands free, she went to work taking off the twins' shirts and shorts.

It was not a graceful operation but luckily the pool was so small it didn't take much to put a few inches of water into it, and the girls had on only shorts and T-shirts over their diapers.

With both things accomplished, she took the hose with her to turn it off and by the time she'd done that, the babies had climbed into the water.

"Coad!" Mandy complained, getting right back out.

"I know it's cold. I'm going to get some water from inside to heat it up."

But she couldn't leave Mel in the water while she did that, so she again lifted the baby out of the pool, making her scream bloody murder because she didn't want to get out.

"Go find the ball. You can take it into the pool with you," Kira said, hoping to distract Mel.

But it was Mandy who found the ball—and threw it into the water from a safe distance away—while Mel merely tried to get back in herself.

So, keeping an eagle eye on Mandy but leaving her in the yard, Kira took Mel into the house with her.

She was glad to see that Cutty was no longer on the telephone. If he had been he certainly wouldn't have been able to hear his conversation over Mel's crying and demanding to *sim* again. Instead he'd already filled a bucket with hot water.

"Thanks," Kira said, pretending not to notice that

he was amused by the spectacle of her swimming-pool comedy of errors.

She took the screaming infant and the bucket back outside but she needed two hands to pour the warmer water into the pool. Which meant she had to put Mel down.

But the minute she did, Mel climbed in again.

Kira was afraid she might burn the baby, so she took her out.

Mel's feet no sooner hit the ground than she climbed in.

Kira took her out.

Mel climbed in.

So Kira took her out, took her to the farthest end of the yard, and then ran as fast as she could to pour the water in before Mel got back, too.

Kira could hear Cutty laughing from inside the house so she knew he was watching, but she was just glad she'd managed to get all the hot water in and do a quick test of the temperature before Mel climbed into that pool again.

Then Kira turned to Mandy who was stomping her bare feet into the puddle left when Kira had rinsed the pool initially.

"The water is warm now, Mandy. Do you want to swim?"

"No."

Of course not. And no amount of coaxing could get the other baby anywhere near the water her sister was happily romping in now.

Kira was slowly learning to pick her battles and

forcing Mandy to swim didn't seem like one she should wage. Besides, after all that, she was ready for a breather herself. So rather than saying any more, she took a lawn chair to the edge of the wading pool where she could sit and watch Mel and Mandy at once, and sat down.

"Can I put my feet in?" she asked Mel.

"Sim?" Mel responded in invitation.

"No, thank you. I'm too big to swim. But I'll put my feet in," she said, taking off her own sandals and rolling up her jeans so she could do just that.

"Toes," Mel said, pointing to Kira's.

"Toes," Kira confirmed.

That drew Mandy's interest and she came to the pool's edge, too, bending over to get a look at Kira's feet, as well.

Kira wiggled her toes for them and that made them laugh.

Then Mandy left, dragged one of the two infant-size lawn chairs to Kira's side and tried to do what Kira was doing—sit in the chair and dangle her feet over the edge of the pool.

Her judge of distance was off, though, and she was too far away. So Kira helped out by moving Mandy and her chair close enough for Mandy's pudgy feet to reach.

She promptly wiggled her toes, too, and it must have looked like more fun than Mel was having because she climbed out of the pool, clumsily maneuvered her own pint-size chair to Kira's other side and wasn't happy until she was doing exactly what Mandy and Kira were doing.

And there they sat, three girls soaking their feet on a hot summer's day, wiggling their toes, making trails through the water, kicking up a light splash just for the heck of it.

And that was when it struck Kira that somewhere along the way she'd turned a corner with her nieces.

That not only had they accepted her, they might even like her.

And nothing she could think of pleased her more.

"If you do that over here I can help," Cutty informed Kira when she came down the stairs carrying a basket of clean laundry to fold after getting the twins to sleep that night.

"I won't pass up that offer," she said, struggling not to let anything fall from the mountain that peaked well above the top of the basket.

Cutty was in his usual position on the couch with his foot propped on top of pillows on the coffee table so Kira put the basket in front of the sofa and joined him on the other side of it.

Oddly enough, sharing the simple chore seemed like a nice way to end the day. A day Kira had enjoyed even more after the realization that she'd made headway in the twins' affections.

"Can I say *I told you so* now?" Cutty asked as they worked.

"About what?"

"The girls. Didn't I tell you they'd warm up to you if you just gave them a little time?"

"You did."

"And now they're passing up their dear old dad like a dirty shirt," he pretended to complain.

"You could have read their bedtime story if you wanted to," Kira pointed out, believing he was referring to the fact that the twins had decreed that "Kiwa" do the honors tonight.

"No, they made their choice and it wasn't me."

"Mel even wanted to give me a good-night kiss," Kira bragged. "Then, not to be outdone, I got one out of Mandy, too."

"You're on the A-list now."

Kira just smiled, keeping to herself how good that made her feel. And at the same time trying not to take too much notice of Cutty.

He had on casual Sunday clothes—a pair of jeans and a simple navy-blue crew-neck T-shirt—but every time he reached for something to fold his carved biceps slid out from under the short sleeve and Kira's gaze kept getting stuck on how sexy that looked.

"You're very patient with the girls," he said then.

"Why does that seem to surprise you?"

"Well, for one, they're a handful."

"And for two?"

He didn't seem eager to answer that because there was a moment's pause before he said, "I guess it comes from the image I have of the way you and Marla were raised."

"The *image* you have? Didn't Marla talk about the way we were raised?"

"No, as a matter of fact, she didn't. I made certain assumptions based on my experience with your father, but she said I was wrong."

"What assumptions did you make?" Kira asked.

"To be blunt? That he was domineering. Demanding. Dictatorial. Controlling in the extreme. Really, that he was just plain mean and that he ran his household like boot camp. And even though Marla swore he was never violent, patience was definitely not what I figured anyone learned from him."

"No, he wasn't violent—that part was true. But Marla denied the rest?" It was Kira's turn to sound surprised.

"She said her father was a model parent. That at times he could be a little stern but that didn't make him any less great. That I'd only seen him one night when he'd been upset, and that he'd had good reason to be angry."

"Oh."

They'd finished folding the laundry and they piled it back in the basket. A lot of the things were baby clothes, and Kira couldn't go into the nursery to put them away while the girls were sleeping, so she took the basket into the foyer and left it at the foot of the stairs, wondering the whole time at her sister's description of their father.

Then she rejoined Cutty on the couch, sitting slightly sideways so she could face him.

"Are you sure Marla was talking about *our* fa-

ther?'' Kira asked then, making a little joke. "Because the father I had was a lot more like your description than what I would consider a model parent.''

"It was important to Marla to have a good face on
things,'' Cutty said, sounding a little sad. But it was
short-lived. "So tell me what he was really like.''

Kira had the sense that Cutty's curiosity came from
more than merely a desire to know about her childhood. But even so she didn't see why that curiosity
couldn't be satisfied. In fact she didn't understand
why Marla *hadn't* satisfied it.

"Boot camp—that pretty much hits the nail on the
head,'' Kira confirmed what Cutty had said moments
earlier. "One of my earliest memories of Tom Wentworth is of this big man towering over me and yelling
because I hadn't made my bed the minute I got out
of it—and made it complete with the sheet folded just
so over the top edge of the blanket, the pillow centered and the spread exactly the same distance from
the floor all the way around.''

"And you were how old when your mother married
him?''

"Three. I don't know how soon it was afterward
that I was in trouble for not making the bed, but I
don't think it was too terribly long a time. I do know
that there were always high expectations of me and
some of the things he made us do seemed unnecessary.''

"For instance?''

"Well, for instance, besides the specifications for
how the bed had to be made, at night our clothes

either had to go into the hamper or be folded in a pile at the foot of the mattress, and our shoes had to be side-by-side under the bed—far enough under to be out of the way, not so far that the heels couldn't be seen. And if the shoes weren't where they were supposed to be or weren't absolutely side-by-side, he would wake us up with a scream that would scare us to death and make us do it the way he wanted it.''

''So you were afraid of him even if he didn't hit you?''

''Oh, yeah,'' Kira said emphatically but matter-of-factly and without feeling sorry for herself.

''I know I'd never seen anyone as petrified as Marla was about telling her father that she was pregnant,'' Cutty put in.

''And then you met him and understood.''

''But there was no hitting?'' Cutty reiterated as if he couldn't believe it.

''No, he never hit us. Although there were a few times when he'd flick our ears—which hurt a lot. But that was as far as any physical consequences went. It was more that there were average punishments that he'd take a step—or ten steps—further.''

''Like?''

''Like we didn't just have dessert taken away, we wouldn't get a meal at all. Toys wouldn't just be off-limits for a while, he'd pack everything up and give it to charity, and we wouldn't have anything to play with until the next Christmas or birthday. Extra chores didn't mean we had to sweep out the garage, it meant that we had to completely take the garage apart, scrub it down as if it were an operating room and put it back together. Extremes—he always did everything in the extreme. Including his reaction if we did step out of line or didn't perform to his standards. He could be very scary. And loud. If I disappointed him or made him mad I dreaded his reaction as much as I dreaded his punishments.''

"And your mother let this go on?"

"He was as hard on my mother as he was on Marla and me. He saw everything and everyone as a reflection of him, and that reflection had to be flawless. It was important that people marveled at how exceptional everything he had contact with was.''

"That's a lot of pressure."

"A lot," Kira confirmed.

"And he was the same with your mother?"

"Dinner at six o'clock every night. If she served it at five after he was likely to throw it against a wall. She couldn't be seen without makeup. The house had to be spotless and everything had to be in exactly the order it had been before we moved in—the way his first wife had decorated it. Once he didn't speak to my mother for six months because she'd dusted the living room and moved a lamp to a spot she thought needed more light.''

"You're kidding?"

"I wish I were. The lamp was where Marla's mother had put it and that meant it couldn't be moved.''

"Was the place a shrine to his first wife?"

"To him it was more that his first wife had set the

standard my mother had to live by. Just the way Marla was the standard I was supposed to live by...well, in terms of getting straight As and minding my manners and being as good at everything as she was. At least as good as she'd been up to the point where she got pregnant.''

Cutty shook his head. ''I still can't believe your mother put up with it all—for herself or for you.''

Kira shrugged. ''He wasn't awful all the time. He could be nice. I think she genuinely loved him, even though I admit, I found him a hard man to love myself. But my mother always said that even though he ran a tight ship he was still a good man, that he provided for us and only wanted the best for us. Plus, she never thought she had a whole lot of options. She'd gotten married right out of high school, she didn't have a degree or any work experience, and when my birth father deserted us and disappeared so he didn't have to pay child support when I was a year old, she'd really been left in trouble. To her it was better to put up with Tom Wentworth's idiosyncrasies—that's what she called them—than to be on her own to raise and support me the way she'd been for the two years between her divorce and marrying again.''

Cutty's eyebrows came together in a frown. ''So did Wentworth ease up on you at least after Marla did the biggest no-no of all and got pregnant at seventeen?''

''Ease up?'' Kira repeated with a laugh. ''Oh, no. As a matter of fact, I sort of got punished for it.''

"*You* were punished because Marla got pregnant and eloped?"

"Not directly. But if you thought he was strict with Marla as a teenager, it was nothing compared to what he was with me."

"Did he lock you in a closet or make you wear a chastity belt?"

Kira laughed again. "It wasn't quite as bad as being locked in a closet or wearing medieval armor. But I wasn't allowed any social life. He made my mother take me to school and pick me up at the end of the day, and beyond that I couldn't go anywhere where either he or my mother wasn't supervising, and *never* either with a boy or if boys were being included."

"No boys—under any circumstances?"

"None. If a boy so much as called me about a school project I was in for it."

"Girlfriends only?"

"Right. And I didn't end up with many of those because the older I got, the more my friends wanted to do things without one of my parents having to go along and to be with boys, and since I couldn't—"

"You ended up without even girlfriends?"

"Basically. I mean, I'd see them at school, but—"

"Geez," Cutty said, cutting her off as if he couldn't listen to any more of what she was telling him despite the fact that she was still merely letting him know the way things had been without any sympathy seeking.

Then he said, "I knew what Marla and I did all those years ago had more repercussions than I could have ever imagined, but I never thought it hurt you. I suppose you didn't even get to go to a homecoming dance or a prom or anything.''

''Nope. Not one. I couldn't be anywhere where any boy might get his hands on me,'' Kira confirmed.

Cutty didn't say anything for a moment. He just studied her face with that penetrating green gaze.

Then he reached a hand to the back of her neck, squeezing it gently and rubbing it with his thumb. ''I'm so sorry. I hate that I made your life tougher than it had been before.''

''It's okay. Who's to say I would have even been asked to a homecoming dance or a prom anyway?''

''Oh, you would have been asked. Believe me, you would have been asked,'' he said as if he knew something she didn't.

He was looking into her eyes and his hand had risen to caress the back of her head in a way that made just about everything seem better.

''I feel like I owe you a prom or something,'' he said in a quiet, husky tone.

''At least one,'' she joked, her own voice barely above an intimate whisper as she had a flashback of an old teenage fantasy of doing just that—of going to a prom with a guy so terrific looking that everyone there would be envious. Of dancing all evening with him gazing into her eyes alone—much the way Cutty was gazing into them right at that moment. Of being taken home afterward and being kissed good-night.

As if he knew what she was thinking, Cutty used that hand in her hair to pull her slowly nearer. Near enough to press his mouth to hers and actually give that good-night kiss the young Kira had longed for. So near that to keep from falling into him she had to turn more toward him, facing the back cushions, facing Cutty.

He kept that hand cradling her head but his other arm came around her, adding a dimension that hadn't been there in either of the kisses they'd shared before—holding her, bracing her, keeping her close as his lips parted over hers and deepened the kiss.

Kira answered in kind, letting her lips part, too, savoring the feel of that muscular arm across her back, of his hand doing that gentle massage.

Lips parted even more and his tongue came to say hello, testing the very edges of her teeth, taking a leisurely course to meet her tongue, tip to tip.

She didn't retreat from that, either. She welcomed it, welcomed the deepening of that kiss, following his lead circle for circle, being chased and giving chase.

He pulled her closer still, until she was half-way sitting on his lap, resting against the breadth of that massive chest.

She wrapped her arms around him, too, letting her palms ride the expanse of his shoulders, savoring the feel of all that strength and power. Savoring, too, the feel of her breasts against him as her nipples turned into hard knots and nudged at him.

No kiss she'd ever imagined and none she'd ever had before compared to that one. She lost herself in it, in the pure sensuality of it, the pure sensual pleasure of mouths opening ever wider, of tongues doing a passionate dance that was awakening things inside her that were hot and fiery, things that made her feel alive with needs, with desires, with hungers she didn't even know she had.

And she was a little afraid of that, of where letting herself get too carried away might lead.

And maybe Cutty sensed it. Or maybe he'd been struck by a similar thought, because at the same moment Kira began to ease out of that kiss, he did, too.

"Maybe we should call that one consolation for missing the prom," he suggested with a frustrated-sounding chuckle, as if every time he kissed her there needed to be an excuse.

"Want to hear about the math camp I had to miss?" she joked in response, as if he could compensate for that, too, while he was at it.

Cutty laughed, but he didn't kiss her again.

He also didn't let go of her, though. Instead he held her there. And she didn't try to move.

After another long moment of looking down into her eyes he finally said, "Tomorrow night Northbridge is giving Ad and me some kind of award—"

"For saving that family from the fire?"

"Mmm-hmm. Will you go with me?"

"To watch Mel and Mandy while you accept your award?"

"No, there's a teenage girl down the street who baby-sits for me here and there. I thought we could call her to stay with the twins and just you and I could go."

"Because I missed a few high-school dances?" she

asked, worrying slightly that he might be asking her out of guilt or pity or something after what she'd told him.

"No, not because you missed a few high-school dances," he said as if he didn't know where that had come from. "Because I'd like you to be there with me."

He said that as if he genuinely meant it, as if there couldn't possibly be any other reason, and it washed away that momentary fear born of her own self-doubt.

"I'd like to be there," she heard herself say, contrary to all the reasons she could think of *not* to.

"Then it's a date."

"Okay."

He kissed her again and it was in that moment that she realized their relationship had reached a new level. A more personal level.

A level that was different than where this had begun.

A level she'd never intended to reach.

Just then she sat up straighter, away from Cutty, to put an end to this evening.

"I'd better let you rest up for your big night tomorrow night, then," she said, wishing it hadn't come out sounding as if there was more than an awards ceremony that he needed to rest up for.

Cutty smiled a smile that let her know he'd heard it that way, too. "Uh-huh," he said with a healthy dose of innuendo. But then he let her off the hook. "I'll call Tiffy first thing in the morning to see if she can sit."

"Great," Kira said, getting to her feet. "I'll just see you tomorrow then."

Kira insisted he not get up and walk her to the door when he tried and instead hurried through the kitchen and outside to the backyard before she was tempted to take him up on the offer.

As much as she would have liked to have even a few more minutes with him, it just seemed too likely that if he walked her to the door it would put them in a position where he might kiss her again.

And the bottom line was that thought was just too appealing.

But she couldn't help regretting what she'd denied herself as she crossed the yard to the garage apartment.

Or wondering if maybe some of the self-restraint lessons she'd learned from her father did her more harm than good.

Chapter Six

"It's okay, Kira. It's not a big deal."

"It *is* a big deal. Betty told me how Marla kept the house. She told me how it was all supposed to be done. And now she'll come here and see that I still haven't managed to get on top of it."

"Kiwa wunnin'," Mel observed.

"Funny," Mandy contributed.

The twins had just gotten up from their Monday-afternoon naps. They were in their high chairs having crackers and milk, watching Kira rushing around the kitchen, frantically cleaning up.

Cutty had taken a call from Betty, who had said she had some free time and wanted to take the girls to the park. He'd encouraged her to come right over, thinking it would give Kira a break.

Then he'd hung up the phone, told Kira and all hell had broken loose.

Mel and Mandy seemed to find it very entertaining. Cutty didn't.

"A few dishes in the sink, some crumbs on the counter, toys on the living-room floor—don't worry about it. The place still looks better than it did before you got here."

"But not as good as when Marla took care of it, and I can't have Betty seeing a mess," Kira insisted.

Cutty shook his head. "It isn't a mess, it just looks lived-in. But if it would make you feel better, you can put the girls in their stroller out front, and I'll wait with them for Betty to get here. That way she won't even have to come in."

"That might seem rude," Kira fretted. "And what about when she brings them back? She'll want to come in then, I know it. And—"

"And by then you can get things straightened up, if it'll make you feel better. But she's not going to do a white-glove inspection. It'll be fine."

"It won't be the way Marla would have had it," Kira reiterated, more to herself than to him. But she did seem to be considering his suggestion. And once she had she said, "I suppose there's nothing else I can do."

Then she made a dash for the stroller.

"Finish your crackers, girls. Betty's coming to see you," Cutty informed his daughters, all the while keeping his eyes trained on the frenzied Kira.

The longer she was in Northbridge with him the

more he was realizing that there were two sides to her. There was this side of her—the side that worried she wasn't doing a good job, the side that never seemed to think she was accomplishing enough, the side that seemed in constant competition with Marla.

Then there was the other side. The side that was more inclined to roll with things. The side that worked harder at winning over the babies' affections than at cleaning the house. The side that paid attention to Mel and Mandy—and to Cutty—before she paid attention to dirty dishes or vacuuming floors.

That was the side Cutty knew he was a sucker for. Which was why he also knew it was the dangerous side. Because that was the softer side. The side that was fun. And sweet. And just a little bit quirky.

That was the side that kept causing him to lower his guard.

"Okay, I have the stroller out front, at the bottom of the steps and the diaper bag packed and ready," Kira announced when she bustled back into the kitchen a few minutes later, still operating at super-speed. "I'll put the girls in it and Betty can push them straight out of the yard as soon as she gets here."

Cutty didn't say anything to that. He just helped Mel finish her milk and wiped her face.

By the time he'd done that, Kira had cleaned up Mandy and taken her out of the high chair. Then she turned to lift Mel to the floor, too.

"I'll grab the sunblock and put it on them outside," Cutty said then.

"Oh, good, that will help."

Kira wasted no time herding the twins through the living room and out the front door.

Cutty watched her go, discouraged by the sight.

Then he grabbed his cane and the bottle of sunscreen and followed behind.

Kira had both twins in the stroller when he limped out onto the porch.

"You promise you won't let Betty inside?" she asked as he joined her.

"I promise."

"But you'll be nice about it so she won't get offended?"

"No, I'm going to tell her you've banned her from coming inside because you're an awful, unsociable person who's holding us hostage in a pigsty."

To Kira's credit she realized he was only being sarcastic and smiled. "Do that and I'll break your other ankle," she countered.

There was that dangerous side again, peeking out at him. And Cutty couldn't help grinning back at her. "In that case I guess I'll have to be nice about it."

"Thank you. Are you sure you'll be okay out here with the girls? It won't hurt your ankle not to have it elevated until Betty gets here?"

"I'll be fine."

But he still kept an eye on Kira as she went back into the house, thinking that witnessing that panic over someone finding a few things out of place was something he should brand on his brain.

He was having more and more trouble keeping in mind that this other side of her existed and it wasn't something he wanted to forget. It was something he needed *not* to forget.

Because, yes, she could pause in her panic and respond to his joke. Yes, she'd stopped long enough to think of him and make sure his waiting on the porch wouldn't cause him pain. But even if there was a part of her that had escaped the effects of having been raised by Tom Wentworth, there was still that other part of her that hadn't. And Cutty knew from experience that that part was nothing to ignore.

He settled himself to sit on the bottom step with the twins directly in front of him and his bum leg extended out to the side of the stroller.

As he slathered the twins with sunscreen he thought about all Kira had told him the night before about her father. He thought about how much it explained for him. But even so, understanding the root cause of something didn't mean that what grew from that root cause didn't exist. It didn't lessen the reality of living with what grew from that root cause. And he knew he had to keep that in mind.

It was just that when it came to Kira, he seemed to have a blind spot. A really big blind spot.

It was difficult not to. Especially when the Tom-Wentworth-influenced side of her was beneath the surface. Pretty far beneath it. And the surface was so damn appealing.

Not just because she was beautiful, either. Although she was. Every time he looked into those big blue eyes of hers it was like staring at a clear sky on a lazy summer afternoon. He loved the way her hair glistened in the sun, the way it fell to her shoulders when she left it loose. And there certainly wasn't a doubt that her body was great, that it was a body his hands itched to get hold of.

But the more he got to know her, the more things he found that he liked about her on top of the way she looked.

He didn't know how long it had been since he'd woken up every morning eager to face the day. He only knew it had been a long, long time.

But every single day Kira had been there had begun like that—he couldn't wait to see her. To hear her voice and everything she had to say. To smell the clean, fresh-flower scent of her. To learn what made her smile, what made her frown, what pleased her and what provoked her, what she liked and disliked. To watch those long-fingered hands at work and at play and wish for a moment when they might accidentally brush his skin. He couldn't wait to learn what she thought of something on the news or see the twins from her point of view, to laugh at them together. He just couldn't wait to be with her, to have meals with her, to tease her, to share every minute and every event with her.

And then what did he do when the day actually did get started? He willed it to pass so he could get to the end of the evening, when the twins were down for the night, and he could have that little bit of time alone with Kira.

As much as he looked forward to the day with her, he looked forward to the end of the day with her even more. He usually even had a contingency plan for how to get her to stay if she seemed inclined to go straight out to the garage apartment after the twins were in bed.

It was nice to sit and talk to her. She was easy to have a conversation with. Easy to confide in. And equally as easy to listen to. And then, of course, kissing her good-night had hardly been a chore.

Oh, yeah, he definitely had a blind spot when it came to Kira. A blind spot that lasted even after she left at night because he'd been going to bed regretting that the day and evening were over. Regretting that he was going to bed alone. And then lying in that lonely bed fantasizing about what it would be like if she were there with him. *Wanting* her there with him. Wishing he could just fall asleep so the morning would come quicker. Not being able to fall asleep at all for hours and hours because he couldn't stop thinking about her.

''Beh-ee!'' Mandy announced, drawing Cutty out of his thoughts as the older woman parked her car at the curb just then.

Mel and Mandy got excited enough to stand up in the stroller and try to get out of it.

''Sit down or you can't go with Betty to the park,'' Cutty warned.

His longtime household helper turned off her engine and got out from behind the steering wheel, waving at the girls as she hurried up to kiss each of them in turn.

"Ooo, my little sweet-cheeks," she murmured affectionately to them both. "I've missed you."

"Beh-ee!" Mel shrieked while Mandy bounced gleefully in her seat.

Then Betty turned her attention to Cutty. "What are you doing out here? You're supposed to have that ankle elevated," she reprimanded.

"I know but I needed some fresh air so I thought I'd wait out here for you."

"How's it feeling?"

"Good," Cutty said.

"Is Marla's sister still here?"

Marla's sister.

Cutty never thought of Kira that way, and it occurred to him that maybe that was something else he should try, that it might narrow his blind spot.

"Kira is working inside, picking up after all of us," Cutty said. "She'll probably say hello when you get back."

"Pahk," Mandy demanded then, as if on cue, just when Cutty needed her to.

"I guess I'll *have* to see Kira when I get back," Betty said. "I can't keep these beauties waiting."

"They probably won't let you," Cutty agreed.

"Oh, I could just eat them up!" the older woman said, bending over to kiss their heads again.

Then she maneuvered the stroller so she could get between it and Cutty. "We'll only be an hour or so," she informed him as she pushed it down the walk.

"I put sunblock on them. The bottle's in the pouch if you need more," Cutty called after them.

"Go on into the house and get that ankle up," Betty ordered over her shoulder as she turned onto the sidewalk that ran in front of the house.

Cutty's ankle was beginning to throb so he knew that was exactly what he needed to do and got himself to his feet.

Marla's sister, he thought as he did to counteract the fact that he was also glad to be going inside because it meant he got to see Kira.

Marla's sister.

But as he lumbered up the steps to the porch he caught sight of Kira through the picture window. She was in the living room, dumping an armload of toys into the toy box in the corner and then straightening the knickknacks on the table nearby and bending to snatch up a T-shirt Mandy had spilled juice on earlier—all at a double-time pace.

Cutty sighed and shook his head, stopping to watch her without her realizing she had an audience, wondering if she had any idea that she was going overboard.

But as he looked on Kira hesitated suddenly. She glanced from the shirt to the entryway and back again.

Then she checked the time on the mantel clock.

Suddenly she crossed to the couch in a hurry, lifted one of the cushions and hid the shirt there, completely surprising him.

Cutty had to fight to keep from bursting out laughing.

And just that quick his blind spot was back in

place, and he had to wonder if he wasn't already in trouble with Kira Wentworth, regardless of whose sister she was.

The awards ceremony honoring Cutty and Ad that evening was held in the school auditorium. It was packed with a standing-room-only crowd as Cutty, Ad, Northbridge's mayor and the entire city council lined the stage behind a podium where a number of people spoke in praise of the two men and thanked them for the bravery that had saved an entire family. Even the dog Cutty and Ad had managed to free just before the beam had fallen and injured them both was in attendance.

The ceremony had a casual, friendly feel to it, and as Kira sat in the first row witnessing it all she was glad for Cutty. It pleased her that what he'd done with Ad—as well as everything else he did for the town—was recognized and appreciated. He really had found a home here and an extended family for himself.

At the end of the ceremony Ad was given his plaque first. His acceptance speech was brief and humorous but then turned more serious and heartfelt as he added his gratitude to Cutty for saving his life.

Kira didn't think there was a dry eye in the place as he openly voiced his affection and friendship and presented Cutty's plaque.

Cutty was obviously moved himself as he limped to the podium on his cane. The two men embraced roughly—the way men do—and then Cutty took over the microphone.

He stared down at the plaque for a long moment as if he was reading it, but Kira thought it was more likely he was getting his emotions under control. That opinion was supported when he had to clear his throat before he could speak.

"This is really nice," he began, unprepared but without any evidence of stage fright. He went on to give his own thanks for all that so many people in Northbridge had done for him over the years, for how much the small town and its citizens meant to him.

Kira listened intently, enjoying the chance to so freely study the impressive sight of the tall man with the broad, broad shoulders encased in a pale green shirt. He wore a tie tonight, a hunter-green tie that set off the color of his amazing eyes. He also had on dark slacks tailored to fall perfectly from his narrow hips, and even though he'd complimented Kira on her champagne-colored V-necked silk blouse and matching slacks, and how nice her hair looked falling free to her shoulders, she thought he was definitely nothing to be overlooked himself.

He didn't talk for long but he did surprise Kira by aiming the last of what he had to say at her.

He sought her out in the crowd with those striking eyes and said, "I also want to thank Kira Wentworth who showed up on my doorstep out of the blue last week and volunteered to use her vacation to chase the twins and wait on me. She's kind of a ray of sunshine in our house and I want her to know how much I appreciate all she's doing for us."

There was nothing inappropriate in his words but

there was a hint of intimacy in the smile he shot her way, making her blush with more than embarrassment at being brought to everyone's attention.

Luckily, though, Cutty ended his speech then and in the applause and cheers and standing ovation that followed, she hoped no one noticed the pink hue of her cheeks.

There was a dinner in the gymnasium afterward, and while a number of people made a point of talking to her and showing an interest in her, Cutty and Ad were the men of the hour and barely managed to eat in the midst of the many well-wishers who wanted to shake their hands.

It was nearly ten o'clock when the evening finally ended. Ad walked with Cutty and Kira out to the parking lot and as he did he said, "Tomorrow night's all set. My sister can't wait to get her hands on the twins."

Cutty made a face. "I was waiting to spring the party on Kira on the way home," he said pointedly to his friend.

"Tomorrow is our boy's birthday," Ad explained to Kira, ignoring Cutty's obvious reluctance to talk about this. "I'm closing down the restaurant for the night. My sister is keeping the twins at her place until the next morning, and I'm throwing him the biggest birthday bash he's ever seen."

"Tomorrow's your birthday?" Kira repeated, aiming the question at Cutty.

He made another face. "It's unavoidable."

"Yes, it is. Birthdays are a big deal and we're celebrating it. Kira included, right?'' Ad said, looking for confirmation from her.

Before she could answer Cutty said, ''I was hoping she would come with me but I wanted to ask her in private.''

''Oops,'' Ad said with an ornery grin.

They'd reached Cutty's car by then and Ad went on to his own where it was parked one spot over, saying as he did, ''Tomorrow night. Eight o'clock. No excuses. Kira, you can bring your dancing shoes even if Cutty can't dance—there'll be music and food and plenty to drink.''

They all said good-night then and Kira and Cutty got into Cutty's car.

''I'm sorry about that,'' he said before he'd even put the key in the ignition.

''That's okay. I wish I had known earlier that tomorrow is your birthday, though.''

''I really don't like a fuss to be made about it. But now that Ad has blown my plan to ease you into the idea, would you like to go with me to a party tomorrow night?''

''What was your plan to ease me into the idea?'' Kira asked rather than answering his question.

''I was going to see if you might like to take a drive tonight, show you the north bridge that inspired the town's name, and then spring it on you.''

Kira laughed, thrilled more than he would ever know by the fact that he'd had a plan at all for prolonging this evening.

''I'd like to see the bridge,'' she said then.

"And the party tomorrow night?"

"I'll think about it until after I see the bridge," she said, as if there was any doubt she would accept an invitation to go with him to his own birthday party.

"Fair enough," he said, starting the engine and pulling out of the school parking lot.

"So there really is a north bridge?" Kira asked along the way.

"An old oak one. Built across the river north of town. Actually, the bridge is more impressive than the river—which isn't much more than a creek anymore."

They were outside the city limits within a few minutes but Cutty kept on driving along a dark country road.

They went about seven miles before he turned onto another road—this one more narrow and less developed than the other, following it through an area that grew more and more densely wooded until they finally came to a clearing.

The bridge was a short distance ahead when Cutty pulled to a stop. He turned off the engine and the car lights so they could see it in the moonlight.

It was indeed a wooden bridge with crosshatch bars running the length of both sides and a railing bracing posts that held a shingled roof over it.

"The only thing it's missing is a horse-drawn wagon clomping across it," Kira observed of the bridge that seemed right out of the pages of a history book.

"That was just what it was built for ninety-nine years ago. It gets its hundredth birthday next year."

"I saw a covered bridge similar to that on a trip to Vermont. Once upon a time," Kira said then.

Cutty angled her way and stretched an arm along the seat back, transferring his focus from the bridge to her. "What were you doing in Vermont?"

"Meeting the parents of a guy I was dating."

Despite the view of the old bridge, Kira went from looking at it to looking at Cutty because he was still a sight she preferred. And when she did she got to see his eyebrows arch.

"You dated a guy seriously enough to go across the country to meet his parents?"

"Why do you sound so surprised?"

Cutty shrugged. "I guess after hearing about how things were for you in the Wentworth household I just didn't imagine you involved with anyone."

"I did eventually move out of the Wentworth household, you know."

"When?"

"About two years ago. I stayed at home while I got my undergraduate and master's degrees, and you're right—I still couldn't really date as long as I was living under my father's roof. Although I did have a little more contact with the opposite sex because of the freedom and flexibility college offered. But beyond having coffee with a guy or lunch or dinner between classes, I couldn't have a relationship that involved much else."

"Even when you hit your twenties? Your father still wouldn't stand for you dating?"

"It wasn't as if there was a magic age at which he started to see me as a flesh-and-blood human being who was entitled to a life. That never happened. I had to *excel* so he looked good. That was all he thought about regardless of how old I was."

"But after you got your master's degree you moved out on your own?"

"I did."

"And your father was okay with that then?"

"He didn't speak to me for six months. I wasn't allowed to go to Christmas dinner that year."

"That sounds like the man I hardly knew and didn't love," Cutty said wryly.

"It wasn't as if he ever willingly relinquished control of anything or anyone, so my moving out wasn't something he could just roll with. But when the silent treatment didn't make me move back in, he eventually had to accept that I'd left and wasn't coming back. Plus it helped that he saw that even though I wasn't living with him, I was still working hard as a research assistant and getting my Ph.D.—which meant I was staying the course the way I was supposed to."

"So even though you were finally out from under his thumb you stayed regimented—you still didn't cut loose?"

Kira laughed. "I definitely didn't cut loose. I moved into the studio apartment I live in now, worked days at the lab and nights and weekends on my doctorate dissertation.''

''Then when did Mr. Vermont come into the picture?'' Cutty asked.

Did he sound a shade jealous?

Kira smiled at that possibility. ''*Mr. Vermont* was my advisor for my master's thesis. As long as I was working on it we kept things impersonal, but when I finished it and we wouldn't be seeing each other again on a professional basis, he asked me out. Although I didn't call him *Mr. Vermont*. I called him Mark.''

''Mark,'' Cutty echoed only with a more distasteful inflection in his voice.

''Mark Myers,'' Kira elaborated, thinking Cutty really might be jealous. And loving it.

''And he was your first…boyfriend?''

''He wasn't the first guy who ever kissed me. There were a couple of stolen kisses that went with those secret lunches and dinners through undergrad and my master's program. But Mark was the first everything else.''

And the last. But Kira didn't add that.

''So if you went to Vermont to meet parents, does that mean you were really serious about him?''

''We were talking marriage,'' Kira confirmed. ''Although I still hadn't been brave enough to tell my parents about him because I knew my father would hit the ceiling. He would have said I was letting someone interfere with my education, that I was going to end up throwing away my life—'' Kira cut herself short. ''Well, you can probably guess what he would have said. But I was serious enough about Mark that I was on the verge of going through all that to have a future with him.''

''What happened?''

''I guess I met his parents,'' she said, trying to make a joke of something that hadn't held any humor for her.

''Was there something wrong with them?'' Cutty asked quietly, apparently sensing the more somber aspects that had returned to stab her even now.

''No, Mark's parents were great. It was just that once I met them things with Mark became a little too clear.''

''What kind of things?''

''Well, I'd always known that Mark thought highly of his mom and dad—his mother in particular. I thought it was nice and I was looking forward to being a part of a family that had good relationships with each other.''

''But the truth was they were as dysfunctional as the rest of us?'' Cutty said, making his own attempt to lighten the tone.

''No, they really were a picture-perfect family. It was just that I didn't know until that trip that Mark considered his mother the epitome of what any wife of his would have to be.''

''Mark Myers was a mama's boy,'' Cutty concluded.

''There was more to it than that. For me, at least. I spent my whole life watching my mother trying to live up to my father's first wife. And never making it. I hated that so much.''

Kira had to swallow back the anger that the mere memory could still rouse in her.

When she had she continued. ''Even though Mark wasn't as controlling as my father, there was still an image of someone else that he expected me to emulate. That he was *demanding* that I fashion myself and my whole life after. I had this vision of making pot roast after pot roast that wasn't as good as the pot roast his mother made, and I knew there was no way I was going to put myself in that position. Almost the same position my mother had been in.''

''So you broke it off with Mr. Vermont.''

''I just had to,'' Kira said, suddenly thinking of too many similarities between the situation with Mark and the situation she was in now.

''Well, for what it's worth, I'm glad you did,'' Cutty said then with a devilish smile that succeeded where his joke had failed to break some of the tension this conversation had caused.

''Why are you glad I broke up with him?'' Kira asked a bit coyly.

''Because if you hadn't you'd probably be so busy making pot roasts that you never would have come to Northbridge, and I'd have to go to my birthday party tomorrow night by myself.''

There was such a glint of mischief in his eyes that Kira could see it even in only moon glow and it made her smile. ''I haven't said that I *will* go to your birthday party tomorrow night.''

"You would turn down a man on his birthday?" Cutty said as if the very idea was unfathomable.

"Maybe I have a mean streak you haven't seen yet."

That just made him grin. "Let's see it then," he said as if he were asking to see something a whole lot more enticing.

He suddenly let his seat slide back as far as it would go and, as if she weighed nothing at all, he half lifted, half pulled her toward him so she found herself facing him and sitting partially on his lap.

Even after the fact Kira wasn't too sure how she'd gotten there but she didn't protest. Instead she played along and said, "I don't show it to just anyone on demand."

"Maybe I can coax it out of you," he suggested, running the tip of his nose along her cheek like the stroke of a sable paintbrush.

"I'm uncoaxable," Kira said in a breathy voice that made a liar out of her.

Not that she cared. She was too lost in thoughts of how much she liked being there with his arms draped around her and his nose tantalizing her.

She closed her eyes and reveled in the tingling, teasing sensation that traveled to the edge of her jawbone, to her earlobe, to the side of her neck where he replaced the whispery strokes of his nose with a kiss. A brief, delicate kiss heated by his breath, warming her from the inside out.

He kissed her chin then. And her bottom lip alone before he finally took her mouth with his. But only playfully. Lips met and separated. Met again. And again, staying only after that third kiss to make it a real one.

Cutty brought a hand to her face, cupping her cheek as he parted his lips and urged hers to follow, allowing tongues to come out and toy with each other.

Kira let her hand rise to the strong cord of his neck, to his hair where it bristled at his nape. In the slightly odd position she was in, her breasts were against the inside of his arm and she felt her nipples tighten there, greeting him all on their own.

For a moment she wondered if he could feel it, too. But her curiosity was short-lived because just then he flexed back at them in answer.

It was a small thing and yet it was enough to make her breasts come to life with a yearning for more than the feel of his muscled arm.

Cutty didn't hesitate to trail his hand from her face even as he went on kissing her, their mouths open wide by then. Firm fingers traced a path to her shoulder and downward until he cupped one breast.

The pleasure was instant and caught Kira's breath, expanding her lungs suddenly and pushing that nipple more deeply into his palm.

His hand closed around her engorged flesh and Kira was torn between how wonderful it felt and desperately wanting the feel of it without the filter of clothes.

Longing for any touch of skin, she untied his tie and pulled it free, then she went to work on the buttons of his shirt until she had them all unfastened so she could plunge her hands inside.

He was hot and smooth and hard muscled, and she suddenly became aware of the fact that there was an insistent ridge letting its presence be known at her hip.

A quiet moan rolled from Cutty's throat as his mouth deserted hers to kiss her neck again, to nibble her earlobe.

Kira let her head fall back to free the way to the hollow of her throat as his hand slipped beneath her silk blouse and coursed up under her lacy bra to envelop that breast that was straining for him.

Oh, but it felt wonderful! And if there had been anything left sleeping inside her before, it all awakened with that touch of his hand. Every nerve ending, every inch of her body was suddenly alive with wanting him.

She brought her mouth to his once again, in a kiss that was lush with need as she writhed beneath his wondrous hand. A need greater than anything she'd ever experienced before. A need to cast aside all inhibitions, all reason, all caution....

That wasn't like her and a part of her froze internally at just the thought.

Froze and then retreated to a safer place.

A place where she wasn't tempted to do anything she might regret.

And she heard herself say, "Maybe we should slow down."

Cutty didn't just slow down. He stopped. He

stopped nuzzling the soft underside of her jaw with his nose. He stopped kneading her breast and merely let his hand curve along her side. He stopped everything to look into her eyes.

"Okay," he said but with confusion in his tone.

"This has all happened fast and—" And she was stammering and flustered and not completely committed to really having this end when her body was still screaming for it to go on, even if her mind had taken a different direction.

"It's all right," Cutty assured her in a voice that was husky and sexy and just made her want to start all over again. "What are we going to do anyway?" he added, "Crawl into the back seat like two teenagers?"

Kira was tempted to shout *Okay, let's do that!*

But she didn't. In fact, she didn't even stay where she was. Without saying anything at all, she moved away from Cutty, back to the passenger side of the car.

She wasn't sure what had happened to his tie but he began to rebutton his shirt front and seeing those big hands at work—those big hands she'd had on her bare skin, on her bare breast, only moments before—was enough to make her mouth go dry.

"You kind of go to my head," she said then, softly, closing her eyes to keep from watching him.

Cutty laughed sardonically. "Like too much to drink?"

"Like *way* too much to drink. It's almost as if I'm

someone else. Someone I'm not sure I even know. And I forget everything and just get swept up and—''

''I know. Me, too.''

There was such understanding, such compassion in his voice that Kira relaxed a little and opened her eyes again to look at him.

His shirt was buttoned once more and tucked into his waistband, and one wrist was slung over the steering wheel so he could angle her way.

''But maybe that's not a bad thing,'' he suggested then. ''I know it feels good to me.''

''Maybe too good.''

He chuckled. ''There's no such thing.''

Kira didn't know whether she agreed with that or not. Yes, he made her feel good. Better than she'd ever felt before. But the thought of letting go as much as she'd wanted to let go a few moments earlier, had terrified her, too.

Cutty didn't seem to notice that she hadn't agreed or disagreed with him. He just started the car then and turned it around, heading away from the covered bridge back to the main road.

Neither of them said anything at all through the entire drive home but the silence that went with them wasn't a tense silence. It was a thoughtful silence. A silence that let what they'd just shared linger in the air.

Only when Cutty had pulled the car into the garage and turned off the engine once more did he let those green eyes settle on her again.

''You still haven't told me if you'll go to the party

with me tomorrow night,'' he said, sounding so normal it brought her the rest of the way back to herself.

Kira considered what he was asking her, knowing it would be wiser for her to stay home with the twins while he celebrated his birthday without her.

But then he'd be celebrating his birthday without her. And she'd just about exhausted her willpower for one night.

''I'd like to go to your party,'' she finally admitted.

Cutty smiled a megawatt smile. ''Right answer,'' he said as if she'd just given him the only gift he wanted.

They got out of the car and went inside to hear the baby-sitter's report that Mel and Mandy had gone to bed without incident and not made a sound since. Then Cutty escorted the sitter outside, insisting that he watch her walk home.

While he did, Kira didn't wait for him. She slipped out the back door and went to the garage apartment because she was afraid of what might be rekindled if she didn't, if they actually said good-night.

But as she undressed and climbed into bed she couldn't help thinking about what had happened tonight.

And about what *hadn't* happened.

And even though she recalled feeling safer not releasing that part of her that had wanted to be uninhibited, that had wanted to throw reason and caution to the wind, that had wanted to make love with Cutty, she couldn't help wishing that just this once she hadn't done what kept her out of trouble.

That just this once she'd been brave enough to do what she wanted to do instead....

Chapter Seven

"Yoo-hoo!"

Kira jumped, startled by the sound of a voice coming through the front screen. She was down on her hands and knees in the hallway that ran alongside the stairs—easily visible through the open door so the visitor hadn't knocked or rung the doorbell, she'd just *yoo-hooed* to announce herself.

"Betty," Kira greeted in return as she got to her feet and went to the screen, pushing it open to let the older woman in. "I didn't know you were coming over," she added, trying to sound happier than she felt by the surprise appearance of the nanny and housekeeper she was filling in for.

Not that she didn't like Betty, it was just that Kira still didn't feel that the house was up to par and at that moment there was even more clutter than usual due to the latest catastrophe.

"I couldn't let Cutty's birthday pass without baking him Marla's special cake," the older woman said once she was inside, holding up the cake container she was carrying and glancing into the living room in search of him.

When she didn't see him, she said in a more confidential tone, "I know this is the second birthday he's had without her and it won't be as hard as the first one was, but still I wanted to bring him a little of her anyway."

It struck Kira that every time it seemed as if the shadow of Marla might be receding just a tad, something—or someone—cropped up to expand it again.

"Cutty is out in the backyard on the lounger keeping an eye on the twins while I pick up this glass," Kira informed the other woman with a nod at the debris just behind her.

What had been a crystal vase on the small hall table was now in pieces all over the hardwood floor.

Mention of it drew Betty's attention to it and she let out a mournful wail. "Oh, no, that isn't Marla's favorite vase, is it?"

"If the vase that sits on this little table was her favorite then I'm afraid that's what it is."

"She loved that vase. And look at that gash in the floor—Marla worked so hard refinishing it. She would just be crushed to see that. What on earth happened?"

"Mandy threw a toy right at the vase and I lunged to try to block it and hit it myself," Kira confessed, feeling more guilty now that she had to answer to Betty than she had with Cutty who had merely said accidents happen and offered to take the girls out of harm's way while she cleaned up.

"I warned Marla that the vase might not be safe there but she said that was the perfect place for it, so it had to go there. And she was always so careful and so diligent that she proved me wrong and nothing ever did happen to it. Even when Anthony was in a fit, she didn't let things get out of control enough down here for anything to get broken. She would be heartsick."

Kira wasn't sure if she should apologize to Betty in lieu of Marla or not. She only knew that, even though the older woman was just talking and not trying to make her feel inept and clumsy in comparison to Marla, that was still what she accomplished.

"Maybe I can replace it," Kira offered.

"I'm sure you couldn't. Marla got it in an antique shop. Like so many of her pretty things. She had an eye for finding the only gem in a pile of rocks. That's why I'm always so careful around here—you can't just go out and find replacements."

Kira hoped Betty wouldn't realize that there was also one less glass banana in the decorative bowl of fruit Marla had kept on the counter in the kitchen. Kira had broken that the day before and she didn't want the other woman to think she was some kind of wrecker's ball going through Marla's house, destroying Marla's irreplaceable things.

"Why don't you go on out back with Cutty and

the girls?'' Kira suggested then. ''I'll pick this up and bring some dishes so we can all have a piece of your cake.''

''It's Marla's cake. I can't take credit for the recipe.''

''I can't wait to taste it.''

''You'll love it. Everybody does. It won first prize at the County Fair three years ago and even got honorable mention in a national contest she entered. That girl could have been a pastry chef.''

''I'm sure,'' Kira agreed as Betty stepped over the broken glass with a sad glance at it and headed for the back of the house.

Kira got down on all fours again to finish gathering the largest pieces of the vase. Of Marla's vase. Of Marla's favorite vase.

Marla's house. Marla's things.

As if she needed Betty to remind her.

Although, there were times when she lost sight of how she measured up to Marla, she realized. Like when she was playing with the twins.

Or alone with Cutty.

Of course some of those times were getting her into trouble, she also pointed out to herself. Those times when she ended up in Cutty's arms.

Or maybe what was happening was that she was finally doing a little of that cutting loose that Cutty had talked about the night before.

That was an interesting possibility.

Maybe she was doing a little of the cutting loose

she'd never done, not even when she'd moved out on her own. Not even with Mark Myers.

It was kind of an intriguing thought.

Cutting loose.

The more she considered it, the more she liked the idea. The more she liked the image that she was even *capable* of cutting loose.

Kira Wentworth, who had always done what was demanded of her, what was expected of her, who had never strayed from the straight and narrow, cutting loose...

Hmm.

"Cake, Ki-wa!"

That call came from the back-door screen to pull her out of her thoughts.

Kira recognized Mandy's voice and it made her smile. "I'll be right there," she called in return.

With the bigger pieces of glass gathered, she stood and took them to the trash, bringing a broom to the hallway to quickly sweep up what remained.

"Ki-wa? Cake!"

That one was Mel and this time Kira couldn't help laughing at the girls and their impatience.

"I'm coming," she said a bit distractedly as her thoughts went on wandering to this new notion of cutting loose.

Maybe even having come to Northbridge on the spur of the moment, staying when she hadn't had plans to, had both been a form of it for her. Baby steps, admittedly. But still it was certainly something her father wouldn't have condoned, and yet she'd done it anyway.

And look at what that had gotten her—Mel's and Mandy's affections and the beginnings of a relationship with them.

Which seemed to be an example of good occasionally coming from veering off the beaten path.

Another intriguing idea.

And if good could occasionally come from veering off the beaten path, from cutting loose, then maybe cutting loose—just a little—with Cutty wasn't such a crime, either.

It certainly didn't *feel* like a crime....

"Cake! Nee cake now, Ki-wa!"

Mel again.

"Just one minute," she said as if that meant anything at all to an eighteen-month-old.

She made sure nothing dangerous to the girls remained in the hall, then hurried to put away the broom and dustpan before she gathered plates, utensils and a knife to cut the cake.

And that was when she realized something else.

She realized that even just thinking of herself as capable of cutting loose gave her a new sense of daring.

Or was she just looking for an excuse to lower some of the barriers she kept telling herself she needed to maintain with Cutty?

It didn't feel nearly as nice to think that.

So she decided on the spot not to.

No, this was just a new dimension of herself. One

she liked. One that was probably long overdue. And she wasn't going to question it. Instead, she was going to accept it. Maybe even embrace it.

"Peez?" Mandy called, trying to lure Kira out with good manners.

But it was so sweet Kira couldn't resist it.

"Here I come," she said, leaving that last doubt behind her as she pushed the screen open with her rear end to join the small group in the yard.

"Cake, Ki-wa! Cake!" Mandy chanted as Mel charged Kira gleefully and hugged her leg in a bubbling-over of excitement.

Kira laughed and let herself revel in the pure joy of those babies. "Yes, we'll have cake," she promised. "But you have to let me get to the table to cut it."

That was enough to send both Mel and Mandy toddling for the picnic table where Cutty was now sitting lengthwise on one of the benches to keep his ankle propped up.

Betty took the top off the cake saver, revealing layers of yellow cake sandwiching whipped cream and raspberries, and topped with a chocolate glaze that dripped artistically down the sides.

"Betty has some news," Cutty said as Kira joined them.

There was something in his tone that Kira couldn't pinpoint but he didn't exactly sound happy.

"Everything's okay with your mother's back, isn't it?" Kira asked as she handed over the knife so the other woman could cut the cake.

"Better than okay," Betty said. "The injection they gave her has given her enough relief to start moving more, and her sister is coming to stay so I can get back to work around here."

Kira's heart sank and that new lease on life she'd been feeling in the house moments earlier threatened to go with it.

She didn't know what to say. She was there to help out while Betty couldn't, but if Betty's hiatus was over...

"Cutty said there was no hurry, that you have everything under control," Betty was saying, "but I just miss these darlings so much it hurts. And if you don't need to get back to Denver, maybe you and I can get to know each other."

Through her shock, Kira finally managed to think of a question. "When exactly will you be back?"

"My aunt should get in around noon tomorrow so I can probably be here after lunch."

"You don't want to spend some time with your aunt?" Kira asked.

"She'll probably be here a month or better so I'll see plenty of her. Besides, those first few hours she's here, she and my mother will be catching up and they won't even know I'm gone."

"Oh. That's nice then," Kira said, trying hard to mean it.

When what she was feeling was that the window of opportunity for more of that cutting loose just might be closing....

* * *

Ad's bar and restaurant looked like an Old English pub inside. The lighting was dim, the walls were paneled in dark wood and the bar was a long stretch of carved walnut with a brass foot rail along the bottom and a beveled-glass mirror behind it.

For the occasion of Cutty's birthday party that night the place that could accommodate a hundred and fifty patrons was well over capacity. All with Cutty at the center of attention where he sat on one chair at a corner table with his broken ankle propped on another chair.

A four-man band was playing live music on the stage at the opposite corner; there was dancing and a huge buffet, a birthday cake waiting to be cut, and even though Cutty was only drinking ginger ale because he was still taking antibiotics to keep the gash in his leg from getting infected, he seemed to be thoroughly enjoying himself.

Kira was enjoying herself, too. Although after two hours of so many people wanting to meet Marla's sister and regale her with more of Marla's accolades, she needed just a few minutes' breather.

She told Cutty she was going for a glass of water and made her way through the crowd. Only rather than asking the already overworked bartender, she went through the swinging doors next to the bar into the restaurant's deserted, brightly lit and much, much quieter kitchen.

Alone in there, she slipped her right foot out of the pointy-toed black mule that went with the dress she'd bought on a quick run to the local boutique while the twins were napping that afternoon. The dress was comfortable—it was a lightweight black-knit ankle-length A-line with a boat neck that looked deceptively prim in front but opened in a wide, low V in back. But the shoes were another story.

Kira arched her foot and wiggled her toes, and when she thought she could stand it again, she put her foot back in that shoe and gave her left one a reprieve, too.

Then she went to the sink and actually did refill her wineglass with water. But once she had she wasn't eager to rush back to the noise and commotion of the party and so she turned around and leaned her hips against the sink's edge to drink her water and enjoy a few more minutes of peace and quiet.

It was only a few minutes, though, before one of the swinging doors opened and in came Ad with a bowl that held only the remnants of potato salad.

He was startled to discover her and stopped short when he did.

Then he smiled and said, "Are you hiding in here?"

"No," Kira denied in a hurry. Then she smiled, too, because she liked Ad and admitted, "Well, maybe a little."

"It's wild out there," he said as if he understood her need for some escape.

"I've never been to a birthday party this big."

"Small town, big parties—it's hard not to invite just about everyone."

"And they all came," Kira marveled.

"Most of them," Ad said as he set the bowl down on a worktable in the center of the room and opened an industrial refrigerator to take out a container of potato salad.

He brought the container to the worktable and began to refill the bowl. "I expected a big turnout," he said. "This is the first time we've really been able to celebrate Cutty's birthday. Or anything else with him. Not many people would have missed it."

"Why is this the first time you've been able to celebrate anything with him?" Kira asked.

"Marla would never have come to something like this. Cutty wouldn't have come without her, so no parties," Ad finished matter-of-factly.

"Why wouldn't Marla have come?"

"It wouldn't have been a place for Anthony, and she wouldn't have left him home with a sitter."

"Ever?"

"She was pretty adamant about being the one to take care of him. She left him with Cutty of course. But no one else."

"Wow. She really was devoted to him," Kira remarked.

Ad didn't say anything to that. He also didn't seem to want to look Kira in the eye and instead became very interested in the potato salad.

For some reason it made Kira suspicious. "Wasn't she devoted to him? That's what Betty said."

"Sure she was."

There wasn't much conviction in that and it sparked a memory in Kira of the evening Ad had come to help with the twins while Cutty did the interview with the college-newspaper reporter. He'd started to say something that night and then cut himself off, saying he didn't want to tell tales out of school. Together with this now, it roused Kira's curiosity.

"Do you know something no one else does?" she joked.

Still, she expected him to say no. But instead he said, "Come on, this is a party. No serious talk."

So there *was* something serious to talk about?

"We're taking a break from the party, remember?" Kira said. "What do you know about my sister that no one else does?"

Ad frowned at her. "It's not like that."

"Then what is it like?"

"I just had a lot of time behind the scenes that other people didn't have, that's all."

"And were things different behind the scenes than they were on the stage?"

"You don't want to talk about this."

The more he tried not to, the more Kira *did* want to talk about it. So she pressed him. "Didn't you think as highly of Marla as Betty and everyone else around here seems to?"

"Marla was one of a kind," Ad said.

"That's the sort of thing that can either be a compliment or a criticism. Which is it?"

"I wouldn't criticize Marla. In a lot of ways she was a tortured soul."

"Because of Anthony?"

"There was more to it than that. Anthony was just one of the ways it came out."

He didn't offer any explanation, though, and in order to encourage him Kira said, "You know, I loved my sister but I didn't get to know her as an adult and from everything I've heard about her since I've been in Northbridge, she was too good to be true. I'd kind of like to know who she really was."

Ad finished filling the bowl, closed the container and replaced it in the refrigerator. Then he returned to stand at the worktable across from Kira.

"How about if I just say Marla was driven and leave it at that?" Ad suggested.

"A driven, tortured soul," Kira repeated. "That's a lot different than anything else I've heard about her."

Ad didn't comment one way or another.

Kira thought maybe if she opened up to him a little he might open up to her, so she said, "You know, it hasn't been easy being Marla's younger sister. It's like she's always been just ahead of me, raising the bar. Even now, it's as if she's some kind of icon around here. I'd really just like to know the truth. Maybe to know she was only human, like the rest of us."

Ad hadn't taken his eyes off her the entire time she'd been talking and Kira could tell she'd gotten through to him, that he was considering being honest with her.

But even when he did speak again he was still hedging.

"Marla was smart and talented and accomplished and good at just about everything."

"But…" Kira prompted with what seemed to be about to come after that.

Rather than continuing, though, Ad said, "Cutty wouldn't tell you this. He'd say it was all water under the bridge. That Marla's gone and none of it matters anymore. He sure as hell wouldn't say it to her *sister,* of all people."

"Then if you don't tell me I'll never know."

"You don't *need* to know," Ad reasoned.

But Kira thought that she did. For her own sake, because she was trying so hard to meet her sister's standards. And because she wanted to know everything she could about Cutty. About his past and what made him tick.

"I'd really like to know the truth," she said. "And I am family. It isn't as if you'd be gossiping."

Ad still wasn't eager to tell her what she wanted to know, and for a moment more he searched her face while he seemed to be deciding what to do.

But apparently her heartfelt, "Please," convinced him because he sighed and gave in.

"Marla was a very intense person. That didn't make her easy to live with. Not that Cutty complained, he didn't. I'm just saying that if I had been in his shoes, I couldn't have been married to Marla."

"Why not?"

"Everybody around here thought she was some kind of saint, or superwoman because that's what she tried to be. That's what she was determined to be. It was like a compulsion or something. She could never give up, she could never accept things the way they were, she could never stop trying to be the best at..." Ad stopped as if he felt he was getting carried away. "Let's just say that it didn't make for any kind of relaxed, balanced life. Not for her or for people who lived with her."

"Believe it or not," Kira said to encourage him, "I understand what you're saying. You could be describing Marla's father—my adoptive father."

"So you know what it's like to live with."

"Too well. My father was more rigid than anyone outside the house knew."

"Rigid—that's a good way to put it. Marla was definitely rigid. And completely intolerant of even small things that went wrong. Or, for instance, something being half an inch out of place. She'd just go ballistic until everything was where she wanted it. *Exactly* where she wanted it."

Which explained Betty, and even Ad, stressing that to her when they'd helped around the house, Kira thought.

"She also had schedules for everything," Ad continued. "Schedules and routines that had to be followed or she just...exploded. And as for that *devotion* to Anthony?"

Ad cut himself short again suddenly, as if he'd said too much already.

"It's okay. This is important for me to know," Kira assured.

Still Ad hesitated. "I don't want it to sound as if I

didn't like Marla. Really, it was just sad. It was really, really sad to watch someone push herself and everybody close to her the way she did. And when it came to Anthony—'' Ad shook his head. ''Well, Marla needed things—and people—to be unflawed.''

''And an autistic child is further away from that than a normal child,'' Kira guessed.

Ad nodded, looking as sad as he'd said the situation was. ''They didn't realize Anthony was autistic until he was about two,'' he continued. ''Before that it just seemed like he wasn't interested in the things babies can be entertained with or distracted by. He was just kind of unresponsive. But the doctor knew it wasn't right and that was when they figured out he was autistic. Marla came unglued when she heard that. She needed things to be perfect and Anthony wasn't. And after she went behind Cutty's back to call your father—''

''I didn't know she'd called him,'' Kira confessed, thinking that her call must have been the contact Cutty had said Marla had with the family after they'd eloped. ''I take it my father wasn't sympathetic?''

''He told her she'd gotten what she deserved. That Anthony being autistic was her punishment. And that he wouldn't have any part of it, nor would he do anything to help out. I believe the you-made-your-bed-now-lie-in-it card was the end of the conversation.''

Kira closed her eyes as her heart went out to the young Marla, imagining the desperation her sister must have felt.

''He was like that,'' Kira confirmed in a near whisper when she opened her eyes.

''After that,'' Ad went on, ''Marla did what she did with everything—she tried harder. She tried desperately to make Anthony normal. To teach him. To control him. To get the autism out of him as if it were something that had possessed him and not just the way he was.''

Ad paused, shook his head again, and then said, ''I'm sorry. This is hardly a story to tell at a party.''

''It's okay. I wanted to know.'' Then, thinking beyond all that Ad had told her, she said, ''None of this could have been good for Cutty and Marla's marriage.''

''No, it wasn't. Plus, it was a teenage, shotgun marriage as it was, and Marla's relationship with Cutty was the one thing she took for granted. The one thing she *didn't* work at. And even though Cutty tried to make it a real marriage—and he tried as hard at that as Marla tried for perfection in everything else—there just wasn't much there.''

''So where did the twins come from?'' Kira asked, not challenging what Ad was telling her, just confused.

''That was my doing.''

Kira's eyes widened and Ad grimaced. ''That didn't come out right. Here's the thing. I knew what Cutty went through trying to please Marla, trying to make the marriage a real one, and I also knew he needed a break himself. They'd never had a honeymoon or a single vacation, so for their anniversary I got together with friends—'' Ad pointed his chin in the direction from which the party was still going strong. ''A whole bunch of us pitched in, made the arrangements and gave them a trip to the Bahamas.''

''What about Anthony?''

''Marla didn't want to leave him, but with popular opinion urging her on, she also couldn't look ungrateful, so she conceded.''

''Who watched him?''

''He was familiar with my sister and me so we moved into the house with him to keep him in his same surroundings.''

''Did he do okay with that?''

''He was fine. But Marla wasn't. She and Cutty were supposed to be gone for seven days but she made him come home after two.''

''And the twins? You still haven't explained how you're responsible for them.''

''There was one night on the trip... That's where the twins came from. One night that ended up making the tension at home even worse and, even though Cutty never said it straight-out, my impression was that it was one night that proved to him that he didn't really have any marriage at all. That they were both just going through the motions. When they got back, Marla moved out of their bedroom into the guest room, and Cutty was sleeping on the couch from then until about six months ago when he got rid of the old bedroom furniture, bought new stuff and started to use the room again.''

''But they never considered divorce?'' Kira asked.

"Marla would have never admitted a failure like that, and Cutty would never have left her or Anthony," Ad said. "So they kept up the appearance of a happy marriage. An appearance that was helped along with Marla's pregnancy and having the twins. But underneath the surface, there was no substance."

Ad finished on a solemn note. He glanced in the direction of the party once more, but it was clear that only Cutty was on his mind and Kira thought he was worrying that his friend wouldn't have wanted him to say all he just had.

"He won't have to know unless you tell him yourself," Kira said, guessing what was going through Ad's mind.

But before Ad could confirm or deny it, one of the swinging doors opened and in popped Cutty's head.

"Hey, what're you two doing? The party's out here," he said jovially.

"You caught us," Ad joked. "I'm trying to steal her away."

"I knew that dress was going to knock 'em dead tonight," Cutty countered. Then he brought his cane through the opening of the doors and waved it like a weapon at Ad, laughing as he threatened, "Don't make me use this on you."

"My skull's already cracked," Ad joked in return.

"I'm headed for the facilities but when I get back I'd better see you filling out the ranks of this party," Cutty said then. "If I have to do this, so do the both of you," he added as if he wasn't having a good time when it was clear he was.

"On our way," Ad answered.

"You better be."

Cutty retreated and the doors swung shut after him, leaving Kira and Ad alone again.

Kira pushed off the sink's edge as Ad picked up the bowl of potato salad so they could follow him.

"Thanks for telling me all this," Kira said along the way.

They reached the doors and Ad raised a hand to one of them to push it open. But before he did he paused to look down at her.

"I might as well tell you one more thing while I'm at it," he said.

"There's more?"

"Only about Cutty. That big mug he just poked in here? I haven't seen it as happy as that until this last week you've been around. Call me silly, but I'm beginning to think it has something to do with you."

Ad pushed open the door and waited for her to go through it ahead of him.

Kira did, working to hide the fact that while everything he'd told her about Marla hadn't been as much of a shock to her as he might have thought it was, that last comment had really rocked her.

The party didn't end until after two in the morning, despite the fact that it was a Tuesday night. With the exception of Ad—who lived above the restaurant and also needed to lock up—Kira and Cutty were the last to leave after Cutty had said good-night to each of his guests and thanked Ad for everything.

The drive home was quick since the restaurant was only a few blocks from Cutty's house. Along the way Cutty and Kira talked about the wisdom in taking Ad's sister up on her offer to have the twins stay at her house for the night. They agreed they would have felt guilty if teenage Tiffy had been waiting this long for their return.

There was no one stirring on the block as they pulled into the driveway, and not so much as a light on in any house. Maybe that was why neither of them said anything as they got out of the car and walked up to the front door. Even as Cutty unlocked it and opened it for Kira they didn't disturb the silence of the sleeping night.

Only after the door was closed behind them did Cutty say, "I know it's late but I don't feel tired."

Kira didn't, either. Or maybe it was just that after a busy day and evening full of well-wishers, what she did feel was that she had barely seen Cutty and that she wanted to have that end-of-the-evening time alone with him in spite of how late that particular evening was ending.

"We're still probably wired from all that celebrating," she said. "But it *is* late," she added, just because it seemed as if she should.

"Yeah, I suppose it is. How about if I at least walk you all the way to your door tonight, though?"

"Your ankle isn't killing you?"

Cutty smiled a devilish smile she could only see in the moon glow that came through the glass in the upper half of the front door since they hadn't turned on a light. "I'm not feeling any pain at all," he assured.

"Magic ginger ale?"

"It must have been."

They went down the entry hall to the kitchen, not turning on a light there, either, and out the back door into the stillness of the backyard.

"So, did you have a good time?" Cutty asked as they crossed slowly to the garage apartment. "Or were you bored out of your mind being with so many people you didn't know?"

"I had a great time," Kira said, meaning it. "I haven't met anyone in Northbridge I haven't liked."

They reached the garage but Kira was still in no hurry to lose Cutty's company so even though she unlocked her door, she didn't open it or make any move to say good-night.

Cutty didn't, either. Instead he said, "What were you and Ad talking about when I found you in the kitchen? It seemed serious."

That was a question Kira had been hoping he wouldn't ask. But now that he had, she opted for being vague. "We were talking about you." Sort of. "You're really close—you and Ad—aren't you?"

"I never had a brother but I don't think I could be closer to one than I am to Ad."

"From what I've seen I'd say he feels the same about you," Kira said, hoping that was as far as the subject went.

It was, because Cutty seemed more interested in her than in talking about Ad as those green eyes did a slow roll downward and back up again. "You know, you look spectacular tonight," he said then.

"I wasn't ashamed to be seen with you, either," she countered, taking in the sight of him in a pair of charcoal-colored slacks and a black mock-turtleneck dress T-shirt that made him look far too dashing to be a small-town cop.

"I had two different guys grilling me about you," Cutty told her. "They both wanted to know if they could give you a call and ask you out while you're here."

"And what did you tell them?" Where did that coy, flirty tone of voice come from?

"I told them to keep their distance," he said in a way that left her wondering if he was kidding her.

"Would I have liked them?" she countered.

The devilishness quotient in his smile increased. "Not as well as you like me."

Kira laughed. "Who said I like you?"

He leaned over and whispered in her ear, "A little bird."

Then he tugged at her lobe with his teeth.

"You've been talking to birds?"

He straightened up and looked into her eyes. "They know a lot of things."

"Birds do?" she said skeptically, enjoying this game just because she was playing it with him.

"They fly around up there, watching us, listening to us. They see all and know all."

"But they eat worms so how can their judgement really be trusted?"

"Does that mean you *don't* like me?" he asked with enough of a bad-boy look in his eyes to let her know he was confident that wasn't the case.

"You never know," she said aloofly. "Could be I do. Could be I don't."

"Maybe I could win you over. If you don't."

"How?"

"How about like this?"

He leaned forward again, only this time he kissed her. A soft, simple kiss full of promise. A kiss that ended all too soon.

"Not bad," Kira judged when he drew back again. "But who knows? One of those other guys might have done better."

Cutty laughed. A low, sexy rumble of a laugh. "Guess I'll just have to try harder."

He propped his cane against the wall behind Kira, freeing both hands to hold her face on either side, his palms cupping her cheeks, his fingers in her hair as his mouth came to hers in a kiss much better, much more serious than the other one. A kiss that claimed her.

But it, too, ended after a few moments and he straightened away from her again.

"Well?" he said in a husky voice.

"Improving," she declared imperiously.

His laugh was sexier still. "I guess I'm on the right track then," he said before his mouth met hers once more.

No matter what she said, he was winning the game because her knees were getting weaker by the minute and she was having trouble not melting into that big body of his. Enough trouble so that she raised her palms to his chest to keep from giving in. Or at least to keep from giving in too easily. Plus it was nice to be touching that honed wall of muscle.

This time when he stopped kissing her he said, "Shall I call them tomorrow and give them the green light?"

With her eyes still closed she said, "Who?"

"The guys who want to ask you out," he answered with one more raspy chuckle before he recaptured her mouth, wrapping his arms around her to pull her close against him with those agile hands against her bare back where it was exposed by the V of her dress.

Oh, what the feel of his hands did to her! His skin pressed to hers was all it took to whisk her back in time to the previous evening. To reawaken everything inside her that he'd brought to life then.

Only tonight it didn't come with the fear of letting go. Tonight other things were racing through her mind.

Things like the fact that Betty would be taking over tomorrow and Kira didn't know where that would leave her. Or if she really would stay or go.

Things like the fact that she'd enjoyed the idea she'd fostered all day of cutting loose. Enjoyed that vision of herself. Enjoyed the possibility that she could.

Things like the fact that after she'd done what she'd thought she should do last night and not allowed this to go all the way to making love, she'd regretted it intensely. She'd gone to sleep wishing that just once she'd been brave enough to do what she wanted to do.

What she wanted to do right now.

Without breaking off their kiss, Kira reached behind her and found the doorknob, turning it and pushing the door open.

Cutty abandoned her lips to see what she'd done.

"Oh-oh," he said, clearly thinking she was going to leave him there.

But Kira picked up his cane and stepped over her threshold, taking it with her.

"You know that where the cane goes, I go," Cutty said with a wicked crook to one corner of his mouth.

"Is that so?" she said. Then she tossed the cane onto the bed.

Cutty laughed and his eyebrows rose. But he stayed in the doorway. "What about last night and moving too fast and—"

Kira answered him only by kicking off her shoes.

But it was enough for him to get the message, because he finally followed her inside, shutting the door behind him.

He still didn't actually come into the single room apartment, though. Instead he leaned back against the door, watching her through the moonlight that streamed in through the windows to provide the only illumination here, too.

"Tell me you know what you're doing," he said quietly.

"I'm doing just what I want," she said without

wavering because the longer she looked at him—at his sable-colored hair going every which way on top, at his ruggedly striking face, at that big body that seemed carved by an artist's hand—the more her whole being cried out for him.

"No doubts?" he asked.

"No doubts."

Still he stayed at the door, drinking in the sight of her just as she was him. Then he chuckled a little, took off his single shoe and sock, too, and came to where she waited beside the bed.

"This is really going to happen," he said as if that fact was just sinking in.

Kira only nodded, basking in his gaze as it seemed to savor her.

Then Cutty raised one hand to her upper arm and let it glide down to her wrist so he could bring that wrist to his lips to kiss the soft inner side, all the while holding her eyes with his.

His breath was warm against her skin. Sensuous. And she stepped nearer to close the small distance between them so he could kiss more than her wrist again.

Which was exactly what he did as his arms came around her once more. Only this time those hands of his delved into the sides of the open V of her dress, slipping up to her shoulders and moving forward to slide it off as his mouth opened over hers and his tongue came to pitch a little woo.

With very little encouragement her dress fell around her feet, leaving her only in her panties, and

Kira refused to be the only one of them without much on.

She wasted no time freeing his shirt from his slacks, interrupting the play of mouths and tongues to pull it off over his head.

With his chest bare, Cutty pulled her against him so her breasts could meet the hot silk of his pectorals as kisses turned urgent. Hungry. Demanding.

He didn't wait for her to deal with his pants. He took something from his pocket and then dropped them to join her dress on the floor before he divested her of her lacy thong, too.

He stopped kissing her then and searched her face, her eyes, as if to reassure himself she was real. And only after he seemed convinced did he reach around to set what he'd taken from his pocket on the nightstand so he could clasp her hands in his as he sat down on the mattress.

He left her standing a moment while he looked at her and a smile of appreciation lit his oh-so-handsome face, wiping away any self-consciousness Kira might have felt.

Then he pulled her to the bed, too. To lie on her back next to him as he lay on his side, their hands still together until he let hers go to brace his weight with one, to slip the other behind her head as his mouth found hers once again in a kiss of parted lips and tongues dueling in delight.

She raised her own hands to his head, to his hair— bristly and soft at once—and he caressed her face lovingly before trailing his hand down her neck, to the hollow of her throat, to her collarbone and shoulder.

He stopped there. But she didn't want him to. Not when her breasts were screaming for his touch.

She covered his hand with hers and urged it on, making him chuckle even as their mouths continued to cling.

Then to tease her he let only his fingertips trail a scant path, skimming just the surface of her skin, at a torturously snailish speed.

Kira groaned her complaint even as her tongue did a little pursuit of its own. But still Cutty took his time, letting those feathery fingertips glide all the way down the upper swell of her breast to her nipple.

Taut. Tight. That crest became a knot that greeted those fingertips and held its own as he took it gently between thumb and forefinger and tenderly rolled it back and forth.

Kira's groan became a moan when he finally took her breast into his palm, enclosing it in the warm strength of that hand she craved.

Kisses grew even hungrier. Even more urgent. Faster and freer, falling on lips and cheeks and chins.

Kira's hands filled themselves with his back— broad and strong and well muscled.

He was beside her and above her, his mouth a rain of kisses, his hand a miracle of kneading, of teasing, of tormenting, every movement of it raising her temperature, making her want him with an even greater intensity.

His mouth abandoned hers for good then, kissing

a leisurely route to her other breast, finding it first with his tongue to taunt that nipple, too.

Her back came off the mattress in response, leaving no doubt that she wanted more.

And more was what he gave.

He took her breast into the hot, wet darkness of his mouth, still using his talented tongue to toy with her nipple, circling it, flicking it, bringing it to life along with every other inch of her body.

Her own hands went traveling. Exploring. Seeking. Down the V of his back to the firm rise of that derriere she'd only glimpsed before that moment.

Lower, to the back of solid thighs.

Up again to his hips, giving him a bit of his own medicine when it came to tantalizing with anticipation.

It was Cutty's turn to groan and hers to laugh. But she granted his wish and let one hand course around to his front.

His moan was deeper and more gravelly than hers had been as she took him in hand, closing her fingers around that long, thick shaft of steel, reveling in the heat of him, the power, the potency.

But that seemed to be all he could take because he rolled away from her briefly, reaching for what he'd left on the nightstand.

"You came prepared?" Kira whispered.

"Just because of a hope-filled fantasy," he said, sheathing himself before he returned to rise above her, fitting himself between her thighs.

Thighs that Kira opened willingly, wanting nothing so much as to be completed by him.

He slid into her then as smoothly as if he had been carved from her. Filling her. Lowering his body to hers in a flawless joining of flesh.

He kissed her again then, easing himself more deeply into her, only to draw back and do it all again. And again until they were moving together too rapidly, too fiercely, for him to keep kissing her.

Kira just closed her eyes and let him carry her along, giving herself to him totally, relinquishing all control and allowing him to take her with him into sensations more incredible than anything she'd ever felt before.

Faster and faster, they moved as if their bodies had become one—in unison, in perfect rhythm. Striving. Straining. Working together until Kira felt as if she were no longer earthbound. As if she'd broken the ties of gravity to soar into the sky. Higher and higher until she burst through the clouds into a blindingly brilliant white bliss that stole her breath and left her cocooned in an eternal moment of unequaled ecstasy...

And then it retreated. Little by little they both came back to themselves. Muscles relaxed. Heavy breathing filled lungs with air again. And an exquisite calm settled them into each other's arms.

"Wow," Cutty said, sounding as awed as Kira felt.

"As good or not as good as your hope-filled fantasy?" she asked.

"The fantasy was surpassed a thousand times over. Are you okay?"

"*Okay* was surpassed a thousand times over, too."

He smiled down at her and then buried his face in her tousled hair to kiss her head as he rolled them to their sides, keeping her close.

And that was how they stayed—his chin atop her head, his arm across her side, his leg over her hip— as total depletion of strength and energy overcame them.

Kira felt Cutty fall asleep but she didn't mind. It was just too nice to be there like that, with him, for her to care about anything.

Then she closed her own eyes, reveling in that moment, that afterglow, and all the warm feelings that went with it.

And when thoughts of what the next day might bring threatened to intrude she just pushed them away.

Chapter Eight

Cutty woke up the next morning in a haze of contentment, the likes of which he couldn't remember ever feeling before.

Without opening his eyes, he reached to the other side of the bed for Kira, expecting to find her there the way he had during the night when he'd drifted partially out of sleep and wanted to touch her or hold her.

But she wasn't there.

Even with his eyes closed he could tell morning light was all around him, so he thought she was probably in the bathroom and he let himself lie there, basking in that contentment that felt so damn good.

He knew he should probably get up. That Ad's sister would be bringing the twins home before long.

But still he stayed in that bed, enjoying the lingering memories of the remarkable night that had just passed. And the best birthday he'd ever had.

So this is what it's like to feel genuinely happy.

That was a bizarre thought to flash through his brain. Where had it come from?

Obviously from the way he was feeling. But still it struck him as odd.

Genuinely happy? Had he never been *genuinely* happy before?

Cutty rolled onto his back, eyes remaining closed, and began to dissect that possibility.

He didn't consider himself an *un*happy person. He made the best of what he had to work with. There were things he liked to do. Foods he liked to eat. Friends he liked spending time with. There were the twins. His job. Baseball, basketball, football games with the Northbridge Bruisers—he liked all of that.

But none of it had made him feel the way he did right at that moment. This was the kind of happiness he honestly didn't think he'd ever felt before.

He definitely hadn't felt it as a kid. There had been happy times, but a general, overall deep-rooted happiness? No, he couldn't say he'd felt that. Not while he was worrying about his dad and his dad's drinking, and how to cope with whatever came as a result of it.

Then there had been Marla.

Happiness wasn't something he thought of when he thought about Marla. Oh, sure, he'd been happy to hook up with her in high school. But like everything with Marla, even the start of the relationship had been complicated and so no, pure, unadulterated happiness was not the primary emotion he recalled.

Then she'd told him she was pregnant. That certainly hadn't made him happy. Neither had meeting Tom Wentworth or fighting with him or being in a position of having to elope. And happy wasn't how Cutty would describe having to come to Northbridge to live off the charity of his uncle.

Discovering that Anthony was autistic—there was no way *that* had been happy news. And the realities of living with Marla, of dealing with her relentless need for perfection. That hadn't put him in a state he would consider genuinely happy, either.

Even the birth of the twins had been marred by Marla's unhappiness at finding herself pregnant again. And what little marriage they'd had crumbling around his feet had been anything but happy.

And then there had been the accident. Losing Anthony and Marla. No matter how bad things had been at home before that, their deaths had struck a blow that he'd been struggling with ever since.

Still, it wasn't as if he'd had a miserable life, because he hadn't. It wasn't that he suffered from depression or anything like that. But when he thought about the course of things all strung together, he guessed he *could* say that he'd never really felt genuine, deep-rooted happiness.

The way he did now.

And it didn't take much to figure out why he felt that way now.

It was because of Kira.

It was as if she'd brought a light, a joy, into his life that had never been there before. He could relax with her as he'd never been able to relax with Marla. He could be himself without worrying that he was disappointing her somehow or letting her down. He just felt good when he was with her.

He felt happy.

Where was she, anyway? he wondered, finally opening his eyes.

Oh, yeah.

He wasn't in his own bed. He was in the bed in the garage apartment. He'd forgotten that.

It was the first time in ten years that he'd awakened there. And even though the place had been painted and the furniture was all new, even though it looked altogether different than it had when he and Marla and Anthony had lived there, finding himself there now was like being sucked backward in time. If Marla had charged out of the bathroom and screamed at him for laying around in bed, he wouldn't have been surprised.

And just that quick his sense of genuine happiness was tinged with an old familiar anxiousness.

Cutty sat up in bed, wanting to hang on to the good feelings, wanting to escape the not so good ones.

"Kira?" he called.

Then it occurred to him that he hadn't heard a single sound come from the bathroom and that was the only place she could be where he wouldn't be able to see her.

So where was she?

Cutty glanced at the bedside clock for the first time and was shocked to find that it was already after ten. He hadn't thought it was *that* late. And Ad's sister had mentioned bringing the twins home around nine.

Had Kira heard the doorbell ring from out here?

He knew that wasn't likely.

But what *was* likely, he slowly began to think, was that Kira had left him in bed hours ago and gone across to the house to clean before Betty came this afternoon.

If memories of Marla hadn't totally deflated his joy moments earlier, that thought did the trick.

Cutty swung his legs over the side of the mattress.

His ankle shot pain up his leg in protest over the drop in altitude and he waited for it to ease up. Then he reached for the cane that was now propped against the nightstand rather than on the floor where it had rolled when he and Kira had joined it on the bed.

She must have picked it up and put it there. Just as it had to have been Kira who had neatly folded his pants and shirt on the nearby chair and so precisely situated his single shoe and sock immediately under it.

Thoughts of Marla again invaded at the sight of all that orderliness.

Thoughts about the similarities between Marla and Kira.

It left him all the more convinced of the reason Kira hadn't been there in bed with him when he woke up.

Damn.

Using the cane, he hooked his clothes and dragged them to him, his spirits deflating even further as he pictured Kira going through the house like a whirling dervish, cleaning and straightening and perfecting everything in her path. The same way Marla would have been.

He pulled on his shirt from the previous night, then his slacks and stood to bend over and grab his shoe and sock. But he didn't put them on. He just carried them with him out of the garage apartment.

And if what he'd felt when he first woke up had been a high high, trudging across the yard thinking that he was going to find Kira frantically whipping the house into shape to impress Betty was pretty close to a low low.

As he went in the back door he expected to hear the vacuum or water running, or something that would give him a clue as to where Kira was. But the house was quiet and he didn't find her anywhere on the first floor.

She's probably upstairs scrubbing down the walls or something, he thought as he made his way to the second level.

Again no sounds greeted him and in search of Kira and the twins, Cutty headed for the nursery.

The door was open and as he approached he finally spotted Kira.

She wasn't cleaning or folding clothes or any of what he'd assumed she'd be doing in anticipation of Betty, though. She was sitting cross-legged on the floor with Mel to her right and Mandy to her left, and they were putting the oversize pieces of a wooden puzzle together.

Intent on what they were doing, no one noticed him and Cutty stopped in his tracks. He'd been so sure he would find Kira in a panic to spruce up the place that seeing her like that actually shocked him.

Had she forgotten Betty was coming? That Betty would see the toys scattered in the living room? And laundry in the basket? And a baby handprint on the television screen?

He couldn't imagine that she had.

Yet there she was, playing with the twins rather than scurrying to make sure everything was impeccable.

Cutty stood there for a moment and watched the scene. Then, without letting Kira or his daughters know he was in the house, he went into his own room, closing the door quietly behind him.

"You jumped to that conclusion, didn't you, you jerk?" he muttered to himself.

But he really was a jerk, he thought, when one minute he was marveling at how terrific he felt all because of Kira and the next minute he was ready to condemn her.

And now here he was, wanting to hurry up and shower so he could be with her again.

"Maybe you should make up your mind," he advised himself as if he were talking to someone else.

He tossed his shoe into the closet, dropped his sock to the floor and stripped off his dress clothes to make a pile over the stocking. Then he headed for his bathroom.

But as he wrapped his cast to keep it dry and stepped into the shower, he started to consider that making-up-his-mind advice he'd just given himself.

He'd already recognized that there were two sides to Kira. That there was the side of her that was like Marla and the side of her that might have fretted over leaving the housework to go to the softball game but had gone anyway.

So if the side existed that could be persuaded to go to the softball game anyway—or sit and do a puzzle with the twins as she was right now—why had he been so quick to believe that it was the side like Marla that would prevail?

Standing under the shower's spray Cutty thought about it, trying to figure out whether he was being unfair to her.

He might be.

Because besides the softball game and finding her with the babies this morning, he also remembered this past Sunday when she'd set up the swimming pool in the backyard and ended up soaking her feet in the water with the twins rather than doing housework.

Plus there were a lot of times he recalled now that were smaller incidences of the same thing. Times when she'd read a story to the girls to distract them from mischief. Times when she'd patiently suffered the complications of one of the twins wanting to help her sweep the floor or dust the furniture. Times when a trip upstairs to do laundry had instead had Kira standing at the nursery door watching the babies sleep.

Times when the housework and laundry and dishes and other things left undone to vex that perfectionistic side of Kira had only been left undone *because* she was more likely to leave the chores in order to take care of him or the babies, to go with him when he asked her to, to play with Mel and Mandy....

That was a very big realization for him.

Big enough to cause him to pause for a minute to let it sink in.

And as it did, he had to admit that while, yes, there was a side of Kira that was like Marla, Marla had never had that other, softer, more flexible side that Kira had to balance it out.

Would Marla ever have left dishes in the sink or mud on the floor to go to a softball game with him?

Never.

Even during the brief month after Mel and Mandy were born, Marla had fed them, bathed them, dressed them and then handed them off to Betty to hold while she'd made sure no speck of dust was left to mar her sense of order.

So what did that mean? Cutty asked himself as he finished his shower, turned off the water and grabbed a towel to dry off.

For one thing, it meant that Kira was more fun.

And for another thing, it meant that she was easier to live with—even considering the fretting and the periodic mad dashes to clean.

That thought made him smile because it reminded

him of the day Betty had come to take the twins to the park, when Cutty had spotted Kira through the living-room window stashing that soiled baby shirt under the couch cushion. That was definitely not something Marla would have done.

So maybe Kira and Marla weren't as much alike as Cutty had thought.

And maybe given the fact that Kira had that softer side, that Kira *could* be persuaded to temporarily ignore a little debris in favor of the people in her life, made it easier to overlook those times when she was in a frenzy over a minor detail.

Cutty unwrapped his cast and limped to the sink to shave, thinking as he did about the way he'd felt when he first woke up this morning. The way he'd felt more and more the longer Kira was around.

Genuine, deep-rooted happiness.

Was that feeling worth the times when Kira was a little nuts?

It must have been, because there he was, lathering his face with shaving foam and grinning as that feeling washed through him again.

As that feeling washed through him again at the thought of having Kira around *all* the time to make him continue to feel that way.

Did he want her to be around all the time? he asked himself.

But that was a no-brainer. He sure as hell didn't want her to leave. He sure as hell didn't want to lose her or this feeling.

"So you take the good with the bad," he told his reflection.

But that wasn't really fair, either. Because the *bad* wasn't really bad, now that he thought about it. Sure, Kira had come across the yard at the crack of dawn in the mornings to try to get a head start on keeping an impeccable house. But she hadn't roused him out of bed to do it, too. The way Marla would have.

Sure, Kira had strived for perfection, but she hadn't been so obsessed with it that she'd made things around there miserable by demanding that he meet her unreasonable standards, too. The way Marla had.

Sure, Kira had *wanted* things to be tidier and more orderly, but if they weren't she had still been capable of separating herself from it long enough to have a good time—to sit and talk with him at the end of the day, to go to his birthday party, to go to the awards ceremony and the softball game, to play with the babies. And to let him do all those things, too. Without guilt. Without berating him and making him feel guilty for it. And that wasn't at all like Marla, either.

In fact, Cutty thought sadly, he didn't think Marla had ever really found much joy in anything.

And the truth was, she'd ridden him so hard she'd taken all the joy out of him, too.

Joy that Kira had put back.

So, no, the *bad* part that went with the good of Kira wasn't really all that bad. It was really just a matter of her being harder on herself than on anyone else.

And the good part? That wasn't just good, either. It was great. It made him happy. *Genuinely* happy.

Happy enough to want to hang on to her.

Even if she did periodically freak out over how much dust there was on the coffee table and who might see it.

Kira was what he wanted.

Kira and that joy and genuine, deep-rooted happiness that only she brought him.

And suddenly, as he took his cane and went back into his bedroom to put on a pair of jeans and a T-shirt, he decided he was going to do something about it.

Kira had just gotten the twins into their high chairs for lunch when Betty arrived.

"My aunt got here early, so I thought I'd come right away," the older woman announced.

For once Kira was glad for the distraction of the housekeeper and nanny. Cutty had only joined Kira and the girls about an hour earlier, but for Kira it had been an awkward hour.

Making love the night before had changed things, and she wasn't exactly sure how to behave. There they were, just like every other day since she'd come to Northbridge except that now she didn't know what to expect. She didn't know if they should talk about what had happened or pretend it *hadn't* happened, or what.

And Cutty was no help. He was being particularly quiet, and she kept catching him watching her all the while she was straightening up the living room and trying to entertain the girls.

Betty hadn't been in the house ten minutes when she started her usual commentary on the wonders of Marla and where Marla liked this and that, and how Marla would have done what Kira was apparently doing wrong when she gave Mel and Mandy slices of bologna to munch on rather than cutting the lunch meat into pieces for them.

But the older woman was barely getting warmed up when Cutty came into the kitchen and said, "Think you can handle this on your own for a while, Betty?"

"That's what I'm here for," Betty answered, seeming thrilled to take over for Kira, who was surprised by the request. And confused and curious about it, too.

Cutty took her hand then—shocking her even more by the display of familiarity—and led her out the back door.

In the direction of the garage apartment.

But surely he couldn't be going there, she thought. He couldn't be thinking of repeating the lovemaking of the night before. Not in the middle of the day, with Betty only a backyard away.

The garage apartment was just where Cutty was headed, though, and within moments Kira found herself behind closed doors.

Where the bed hadn't yet been made.

Just the sight of it did two things to Kira—it gave her an instant flash of vivid memory of what they'd done there and also inspired a sharp desire to do it again.

But if that really was what Cutty had in mind, she just couldn't do it, so she turned her back to the bed and faced him with a questioning glance.

Cutty was perceptive enough to catch it and even to know what was on her mind.

He smiled a one-sided smile and said, "Do you honestly think I brought you out here to ravage you in broad daylight while Betty baby-sits?"

"I hope not," Kira admitted.

"You can relax, that's not what I have up my sleeve. Much as I wish it was."

Kira refrained from saying *me, too.* "What *do* you have up your sleeve?"

"I wanted to talk to you. Without anyone overhearing. In all the birthday commotion yesterday and last night we never got into what's going to happen now that Betty is coming back to work."

"No, we didn't," Kira agreed, although the subject had been weighing on her.

"Well, we need to talk about it."

"Okay," Kira said, waiting to hear what he had to say.

He came to stand close in front of her, reaching a hand to her arm. A hand that sent ripples of wonderful sense memory all through her and made it difficult to concentrate on what he was saying.

But she put some effort into it in time to hear, "I woke up this morning feeling incredible. And I realized that you're the reason."

Kira couldn't help smiling. "I'm glad."

"I also realized that with Betty coming back it could mean that you might not stick around much longer and the thought of you leaving was..." Cutty chuckled wryly and shook his head. "Well, I didn't like it."

The man knew how to make her feel pretty darn good, too. In more ways than one.

But she didn't say that. Instead she made a joke. "So what do you want to do? Hire me on as your own private microbiologist?"

"I want you here, that's for sure," Cutty said in answer to her jest. But he wasn't kidding. He was serious.

"I thought a lot about it this morning," he went on. "I know you came to find the twins, that you only stayed to help out and to get to know them, to start to build a relationship with them. But in the meantime you've also built a relationship with me. A pretty terrific one, I think. And I don't want this to be all there is to it."

Kira didn't know what *this* entailed. But she was beginning to have nervous butterflies in her stomach and she tried to calm them as he continued.

"You know, when you first showed up here I expected you to be just like Marla. I figured the house—and the girls and I for that matter—would be whipped into the kind of shape Tom Wentworth would have been proud of. I definitely didn't think I'd have someone sitting with me at the end of the day, or going to the softball game, or my birthday party, or someone who would be playing with the girls.''

Those good feelings began to fade in Kira because to her that seemed on the brink of criticism. The kind of criticism her father would have dished out—although more harshly—for slacking off when there was work to be done.

''But I finally came to realize,'' Cutty was saying, ''that you're different from Marla. That in some ways you really aren't Tom Wentworth's daughter. That only Marla was. And I guess it finally sank into my head that that part of my life is over. That it's time to move on, to start fresh—all those platitudes that are making a lot of sense to me today. So I just want to know if we can work this out.''

Kira wasn't sure what he meant by *work this out,* either. But her confusion wasn't what was uppermost in her mind. What *was* uppermost in her mind was what he'd said about her being different than Marla. To her, being different than Marla meant not as good as Marla....

And suddenly it seemed very important that it had been Ad who had said Cutty and Marla's marriage had been troubled, that it hadn't been Cutty himself who had told her. And that maybe, looking in from the sidelines, Ad had been wrong. That the way Marla had done things was the way Cutty had liked it. Or at least what he expected.

What had he said? she wondered suddenly when it occurred to her that her own thoughts had interrupted the course of this conversation. He wanted to know if they could work this out.

"I'm sure we can work out when I come to Northbridge to see the girls and other times when they can come to Denver to be with me, so you can have some freedom to get on with your life," she said, interpreting what he meant while her mind was still really on the idea that Cutty, of all people, had compared her unfavorably with her sister.

He frowned at her, his expression confused now. "I wasn't talking about visitation with the twins," he said as if he'd thought that was perfectly clear. "I was talking about you and me. About you staying."

"Staying? I don't know how I could stay," she said, trying to ward off the hurt that was beginning inside her and wondering if there would ever be a time when she wouldn't be in her sister's shadow. "I have my apartment and my job teaching at the university—"

"So give up your apartment and get a teaching job at Northbridge College. I know it wouldn't be as prestigious as working at a university and it probably wouldn't pay quite as well, but I have some influence with the powers that be and I'm sure I could get you onto the staff."

And not because of her own merits. Because of who he was and probably because the dean and the board of directors had all thought so highly of Marla that they would hire her sister...

"I don't want to get a job that way. I got the one

I have because I'm known for my work, for my accomplishments.''

"Then your credentials will get you on here, too," Cutty countered as if it were inconsequential. "I'm just saying—"

Kira cut him off with a resounding no. "I can't stay in Northbridge."

"I don't know why not," Cutty protested, taking his hand away from her arm.

"I just can't, that's all. I won't," Kira said firmly as she endured the regret that washed through her at losing his touch.

Cutty frowned a confused frown. "What did I miss here? I thought…especially after last night—"

"Last night was…nice." And that was a vast understatement. "But it can't change the whole course of my future. I can't give up everything I've worked for and accomplished just because of it."

"I'm only asking you to consider making a few adjustments to have what you said you came here to find in the first place—family."

"The twins will still be my family." The twins who never knew Marla, who would never compare her to Marla, who would always take her only for who she was on her own.

"The twins," Cutty parroted as if that clarified something for him. Something that struck a blow.

But Kira forced herself to stand her ground by reminding herself of all the times she'd thought *Marla's house, Marla's things.* By the idea of living with so many people like Betty and Carol the saleswoman and so many others she'd met while she'd been in North-bridge who couldn't see her for anything but Marla's sister. By remembering that Cutty thought she paled in comparison, too…

Despite the ache that was rapidly wrapping around her heart, she said, "I guess really, since Betty is back and you don't need me anymore I should probably just go ahead and pack my things to go home."

Cutty's deep green eyes were piercing as he stared at her. "I can't believe this."

"There's nothing to not believe. I worked hard to get my degree, to get my teaching job. I had some free time to come here and now I'll go back."

"As if your degrees and job are more important?"

"They might not be important to you, but they are to me."

"More important than anything—or anyone—else? Like a true daughter of Tom Wentworth?" Cutty shook his head again. "You've either fooled the hell out of me since you got here or you're fooling your-self right now."

Kira didn't understand that, either. But he'd struck a blow of his own with that *daughter of Tom Went-worth* remark and so she merely raised her chin de-fiantly, leaving him to think whatever it was he was thinking while she fought to keep from breaking down and letting him know how difficult this was, how much she wished it could all be different, how much it was hurting her.

Then she said, "I'll pack and say goodbye to the girls and be out by the end of the day."

"No!" Cutty nearly shouted. "How did we go from everything being okay when I brought you in here, to you being gone by the end of the day?"

Kira couldn't go on looking at that handsome face, at that body she'd been so intimate with such a short time before, and stick to her guns. So she turned her back to him and said, "It's for the best. Betty is back and can handle everything. The girls love her. I might as well get home."

"This doesn't even make sense. What did I do? What didn't I do? Or say? Or... One minute we're going along great—better than great—and the next minute not only aren't you staying, you're leaving right away?"

"I just think it's for the best," she said quietly, around a throat full of tears.

"And you're just going to let me hang, wondering what the hell went wrong in the last ten minutes?"

"Nothing went wrong," she said because she couldn't tell him the truth about what she felt, about how much of a mistake it had been for her to put herself in a position where she was being compared with her sister once again. About how much of a mistake she knew it would be to put herself into that position forever. "We just see things differently."

"Apparently," Cutty said sarcastically.

For a long moment neither of them said anything at all, and in the silence Kira fought not to cry.

Then Cutty said, "So that's it? You're really going?"

Kira could only nod confirmation.

A few more minutes of that tense silence passed and then Cutty said, ''I'll never understand this.''

But he must have given up trying to because then Kira heard the apartment door open and he was gone.

Chapter Nine

It was two o'clock the next morning when a weary Kira unlocked the door to her Denver apartment. She turned on the table lamp just to the right of the threshold and carried her overfilled suitcase in before she noticed her best friend Kit on her couch.

Kit had obviously been asleep, but with Kira's entrance she sat up and squinted against the sudden light. "Hi," she said simply enough, as if her being there like that wasn't an unusual occurrence.

"Hi," Kira answered with a question in her tone as she closed the door behind her. "How come you're sleeping on my couch?"

"You sounded so bad when you called that I wanted to be here when you got home," Kit explained.

Kira had called from the Billings Airport early in the evening and although she hadn't given Kit any of the details, she had told her things had taken a turn for the worse with Cutty. She also hadn't been able to conceal how upset she was.

"You didn't have to do that," she said. But she was glad Kit had. Despite the hour, Kira knew she wouldn't be able to sleep and she really didn't want to be alone.

"I brought cake," her friend said. "Chocolate fudge. Guaranteed to lift the deepest doldrums."

Kira made an attempt to smile. "Thanks but I don't think I can even eat that right now."

Under Kit's scrutiny, Kira turned on another lamp, kicked off her shoes and dropped into the matching plaid armchair that was positioned at a forty-five degree angle to the sofa.

"You look awful," Kit observed. "You cried all the way home, didn't you?"

"I tried not to but I couldn't seem to help it. It was embarrassing. The woman next to me on the plane thought I must be going to a funeral."

"Tell me what happened."

First Kira told Kit how good things had gotten between herself and Cutty since she'd talked to Kit on the phone on Sunday. She told her about everything Ad had said about Marla, and about Cutty and Marla's marriage. She told her about sleeping with Cutty after his birthday party. And then she told her about what had happened the morning after the party.

Kit listened without saying much, letting Kira pour

it all out. At one point, she did get up and go into the bathroom to bring back a box of tissues so Kira could blow her nose and mop at the tears that just kept coming, though.

"So here I am," Kira concluded when she'd finished. "I just left. I packed up and went back into the house to say goodbye to the twins—"

"That couldn't have been easy," Kit interjected.

Proving her friend's point, the tears Kira had gotten under control began to run down her cheeks again. "It was horrible. I just wanted to pick them up and run with them. But at least Cutty was upstairs so I didn't have to see him again. I don't think I could have survived it."

"How about a cup of tea?" Kit offered.

Kira nodded her agreement as she blew her nose yet again.

Kit went around the island counter that separated the tiny studio apartment into living-sleeping space and kitchen, and made the tea. By the time she returned, Kira had managed to stop crying again.

Kit handed her a mug and then took her own with her to sit on the couch again.

After a few sips, Kit said, "Tell me again *exactly* what Cutty said about Marla."

"He said that he expected me to be like her," Kira complied with a hint of anger in her voice. "He thought I'd whip everything into the kind of shape my father would have been proud of, and that he hadn't thought I would end up sitting around or going to a softball game or a birthday party or that I'd play with the twins instead of doing the work that needed to be done.''

Kit frowned at that. ''But when we talked on Sunday didn't you say that he kept encouraging you to leave things until the next day and not to worry about what didn't get done?''

''Yes. But maybe it was some kind of test or maybe he didn't really mean it or something.''

''You think it was a trap?'' Kit asked.

''I guess not. But I don't know why he said that kind of thing all along and then held it against me when that's what I did.''

''Are you sure he *was* holding it against you?'' Kit asked kindly.

''What do you mean? What else could he have meant?''

''I'm on your side, Kira. I really am. I'm behind you a hundred percent. It's just that I'm also wondering if you took some of what he said at the end differently than he might have intended it.''

But rather than pursuing what Kit was suggesting, Kira seized the one word that spurred her memory. ''*Different*—that's the other thing he said—he said he finally realized I was different than Marla. That I wasn't really Tom Wentworth's daughter the way Marla was.''

''But, Kira, isn't that a *good* thing?'' Kit asked somewhat cautiously. ''That's what I was getting at— what I hear in that isn't bad. You know he didn't care for your father. That he thought he was a tyrant— which, by the way, from what you said Cutty's friend told you, sounds like what Marla was, too. It seems to me that it's a compliment that Cutty thought Marla was like your father and you aren't.''

That was definitely a different point of view. One Kira hadn't considered.

But Kit continued before she had a chance to confirm or deny it.

''And as for you thinking Cutty was criticizing you for sitting around or going out or playing with the babies rather than doing housework—maybe he was saying that was better than the way it had been with your sister who wouldn't have even gone to a birthday party for him.''

''Don't forget, though, it wasn't Cutty who said Marla had done anything wrong. It was his friend,'' Kira said, defending her interpretation even as a spark of hope sprang to life that Kit might be right.

Kit had an answer for that, too. ''His friend also told you that Cutty *wouldn't* say anything against her—especially to you. And unless I'm missing something, Cutty never said anything particularly positive about Marla. He also wasn't the one who threw it up to you that she'd done things better than you were doing. That all came from that Betty person. The same as all Marla's accolades came from people on the outside. It was also that Betty who acted the way your father did with your mother about making sure everything of Marla's was kept just the way she left it.''

That was actually true, Kira realized when she thought about it. It *had* always been Betty and outside people who had touted the glories of Marla. It hadn't been Cutty.

Still, she didn't think she could have been so wrong and she tried hard to remember a time when Cutty had insisted that things be kept the way Marla had kept them, or that Kira had to do anything the way Marla had.

The problem was, no matter how hard she tried, she couldn't come up with a single instance.

In fact, it suddenly occurred to her that after her first disastrous day of trying to take care of the house and the twins he'd actually told her she needed to have *less* concern for doing things the way Marla had. And even when she'd broken Marla's favorite vase, Cutty had taken it in stride. It had been Betty who had made Kira feel bad about it.

And when it came to keeping Marla's memory alive the way Kira's father had kept his first wife's memory alive? Cutty couldn't be accused of that when he hadn't even wanted to talk about Marla.

Which could also have been some of the reason Cutty hadn't been the one to tell her about the way things had been in his marriage...

Kira closed her eyes as everything Kit had brought to her attention began to sink in. "Do you think I just jumped the gun because of my own warped competition with Marla?" she asked her friend.

"I think you heard what Cutty said and saw things with competition coloring it, yes," Kit admitted tactfully. "I just think you've spent so much of your life being compared to Marla and feeling like she was the standard you had to live up to that it's hard for you to see it any other way. I also think that this time around you might have won the competition—in Cutty's view at least—but that you're so used to believing you're not as good as Marla that you didn't recognize it."

Kira had opened her eyes again to look at her friend. "But that's another thing, Kit—even if I won the competition in Cutty's view, and even if Ad had reservations about Marla, there's still Betty and a whole town full of people who adored Marla and never saw me for myself. Do I really want to even consider being in a place where the general consensus will be that I'm not as good?"

"I'm not thrilled about even the possibility of you moving," Kit qualified, "but who cares what anybody thinks? There's a great guy who you're crazy about and who seems crazy about you, and two babies you adore who adore you back—why would it matter what anyone else thinks? Maybe in that you are being too much like Marla and your father."

Kira laughed a small, humorless laugh. "So what it all boils down to is that you just think I've been an idiot and that I've completely blown something that could have been the best thing that ever happened to me?"

"You know I don't think you're an idiot. I think that you just saw this from a perspective based on your own experiences. We all do that. But I also think that you should get some sleep and then call this guy and talk to him, find out if I'm right or if you are. What harm is there in that?''

After only about two hours of sleep Kira did more than merely call Cutty the way Kit had advised. She caught a plane to Montana, rented another car and was within a few miles of Northbridge again by three o'clock the following afternoon.

She was also wondering if she'd just gone off the deep end to be doing this.

But she pushed that thought out of her mind and forced herself to focus only on the reason she'd done this in the first place—to see if she honestly had a chance with Cutty.

Because once Kit had left her alone, Kira had still had trouble falling asleep and in that time before she had, she'd thought a lot about all her friend had said. She'd also thought a lot about what Ad had told her. And she'd thought a *whole* lot about Cutty.

What she'd realized was that Kit really might be right and that she might have been wrong in just about everything that had caused her to make her decision to leave Northbridge and Cutty and the twins behind.

Because despite going over and over almost every moment she'd had with Cutty she still couldn't think of even one time when he'd criticized her. She couldn't think of even one time when he'd compared her to Marla. One time when he'd told her she had to do anything the way Marla had done it.

And as for the feelings the other people in Northbridge had for Marla? Sometime around four that morning Kira had decided that was something be-longing to Marla. That love, that respect, that admi-ration her sister had worked hard to achieve *shouldn't* be challenged. It should be left to Marla and Marla's memory. Especially when it had come at what might have been a very high cost.

And more important, for the first time in Kira's life, she'd come to realize that she really could be free of the shadow cast by Marla if she stopped comparing herself to her sister. If she stopped expecting herself to live up to her. She'd realized that Kit was right when she'd said that what a whole lot of other people thought wasn't the issue if *she* didn't think she was somehow less than Marla. Certainly what other peo-ple thought shouldn't have the power to influence her or her decisions when it came to Cutty or the twins.

Because as long as it wasn't Cutty who was deter-mined to keep Marla alive—the way Tom Wentworth had tried to keep his first wife alive—as long as it wasn't Cutty who was comparing Kira to Marla, then nothing else mattered.

Except maybe if Kira's response the day before had closed whatever door Cutty had been opening for her. *That* was definitely something that would matter...

The gas station Kira had stopped at for directions the first time she'd arrived in Northbridge came into view just then and knowing how close she was to Cutty's house set off butterflies in her stomach.

What if Kit was wrong and I was right, though...

That thought had flashed through her mind a dozen

times on the return trip, and she'd dismissed it. Only suddenly it wasn't as easy to shake.

What *if* Cutty had been saying he accepted the fact that she wasn't as good as Marla but he wanted to work things out with her anyway? And what exactly did *working things out* entail? Had he wanted her to just stay in Northbridge in general? Or in the garage apartment? Or had he been talking about more than that?

"You're here to clear everything up," she reminded herself. "*Then* you'll make a decision. If he isn't offering what you want, you can just say no and go back to Denver."

That was how she'd gotten up the courage to do this at all—she'd decided she was just going to go back to Northbridge, find out exactly what Cutty had meant the previous morning, and then—and only then—would she make up her mind what she wanted to do.

Kira pulled up to the curb in front of Cutty's house.

She couldn't take her eyes off it as she fumbled to turn off the engine in the unfamiliar car.

Betty would probably be there, she knew, and she didn't relish facing the woman after the quick, tearful goodbye to the twins that the other woman had witnessed the day before.

But she hadn't come all this way to chicken out just because Betty made her nervous and so she took the key out of the ignition, slipped from behind the wheel and headed for the house with her heart beating a mile a minute.

The front door was open, just as it had been the first time she'd climbed those porch steps. But now Cutty wasn't at the hall table, talking on the phone. She spotted him through the picture window, sitting on the sofa with his leg propped on a pillow on the coffee table.

She didn't hear the sound of the television or even the radio or stereo and he seemed to be just staring into space. With a very dour expression on his handsome, clean-shaven face.

He spied her then and the dour expression transformed instantly into one of surprise. Surprise that got him off the couch in a hurry so that he reached the front screen when she did.

For a brief, fleeting moment Kira wondered if he was going to slam the door in her face and lock it to keep her out.

But that wasn't what he did.

He pushed the screen open wide and said a tentative, questioning, "Hi."

"Hi," Kira responded the same way.

"You're about the last person I expected to see," Cutty informed her. "Come in."

Kira did, thinking that no man should be allowed to look that good in a plain pair of jeans and a white T-shirt, and that if she ended up having to turn around and leave him again it was going to be even harder than it had been the day before.

From the entryway inside, Kira glanced around in search of the twins and Betty, but she didn't see or hear anything that gave her a clue as to where they were.

"Betty took the girls to the park. You just missed them," Cutty said, guessing what she was looking for.

"Good," Kira said. "Then we can talk."

Cutty motioned with his cane toward the living room and Kira went ahead of him, keeping her fingers crossed that she hadn't made a mistake by coming here and thinking that maybe Kit had been as right about doing this over the phone as Kira hoped her friend had been about everything else.

But it was too late now and so all she could do was go through with what she'd come for.

Nervous, though, she began to pick up the few toys that were on the floor.

"I thought you came to talk?" Cutty said from behind her.

Kira dropped the toys into the toy box and turned back to find him still standing, his weight braced on the cane, watching her.

Now or never...

"I did."

"What do you want to talk about?"

Kira screwed up her courage and said, "I need to know if I misunderstood what you said to me yesterday morning."

Cutty's frown was dark and intense. "I thought I made myself pretty clear. I asked you to stay. You said no."

And obviously he wasn't only confused the way he had been at the time. He was angry now, as well.

"What you said about my staying wasn't altogether clear, either. But maybe we can get into that after you explain the rest of what you said."

"The rest?"

Kira took a deep, fortifying breath. "This is what I thought you were saying to me—" She went on to tell him the way she'd taken what he'd said. Honestly. Openly. Sparing nothing, including the depth of her own insecurities when it came to being compared to her sister and the need that had been ingrained in her to do everything she could to be as good, to excel.

The longer she talked the more Cutty's expression and stance relaxed until, by the time she was finished, his eyebrows were arched in disbelief.

"You are so far off the mark," he said then in regards to what she believed he'd been telling her the previous day. "I know Ad told you how things were between Marla and me—he confessed that last night. He said he did it because he knew I'd never tell you myself and he was right. I wouldn't have. But not because it isn't all true. I won't say anything against Marla because she's gone and everything that happened, everything she was and did, is over. Nothing can be served by rehashing it. Plus she needed so badly for people to think of her the way they did— the way they do—I couldn't ruin that for her when she was alive and I can't do it to her memory, either."

Kira had to admire his loyalty even if it had tweaked those insecurities of hers. But she still needed to know just how true what Ad had said was.

"So the marriage wasn't all Betty and everyone else around here believes it was?"

"Had Marla not turned up pregnant we probably wouldn't have even *dated* another month, Kira. We were just teenagers. No, the marriage that came out of that wasn't what people think it was. When you first showed up here and offered to help out, all I could think was that you were bound to be like Marla and I couldn't get into that again. So your friend was right—I was thrilled to figure out that the biggest part of you *is* different from Marla. I was *glad* that you were willing to overlook a few things to go to the game and the party and the awards ceremony with me. And the fact that you were playing with the twins when I expected you to be working like mad to make everything perfect before Betty came back? That's what made me realize I wanted you to stay."

Relief washed through Kira so thoroughly she almost felt weak. But at the same time there was that *stay* part again and she still didn't know what, exactly, he had in mind.

"Now explain what you mean when you say that you want me to stay," she said more bravely.

A slow, sexy smile brightened his features and he used the head of his cane to hook her upper arm and pull her to stand close in front of him.

"I really didn't make myself clear yesterday, did I?" he said. "*Stay* means I want you to move to Northbridge and marry me. It means I want you to be Mel and Mandy's mom, and I want to have a couple more kids with you. It means I want to spend every day for the rest of my life with you. It means—'' he was suddenly giving special enunciation to each word ''—that I'm so in love with you that I'm damn near giddy.''

It was Kira's turn to smile. ''And you can live with your whole town probably thinking you've traded down?''

''They're all going to love you as much as I do,'' Cutty assured. ''And one way or another, the only thing I care about is you saying a big fat yes to being my wife.''

There was one more thing Kira had thought about when she'd considered the possibility of a future with Cutty and she thought she had to say it now. But she was reluctant to and it must have shown on her face because he said, ''What? You're going to say no?''

''I have just one condition,'' she ventured. ''But it's a huge one.''

''Let's hear it?''

''The whole time I was here I just kept thinking that this is Marla's house, that everything in it is Marla's.''

''And you don't want to live in Marla's house with Marla's things,'' Cutty guessed.

Kira grimaced. ''I'm sorry. I know this is your home, too, and they're your things, too. But—''

Cutty chuckled slightly. ''Gone!''

''Me? Or the house and the things?''

''Not you. The house and the things. You're more important to me than all of it. I think we *should* start fresh. Although I will have to keep Mel and Mandy," he joked.

Kira laughed as even more relief flooded her. "I wouldn't give them up for anything."

"So where's the big fat yes to marrying me?"

"Big fat yes!" she repeated with enthusiasm.

Cutty pulled her the rest of the way into his arms then and kissed her a kiss that initially just seemed to put a stamp on the deal.

But it took only a few moments for the kiss to become more than that. To rekindle what they'd shared after Cutty's birthday party and ignite a desire hotter than the sun.

Cutty stopped then and glanced at the clock on the fireplace mantel. "Hmm. You know, we might have half an hour yet to ourselves."

Kira knew what was going through his mind and she merely smiled.

But apparently it was enough consent for Cutty because without another word he took her hand and led her through the kitchen and out the back door, all the way to the garage apartment where Kira had stripped and remade the bed before she'd left for Denver.

With time limited, they didn't waste any of it.

Clothes were shed as mouths clung and then Cutty laid Kira back on the mattress where a passion even greater than what they'd shared before erupted.

There were no inhibitions. There was no timidity. Hands explored and aroused. Lips parted and tongues teased and tormented and claimed each other. Bodies came together in one graceful motion and moved like the rhythm of ship and sea to reach an all-new height, to find a glorious, unguarded ecstasy that left them breathlessly holding each other as Cutty rolled them to their sides and pressed tender lips to the top of her head.

"It's a good thing you said yes or I think I'd just keep you prisoner out here for the rest of your life," he said after a moment, his voice raspy with the remnants of lovemaking so divine Kira felt as if she were floating on air.

"What would I be? Your love-slave?" she asked.

He grinned a satiated grin. "Love-slave," he repeated as if trying out the sound of it. "I like that."

"But think of the scandal when, one day, Betty happened upon me handcuffed to the bed. Small Town Cop Keeps Microbiologist For His Own Personal Pleasure," Kira said as if reciting a headline.

"You'd have sympathy in your favor, though, and the whole town would make you its new idol."

Kira laughed, realizing just how unimportant that seemed now, in Cutty's arms, knowing he was hers. "That's okay. I think being your wife will be enough for me."

He reared back to look into her eyes and his expression surprised her because it seemed that her simple comment had genuinely moved him.

"I hope so," he said softly.

Kira pressed one palm to the side of that face she knew she'd never tire of and kissed him. "I love you, Cutty," she said then, her own full heart echoing in her voice.

"I love you, too. More than I even knew until you walked out of here yesterday. Don't ever do that again."

"You're going to have to get a court order if you want to get rid of me," she told him.

Commotion from inside the house then let them know Betty was back with the twins.

"We should get up and get dressed before she catches us," Kira said.

Cutty grinned. "Yeah, I suppose we should," he agreed as he kissed her one more time.

Then they both made quick work of dressing and finger-combing hair and making sure all evidence of how they'd spent that half hour was concealed.

But regardless of how concealed it was, Kira carried with her the warm glow left by that and by the knowledge that she'd finally found her own heart's true desire. Her own heart's true love. That she'd found it in Cutty.

And that along with him came two beautiful babies she couldn't have loved more if she'd given birth to them herself.

Two beautiful babies who were just a wonderful bonus to make her life complete.

*   *   *   *   *

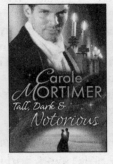
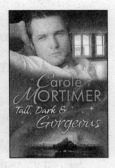

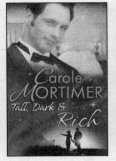
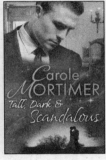